Diary of a Ryde

JOANNA RYDE

Gimme Hope

Joanna Ryde xxx

BOOK REPUBLIC
A BOUTIQUE PUBLISHING PRESS

Published in 2011 by Book Republic, an imprint of Maverick House Publishers.

Office 19, Dunboyne Business Park, Dunboyne, Co. Meath, Ireland.

www.bookrepublic.ie

email: info@bookrepublic.ie

ISBN 978-1-907221-27-9

Copyright for text © 2011 Kolyn Byrne

Copyright for typesetting, editing, layout, design

© Book Republic

10 9 8 7 6 5 4 3 2 1

The paper used in this book comes from wood pulp of managed forests. For every tree felled, at least one tree is planted, thereby renewing natural resources.

The moral rights of the author have been asserted.

All rights reserved.

No part of this book may be reproduced or transmitted in any form or by any means without written permission from the publisher, except by a reviewer who wishes to quote brief passages in connection with a review written for insertion in a newspaper, magazine or broadcast.

A CIP catalogue record for this book is available from the British Library.

This book is dedicated to me ma and da, for puttin' up with me and bein' the best parents anyone could ever wish for!

Thanks to everyone who's shown love, support and appreciation over the years. Yiz are all rydes.

God bless!

January

Jayzis, the 1 January already. I can't believe it's 2005. I can remember last New Year's Eve like it was only yesterday which is more than I can say for this New Year's Eve and that *was* only yesterday.

We all went over to Bernie's last night. Bernie's me best mate. I know her years, like since I was borned like. She's mad though. Her ma and da went the Canaries last Saturday, the lucky bastards. I mean they have the right idea, d'ya know what I mean? So Bernie says, 'Right. Fuck them, goin' the Canaries without me. We'll have a party.' So we all headed over to her gaff last night. Jasmin made a punch or so she called it and god only knows what the young-one put into it. The thing was purple. She said it was Vodka, Malibu, Bacardi, Blue Aftershock, orange juice, pineapple juice and Lucozade but I'd say she added a few more ingredients, like Calpol and Domestos. I think I had two glasses and the room was spinnin' and I don't get drunk, Bernie will tell ya. Tracy was gonna bring over her karaoke machine but we told her not to. The last time that karaoke machine appeared at a party we couldn't get Concepta Cooney off the thing. I was gonna shove the microphone up her arse at one stage. I wouldn't mind but she can't sing a note. Concepta's the one with the arse as wide as O'Connell Street and a mouth not too far behind. She's the only person I know who'd be able to walk down the quays on both sides of the Liffey. She's like the Straits of Gibraltar, I'm not jokin' ya. Anyway, there was no way we were goin' to listen to her singin' – or screechin' would be more like it – so we told Tracy to leave the karaoke machine at home.

I don't know what time it was when Bopper showed up. Bopper's me brother. He's a year and a half younger than me but we do have a bit of buzz. He likes comin' out with me and me mates and I don't really mind coz he brings his friend Paulo with him and he's a ride. He's from Bosnia or somewhere originally, one of these Scandinavian countries that I can't pronounce anyway but he's been here eight or nine years so his English is perfect. Well better than mine anyways. I do always be chattin' him up, havin' a bit of a laugh with him but we never do anythin'. I think he fancies me but we wouldn't do anythin' coz he's like, Bopper's best mate and he respects me. Not that I fancy him or anythin', I mean, he's gorgeous but I don't fancy him.

Anyway it was a great night from the little bits I remember. I woke up in Bernie's conservatory half naked for some reason with only a blanket coverin' me. If I end up with frostbite I'll sue the bitch, don't think I won't. I found me bra hangin' off of the extractor fan in the kitchen. God only knows how it got there. It was definitely mine coz I'm the only one that has the lace underwire support, €16 in Dunnes, ya can't go wrong.

I said to meself the other day that I'm gonna make a few New Year's revolutions and stick to them. I can't remember what last year's ones were but I'd say they lasted about 20 minutes knowin' me. Me first one this year is to write down a few things goin' on in me head coz its nice to have somethin' to remember the year by. I want to write down a few of me thoughts, ya know that kind of a way. Jayzis, can ya imagine Jasmin havin' a thought? It'd die of loneliness. So here it is. Kind of a diary. Like your woman Florence Nightingale.

Me second revolution is to give up the smokes. I remember sayin' it last year. There was a time in this country when ya didn't have to stand outside a pub in the rain to smoke. Jayzis that'd be deadly, and that's on top of the early closin' times and the other mad laws. This country is like the ~~Soviet Socialist, Union of Socialist,~~ fuckin' Russia. Can ya imagine someone tryin' to tell Concepta Cooney to put out her smoke in the pub? She'd floor the bastard and then shove the cigarette up their hole. I do have to give up though. I'll save a few quid anyways. I'll put a few quid a week away for a holiday. Oh Jayzis, there's another revolution. That's three now.

What else? Oh I'm gonna try and put meself out there a bit more, ya know with me singin' and radio presentin'. I'll try get a job on a station. I know a few of the lads on CRAC, or Community Radio Cabra to give it its proper name. I'd be deadly I would. I could do the traffic or somethin' first. 'Traffic is heavy on the Navan Road headin' into the city as usual. Get the fuck out and walk.' Can ya imagine?

I need one more revolution to make it five. Tracy says she's gonna be more assertive and I would too if I knew what it meant. When I find out I'll tell ya. I thought she said she was gonna be a surfer the first time she said it. Can ya imagine Tracy Murtagh on a surfboard out in Portmarnock, now I ask ya? Concepta's goin' on a diet, about time. If someone like Vodafone were to lose as many pounds as she needs to, they'd go bankrupt. Jasmin's gonna learn Spanish as one of her revolutions, god help her, the poor young-one struggles with English. What did Bernie say? Oh yeah, she was gonna have more sex. I think that'll be me fifth one. I haven't had a ride in two months. Jayzis.

✳✳✳

Well me head is melted, right. I'm in work in a while and I can't think straight at all and I mean, I wasn't even drinkin' last night. Maybe that punch is still in me system. Jasmin Spi will be gettin' a punch when I get her, the bitch.

I went back to bed when I went home yesterday and then watched *Grease* when I got up. I love that film and I was ragin' coz I missed *The Sound of Music*, ya know yourself. So the evenin' came and I says to meself 'Fuck this, I'm not stayin' in watchin' the telly.' So I give Bernie a ring and she's in the gaff just finished cleanin' up. So I throw on some cloths and knock down to her house which I have to say, she's cleaned up grand after the party. Her ma won't even know. She even unclogged the toilet which is a miracle considerin' what Concepta Cooney left in it the night before. It was sickenin'.

Anyway we were gonna ring a curry but neither of us had any money so we decided to go into town to get some money out and get food in Eddie Rockets or somethin'. I don't see why the fuckers don't put more bank machines around. It's a pain in the hoop.

So off the two of us went into the freezin' cold and onto the bus which wasn't much warmer. Me nipples were like rockets all the way to town it was that cold and I was wearin' a jumper and that lovely new jacket I got for the Christmas in A-wear. Eddie Rockets was black, wouldn't ya know it, so we said fuck it and went to McDonalds instead. I was gonna get a Mcflurry but I thought I'd probably freeze to death on the bus on the way home if I did.

Now who do I see as I get off the bus on the way back to Bernie's only Paddy. Me and Paddy have a strange history. I met him over the Halloween weekend in Boomerangs or maybe it was Club M, one or the other, I was probably too drunk at the time to remember which. He was kinda givin' me the eye and I was givin' him little subtle hints back like grabbin' his arse when I was passin' by. So he comes over this night and starts talkin' to me and I was delighted with meself. One thing led to another anyways so I was like, deadly. Now me ma and da were away at the time and Bopper was off somewhere — god only knows where with that young-fella. So I asks Paddy to come back to mine. Now before ya get any ideas, let me just tell ya that I'm not usually like that. The others are but I'm not. I never asked anyone back before that. So he says yeah and we get the Nitelink home. Bernie was with me too that night, tell a lie it was Tracy. I remember coz she was wearin' me red poncho I got in Top-Shop and left it somewhere, the bitch. I nearly battered her only for Paddy was there.

So we go home and flick through the music channels as ya do and eventually, not before time, good jayzis I was fallin' asleep, we end up in the bedroom. Well not my bleedin' bedroom, it was Bopper's. He has a double bed and I only have a single and me ma was only after gettin' me a lovely new quilt cover in Guinneys. Thank god she got rid of the bunk beds when me sister Wanda moved to Australia! So anyway to cut a long story short, he was amazin'. The best ride I'd had in a long time. The only ride I'd had in a long time let the truth be told.

So I was textin' him over the next few days and he asked me to go the pictures, some shite with your woman Angelina Jolie in it and other than I like her, it was a load of me hole as far as I remember. After the pictures we went back to his gaff and nearly destroyed his sofa. He lives in Cabra so it's not that far away. I think his ma was out lookin' after his nanny after only gettin' her catamarans done or whatever that thing is in your eye and his da's dead. He was hit by a truck comin' home from the pub one night. It took three days to get all the bits of him out of the radiator I'm told.

So I text him the next day askin' him to meet me after work and he sent me back a message somethin' like 'I think we're movin' too fast, I just broke up with a young-one, blah blah blah.' I have to admit, I was in the height of it. Concepta Cooney wanted to batter him.

So I've seen him around a few times since and said hello, had a bit of a chat, that kinda thing. Last night right, as I was sayin', I saw him when I got off the bus and he was talkin' to meself and Bernie for ages and then when we got back to Bernie's, the minute I walked in, I got a message off him askin' me did I want to go for a drink sometime. Bernie was havin' none of it and told me to tell him to fuck off. I don't know what to do though. I didn't text him back or anythin' but now he's after textin' me again. Jayzis, I don't know what to do.

**

Well I'm delighted with meself coz I'm still off the smokes. Now when I say off, I had three yesterday which ya have to admit isn't bad. I'm doin' better than Concepta's doin' on her diet anyways. I rang her last night and she was on the way back from the chipper. She's unreal that young-one.

Anyway I told her about Paddy askin' me to go out and she nearly jumped down the phone at me. I'd say there was people asleep in Carlow that woke up, she was that loud. She says I'm mad if I go for a drink with him after what he did to me the first time and I have to be honest, I'm kinda agreein' with her, especially after she got Tracy to ring me.

Now I have to be honest, Tracy is the one I listen to most. Brains to burn has Tracy Murtagh. She's studyin' English and Psychology out in UCD, nerdy cow, but fair play to her. Tracy was sayin' that Paddy was just tryin' to be with me to see if he could and that if I was to go for a drink with him and things started again he'd get bored with me. The only thing is, Tracy tells me, is that if I say no, he'll think I'm a challenge and be wreckin' me head, askin' me out and ringin' me and that. So straight out Tracy asks me, she's mad into this psychology stuff, analyzin' everythin'. I can't even spell analyze. So she asks me do I like Paddy. I think about it for a minute and I realised he's not all that great, fair enough he was good in bed, or on his sofa anyway, and he has a big enough willy but he's not the best to look at and he's a bit of a gobshite, let the truth be told. So Tracy says I've two solutions. I could either; A – just get me bit and let him get bored with me, which I'm thinkin' about coz I'm dyin' for me hole, don't mean to be vulgar but I'm not one for beatin' around the bush; or B – tell him to fuck off and ignore him if he tries to ring me or whatever. I asked Tracy what about C – lettin' Concepta beat the shite out of him but she doesn't think that's feasible, whatever the fuck feasible means.

So I have to admit, I kinda have me mind made up now thanks to Tracy. She's only deadly although I'd never tell her that to her face, I mean she already thinks she's all that and a packet of Fruit Pastilles coz she's goin' to college and the rest of us can't even spell it. But she'll make a deadly psycholologist one day or somethin' else to do with English. I mean what type of job will she be able to get with English? Although sayin' that maybe she has to learn how to speak proper with the psychology so she'll be able to talk to all her patients. She says she'll gimme this book to read about stoppin' smokin', but as I said, I only had the three yesterday so I'm doin' well and stickin' to me revolutions. I still haven't had any sex yet though.

***

Sunday mornin' and I don't have a hangover, good sufferin' jayzis. I can't remember the last time that happened and I wasn't even workin' today. I can't believe I stayed in on a Saturday night. It was crazy but nobody was in the humour of goin' out what with the Christmas and New Year just over. I'm loaded though so I was sayin' it to the others about goin' away for a week in February, somewhere like the Canaries or somethin' and they all seem up for it. Can ya imagine the buzz we'd have?

I'm gettin' a cold I think or else its still the after effects of Jasmin's punch from the New Year's party in Bernie's. I just feel shite. Did ya ever get one of them days where ya wake up and ya just don't feel right? And as I said, it couldn't have been a hangover coz I wasn't drinkin' last night.

I was tellin' Tracy about this thing I'm tryin' to write and she was sayin' that it was Anne Frank that wrote the diary and not Florence Nightingale, whoever the fuck she is. Bopper thinks she sounds like a drag queen although how he knows what a drag queen's name sounds like is a mystery to me.

After work, Bernie met me and we went to my gaff to watch a DVD. Bopper got a lend of his favourite film, *Moulin Rouge*, off Paulo and the three of us watched it and finished the last of the tortillas and dips me ma got in for over the Christmas. She'll kill me if she finds out. That *Moulin Rouge* is a weird film. Now I'd never seen it before but Bopper loves it, he's a huge fan of Obi Wan Shinobi or whatever it is that Scottish fella's name is from *Star Wars*. I thought it was a bit weird though. The music was great, don't get me wrong but I felt dizzy lookin' at it a couple of times. Bopper was givin' us a runnin' commentary on it as usual and I nearly ended up suffocatin' him with a cushion. He's a fucker for it. I remember we went to see *Titanic* and he told me the endin'. I was ragin' as well coz I sat there through the whole film knowin' the ship was gonna sink — the bastard.

✳✳✳

I'm really startin' to scare meself now. The girls all think I'm a new and improved Joanna and I'm startin' to agree with them. I got a phone call last night off Bernie as I was watchin' some shite on the telly about a temple in Istanbul or some other mad place in India, I can't remember. Me da was watchin' it and I was just sittin' there really coz I had fuck all else to do. Anyway Bernie rings and asked me to go to Coyote for the RnB night. Now I wasn't really in the mood for goin' out let the truth be told but I said fuck it, I may as well, I do enjoy an RnB night in Coyote and the last time I was there some young-fella gave me his number which I lost wouldn't ya know, although it was his fault for writin' his number on the back of a Dunnes receipt, the spa.

Anyway I couldn't find Bopper for the life of me and he wasn't answerin' his phone. Paulo, the ride, was around in the gaff, this must have been about half seven, and they said something about bingo before runnin' out the door. I don't know what sort of places them two young-fellas do be goin' to.

We would have asked Jasmin but she's down in Kilkenny with her ma and da, her brother Andy and her sisters, Sandy and Mandy. They're triplets. I do get very confused. All three of them look the same, even Andy since he started growin' his hair. He's one of them teenage mosher spas that hang around the Central Bank on a Saturday shoutin' at the auld-ones passin' by and goin' to shite gigs in the Temple Bar Music Centre by bands with shite names like The Left Testicles.

Tracy couldn't come coz she's workin' on some project about Charles Dickens. I think he's your man that wrote *Matilda* which is one of me favourite books so I'll be able to give her a hand.

Concepta had to work late so she couldn't come either. I was wonderin' what sort of factory opens on a Sunday night but she was sayin' that there was some kind of problem over the Christmas so they're all doin' overtime. She works in a sweet factory. No wonder she's the size she is but now in sayin' that, she's always bringin' us home a few bags of jellies which they must give her. Nobody, not even Concepta, would be able to smuggle that many jellies out of a factory. There's a press in our kitchen that's like the pick and mix in the cinema there's that many jellies in it. Me ma's thinkin' of openin' her own shop and sellin' them at this stage. She keeps makin' us eat them to try to get rid of them, puttin' them into the trifle and ice cream and that. I swear to jayzis, she put some in the stew last week. I was convinced I saw little jelly babies floatin' around in it.

Anyway where was I? I keep goin' off on tandems. Oh yeah, me and Bernie in Coyote. Yeah I scared the shite out of meself coz I didn't have one drink and all I had was one smoke that I robbed off some fella in the queue as well. I was on the pints of Coke all night and the stuff was goin' right through me. I was pissin' like Viagra Falls. The splash was drownin' out the music and that was just the dribbles. It was weird though coz I'm mad without the drink, I mean I was talkin' to people and all and I never do that. I must ask Tracy why that is now when I see her. The money I'm savin' by not drinkin' is great as well. The pints of Coke are less than half as much as the bottles of Smirnoff Ice or Bacardi Breezer or whatever I do be drinkin' normally so I'm savin' loads.

The only other thing though, other than the pissin' like an elephant is I wasn't able to sleep, although that could have somethin' to do with the cold I still have as well. I took everythin' I could find for it, although I only had three spoonfuls of Calpol which is good for me coz I usually go through a bottle a day when I'm sick. I do just love the taste of it. They should bring out a Calpol flavoured drink or somethin'. It'd be deadly. They could have it in little purple bottles or somethin'. I found a bottle of that Milk of Malaysia or Magnesia or whatever it is it's called but I didn't really know what it does so I didn't take it. Maybe I'll have another spoonful of Calpol. Or maybe two. Calpol and vodka shots. I'd buy them.

✳✳✳

I decided to go into town for a bit of shoppin' today although to be a hundred percent honest with ya, I wasn't really feelin' up to it. I'm still dyin' with this cold and no amount of Calpol or that Benilyn 4 Flu stuff me ma got is doin' any good. Me throat is in a heap and me nose is runnin' like one of them American runners at the Olympics, the ones that are mad into the drugs.

I wasn't in the humour for goin' into town as I said but Concepta had no one else to go with so I said I may as well get out of the gaff for an hour. Me ma's cleanin' everythin' coz she took down the Christmas decorations and if I inhale any more Domestos me stomach is gonna start turnin' yellow.

I got fuck all in town though. Bopper got me a HMV voucher for Christmas, €25, Jayzis, so I got meself a CD. All I got him for Christmas was a Lynx set so I was thinkin' of gettin' him somethin' else coz I feel kinda guilty. That and the fact that me birthday is next week and I want somethin' nice off him for that.

Concepta brought back a top her auntie had got her in A-wear coz it was too small. The auntie must be blind though coz she got a size 10 and Concepta can't be any smaller than an 18 and that's just me bein' nice. Ya wanna see it, a belly top, halter neck type thing in a kind of a biscuity colour. I could only imagine Concepta Cooney wearin' somethin' like that. The thing would have been lucky fittin' on one of her fingers. She changed it anyway and the two of us went to Burdocks for the usual battered sausage and curry chips. I can't pass Burdocks as much as I wanted to but Concepta persuaded me to go in, although she's meant to be on a diet. Diet me hole. I left a few chips and the end of me curry sauce when I was goin' the toilet and when I came back she had them eaten and all and then she wanted to go to for ice-cream as well after it. There was no way though. I put on eight pounds over the Christmas as it is, ya wanna see the size of me. I'm no Concepta now but she was my weight once, when she was about four but still.

We popped in to see Paulo in Clery's as well. Jayzis he looks gas in his suit. He's not the type of young-fella ya see workin' if ya get what I mean. It doesn't seem to be his type of thing but he's a ride in that suit. I'll definitely be shoppin' in Clery's more often, although not if Concepta realises there's a restaurant in it.

＊＊＊

I'm knackered. I swear to god, that Coke has me awake all night. Never again. Tracy thinks the caffeine has become a substitute for the nicotine. I mean jayzis, I only had nine pints of Coke. I told her it's the cold that's keepin' me awake but she said I had more energy last night than Poolbeg has in a year, whatever the fuck that means. I was pissin' like mad though so I might just take her advice and lay off the Coke for a while. That and the Calpol. I got the Calpol 6+ there yesterday but it's just not the same.

We weren't even goin' to go for a drink but Jasmin was back from the arse end of nowhere so we decided to go for one which as usual ended up with us in the pub for the night, just the local now, Farley's its called, lovely little spot but a bit quiet, full of auld-ones but grand if you're not that bothered. I was surprised now for a Tuesday coz a few of us went. There was meself, Jasmin obviously, Bernie of course, the Tracy one, Bopper and Paulo, the ride. Concepta had to work, as if we missed her greatly. She's still doin' the late shifts in the factory. She won't tell us what happened over the Christmas but we're convinced she ate all the jellies and now they're behind in their orders or somethin'. I know she was involved somehow coz otherwise she would have told us. She's mad for the gossip, Concepta.

Bopper and Paulo disappeared about 11 o'clock to go to some club in town and we were all set to go with them but they said it wouldn't be our type of thing so we said fuck it and stayed where we were. Bopper Ryde wasn't in bed when I leavin' this mornin', the dirty fucker. I wonder where he stayed, although knowin' his luck with young-ones, he probably stayed in Paulo's. I actually haven't seen our Bopper with a young-one in ages now that I think of it. He's gone very secretive lately. I wonder if there's something wrong with him, jayzis.

Meself and the girls had a good laugh in Farley's. Needless to say, they couldn't get us out of the pub. Usually I'd be locked out of me tree but it was mad bein' sober at the end of the night, especially coz the others were locked, although sayin' that, Tracy doesn't get that locked but Jasmin and Bernie were. Meself and Tracy had to carry them home. Thank jayzis Concepta wasn't out with us, I mean, can ya imagine tryin' to carry her home. Ya'd need to rent a crane.

✳✳✳

Mental, bleedin' mental. I was in work today and there was war. I can't remember if I said already but I'm workin' in the Spar down the road. Now I know it's not somethin' I want to have as me career or anythin' but it's grand for the minute.

Anyway there was killin's in the shop earlier on. That Julie Walsh one. Now whatever about Concepta, Julie Walsh must be twice the size of her and she's really sweaty as well. I've seen her sweat after walkin' from one end of the shop to the other and believe me, it's not that big, although to be honest, the fat cow rarely gets up off her hole to do anythin'. I've seen her, now no word of a lie, comin' in for an eight-hour shift and only gettin' up off the stool at the tills for her break. She'll even make someone else press the buttons for the smokes or get somethin' she can't reach, the lazy cow. She's always gettin' poor Sheila to do stuff for her and Sheila's very quiet. She wouldn't say no. She's from China, Sheila. A lovely young-one. I don't think that's her real name now that I come to think of it but it could be, I don't know. I would ask her but the silly cow hasn't a clue what I do be sayin' to her. It's gas, the poor young-one comes over here to learn English and the only thing she can understand is 20 John Player blue.

As I was sayin' anyway, there was killin's in work. Julie Walsh had a fight with one of the customers. I mean a real fight. The two of them were batterin' each other in the middle of the shop. What it was over I couldn't tell ya. I don't think Julie Walsh could tell ya let the truth be told but it was like somethin' off the wrestlin' on the telly in the middle of the Spar. I thought we were bein' raided at first. I swear to jayzis, I got the fright of me life. Julie Walsh was in bits after it though. She had to be calmed down by about 11 of us. I wouldn't even mind but she didn't even know the customer. Accordin' to Sheila it was somethin' to do with a pair of tights but knowin' her English it could have been over that Julie Walsh one bein' a snotty cow as usual. She's an awful bitch to the customers. I don't know why they keep her on. The fat cow does nothin' anyway.

I'm just thinkin', I haven't heard from any of the girls now since Tuesday night when I was in Farley's which is a bit weird. I was dyin' to ring them to tell them about Julie Walsh but I was up to me tits, ya know the way it does be. We'll probably end up headin' out tomorrow night, ya know yourself. Friday does be a bit of buzz.

Bopper still has me very confused. I don't know where he went on Tuesday but he's keepin' very quiet about it. Very strange, although it is our Bopper and he is very strange. I do worry about him though. He's me little brother and I have to look after him. If there's anyone givin' him shit, I'll kick lumps out of them. I text Paulo to see if I could get a bit of gossip on Bopper but he never text me back. That young-fella never uses his phone. He has one of them new Nokias and he showed it to me there last week and I swear to Christ, it's in Romanian or whatever language they speak in Bosnia. Jayzis.

✻✻✻

I was around in Bernie's last night coz she rang me and asked me to come around, ya know yourself. So we were lookin' for a video to watch coz we've seen every DVD she has about 15 times. I know every word from *Muriel's Weddin'* I've seen it that many times. I have to say though, it has to be one of me favourite films. Your one that does Muriel, Colette somethin' I think her name is, she's only deadly. She was great in that *Sixth Sense* as the ma. I love the bit when they do *Waterloo* on the holiday, in *Muriel's Weddin'* not the *Sixth Sense*. Bernie and meself do always be doin' it in the sittin' room for the laugh.

Anyway we're lookin' through the videos and what do we come across only a video of a show we did in primary school years ago. We were only about nine or 10 in it, or maybe it was 11 coz it was in 5th class in school but ya wanna see the state of us. There's a bit in it near the start and it's me, Bernie and Tracy doin' the *Shoop Shoop Song,* ya know that one that Cher does in *Mermaids*, seriously, the state of us. Tracy Murtagh was wearin' a pink tutu, a black shirt tied at the end, a pair of her ma's pink high heels and her hair all tied back. Bernie's in a little black dress, big hoopy earrings, a pair of black sandals, like somethin' Moses would wear, with her hair in pigtails. Not much has changed there then. And then there's me in a pair of these jeans with flowers down the side of them, a pink bellytop and a pink headband to match and the three of us are dancin' around, lookin' deadly and lip syncin' to the words. Britney Spears would be jealous we were that good at the mimin'. I have to say, now I'm not bein' big headed or anythin' but we were only mafis.

Then there's a bit with Concepta Cooney who was in 6th class at the time, she must have been coz she's a year and a half older than me but she's singin' that song by Whitney Houston, ya know, *I Believe The Children Are Our Future*. Ya wanna see the state of her. The poor cow was the same size then as she is now. God I remember we used to give her an awful time about it, I mean now we only slag her behind her back.

Then in another bit, Jasmin and our Bopper are doin' *You're The One That I Want* from *Grease* with loads of other young-ones and young-fellas. They were in the same class Jasmin and Bopper, that's how we got to know her as far as I remember. Jayzis the state of her. She had these big glasses that looked like the bottom of beer bottles and big goofy teeth. She has the contacts now. Jayzis I don't know how many times I've seen the dizzy cow tryin' to put them in backwards. Our Bopper looks gas in his little denim jacket and his jeans. He's givin' it socks, ya wanna see him and he keeps lookin' out into the audience thinkin' he's all that and a mint Aero.

So anyway its great and all the rest of it and just before the end who comes out only meself and the Bernie one in bikini's and sunglasses mimin' to *Cruel Summer* by Bananarama — no, tell a lie, it was the Ace of Base version. Well ya wanna see us, we were only deadly and I wouldn't say we were any older than 11. The crowd were goin' mad and all. I remember we nearly got one of them standin' rotations.

It's gas though. Me and Bernie have been mates like forever. I'll be 18 next week, I can't remember if I mentioned me birthday already, and she'll be 18 in a few months so its like 19 years we've been best mates, all our lives almost. It's weird now that I come to think of it. We were sittin' there watchin' the video and I was like, jayzis, it's mad growin' up with someone your whole life, d'ya know what I mean? I know Bernie longer than Bopper even and he's me brother. As I said, we only started hangin' around with Jasmin when we went into secondary school. She was a year behind us, although sayin' that, she's a year behind most people. I told her a joke on Christmas Eve and she only started laughin' today. Tracy we know a bit longer. She moved to our school when we were in third class and she was very quiet, a bit of a drifter so meself and Bernie took her under our wing kind of thing. She was a brainy bitch even back then. I copied me homework off poor Tracy for years. Meself and Bernie knew she'd do well and here she is goin' to UCD.

I'm not really sure how Concepta started hangin' around with us. As far as I remember we met her one night in the Temple Theatre at an under 18's or somethin', we were only gone into 3rd year. She did the transition year so that's how we ended up in the same class but she just ended up bein' around us all the time and hasn't left since, more's the pity.

But me and Bernie, we go back a long way. Her ma and my ma are best mates as well so we're like sisters. I remember people used to say that to us all the time. We used to think we were only the business when people said it, although sayin' that, we look fuck all like each other. I'm much better lookin' than she is for a start.

It was weird lookin' at that video, ya know, with me birthday comin' up and all. It makes ya think where life is goin'. It also made me think where I could get a pair of them jeans that I was wearin' doin' the Shoop Shoop song. They were only mafis.

✳︎✳︎✳︎

Well me cold is nearly gone thank merciful Jayzis coz it was really startin' to wreck me head at this stage. I hate bein' sick.

We decided to go out last night into town; meself, Bernie, Jasmin, Tracy and Concepta. There was no sign of Bopper and Paulo. I text them both but didn't hear anythin' back from them. God only knows where they were or what they were doin'. Bopper does seem to be back to his old self though. His limp seems a bit better anyway. He did somethin' to his back on Tuesday night and was walkin' around like John Wayne the past few days. He was tellin' me that Paulo was tellin' him that Concepta keeps textin' him askin' him out, fair play to her although as I said, Paulo fancies me.

So it was only the girls headin' into town so we decided to go to Fitzsimons which, I have to say, is a good spot although it can be a bit touristy at times, nowhere near as bad as Club M but there still does be loads of foreigners there, not Irish foreigners but foreign foreigners, like people here on holidays.

So we're sittin' there havin' a few drinks, me back on the alcohol coz this cold is nearly gone and I can't remember why I stopped drinkin' in the first place. Who walks anyways only Paddy, ya know your man who destroyed me on his sofa, and his mate Phillip so needless to say, I pretend I don't see him but Jasmin, spa that she is, runs over and its all hugs and kisses and 'Howaya Paddy?' and 'Ya look great Paddy' and 'I'm here with Joanna and the girls Paddy.' I felt like streelin' out of her, I'm not jokin' ya. So she brings them over and he tries to hug me and I move away and he's like, 'What's wrong Joanna?' and I just give him a dirty look so its all tension and Phillip and the girls are there starin' at us to see what's goin' to happen and then Paddy says, 'Why haven't ya answered me texts?' Next minute, Concepta Cooney was flyin' for him and only for he moved he would have ended up in A&E. Her and Bernie start givin' it loads about him only bein' out for one thing and how he can't just expect me to go out with him just coz he text me a few times so he starts shoutin' back at them and I start shoutin' at him and Phillip starts shoutin' and poor Jasmin is standin' there without a clue of what's goin' on as per usual. So eventually Tracy tells us all to shut the fuck up and explains to everyone that Paddy might just be afraid of commitment especially coz me and him happened just after he broke up with his girlfriend back in October. So Tracy tells everyone to go to the bar to get two shots and nobody even questions her coz as I've said before, we all listen to Tracy coz she's the smart one so she knows what she's talkin' about. We're standin' there around the table with 14 shots in front of us and Tracy counts to three and we all lower the first one back followed straight away by the second and Concepta and Bernie ran straight to the bar while I stand there nearly heavin' over the taste of it.

We had a good night though. We had a good laugh with Paddy and Phillip and I'm startin' to think Paddy's gettin' the hint that I don't like him. Phillip's a great laugh. He's very quiet but he's very funny. He's a lovely young-fella, not one of these spa's ya do see around.

Concepta found an English stag party in the middle of Fitzsimons and ended up snoggin' three of them, the dirty slapper although fair play to her. Palatic is not the word though. She couldn't see straight, or at least I hope she couldn't coz the state of the fellas she was with.

I was gettin' chatted up by some fella who said he was from Belgium but I think he was takin' the piss coz I asked him where in Belgium he was from and he said Flanders. Now come on, everyone knows that Flanders is your man in the *Simpsons*.

✱✱✱

That Julie Walsh one is unreal. I swear to Jayzis, I was gonna murder her yesterday. I was tellin' ya there was war the other day between her and one of the customers. It's all anyone's been talkin' about since. She nearly got sacked over it. Greg, the manager, wasn't impressed at all. He called her into the office and gave out stink to her, we know because we were listenin' at the keyhole. She's in the height of it though. She said the security team wasn't quick enough to deal with the situation. The only thing is, we don't have a security team. She was goin' mad as well coz she lost one of her earrings and it was a good one she got off her ma for Christmas from the Elizabeth Duke Collection in Argos. She's thinkin' of suein' because of the stressful circumstances she was put under. What about the stressful circumstances we have to put up with everyday havin' to work with her? Ya don't see us suein' them, do ya?

That Julie Walsh one is always gettin' herself into trouble, I was tellin' Sheila. She couldn't understand a word I was sayin' but I was tellin' her anyways. I should learn Chinese, can ya imagine? I wonder what the Chinese is for 'Julie Walsh is a horrible cow.' But as I was tellin' Sheila, she's always gettin' herself into trouble. We went out for the Christmas party there a few weeks ago, I don't know where Sheila was but she wasn't there, but we went the ThunderRoad Café for a meal and then to Club M and needless to say, Julie Walsh was locked out of her head. So we're in Club M and she's on the podium, although how she fit up on it is a mystery to me, and some young-one is standin' behind her waitin' to get up on it and she tugs on Julie Walsh's leg and she turns around to the young-one and kicks her in the face. Now there was murder and Julie Walsh was kickin' and screamin' and the young-one was doin' these mad Power Ranger kicks and all. I thought she was havin' a fit, ya wanna see her. Anyway the two of them got kicked out and that was the last we thought we'd see of Julie Walsh for the night until there we are in Burger King on Grafton Street and who walks in only Julie Walsh and gets sick all over the place, I swear to Jayzis, it was a disgrace and I wouldn't mind, I had only taken one bite out of me Whopper and I was totally put off. I couldn't stomach another bite after seein' her, dirty bitch. And ya'd think she'd be scarlet the next day in work wouldn't ya. Jayzis no. She thought it was the funniest thing since the time a bottle of Coke fell on a customer and knocked her out.

She gets on me tits. If I have to hear anythin' else about that fight, I'll kick her so hard up the hole she'll have somethin' else to sue us over, the stupid cow.

※※

I was sittin' at home last night watchin' some shite on the telly when a knock comes on the door and who is it only Jasmin, god love her. The poor young-one looked frozen. I think she was wearin' three jackets, it's that cold at the moment. There's a nasty chill in the air. I'm walkin' around all the time with nipples ya can hang your keys out of and that's even under me clothes.

Anyway Jasmin comes in and the two of us go up to me room, a bottle of Smirnoff Ice each, and put on a bit of music and have a chat and now, I have to say, it was a nice chat which is a bit weird when Jasmin is involved. After all, we're convinced she's a bit slow. She's not the brightest spark in the box, d'ya know what I mean? The other thing about Jasmin though is that she speaks with a very bad lisp. I mean sometimes it does be impossible to understand a word she does be sayin'. She's worse than Sheila — and she's Chinese. Jayzis, the slaggin' we used to give poor Jasmin when she was younger with her lisp and her big beer bottle glasses. Her and Bopper used to go out when they were in the same class in school and the slaggin's we used to give him over her. Believe it or not, Bopper and Jasmin were the best of mates up until a year or two ago and he kinda drifted for a while and she started gettin' closer to meself, Tracy, Bernie and Concepta. She was always kind of around before that but ever since Bopper started hangin' around with Paulo she's become one of us.

I have to say, she's a lot better lookin' now. She was a bit of a tomboy before but we kinda groomed her, got her wearin' all the right gear and that and she got the contacts instead of the glasses and got her hair done properly and all. It was like that film *Clueless*, although meself and Bernie did the same for Tracy in third class. What can I say? *Off The Rails* hasn't a patch!

Anyway Jasmin said she finally found out what happened at the jelly factory and why Concepta's workin' all the mad hours all of a sudden. Apparently now, accordin' to Jasmin's uncle's friend's sister's brother-in-law's nephew, they were doin' their usual random taste test where they pick up every couple of jellies and taste it to make sure its alright. I wonder if that's what Concepta does, it would explain why she's so fat. Anyway one of the tasters found a sugar-coated tampon on the conveyor belt. It wasn't used or anythin' but its still disgustin'. I was nearly gettin' sick after Jasmin told me, I swear to Jayzis. She said they had to shut down the factory and do loads of checks and everythin'. I'm tellin' ya now that had somethin' to do with Concepta Cooney. It has to have. She probably did it as a joke coz I know Concepta and she would have told us about it. I bet ya she said nothin' coz she's afraid they'll sack her if they find out. I'm goin' to have to ask her. Jasmin asked me not to say anythin' and pretend I don't know but fuck that, I'm dyin' to find out. It makes ya think though. Imagine that tampon hadn't of been spotted by the tasters. Jayzis, I hope they were only jelly babies floatin' around in me stew last week.

***

I spent a fortune yesterday. I swear to god, I don't know how I spent that much money.

I was sittin' at home not really doin' anythin' and I get a text message off Bernie sayin' 'Wot U up 2?' so I sent her one back sayin' 'Not much. U?'. So next minute the house phone rings and its her and she asks me do I want to go to the Blanchardstown Shoppin' Centre to get a few bits in the sales, so ya know me. I says fuck it, I may as well. So the two of us get the 220 up, don't even get me started on that bus service. Forty minutes we were waitin' on a bus. Forty minutes like spas at the side of the road and when one did come along it was full and wouldn't let anyone on. Luckily enough a gang of young-fellas decided to get off while I was shoutin' at the bus driver coz I was about to get violent. I mean its ridiculous at this stage. Forty minutes is a bit much.

So anyway we get to the centre eventually and the two of us went crazy. The sales are only deadly. Boots have loads off the make-up so we bought a good bit and it's the good stuff, Max Factor and No7 and all. They even have that good foundation that I like for half price so I had to buy four things of it. Bernie got a lovely brush set and only for I have millions of brushes, I would have got one meself. I got one for Jasmin though coz she's always robbin' mine when we're out.

Ah ya wanna see the stuff I got in Dunnes. It was all that Savida stuff, ya know the designer stuff they do, the stuff that's usually a lot dearer than their own stuff. I got a lovely suedette Indian style boob tube in a beige and an Indian style laced skirt in a kind of a chocolatey colour. I swear to god, they're only mafis and I got a lovely pair of light brown knee high boots to go with them. They're doin' some lovely stuff at the moment. I even got meself one of them extra support underwire bras down to €12 from €16, I mean now where would ya get it? Ya can't go wrong.

I picked up a lovely candle set as well for me ma in the homewares, a beautiful little thing it is, and some of that room scenter stuff. They had these glass beads as well and a lovely marine coloured vase as well that'd look lovely in our sittin' room. I don't usually buy stuff for the house but ya can't pass the stuff. I even got our Bopper a lovely tee-shirt reduced from €20 to €5. Now I mean, where would ya get it? Ya can't go wrong.

I was ragin' coz French Connection's sale doesn't start 'til next week and a lot of the stuff in Top Shop and Miss Selfridges is already gone. Debenhams have a few nice things as well. I got two lovely halternecks for half price and a pair of Miss Sixty jeans with turquoise beads goin' down the side of them. They're only mafis. They're like a pair that Tracy has only hers are bell-bottoms with embroidery down the side instead of beads. I'm always tryin' to rob them on her. I couldn't find them anywhere. Her ma bought them in America or somethin'.

Meself and Bernie were knackered after all that shoppin' so we went to Eddie Rockets for somethin' to eat. I had one of them classic burgers and chicken tenders and I could have fit twice as much in I was that hungry. That's a very Concepta thing to say.

I'm delighted with me bargains though, I am. I love the sales, especially when I have a few quid to spend in them. I'm dyin' to wear them out now. The girls probably won't be doin' anythin' 'til Friday though. Ah I'll give Jasmin a ring to see what she's up to. I can't wait to wear all me Indian style gear that I got in Dunnes, although I'll probably end up lookin' like Pocahontas.

✱✱✱

There's goin' to be war. They want me to come into work on Sunday and I'm havin' none of it. Ya must be jokin, workin' on me birthday. There's no way! I did mention that its me birthday on Sunday didn't I? Me 18th. I'm all excited but there's no way I'm workin'. See what happened is, that Julie Walsh cow is off sick sayin' she's sufferin' with stress after the fight last week and that it affected her mentally and she's unfit to work as a result. If I ever get me hands on the cow she won't be able to work for the rest of her life. I told Greg I wasn't comin' in. I said there was no way and he may as well go to Julie Walsh's gaff and reef her into work coz he'd have a better chance of that than me comin' in. Not that I have loads planned but we'll probably end up goin' out Friday, Saturday and Sunday night and with a bit of luck I'll be too busy sufferin' with a hangover Sunday mornin' to come in and work. I don't think Greg understands though although he never does, especially if he's talkin' to Sheila. He's from South Africa, Greg. Some place near the sea as far as I know. I can't remember what the name of the place is for the life of me but I know it's near the beach coz he does always be tellin' me he used to go surfin'. He can be as narky though sometimes and he scares the shite out of me when he's angry. He's about seven foot tall and bald and real muscley and he has the mad accent that sounds like German or somethin'. He thinks the Irish are all mad and that we're all alcoholics but I don't know where he gets that idea. I asked him to come for a drink for me birthday so he said he might come out Saturday night or if not it'll be Friday or Sunday. The last night he was out with us was the Christmas party when Julie Walsh got kicked out of Club M. Thank jayzis she isn't comin' this time. I don't think I could stomach her gettin' sick in Burger King again. I'm still gettin' over the last time. That's one of the good things about her not bein' in. I don't have to ask her to come out with me for me birthday. I'd end up killin' her, I know I would. She'd annoy me to such a stage where I'd have to get up and give her a dig.

    Somebody found her earring by the way, the one she lost in the fight. Sheila was tellin' me, although as I said before, I never understand what Sheila does be sayin' but I think she was tryin' to tell me that someone found it in a cup of potato wedges and brought it back to complain. I swear to god, if I hear another story about people findin' things in their food, I'm never eatin' again. Maybe we should try that with Concepta although nothin' would turn her off her food. I wouldn't mind but ya wanna see the state of the earring and here's me thinkin' it was goin' to be solid gold with real diamonds. Me arse, and I bet ya that dirty Julie Walsh cow is gonna put it back in her ear after it bein' in a cup of potato wedges, the manky bitch.

Anyway as I was sayin, there isn't a hope of me workin' Sunday. I'm hopin' to be way too tired to do anythin' after Saturday night if ya know wha I mean? I might just get an extra special birthday present. I bleedin' better.

✳✳✳

I was on me way home from work last night, on a late shift til 10 o'clock I was, and who do I spot only Paulo. So I was like 'Paulo. Paulo. Come 'ere.' So he stops anyway and waits for me to catch up with him and then he gives me a big hug like he usually does. So he tells me he's on his way over to see our Bopper and I was like 'Right, grand, ya can walk me home so.' And I give him a little nudge and a wink kinda messin' sort of thing. So we were there walkin' and havin' a great little chat. He was tellin' me about his job and about the people that he works with and this manager that tried to feel him up in the stockroom but he was havin' none of it. Jayzis I could imagine Greg comin' onto me in the stockroom. I'd leave him there for dead and have him sent back to South Africa in pieces. So he was sayin' as well about the Concepta one askin' him out and I thought it was only gas coz I could imagine the look on his face after gettin' a text message off Concepta askin' him to go to the cinema with her. Jayzis the thoughts of it. I couldn't imagine Paulo and Concepta together and as I was sayin' before anyways, and especially the way he was actin' last night, I'm convinced he fancies me. I told him about what Jasmin's uncle's friend's sister's brother-in-law's nephew heard about what happened in the jelly factory and he couldn't believe it. D'ya know I actually haven't seen her since I heard it meself to say it to her. I must knock around to her house and pretend I want a lend of a CD or somethin' or maybe to get back one of the 47 she had belongin' to me, and me Discman as well. Come to think of it she has me electric shaver as well. She can keep it. I won't be goin' anywhere near it again after she was usin' it to shave her bikini line. Jayzis, ya'd catch scabies or somethin'.

Paulo said he'd come out at least one of the nights for me birthday as well so fair play to him, although he says he might have to go out to meet someone on Saturday night so ya know me. I tried to get all the info out of him but he wouldn't tell me who it was. He's very quiet about things sometimes, Paulo. He won't let ya know what's goin' on or anythin', kinda likes to keep himself to himself. I usually just ask Bopper if he wont tell me and get all the gossip that way but you do kinda feel that he does be hidin' somethin' sometimes, like he has a secret or somethin' or maybe that's just the way people from Bosnia are. I wouldn't know now coz Paulo is the only one I know. Oh there was that young-one Jodie that was in school with us for a while. She was from Bosnia. Tell a lie, she was from Offaly. She was only in the school a few months so I can't really remember.

Anyway I didn't find out who Paulo is going out with on Saturday so I'll get it out of Bopper soon enough. Paulo ended up over in the house for ages and meself, himself and Bopper watched the telly for a while and got a curry that Paulo paid for and all fair play to him. He even did the washin' up. I wouldn't mind but we have a dishwasher — the spa.

✳✳✳

Oh good Jayzis! Well I finally got all the details out of Concepta about what happened in the jelly factory and I'm really starting to prefer she hadn't told me.

I knocked over to her last night pretendin' to be lookin' for me *Mariah Carey's Greatest Hits* CD which I wouldn't mind, I never got off her in the end. I don't think I've ever seen that cow buy a CD. She just robs everyone else's. Ya wanna see the size of the collection she has and they're not only mine. She has CD's belongin' to Jasmin, Bernie, Bopper and even Paulo as well. Tracy won't let her anywhere near hers though. She's mad when it comes to CD's, Tracy. They're all in alphabetical order and all. She had an eppo one day when she realised Concepta had taken her Madonna's *Immaculate Collection*. The two of them nearly battered each other over it and I wouldn't mind but Concepta already had a lend of it off me.

Anyway gettin' back to the point. I don't know if ya noticed but I keep goin' off on tandems, talkin' about somethin' else and I end up forgettin' about what I was talkin' about in the first place. It's just this habit that I have. I don't know where it came from, maybe its just coz I talk very fast or somethin', I don't know. Maybe Tracy would know. I must ask her although I'll forget. I'm always sayin' I'll ask Tracy about things and end up forgettin'.

So the jellies anyway. Yeah, Concepta said they did really find a tampon but wait and ya hear this. Concepta said she had it down her bra coz she was waitin' to go on a break and ya know, use it if ya know what I mean but its hard not to be vulgar when you're talkin' about shovin' a tampon up your thingy. So anyway she had this tampon in her bra and whatever happened, she said she must have bent over the conveyer belt but when she eventually got to the toilet, the tampon was gone and she was just about to go back and tell one of the other young-ones she works with when all hell breaks loose. There was alarms goin' off and people runnin' everywhere and flashin' lights and next minute the whole factory stops and the manager comes out of the office to see what's wrong and he goes mad when he realises that one of the tasters found a sugar coated tampon, which I have to add was out of the packet. Ya know Concepta, not one for class. She'd be no Myleene. And if that wasn't bad enough, who was in the factory at that exact moment only one of the health and safety people that the government send out to see how clean the place is. Can ya imagine? Poor Concepta nearly shit herself as if the tampon in with the jellies wasn't bad enough.

So anyway that's why the factory got closed down and why they were workin' all the overtime and all and that's why she never told us, coz they'll murder her if they find out. Concepta Cooney and her tampon. Now there's one period she'll never forget.

✳✳✳

Oh good God. I'm not even goin' to try and explain about last night. Alright I will. One word to begin with – Jayzis. It was only mental. Where do we decide to go only the Red Box and I mean it's been years since I was there. I think the last time I was there I was 14 and at some under 18's yoke that was on. They used to have them all the time but ya don't hear of them much anymore. They used to do nights in the Temple Theatre with Mark McCabe. I wonder does that still be on. The Red Box used to be great for the under 18's. It's unbelievable now though. They've done it up since the last time I was there and its real like Ibiza or one of these places. Not that I've been to Ibiza but ya know what I mean.

Now the music wasn't exactly my thing. I prefer Beyonce and Britney to that pump pump pump dancy shite but I got onto the floor and gave it a bit of a go, ya know yourself. I was locked out of me head. I wouldn't even mind but I can't remember where half the drink came from. I think I was just pickin' up drink off counters or whatever and drinkin' it. I know at one stage I had a few shots but what they were I couldn't tell ya. Jasmin got me one so there was probably vodka and fairy liquid in it knowing her!

Whatever about me bein' locked though, there was loads of people there mad out of it and I really mean mad out of it. Space cadets like. I don't know how many times I got asked for yokes and ya know me when I'm locked, I was huggin' the fuckers and all and tryin' to have a bit of a chat with them and all the rest of it. They must have thought that I was on something coz I was so locked but I'd never go near any of that stuff, wouldn't go near it. Its not my scene and none of me mates are like that.

There was all these young-ones and young-fellas as well wearin' all that mad illuminous glow in the dark shite, ya know the type of thing, yellow and orange and green and blue and turquoise. More flashin' lights than Funderland. I thought it was deadly though. I was goin' up and talkin' to them and puttin' the things on meself. I looked like a Christmas tree at one stage. All I needed was some stupid fucker to spill a drink on me and I'd end up electormicuted. Can ya imagine? Me lyin' in the Red Box burnt to a crisp and covered in illuminous lights. Jayzis.

I had a good night. There wasn't many of us mind but it was still a laugh. There was just me, Bernie, Jasmin and Bopper at first and then Bopper disappeared after about 40 minutes. He said somethin' about meetin' a friend and the two of them goin' off somewhere. Me and the girls stayed in the Red Box though and had a great night. There was this chillout room upstairs and me and the girls were up there for ages. It was deadly coz ya can look down on all the clubbers givin' it socks downstairs below ya. We kept losin' Jasmin and we'd find her leanin' over the balcony lookin' down. I think it was all the colour. Jasmin gets excited very easily.

We were talkin' to a young-one and young-fella in the chillout room from Armenia which accordin' to them is nowhere near Bosnia where Paulo comes from. They were lovely people. I've never talked to anyone from Armenia before but they were nice. I don't even know where Armenia is but I was never any good at history in school.

No I have to say, I enjoyed the night although I didn't wear me new gear I got the other day in Dunnes. I'm savin' it for tomorrow night for me birthday. I did mention its me birthday tomorrow didn't I? Although let the truth be told, I don't like makin' a fuss about me birthday. I'll just have me three nights out and that'll be it.

**

Happy birthday to me, happy birthday to me, happy birthday to JoJo, happy birthday to me. Jayzis. Can ya imagine? Here I am the big 18. I thought I'd be really upset coz I'm gettin' old but I think I have too much of a hangover to think about it.

Is it any wonder I have a hangover after last night? We went up to Heaven in Blanchardstown coz it's been a while since we were up there and I do enjoy a night up there. It does always be a great bit of buzz. I can't remember a bad night up there let the truth be told and the people are always lovely. I'm always bumpin' into people I know. I know a good few people from Blanch from school and that, lovely people most of them. The other thing about Heaven is that there's always loads of rides and when I say rides, I mean it. Gorgeous lookin' fellas, real good lookin' fellas now, very handsome and that and sound as well.

Anyway we're standin' there in Heaven. There was me, Tracy, Bernie and Sheila, Dymphna, Greg and Marie from work and who walks past us only Julie Walsh. Now it wasn't me that spotted her, it was Dymphna and to be honest, Dymphna hates Julie Walsh more than I do if that's possible. I think it has somethin' to do with Julie Walsh callin' Dymphna a smelly, flea-ridden, scruffy, infested toe-rag but I could be wrong and whatever about there bein' a bit of a bang off Dymphna, which I have to say, can be a bit bad at times especially after she's been on the hot food counter for a few hours but Julie Walsh isn't much better.

So we were standin' there and Dymphna spots her and calls her over and she turns and waves, kinda scarlet that we seen her in the pub when she's out sick. I'd say she was drinkin' there thinkin' we'd be goin' into town but then she spots Greg and I've never seen Julie Walsh move as fast in me life. She must have got the fright of her life. So Greg, not bein' one to miss an opportunity, follows her and finds her and accordin' to eyewitnesses, I wish I had of been there, it was a friend of Tracy's told us, Greg starts shoutin' at her and givin' it loads and Julie Walsh is just standin' there scarlet. Pure morto I'd say she was coz Greg can do that to ya, especially with half the pub lookin'. She told him though she was only in the pub coz the drink helps calm her down after the fight last week. She's a spa of a young-one, I swear to jayzis. Lucky she left soon after coz if I had of seen her I'd have battered her. It'd be more than an earring she'd be losin'. She'd be lucky to leave with all her limbs attached. The stress of the pub was probably too much for her. Stress me arse. The only stress Julie Walsh knows about is when the floorboards struggle to take her weight. That lazy cow just doesn't want to work. She'll just spend all the rest of her time off sittin' on her arse watchin' *Ricki Lake* and *Murder She Wrote*. Seein' her really pissed me off though coz I was meant to be workin' on me birthday coz of her. Fair play to Dymphna now for doin' it for me but that Julie Walsh one really gets on me tits. Other than that it was a great night.

***

I'm never drinkin' again. Never. I'm in some state let me tell ya. God only knows what I had to drink last night. I certainly don't remember. Everyone kept goin' to the bar and gettin' me drink so I was out of me face. I think Jasmin wanted to get me a drink at one stage but I said no way. Knowin' Jasmin I'd end up needin' me stomach pumped. She was on the Baileys and Lucozade the last I heard.

Now it was a great night from what I remember and there was loads of us – meself, Bernie, Jasmin, Tracy, Concepta, Bopper, Paulo, me Uncle Dessie, Paddy and his mate Phillip and Sheila, the Chinese young-one from work. We weren't really sure where to go but Paulo suggested Break for the Border coz there was this 70's and 80's night and nobody really had any other ideas apart from the RnB in Coyote so we ended up havin' a bit of a vote and I decided to go to Break for the Border for a bit of buzz and we really ended up havin' a great night. The only thing about the 70's and 80's is that I wasn't alive for the 70's and most of the 80's but that doesn't mean I don't know any of the music. I love a bit of Abba and ya can't get me off the dancefloor when Bananarama come on. 'I'm your Venus, I'm your fire, your desire.' Its only great. Ya can't beat it. Me and me Uncle Dessie were givin' it loads. He's me ma's brother and he got separated from his wife, me Aunt Doris, there last year and ever since he's been around all the time and even started comin' out with me and Bopper all the time. He's mad, I swear to God, mad. Ya wouldn't think he's a 48-year-old auld-fella. He's kinda goin' through some sort of second childhood or somethin' since him and me Aunt Doris separated. He's after gettin' mad into all the hip-hop music and everythin'. He loves Eminem. That's half the reason why I didn't want to go to Coyote. If ya saw me Uncle Dessie gettin' down with his bad self as he says, ya'd know what I'm talkin' about. I do be scarlet. He does be goin' around shakin' his hole and feelin' up all the young-ones. I swear to god, he's been watchin' too much *Ricki Lake* and *Save the Last Dance*. They all love him of course. Think he's only the best thing since Vanilla Ice. He goes home with more phone numbers than the rest of us put together and I wouldn't mind but me Uncle Dessie wouldn't be the best to look at by a long way and anyways, he's old. Jasmin loves him. Thinks there's nothin' like him. Worships the ground he walks on. Ya wanna see the two of them together. It does be sickenin'. Now he never like does be doin' anythin' with her coz if he did, I swear to Jayzis, I'd kill him if Bopper and me ma hadn't got there first. The two of them do be dancin' and doin' all the moves and all and I wouldn't mind but Jasmin wouldn't be the greatest dancer. I'd be a lot better now although Bernie would be the best dancer out of us all let the truth be told. I mean credit where its due. But Jasmin and Dessie do be laughin' and jokin' and all the rest of it, the best of buddies on a night out, sittin' together on the Nitelink, sharin' chicken baguettes in Abrakebabra on the way home and they have all these private jokes as well that none of us know what they're talkin' about. I have to say, they piss me off at times but I love me Uncle Dessie to bits, now I do.

Bernie was in the height of it over somethin' last night and for the life of me I can't remember what it was over or who it was with or anythin'. All I can remember is her shoutin' at somebody and stormin' off and Concepta and Tracy runnin' after her. Jayzis I must have been hammered coz I can't remember what happened after that or even who I was talkin' to at the time. Tell a lie, it was Phillip. I waffled the ears off the poor young-fella half the night. I have to say, he's a lovely bloke, much nicer than Paddy and better lookin' if I'm honest. I don't even know what I was talkin' to him about but he was listenin', fair play to him. I know I wouldn't listen to me if I was locked out of me tree and talkin' shite. He even gave me his number although I had a look in me phone today and its not there. Hold on now and I have another scroll through me P's. Oh he is there. He's in as Pilp. That'll tell ya just how locked I was although sayin' that, I probably have the wrong number as well with 2's and 4's all over the place. I'll be ringin' Russia. I'm sure someone else'll have his number though. I must text him coz as I said, he's a nice young-fella.

Poor Tracy wasn't drinkin' last night coz she's still busy with her project on Charles Dickens. He didn't write *Matilda* she tells me. Charles Dickens was your man that wrote *Oliver* and the *Christmas Carol*. I knew I'd heard of him. I told her I'd help her with her project if I can coz I've seen the *Christmas Carol* loads of times. It was the one with the Muppets in it now but I'm sure it's the same thing. Jayzis aren't the Muppets great.

Talkin' of Muppets, the slaggin's we were givin' Concepta all night over the tampon thing. The poor young-one is scarlet. It has to be the first time I've ever seen her go red. Concepta doesn't get embarrassed, the girls will tell ya. She's just hopin' they don't find out it was hers though coz they're lookin' for someone to blame over it she tells us. I felt kinda sorry for her let the truth be told. She hasn't really been herself the last few days. She's even stickin' to her diet and that's sayin' somethin'. Ah I hope she doesn't get in trouble over it, honestly now.

Bopper and Paulo were locked out of it. I don't know if I saw them off the dancefloor. Bopper was givin' it socks to all the old Kylie and Madonna songs and he loves the Abba as well, knows all the words. He's always listenin' to the Abba *Gold* CD in the gaff. They're mad the two of them when they get together. They have all these little phrases that we don't understand. They do always be talkin' about people we don't know with weird names. I'm tellin' ya, them young-fellas are loopers.

Poor Sheila was locked after two bottles of Smirnoff Ice. Ya wanna see her dancin'. I thought Jasmin was bad. She's gas and ya wanna see her goin' around talkin' to all the fellas and all. I wouldn't have the balls now but fair play to her, although I'd say half the people she was talkin' to hadn't a clue what she was sayin' to them. I don't know how she remembers to speak English when she's locked, I mean I forget how to speak English when I'm locked and I'm not even Chinese. I have to say though, she's a great young-one and all the others think she's lovely. She just knows how to have a good laugh, d'ya know wor I mean?

I can't remember what happened to Paddy but he definitely left before the rest of us, even Phillip coz he came up and said goodbye to us before he left. I can remember Paddy talkin' to Bernie for a bit but that's it.

Overall though, it was a great night. I really enjoyed it and it was worth the hangover although as I said, I'm never drinkin' again. Well until next weekend.

✳✳✳

I have a rash. I swear to god. It started out on me hand and it's spread all down me left leg. Now at first I thought it was an insect bite coz it was only a little red dot on me left hand but then I was thinkin' how many insects do bite ya in Ireland in the middle of January, although me Aunty Linda said that she was bitten twice by mosquitos in Wexford at New Years, and then it started gettin' bigger, me rash, not Wexford. I was like, Jayzis. Now I thought it might have been a hive or somethin' coz I mean it's definitely not a heat rash. Not with the weather we've been havin' and I don't think its frost bite coz I think, although I'm not too sure, but I think your hand does fall off with the frostbite. I heard that somewhere although it was probably off Jasmin and we all know that if she had a car, people would get her penalty points mixed up with the points she got in the leavin' cert. Can ya imagine Jasmin with a car? There'd be no one safe. The poor young-one has trouble tellin' her left from her right. She'd have to write a big L and R on her hands so she wouldn't forget. Although then she'd forget what the letters meant, the dope.

Anyway I woke up this mornin' and me rash was spread right the way down me leg. It's reefin' itchy and ya know yourself, ya try not to scratch it but ya just have to. It's one of them things. What if it's chicken pox? That's meant to be very dangerous to get when you're older. All the mas on the road will be sendin' their kids around to my gaff so they can catch it off me. I remember my ma did that to me when I was a young-one, the heartless cow. I mean how cruel would ya have to be to send your child out to catch a disease? I was in bits with it for weeks I remember. Half the class in school was out at the same time over it. The teacher would have been delighted only she caught it as well.

I hope its not one of them DDT's although now that I come to think of it, there isn't a hope that its a DDT. It's been that long since I've had sex. Talk about the immaculate conception, that'd be more like the immaculate infection. I bet its just that me ma changed the washin' powder. I said it to her there the other day, I said ya'd be better off stickin' with the Daz but d'ya think she'd listen to me? Now that's the second time I got an infection over the bitch.

✳✳✳

I'm only hearin' things today about what happened on Sunday night and I must have been more locked than I usually am coz loads of stuff happened that I can't remember and I usually remember everythin'. The girls and our Bopper will tell ya.

First of all the girls are sayin' that I kissed Phillip after Paddy left and I'm tellin' ya for a fact that never happened, not for want of tryin' mind you. I'm goin' to be honest with ya, I do have a bit of a thing for Phillip, as I said he's a lovely young-fella, but there's no way I kissed him. That's somethin' I would have remembered although sayin' that it was definitely him that was helpin' me walk when I left the club. I must ask Tracy coz she was sober. It was Bernie and Concepta that said it to me and they're messers sometimes. Luckily I haven't text Phillip, or Pilp as he's still called in me phone, coz I'd be scarlet if I did kiss him and didn't remember.

Oh yeah and Bernie was in the height of it over Paddy. She said she was talkin' to him for ages and then he tried to kiss her but she was havin' none of it. She says he asked her earlier in the night if he had a chance and she kinda said no because of the way he was with me and because he just asked me out there last week and he's been textin' me and that. She's decent like that Bernie although I'd be glad if she was with him coz then the fucker would leave me alone. But anyway, he tries to kiss Bernie and she tells him to piss off and he tries again so she started goin' mad at him and had to be held back by Tracy and me Uncle Dessie. I'm ragin' I missed that. I'd say it was gas although the way Concepta told me the story ya'd swear there was after been killin's. Exaggeration should be that young-ones middle name. Although it wouldn't be as funny as her real middle name. Its Cleopatra believe it or not. Concepta Cleopatra Cooney. Her ma and da must have been on somethin' and it can't have been a bet coz she has a sister Veronica Aphrodite, who I believe was named after some Roman goddess back in the old days, and two younger brothers, Malachy Achilles and Herbert Hercules, who were these people from Greece. I know that coz I saw that film *Troy* and Disney's *Hercules*. I mean for Jayzis sake, that's cruelty. Somebody should get the child welfare people on to Concepta's ma and da for givin' the kids names like that and if it wasn't bad enough Concepta gettin' slagged over her weight in school.

Anyway where was I? I was goin' off the subject again. As I said before, I have a habit of doin' that. I do be talkin' about one thing and then go off and start talkin' about somethin' else. I was meant to ask Tracy why I do that but I never got around to it. That's always happenin'. I'm always forgettin' to ask her things although the poor young-ones up to her tits at the moment with her project.

Yeah so anyway gettin' back to what I was sayin', Paddy tried it on with Bernie and she was havin' none of it. That's why he left early I think. I mean he was probably scarlet after causin' a scene. I know I would. I wouldn't even say goodbye. I'd be gone.

The only other thing about the other night was that Paulo got a hickey. Concepta was tellin' me coz she saw him in Clery's on Monday although he won't say who he got it off and nobody remembers seein' him with anyone on Sunday night and he came home with us and Bopper stayed in his gaff so someone would have noticed him bein' with someone. I must ask Bopper. Maybe he knows where Paulo's hickey came from.

✳︎✳︎✳︎

Well the Julie Walsh one was back in work today luckily enough for her coz from what I hear, they're lookin' for a way to get rid of her. I mean would ya blame them? She threatened to sue them over that fight last week and they can't sack her over that now in case she does and they can't say anythin' about her bein' out sick even though Greg saw her in Heaven coz she has a doctors note sayin' she was sufferin' from stress. Stress me hole. The only stress that one knows is when she tries to fit into a size smaller than a 22. She came in today thinkin' she was all that and a packet of Wrigley's Extra Green, sittin' on her stool tryin' to get everyone else to do her job. I caught her tryin' to get poor Sheila to do the phone credit machine for her so I called Sheila aside and I says 'Sheila you don't be doin' what that one tells ya. Ya have your own job to be doin'. Let her get up and do it herself.' But ya know Sheila, she's too nice to say no. That or she didn't understand a word I said to her. So I caught Julie Walsh askin' her to get a packet of cigarettes a few minutes later so I went through her for a shortcut. 'Here you' says I. I was standin' there with me hands on me hips starin' Julie Walsh out of it and she turns around and I says 'How dare you be tellin' Sheila what to do. She has enough work to be doin' without doin' yours as well. Now the next time get up off your arse and get the cigarettes yourself or it'll be more than an earring you'll be losin'.' The look on her face. I swear to god, she nearly died. It had to be said though. I've had enough of her, I really have. I mean normally I wouldn't say anythin', I'd let it be if ya know what I mean. If I have a problem with somebody I'll talk to me mates or whatever but I wouldn't say it to their face coz that's just how arguments start. Call me two faced if ya like but to be honest I couldn't give a shite. We all bitch about people behind their backs and I'm not goin' to be one of these high and mighty gobshites who pretends they don't.

Anyway as I was sayin', somebody had to say it to Julie Walsh coz she was only back in the door five minutes and she was tryin' to get people to do things for her. Believe me, there's a lot more I could have said but I was just annoyed over poor Sheila and she wouldn't stick up for herself, ya know that kind of way. No, I could have said a lot more to Julie Walsh but I didn't want to cause another scene. Believe me, her day will come and I'll be there ready to break me shite laughin' when it does.

***

We had a quiet night in last night. Just meself and Bopper, and Bernie came around for a while. We decided to watch

Findin' Nemo on the DVD coz Concepta got it for me for me birthday. I have to give it to Concepta, she's great at pickin' out presents. I was only delighted with *Findin' Nemo*. It has to be one of me favourite films. Your one Dory reminds me a bit of Jasmin.

So anyway it was just me, Bopper and Bernie and we got a lovely curry, mafis now, the nicest curry I've had this long time. The chicken balls were just right and the batter was lovely on them and not one bit fell off the chicken like it usually does. Even the rice was lovely coz I mean there's often times when ya do get a bad bit of egg fried rice. We were goin' to have a few jellies as well but they haven't been touched since we heard Concepta's tampon story. The only things is, she hasn't brought any home since so they're not really startin' to build up in the press again. I told me ma she should send them to the starvin' kids in Africa but she said they mightn't like cola bottles. I told her to send the jelly babies instead but she told me they mightn't like them either. I know if I was dyin' of starvation I wouldn't give a shite if it was a cola bottle, a jelly baby or a sugar coated tampon, I'd still eat it.

Meself and Bernie were tryin' to get all the gossip out of Bopper about Paulo's hickey but he hasn't a clue. Now Jasmin tells us she walked to Paulo's house with him and Bopper and he definitely didn't have it then although she was palatic and wouldn't see an ice-cream van parked on his neck never mind a hickey but we left them only five minutes earlier and it wasn't there, well, so Bernie says. I couldn't even see Paulo that night, let alone his neck. Bopper knows nothin' though. He can't remember seein' it at all. But as I said before, Concepta saw it the next mornin' in Clery's when she was talkin' to Paulo so unless he got it that mornin' on the way to work. Its weird now I have to say. I don't even know why Bopper does stay in Paulo's. They don't have any spare beds and our own house is closer than Paulo's from where we get off the Nitelink and he had to leave early on Sunday mornin' anyway coz Paulo was in work. Them young-fellas are mad.

✳✳✳

I text Phillip yesterday, ya know Paddy's mate, and believe it or not, I actually got the number right when I was locked although as I said before, I wrote his name down as Pilp. Now all week I was sayin' will I text him, will I not text him so yesterday I says fuck it and whipped out me phone and sent him a message, somethin' like 'Heya wots da story? Wot u up 2?' So we were textin' away for a while, ya know all the usual shite, 'r u workin 2day?' 'U goin out da wkend?' and all this so I says to him eventually, 'So do u wanna meet me sum nite 4 a drnk?' ya know yourself, grabbin' the bull by the horns coz it didn't look like he was gonna ask me. If he's anythin' like his mate Paddy then it'd be three months before I got asked out and at this stage, I'm not waitin' that long. So he doesn't text me for a while and I'm wonderin' what's goin' on like and whether I should text him again or whatever when I eventually get a message off him sayin' that he likes me and all but he doesn't think it's a good idea that we go out coz of what happened with me and Paddy coz Paddy is his best mate and all this shite. I says, well Bernie's my best friend and it didn't cross Paddy's mind when he was tryin' to get stuck into her on Sunday night. But he said Paddy's still into me and he wouldn't do that on his best mate and as much as I'm ragin' that he's not comin' out with me, I kinda get where he's comin' from, d'ya know what I'm tryin' to say? This'd be lost on poor Jasmin. The amount of times we have to go over things two or three times with her until she knows what we're talkin' about. Tracy does always be drawin' her diaphragms to explain things. She had herself convinced there was 12 colours in the rainbow the other day, convinced of it. Wouldn't let the rest of us tell her any different. She must have been countin' them twice coz everyone knows there's only six colours in the rainbow, the sap.

Anyway, that's beside the point. Its miles away from the point but where was I? Oh yeah, Phillip. Yeah I wasn't really bothered so I text him and said it was grand and could we be mates and all the rest of it and he was delighted that I wasn't pissed off with him. No I couldn't be. As I said, Phillips a lovely young-fella. I'm not goin' to get me bit off him but he's still nice.

✷✷✷

We were out last night. There was meself, Bernie, Jasmin and Concepta. We were tryin' to get Tracy to come out but she's still doin' the project on Charles Dickens, fair play to her. She says she's goin' to give me a lend of a book called *A Tale Of Two Cities* to read coz she says I'd like it. Sure I'll give it a go and see what I think. I'm not usually one for the readin' but if Tracy says its good I believe her. She had to read every single book Charles Dickens ever wrote. I bet ya she's cursin' the fucker for writin' so many.

We tried to get Bopper and Paulo to come out with us but they were gonna just sit in our gaff and watch a video, the borin' fuckers. It was only the two of them now coz me ma and da were goin' to some 50th and came home later than I did I might add. And they give out about me and Bopper comin' in at all hours.

We had a good night as usual. We were goin' to go to Fitzsimons but Concepta said how about goin' to Bad Bobs instead? Now usually when Concepta makes a suggestion we try to ignore her but Bernie and Jasmin were agreein' with her so I didn't want to be awkward and I have to say, I like Bobs anyways. There does be a good atmosphere. The only thing is, if you're on the top floor and want to have a smoke, ya have to go down three flights of stairs and before ya say anythin', I'm not back on the smokes. Well not really. Well I am kinda. I'm smokin' less than I did before Christmas anyway.

Yeah so we were doin' the usual, havin' a few drinks, dancin' away to all the tunes. Concepta was goin' around chattin' to anyone drunk enough to listen to her. That young-one would talk to shite. I've seen her go into a pub and talk to every single person in it before the end of the night. She's always goin' missin' but we don't have to worry about her. She usually turns up at the end of the night especially if she knows we're goin' for somethin' to eat before goin' home. Jasmin is a different story altogether. I don't know how many times we've nearly had to send a search party out for that young-one. We found her one night, now this is no word of a lie, we found her on the roof of Spirit. How she got there I couldn't tell ya but there was this big commotion and the bouncer came and found Tracy or somethin'. The fuckin' roof. She could probably hear pigeons or somethin' and wanted to know where the sound was comin' from, the dizzy cow. Jasmin wouldn't be able to get home from town only she gets the taxi with us and we'll usually drop her to her house if

Paulo's not with us coz he shows her which house is hers if he's with us coz he lives near her.

So last night anyway, meself and the girls, Bernie and Jasmin it was, Concepta was off doin' her meet the crowd shite, we got talkin' to these young-fellas from Kerry. Total boggers they were. The woolly jumpers and all. I was half expectin' a few sheep to appear from somewhere. So we were talkin' to them for ages and havin' a dance and the rest of it and one of the fellas, Dermot his name was, the nicest lookin' of them all let the truth be told, a bit of a ride, he was mad into me, givin' me all the lines and the rest of it and one thing is leadin' to another and we end up kissin' there in the middle of the second floor in Bad Bobs and he was even a good kisser for a culchie. Not only that but Bernie was with one of them and then Jasmin was and even Concepta ended up with one of them when she came back although hers was the biggest bogger of the lot. He even smelt like a farm if ya know what I mean. So we're all leavin' anyway, well we had to, the club was closed, and they asked us back to the hotel they were stayin' in, some place in Ballsbridge, out near Funderland but Concepta really wanted to go home. I think it was because your man was a minger but she says it looked like they didn't have a hotel out in Ballsbridge and it was probably their caravans in some field they were bringin' us back to. In other words, she was tryin' to make out they were knackers or travellers or itinerys or whatever it is ya say these days so people wont think your racist or whatever the word is when ya don't like knackers. So anyway to cut a long story short, we decided to go home although I did give Dermot me number and he promised to give me a ring the next time he's in Dublin. He says he does a lot of travellin' so it should be soon. 'He does a lot of travellin'.' The Concepta one said in the taxi on the way home, 'Does he travel in a High-Ace van?'

✽✽✽

I was sittin' on the toilet this mornin' as ya do, well unless ya have a willy and can piss standin' up, and next minute all I hear is this ringin' noise. Now I haven't a clue where it was comin' from. There was no one else in the house at the time. Me da was in work, Bopper was over at Paulo's or somethin' and me ma was at the doctors coz she's convinced she has a lump on her diddy. Me da keeps tellin' her its her nipple.

So there I was with me knickers around me ankles wonderin' where the noise was comin' from when it suddenly dawned on me that it might be me phone ringin'. I jumped up like a kangaroo and ran to me bedroom, difficult as it was with me knickers trailin' along the floor at me feet, me nearly leavin' a trail of piss along the landin' floor from the bathroom to the bedroom. Me phone was on the bed and I picked it up to answer it and the ringin' stops all of a sudden, wouldn't ya know. Typical isn't it? All of that and I still missed the call. The ringtone was changed to Like A Virgin again I might add. When I get Bernie Boland I'll kill her. She does that every time we go to the pub.

I looked to see who it was that was tryin' to ring me, hopin' I hadn't given me number to anyone I wasn't supposed to on Saturday night or that Bernie hadn't. She has a habit of givin' fellas my number when she doesn't like them, leavin' me to try and work out who these gobshites are. I don't know how many times some spa has rang me wantin' to talk to Bernie. I was thinkin' of writin' her number on the back of one of the cubicle doors in Coyote but it's probably there already.

Anyway, whoever was tryin' to ring me had their number blocked so I didn't know who it was. So there I was in me bedroom, me knickers around me ankles with me phone in me hand, lookin' out the window at Mister O'Toole across the road hangin' out his upstairs window starin' at me, the dirty fuckin' prevert.

✱✱✱

I was in work yesterday, Julie Walsh wasn't in thank God, and I had a good chat with Sheila, well as good a chat as ya can have with Sheila without callin' in a transvestite or a translator or whatever it is. I must say, I'm gettin' better at understandin' what she's tryin' to say. Well at least I hope I am. One of her friends came into the shop yesterday, a Chinese young-one, and the two of them started talkin'. I swear to god, that Chinese is a mad language and the speed of them. I hadn't a clue what they were sayin'. They definitely said somethin' about Julie Walsh coz they said fat cow a few times so that must mean the same thing in Chinese as it does in our language.

Anyway meself and Sheila were havin' a chat, in English by the way, I haven't a word of Chinese, except maybe *li ping* which means jump I think, and I was askin' her about fellas and all the rest of it, just if she likes any, not gettin' into the ins and outs of her sex life if she has one although she wouldn't be the only one not to if she didn't. Anyway I don't think they teach her stuff like blow-job in the English college, although you'd be surprised. She knows what a joint is although I'd say that has somethin' to do with Marie. I don't think I've ever seen that woman not stoned. She's keepin' some cannabis farm in Thailand or somewhere goin' all by herself and I wouldn't mind, she's married with kids and grandkids and all.

Anyway here's me goin' off on tandems again. I think I was talkin' about Sheila talkin' about fellas. I was yeah. And she wasn't really givin' much away and ya know me, I was tryin' to get all the info out of her. So she says there's no one she really likes at the moment and all the rest of it but she wouldn't mind havin' a boyfriend. Now it was the wrong thing to say to me, Sheila knew by the look on me face. My mind went into overdrive straight away tryin' to think of someone to set her up with. There's no one in work. There's only really Greg and he'd be too old and he's the manager anyway and then there's Boris that does the stockin' the shelves but we do forget he's there and he's from Ukrainia or some other mad country and speaks less English than Sheila and that's sayin' somethin'. There's a few kids that do a couple of hours at the weekend but they're only about 14 or whatever. So I was thinkin' away anyway and next thing a thought hits me. What about our Bopper? They'd be great together and they're both around the same age. So I gave her his number and told her to text him. I just hope she can text in English although in sayin' that, I don't think Bopper can either so they'll be grand.

✳︎✳︎✳︎

I was bored out of me box sittin' at home last night so I decided to knock around to Bernie's for a chat and ended up stayin' for a couple of hours. We watched *Muriel's Weddin'* on the DVD again. That film never gets old. I can tell ya every single line from it I've seen it that many times but there was fuck all on the telly so it was either that or the usual shite: episodes of *Friends* ya've seen 11 times, documentaries on Eskimos, shite American detective programmes on RTE 2, Channel 4, TV3 and Sky, or the news. I don't know why we pay all that money for 100 channels on the digital and still have the same shite to watch. There's even some channels where ya can watch the same shite an hour later, just in case ya missed it the first time or are a sad bastard and wanted to watch the same programme twice in a row.

Yeah so meself and Bernie had a bit of a chat and watched *Muriel's Weddin'*. I was tellin' her about me tryin' to set Sheila and Bopper up and she thinks it's a great idea and all coz they're both single and young and she thinks they'd make a great couple although she says for some reason, that she doesn't think Bopper is into Sheila. Now the last time Sheila and Bopper were out with us as far as I remember was the night of me birthday and I was far too pissed at the time to notice if there was any chemistry goin' on between them. I don't even know if the two of them were talkin' let the truth be told. Bernie said she did but can't remember for how long or what way they were lookin' at each other or anythin'. She's hopeless. I must see if Concepta, Tracy, Jasmin or Paulo noticed if they were into each other. Bernie is helpin' me set them up though. Whether she likes it or not, she's helpin'.

Oh the other thing we were talkin' about was Paddy. I noticed he's kind of left me alone the last week or whatever and was wonderin' has he given up but Bernie says he keeps textin' her all the time. How he got her number, we don't know but he has it and keeps textin' her and askin' her out and all and she's havin' none of it. I told her she should but then she accused me of just sayin' that so I could go out with Phillip, the cheek of her. I'm not like that, now I'm not. It wouldn't be like me to be selfish. All I'm sayin' is if she likes Paddy she should go for a drink with him. Plus Phillip might ask me out if Paddy's goin' out with Bernie. Me selfish? The cheek of her.

✳✳✳

I had to go the doctor today coz that rash I had is after comin' back and it's worse than it was before. Seriously like, it's all down the left side of me body and startin' to spread up me left leg. It started to get very close to me fanjita so I said enough is enough and headed off to the doctor.

Now for some reason the doctor we usually have, Doctor Najima, wasn't there. She's lovely, Doctor Najima. She's been me doctor since I was borned. I used to be amazed goin' to see her when I was a kid coz she's from India and she was the only foreign person I knew. Ya'd never see anyone foreign walkin' through Dublin when I was a kid. Jayzis, how times change. Ya'd be surprised to see anyone Irish walkin' through Dublin these days.

Anyway so there was no Doctor Najima and instead there was this other fella there. A ride I have to say, couldn't have been more than 26 although he looked much younger. Needless to say, I nearly died when I realised it would be him lookin' at me and not Doctor Najima. I thought about runnin' away but there was a few other people in the waitin' room so I couldn't. Your man called me into the room anyway and I sat down on the chair opposite him and he asked me what was wrong with me and I blanked. Me mouth just wouldn't move. I was thinkin' to meself, this fella is a ride. There is no way I'm showin' him me rash. He'll think I'm a dirty whore. He was startin' to think I was a bit slow or somethin' then coz he was lookin' at me, wonderin' what the fuck was wrong with me. So I eventually told him about me rash and he starts askin' me loads of questions about it and that and next thing he tells me to get up on that bed yoke they have in the doctors room and take off me cloths. Well I was havin' none of it. 'Ya dirty bastard,' says I, 'I only know ya five minutes.' And he kind of laughs but deadly serious he says he needs to see how far the rash has spread. So I took off me top and me jeans and was sittin' there in me bra and knickers in the middle of the doctors. Thank god I had just changed them before I left the house. Bad enough havin' a rash without havin' dirty knickers as well. So the doctor kind of looks at me from a distance then takes a closer look and does the usual doctor shit, says 'Ah ha,' writes a prescription, tries to tell me what's wrong with me although I couldn't understand a word of it, I don't even know if he was speakin' English although he was definitely Irish, a bogger but still Irish. I swear to god, I was still scarlet ten minutes after I left and that wasn't just the rash.

He prescribed tablets and a cream called Silcock's Base that I have to spread on the rash. It comes in this big tub and all. Its like a bucket. Our Bopper thought it was hilarious. He got a black marker and rubbed out the sil and the s at the end of silcocks so now it just says cock base. I don't know what does be goin' through that young-fellas mind at times, I really don't. I'm only hopin' that the stuff works though coz there's no way I'm goin' near that doctor again. Ever!

✻

Well our Bopper is havin' none of it. We tried, we really did but he just doesn't want to know. Sheila text him there earlier and he said there was no way he was gonna text her back. I told him that wasn't nice but he says he couldn't give a flyin' fuck, that I shouldn't be givin' his number out to young-ones. I told him I was only tryin' to help, that I was tryin' to set him up with Sheila coz I thought they'd make a nice couple but he doesn't want to know. I'm tellin' ya, he can be as moody at times. I mean the least he could have done was text the young-one to have a bit of a chat with her, even if she can hardly speak the same language as him. I definitely have seen them talkin' before but as I said, whether there was chemistry there or not, I can't remember.

'Do ya not like her then?' I asked, tryin' to get to the bottom of it. Ya know me, always tryin' to be the diplomat. I haven't a clue what that means but that's what Tracy says about me and she does English and psychology in UCD so she knows what she's talkin' about. 'She's a nice young-one,' Bopper says, still in the height of it mind you, 'but I don't fancy her or anythin'.'

'It should be personality that counts,' I told him although let the truth be told, that's a load of shite. If I don't fancy a fella, there's no way I'd be able to, ya know, do anythin' with them. Shallow as a paddlin' pool, Bernie does say but that's me. I wasn't sayin' this to our Bopper. He's still not havin' any of it.

Poor Sheila. I think she was actually quite excited about it, although how anyone can get excited over our Bopper, I'll never know. But I told Sheila, I did, I says 'Sheila, there's plenty more fish in the sea and you'll find your Nemo soon enough.' She thought it was only hilarious although to be honest, I don't think the stupid cow had a clue what I said to her. If she finds it hard enough to understand me then she'd be fucked with our Bopper, although in sayin' that, by the looks of things, she won't.

**

I'm goin' to hell. No really I am. I did a terrible thing. Now it was an accident, I swear to Jayzis it was, but still it was terrible. I wasn't the only one involved either. There was Bernie, Jasmin, Concepta and our Bopper too. It was terrible, really it was. I'm still findin' it hard to come to terms with but we were only tryin' to help, really we were.

We decided to head into town for the evenin'. Tracy couldn't come coz she was still workin' on her project, god love her. She's exhausted over it and Paulo has a rash believe it or not. I gave him some of me tablets and that Silcock's Base stuff. It's only deadly. I swear to god, mine is all cleared up now except for a patch on the back of me right arm, which to be honest, is reefin' itchy.

So anyway there was the five of us in town and we thought we'd try Traffic on Abbey Street for a change. It was a great night, now I must say. We had a great laugh. Meself and Bernie ended up snoggin' these two fellas from Terenure but they seemed to be a bit posh so we ditched them. I mean when they started talkin' about rugby we said fuck that and pretended to go to the toilet. We tried to find the others but they were all off doin' their own thing as usual. Concepta was chattin' to a crowd of about 14 people from Cork about god only knows what. They were all standin' in a circle around her listenin' to everythin' she was sayin', thinkin' she's all that and a tub of Silcock's Base.

Jasmin was standin' at the edge of the dancefloor totally locked, or so we thought at the time. Believe it or not, she says she just liked the lights and thought they were nice. I'm tellin' ya, its weirder that young-one gets although in sayin' that, at least the lights kept her from ramblin' onto the roof or somethin'.

Bopper was talkin' to a French young-fella, well at least I think he was French coz he kissed our Bopper on both cheeks when he saw him. They do that in France the young-fellas. Its how they say hello to people they know, even to other young-fellas. He disappeared for a good hour and a half, our Bopper, but he just showed up again all of a sudden. He must have been dancin' or somethin' coz he looked wrecked and his hair was all messed up.

Anyway we were leavin' the club at the end of the night and we decided to walk towards Capel Street to try to get a taxi. It's a bollix on a Friday night I know but me hoop I was gettin' that Nitelink. So we're walkin' anyway and we were just passin' the back of the Jervis Street Shoppin' centre and we spot this auld-fella lyin' there, completely locked. So we were like, ah we can't leave him like that so we helped him up and tried to get him to stand but everytime he tried, his legs collapsed underneath him and he fell over. So Concepta and Bopper got one side of him each and kind of had him tryin' to walk although I think they just ended up carryin' him coz he wasn't able to walk. All of a sudden Bernie asks us where we're gonna bring him so she looks in his pockets and pulls out his wallet and finds somethin' with his address on it, don't ask me what. Tom, this auld-fellas name was, or at least that's what it said on his cards, we went through all of them. This auld-fella lives up in one of them houses near Smithfield as it happens so we bring him to his house and there's a light on so we were thinkin', should we knock. Before we could even consider it, Concepta has her hand stuck on the doorbell. Some auld-one, who I'm guessin' was his wife, or at least I hope it was, answered the door and nearly got the fright of her life. 'We found your husband in a bit of a state and helped him home.' I announced, very proud of meself for bein' the good samarital, I have to tell ya. So your woman says 'Thanks very much,' and looks around at us and all of a sudden her face drops and I could tell she was panicing and all of sudden she goes, 'Where's his fuckin' wheelchair?' Well we nearly died, all five of us. No wonder the bastard couldn't walk.

February

February already. Can ya believe it? It really doesn't feel like January is over already but like, it is coz it's February and February comes after January. The question is though, where did the month go? I think when ya get older time goes quicker. Now I'm far from a scientist or Tracy or anythin' but its just somethin' I've noticed. Maybe I just slept more or somethin'. Christmas and the New Year seem ages ago though. I don't think I can even remember me New Year's revolutions. Hold on, let me think. First I said I was goin' to stop smokin' and I did, for about a week mind you but I tried. I gave up the drink for a few days as well so at least I tried which is more than I can say about Concepta Cooney and that diet. They're not doin' the supersize in McDonalds anymore so Concepta just gets two regular chips instead, the hungry cow. If ya ask me, she's put on more weight since the New Year instead of losin' it.

Me second revolution was to write this yoke and ya have to give it to me, I'm not doin' too bad. I'm no Charles Dickens but then again I'm not tryin' to be. Jayzis can ya imagine in 200 years time, young-ones like Tracy studyin' me, quotin' Joanna Ryde and all. Now that would be funny, although I'm startin' to think that anyone who reads anythin' that I write is gonna need a transvestite or a translator or whatever them people are to tell them what it means in English coz that's far from what this is.

Me third revolution was to save for a holiday and believe it or not, I have a few quid in the bank and I'd say we're definitely gonna book somethin' in the next few days. Concepta was only sayin' it there to us the other day. She wants to go to Santa Ponsa coz I believe it's meant to be great for our age. I was there when I was about seven as far as I remember but I was only a kid then so I wouldn't have noticed things we'd be into now like clubs and fellas. We'll go somewhere though.

Me fourth revolution had somethin' to do with the singin' and to be honest I've just been a lazy bitch. I haven't really bothered to get up off me hole and put meself out there. Sayin' that now, I've been listenin' to the radio so that's kinda helpin' me.

Me last revolution was to have more sex and since New Years I haven't had any so that one's not really goin' that great but I haven't really been tryin', let the truth be told. I mean I could easily go out and find somebody but at the minute I just want to enjoy me life, d'ya know what I mean? Maybe next month I might try a little harder coz to be honest, I'm dyin' for me hole.

I'm tryin' to think how the girls are doin' with their revolutions. Well as I said, Concepta's diet never even started but lets face it, nobody expected it to. Bernie said she was goin' to have more sex but she's had as much luck as I had. Jasmin, believe it or not, bought a Spanish book and started learnin' Spanish. I swear to Jayzis. She even has a tape that teaches her how to say the words properly and all. She'll be grand though coz they all have lisps in Spain so they'll be able to understand her. It's a pity we can't. What did Tracy say for her revolution? Oh yeah, she was goin' to be in a circus. Hold on, that's wrong. She said she was goin' to be more assertive. A month later and I still don't have a clue what that means. I would get meself a dictionary but I wouldn't know how to use it and anyways, I couldn't really give two fucks. If I don't know what somethin' means, I usually just ask me da or Tracy or ignore it. Anyway, the last time I had a dictionary was in school and we used to just use it to look up dirty words. Vagina — part of the female genitalia. Now how the fuck was I meant to know what genitalia meant? I had to look that up too. Ya know for years I thought Vagina was a place in America that they called Virginia and we called Vagina. I went around tellin' all the kids in me class when I was a young-one that me auntie Linda was on holidays in West Vagina. I wouldn't mind but it was only a few years later that I realised Chicago was in a totally different state altogether as if anyone really gives a fuck.

✷✷✷

Bobsleddin'. Now that's a weird sport. I was flickin' through the channels there and found the bobsleddin' on one of the sports channels. I was about to turn it off straight away but I thought to meself I'll leave it on for a minute to see what its like and two hours later I was still there watchin' it.

Now if ya've never heard of bobsleddin' before or never seen it, I'll explain to ya about it, although I'm shite at this sort of thing, but anyway, there's these four fellas and they're wearin' these skin-tight yokes. I haven't a clue what ya'd call them. They'd be like a catsuit only not leather. They must be made of the same stuff they make the cyclin' shorts out of, Lycra or whatever it is. Anyway, they're skintight and they show off all the bulges and that. I think that's why I ended up watchin' it for so long.

So the fellas are all wearin' these skintight yokes and helmets and they have to push this yoke, its called a sled although I've never seen a sled that looked like that before in me life. Santy would never fit in it, let alone all the presents and there'd be nowhere to tie the reindeer at the front. But they have to push this big sled down a big chute of ice. It'd be a bit like a rollercoaster track. Oh no, d'ya what it'd be like? Ya know one of them water slides. It'd be like that only made of ice and the four fellas push this big sled and then jump in and start flyin' down the chute. Its weird but I have to say, I got very into it and believe it or not, there really is a Jamaican bobsleigh team, ya know like in that film *Cool Runnin's*. Now they're not the same four fellas that was in the film but I'd say they've changed the team since then coz the other fellas would be too old now.

That's a great film though. If ya know nothin' about bobsleddin' then ya should watch that. I mean I was able to watch the bobsleddin' there today and know what was goin' on because of that film. It was in Salt Lake City as well and that's in Canada where they made *Cool Runnin's*. Your man with the lucky egg was gas and his little song as well. Jayzis, it was hilarious.

Whatever about the Jamaican bobsleigh team though, I nearly died when I saw the Irish team. No word of a lie, we really do have a bobsleigh team. I seen them today. And one of our lads, now I'm not only sayin' this coz I'm Irish, but one of our lads had the biggest bulge out of all of them although he probably had a lucky egg down his trousers, or more like a lucky Easter egg. He was huge.

We didn't do too bad today either. Well we didn't finish last so that's somethin' isn't it, especially when ya think that we don't get any snow here. The poor fuckers must have to practice with a sled with wheels on it. Can ya imagine them flyin' down the side of one of the Wicklow mountains in their sled with wheels, like stabilizers on a piece of wood. Fair play to them for tryin' though.

✳✳✳

I'm all excited. We booked a holiday today. Two weeks in Playa Del Ingles the first two weeks of July. I wanted to go earlier meself but Tracy was sayin' somethin' about exams and the rest of us know that college is important and we wouldn't go without her.

There's loads of us goin' so it should be a good laugh. There's me, Bernie, Concepta, Jasmin, Tracy, Tracy's friend Miranda from college, our Bopper and Paulo. Can ya see all of us in the Canaries? They won't know what hit them. It'll be like hurricane Joanna.

I betcha Bernie Boland has already packed. The young-one is unreal. I've never met anyone as organised in me life. Now she wouldn't be organised in the same way as Tracy. Like Tracy is organised with her stuff. All in alphabetical order and that but Bernie would be organised with time like. Say on a night out, Bernie would be the one to text all of us to arrange a time to meet and where we're goin' and the rest of it. I can imagine her on the holiday now. She'll have a piece of paper with times we have to do things at. An itinerant I think it's called. I wouldn't mind but she hasn't a hope with all of us. We're about as organised as Julie Walsh's knicker drawer. Jayzis, the thought of that is makin' me sick.

Concepta said she might have trouble gettin' off work but ya know Concepta, she'll tell them there's no way she's workin' and just not show up. They won't sack her. I don't know why but they won't. I mean, its hardly like they'd miss her coz I'd say she does fuck all anyways. They still haven't found out that it was her tampon that they found covered in sugar. Jayzis, I must be mad goin' on holidays with Concepta. The thought of seein' her in a bikini is enough. I don't even think she shaves her bikini line either. I think I'm goin' to be sick. The thing about Concepta though is that she'll make friends before we check into the apartments. She'll be the most famous person on the island after three days knowin' her. She's great like that, Concepta.

Jasmin's only delighted we're goin' the Canaries coz it means she can speak her Spanish although in sayin' that, we had to tell her the Canaries are part of Spain. She thought they spoke Canarian if there is such a thing. Believe me, we won't be relyin' on her to tell us what things mean, especially when it comes to drink. Everyone knows what she's like when it comes to alcohol. It was whiskey and Red Bull the last night she was out with us. The young-one has a stomach made of steel I'd say. It'd be the only way to explain the shite she can drink.

Tracy will be great to have on the holiday. She'll be lookin' after everyone and makin' sure we're okay. I'd end up in Lanzarote if Tracy wasn't there with us. Her friend Miranda is comin'. Now Tracy was sayin' that Miranda was dyin' for a holiday and that's why she asked her. None of us mind though. We wouldn't be like that. I think I've only ever met Miranda once or twice but I must have been locked coz I can't remember what she was like. Jasmin says she's a bit of a stuck up cow but Jasmin is very quick to judge a person sometimes. I'm sure we'll get on with this Miranda young-one. If Tracy likes her then we should too.

It's great that Bopper and Paulo are comin'. I forgot all about askin' them only Concepta reminded me. It'll be good to have a couple of lads around. We got them an apartment on their own, just the two of them. It'll probably be Tracy, Miranda and Jasmin in one, me, Bernie and Concepta in another and then the lads. Ah I can't wait. There better be nice fellas although I heard it's very easy to get your hole in the Canaries. Well Julie Walsh did last year so I'd say it is.

✷✷✷

Good jayzis, the weather is unreal. I think there must be a hurricane or somethin' flyin' over Ireland. The wind is unreal and it's pissin' down. I wouldn't mind but I had to go to work and home in it today. I rang me da to collect me but he was workin' late so he couldn't. I was cursin' him all the way home. I was carryin' a paper bag as well with a few bits in it and it started fallin' apart in the rain. Me Aeros fell on the ground as I crossed the road and all and when I went to get back to get them, some fucker in a Skoda flies past and drives straight over them. I could have killed him. Not only that but he went through a puddle as well and drowned me, as if I wasn't soaked enough. The dye in me knickers had started to run by the time I got home. I used two towels dryin' meself I was that wet. Me hair was in bits and I wouldn't mind, I'm usin' that new Pantene stuff for winter although its meant to be spring now that it's February. Spring me arse.

The wind is even worse. I was lyin' in the bed last night and I couldn't sleep coz of the noise. It was like it was whistlin' at me. It just kept on goin' all night. Then when I went out this mornin', I nearly got taken off me feet and flown down the road, only I was wearin' heavy shoes. I had an umbrella but that was as much use as a size eight shirt to Julie Walsh. The minute I put it up the wind caught it and turned it inside out and it was a fucker to fix. I hate this type of weather when everyone has umbrellas up. I don't know how many stupid fuckers nearly took the eye out of me walkin' down the road. One cow even got one of the spikes caught in me hair and reefed it as she was walkin'. I nearly battered her when I got her. The stupid bitch should really look where she's goin'. I swear to god, the next person to hit me with an umbrella will be havin' the thing shoved up their holes and then I'll open it, don't think I won't.

Me ma was goin' mad coz the wind knocked her hangin' baskets off the wall out the back and her geraniums are destroyed. She went around today tryin' to fix the garden. In the middle of February, would ya be well? Your one next door mustn't have taken her cloths off the line coz I found about four pair of knickers, a tea towel and a Manchester United jersey in me ma's rhododendrons. Well at least that's what she said it was. I wouldn't know a rhododendron from a piss in the bed. I can hardly even say it. I picked up all the cloths though and dropped them in to Petulia next door. She was only delighted. She thought she'd never see them again, especially her Man United jersey. She's always wearin' it. I told her she shouldn't hang her cloths out in a hurricane and she smiled at me. The type of smile that someone gives ya when they've just done somethin' stupid. The type of smile ya do always see on Jasmin.

✻✻✻

Tracy has a fella. Well, so we think anyway. Well so Bernie thinks and she told me. All the clues are there like. She hasn't said anythin' but meself and Bernie put two and two together and got boy.

First of all, it's been god knows how long since Tracy was out with us and I know she said she was doin' her project but that could have been a cover up. Maybe there was no Charles Dickens project. Maybe she was lyin' all along so she could sneak off with this young-fella without havin' to tell us about it, although let the truth be told, I couldn't see Tracy doin' that. She wouldn't be the type to lie. It's not in her nature. She wouldn't be the type of young-one to make somethin' like that up and she is very serious when it comes to her college work.

Bernie was sayin' as well that she heard Tracy tell Bopper somethin' about a young-fella that she goes to college with that's meant to be a bit of a ride and that she wanted our Bopper to have a look at him to see what he thinks. Now what she'd want to get our Bopper to check out a young-fella in her class for, I don't know. I mean if she was goin' to be askin' advice on fellas would she not be askin' one of the young-ones like meself. Maybe she just wanted a male prospective. Herself and our Bopper have been gettin' very close lately. Oh good god, what if its him? What if Tracy is into our Bopper? What if the two of them were goin' out and they didn't tell anyone? It would explain a lot though like the two of them are very seldom out with us together anymore. I wonder does that be why he does come home with big hickeys all the time. Tracy is givin' them to him. I must text Bernie and see what she says. Tracy and Bopper did seem very pally when we bookin' the holiday Tuesday mornin' although she did have to run off and go to college and our Bopper offered to walk her to the bus stop now that I think of it. Very peculiar. The only person our Bopper usually walks to the bus stop is Paulo.

The last time I was talkin' to Tracy before we booked the holiday, it must have been Monday night, she spent half the night textin' on her phone. Meself, herself and Concepta went to the chipper to get somethin' to eat and I remember sayin' it to Concepta after Tracy ran off for college the next mornin'. Tracy usually isn't one for textin'. Not for the whole night kinda thing. She'd always text ya back mind you but she's not one for text conversations. Many a time I've text Tracy and she'd ring me back. She says it saves a lot of time. The other thing about Tracy textin' is that she always writes the full words in perfect English. She never cuts anythin' down like writin' 4 instead of for. I'd do it meself as well except me spellin' is up me hole. Seriously I'd be fucked without predictive text.

So what was I sayin'? Oh yeah, Tracy textin' all Monday night. So I said it to Bernie when we were talkin' today and she thinks that it could be the new fella that she's textin'. That's probably why she didn't leave the phone out of her hand the whole time meself and Concepta were with her. We'll have to find out now. We must ask her who this fella is. I'm sure she said somethin' about a young-fella called Oliver, although he sounded a bit young the way she was talkin' about him and I think she said somethin' about him robbin' somethin'. I think she might have been talkin' about her Charles Dickens thing now that I think of it.

✳✳✳

Jasmin's got an awful rash. Ya wanna see her. Breakin' out really bad. Like me own, her's started out really small and began to spread and she said its reefin' itchy. She couldn't sleep last night and her skin is in an awful state from all the scratchin'. She's tearin' lumps out of it. Jasmin has very long nails, beautiful nails. I haven't seen real ones like it before. Everyone does be jealous of her. Mine are dreadful. Shite for scratchin' with. I used to get a blunt scissors, an old one we have ages, and open it out and scratch with that. Ya wanna see the lines I had left in me skin but when ya need to scratch, ya need to scratch. Thankfully me rash is gone coz it really was wreckin' me head. I couldn't relax. Kind of on edge all the time, wakin' up a few times durin' the night and gettin' kinda frustrated when I got really, really itchy, ya know what I mean? Like really, really itchy, like reefin'. Like ya just wanna tear all your skin off and jump into a bath full of Dettol. I was tempted on many an occasion, believe me.

Jasmin's not impressed though. It's really wreckin' her head and I wouldn't mind but she's only had it a day or two. She thought it was chicken pox at first, the dizzy cow. I think its coz she heard meself and Tracy talk about it a while ago and thought she might sound smart. She's not foolin' me though. Jasmin wouldn't know what chicken pox is. I don't even think she knows what chicken is. I won't tell ya what she thinks KFC stands for. I'd say she knows what a pox is though coz that's what she goes around callin' everyone. The bitch will probably say she got it off me but I think I got it from the punch she made for New Year so it'd be nothin' more than comeuppance and anyways, Paulo had it as well so she could have caught it off him. I gave her some of that Silcock's Base to rub on herself but knowin' that dizzy cow she'll probably eat it or more likely, mix it with vodka.

✳✳✳

Great night last night, now a great night. We were in Bad Bob's and as I said, it was a great night. I wasn't goin' to go, ya know yourself. I wasn't really in the humour. I would have been happy sittin' at home havin' a bath and watchin' the *Late Late Show* with me ma. I was a bit wrecked after work and ya know the way ya do be when ya come home and sit down and ya don't want to get up. I mean, at that stage I hadn't the energy to get up and find the remote control to turn on somethin' proper instead of Sky News. So there I'm sittin' like a spa tryin' to change the channel like that young-fella from the second X-men film. Ya know the young-fella who doesn't sleep, the one with the glasses. Anyway there I was like a gobshite tryin' to get MTV just by blinkin' when the phone rings. Now I was thinkin', Jayzis, I didn't change the channel but I made the phone ring but I picked it up and realised it was Bernie and that I didn't have special powers after all. So I answer it and straight away she's tellin' me Tracy's after been on to her and they're all goin' into Bad Bob's so I said there's no way, that I was too tired and she's tryin' to persuade me to go out and eventually gives up. The phone's not even down 25 seconds when it rings again and this time it's the Concepta one, same thing, tryin' to persuade me to go out and I just hang up on her as she's half way through a sentence. Then the phone starts ringin' again and this time its Tracy. Well I knew straight away I was fucked. She started all this guilt trip shite, sayin' she hadn't been out with us in ages and she missed us and all this. She's a bitch and I wouldn't mind but she knows exactly what she's doin' coz she studies psychology. I wouldn't be surprised if the three of them were together when they were ringin' me. Tracy probably had it all worked out, the conivin' cow. I had no choice but to go at that stage.

 I'm delighted I did go out in the end. It was a great night, now a great night. There was only the four of us. Jasmin was off doin' somethin' with Andy, Mandy and Sandy, god only knows what. She never told us and we do be afraid to ask with Jasmin sometimes.

 Bopper and Paulo were goin' out to some house party out in Dunboyne of all places and wanted to know if we wanted to go but Tracy was insistin' we go to Bad Bobs, which I have to say, I found a little bit strange coz normally she couldn't give a shite where we go. We could have a drink in the middle of Iraq with bullets flyin' around the place and Tracy wouldn't give a fuck and anyways, Bernie does usually have our weekends planned out a week and a half in advance and we do just go along with what she says. I said it to Concepta, I said, 'This is a bit weird, Tracy gettin' us to go somewhere. It's not like her.' And Concepta agreed. Nothin' else was said though until we got in there and only after about five minutes after we arrived, meself and Bernie were standin' at the bar, Concepta had already made friends with three young-ones form Belfast, and we look over and see Tracy gettin' stuck into some young-fella. 'Jayzis, Tracy's quick tonight,' Bernie says to me but I realise what's goin' on here. 'That's your man Oliver,' I says to Bernie. She looks at me wonderin' what I'm sayin' to her. 'He's your man that Tracy's goin' out with,' says I. 'Go way,' Bernie says and nearly breaks a heel tryin' to get a better look at him. Anyway Tracy eventually brings the young-fella over and his name is Lance. I swear to god, the chap's name was Lance. 'Like the cyclist,' he says to us in a mad Cork accent. 'Who? Stephen Roche?' Bernie asks, the stupid cow. Not even Jasmin would say somethin' that bleedin' stupid but to be honest now, I haven't a clue who this fucker is talkin' about. 'Lance Armstrong,' he says with a big smile, the spa. 'Ah yeah,' meself and Bernie say, even though we haven't a clue what this fella is talkin' about.

I have to say though, he's actually a lovely fella. Very nice and he's mad about our Tracy, ya can tell by the way he looks at her, into her eyes and not at her tits even though she's wearin' my Indian style boob tube that I got in Dunnes. He is a bit of a bogger, bein' from Cork and all but we all have our crosses to bare. He's in college with Tracy so that's how they met. I'm delighted for her though. She seems really happy. She's says they're not really goin' out so that's why she never said anythin' but I knew me and Bernie were right the other day.

Tracy ended up goin' back to Lances and all, fair play to her. We had a good night on the whole. The only pity is that I didn't get me hole. Well at least one of us is gettin' it, although it could have been more dependin' on what Jasmin and more so Bopper and Paulo got up to last night.

✳︎✳︎✳︎

I am never drinkin' again. Oh good god, I'm in a state. I can hardly remember a thing after the *Macerena* but we'll get back to that in a minute.

We decided we'd hit Heaven in Blanchardstown for the laugh. Bernie wasn't mad into goin' out but after her draggin' me the night before, she had no choice. She was goin' even if she had to be forced and I would have, don't think I wouldn't but to be honest she didn't need much persuasion. Needless to say, as soon as she decided she was goin', she had the whole thing organised, where we were goin', who was goin', what time, how we were gettin' home and all the rest of it, all in the space of two minutes and without askin' anyone else I may add.

We tried to get Tracy to come but she was goin' out for a date with Lance, her words not mine. A date! Where does she think she is? California? The only date Tracy ever had was the one she gets once a month. A date? The two of them are probably goin' to watch a film and then to Abrakebabra on the way home. It was far from the word date that Tracy Murtagh was reared. She may be goin' to UCD now but she's a north-sider through and through. She's watchin' too many repeats of Friends, that's what it is. I bet ya she does be out there in UCD drinkin' cappinchinos with all her snobby mates and not even the cappinchinos ya do get in the packets, ya know the Maxwell House, but the real stuff that they make with a machine. €3 a cup, would ya be well?

Concepta came with us as well. The young-one's off her rocker. We all went over to her place for a few drinks first. It was meself, Bernie, Jasmin, me Uncle Dessie and Bopper. Paulo isn't well. He has another skin infection, all down the inside of his thigh, Bopper said. Nothin' like the one he had before, the one I had, the one Jasmin is still sufferin' with. This is all scabby, Bopper said

Anyway we had a few in Concepta's before we went anywhere. We had a few bottles of Vodka and a bottle of Peach Schnapps we found in Concepta's press when she wasn't lookin'. We told her Bernie's ma and da got it in the Canaries that time they were away for New Year. She drank most of it herself so she can't really say anythin' if she finds out. Jasmin was on the Southern Comforts and pineapple juice, although when we got to Heaven it was Southern Comfort and cranberry juice coz they had no pineapple. She caused murder over it as well, the sap. We were all locked when we got there, even me Uncle Dessie and god only knows how they let us in although the bouncers there are all lovely. I think I was only in the place an hour before things started to go blank coz I was that palatic. I can remember at one stage there was loads of us doin' the Macerena. Now whether the song was on or not, I can't remember but there we all were doin' the dance, me, Bernie, Jasmin, Bopper, Dessie, Concepta and about eight young-ones Concepta had made friends with from Hartstown. Well that was at first. We went around gettin' everyone up to do it and ya know Concepta, havin' chats with them all, complete strangers. I swear to god, we had the whole pub up doin' the Macerena and us in the middle of them all havin' started it. I wouldn't mind but Jasmin Spi is hopeless at the dance. She always jumps left when everyone else is goin' right.

God only knows what happened after that. I can't remember gettin' home but I must have coz that's where I am now. I'll ring me Uncle Dessie and see if he can tell me. I would ask Bopper but I don't know where he is. He definitely didn't come home with us, me ma told me that much. I think I saw him chattin' to some young-fella he used to go to school with. Him and Jasmin had the poor young-fella up doin' the *Macerena* with us although where our Bopper ended up goin' I don't know. I hate when I don't remember things. I could have scored and I still wouldn't know about it. Although in fairness, what are the chances of that?

✷✷✷

Whatever about the bobsleddin', that curlin' is a mad sport. Seriously like. I put on that winter sports channel when I was watchin' the telly coz there was fuck all on and I thought there might be a bit of bobsleddin' on but it was curlin'. Now I was about to turn it off coz I was thinkin', this is a load of shite, but I ended up watchin' it for a good two and a half hours. Once ya start watchin' it ya just can't turn it off. When I turned it on there was a great match on, Switzerland against Canada, and the Canadians are meant to be the best in the world, or so the commentator said anyways. They hammered the Switzerlanders.

Now if ya've never seen curlin' before, it's very hard to explain. There's two teams with a few players on each one, five I think it is, and what happens is, they're on ice and there's this big target and they take turns to glide this big round yoke down the ice and the team with their yoke nearest the target after all the yokes are gone, wins. Its kinda like bowls if that makes it easier for ya. I told ya I'm not great at explainin'. Now the mad thing about curlin' though is that there's these people who sweep the ice in front of the big glidin' things just after they're glided and they sweep to heat up the ice so the yoke moves faster or to one side or whatever.

Seriously though, it's very excitin'. The tension does be unbearable. Ya do think one team is goin' to win and at the very end, the other team does a great bit of sweepin' and wins. I'm tellin' ya, ya just find it too hard to turn it off in case ya miss anythin'.

Believe it or not, there's an Irish team. I swear to jayzis, an Irish curlin' team and we don't even have an ice rink. We're shite mind you but we're playin' against countries that are really cold like Scotland so I mean, ya have to give us a bit of credit for bein' there in the first place. Where the fuck would they practice though? I think they were usin' mops instead of brushes, the Irish team. Probably cleanin' ladies from a community centre or somethin'. They probably have a sponsorship deal with Vileda or somethin' as well.

※※※

Guess who's goin' to Galway on Friday? I'm dyin' for it. I can't wait. There's meself, Bernie, Tracy, Jasmin, Concepta and Tracy's friend Miranda, the one that's comin' the Canaries with us. It was Tracy's idea. She said to us last night. Meself and Bernie were around in her place watchin' a film, and she was sayin' somethin' about doin' somethin' for her birthday. She was sayin' she'd like to do somethin' different, not just goin' into town and gettin' locked. So she said what about goin' away and gettin' locked. At first I thought she was talkin' about somewhere foreign. I was thinkin', it's this weekend, how are we gonna get a holiday that quick and anyways, we have the Canaries booked but she said she was thinkin' about somewhere down the country. Anyway the subject was changed and we ended up talkin' about somethin' else. That was it I thought, we're goin' into town to get locked for Tracy's birthday, end of story, until I get a phone call off Bernie this mornin' tellin' me to take the weekend off. She's unreal. She has the train times sorted, a hotel booked, a list of places to go in Galway, how much its all gonna cost and how much we'll need to bring with us. I don't be able for her sometimes.

I'm dyin' for it now though, a girls weekend and its Valentines day on Saturday as well so that should be a bit of buzz. That Miranda young-one, Tracy's friend from college, is comin' too so we'll get a chance to meet her before the holiday and get to know her and that sort of thing so that'll be good. I just hope Tracy enjoys it. In fact she better enjoy it, us goin' to all this trouble so she has a good birthday. I plan to get very drunk this weekend.

※

Did ya ever see that film Outbreak? The one where there's this mad disease and everyone gets it coz it gets passed on. I think that's happenin' to us, my group of friends like. It's the rash ya see. First I had it, then Paulo, then Jasmin and now Bopper and Bernie. I swear to jayzis, it's unreal. Mine is gone now thank god but the rest of them are in an awful state. Our Bopper has had three showers today alone. He must have scrubbed layers off his skin. He was usin' one of them exfoliatin' sponges. It's his own, not mine, although why our Bopper has an exfoliatin' sponge, I'll never know. I gave him some of that Silcocks Base stuff so he's covered in that from head to toe. I wouldn't mind but there's only a little patch on the inside of his left leg, hardly anythin' to get worried about, not yet anyway.

Bernie rang today in an awful state, now an awful state. Hysterical, the young-one was and its not like Bernie. She doesn't get worried over anythin'. She told me what was wrong with her and I calmed her down.

I mean, it's not really that big a deal is it? A few red marks on your skin I told her, once a monkey didn't bite her she's grand but she hadn't a clue what I was talkin' about so I rang Tracy and asked her what the disease is in *Outbreak*. She knows these sort of things, Tracy. Marburg it is, she tells me. For the bit of buzz, I ring Bernie back and tell her she has Marburg and she runs off to check what it is in this huge medicine book she has and comes back hysterical, nearly cryin' down the phone while I was breakin' me shite laughin' at the other end. I mean the young-one only has a rash. It's not the end of the world. It could be worse. She could be Paulo. He has two different types of rashes.

I'm just thinkin', what if its one of them LCD's and Paulo passed it on to me somehow and it started spreadin' from there? That's just dirty that is. I definitely didn't get a rash from havin' sex with anyone, not unless it was meself anyway and it definitely wasn't with Paulo. But can't ya only get an LCD from havin' sex with someone and I don't think Paulo is doin' the business with Bernie, Jasmin and Bopper although ya'd never know and who am I to judge? Anythin' goes in this day and age and he definitely didn't go near me. Believe me, if Paulo did anythin' to me, I would have noticed, the ride that he is. I don't care how locked I would have been.

It's a mystery where this rash came from and how five of us have got it so far and the thing is, I've definitely not been anywhere near a monkey although I do work with Julie Walsh so that could explain a lot.

✱✱✱

I was in work today and who walks into the shop only Paddy. Now it's been a while since any of us have laid eyes on Paddy or Phillip for that matter. Ever since Phillip said he wouldn't go out with me for a drink and Paddy tried to get into Bernie and she was havin' none of it. I've texted Phillip a few times. Once or twice anyway but he never text me back, probably hadn't got credit or somethin', ya know yourself.

Anyway, I'm standin' there at the till today and who walks up only Paddy. Now I didn't notice him at first. I was in a world of me own at that stage. So he says, 'Are ya not goin' to say hello?' and I look up and to be honest with ya, I got a bit of a fright. He's probably the last person I expected to be standin' at the till in front of me. 'Ah howaya.' I say, still kinda surprised at seein' him. I have to say, he looked gorgeous. The nicest I've seen Paddy lookin' this long time. So he says to me, 'What ya doin'?' I looked at him, gobshite that he is and I says, 'I'm workin' Paddy, what d'ya think I'm standin' behind this till for? It's hardly a fuckin' hobby.' So he just smirks at me, the big dopey head on him, and he says, 'Have ya any plans for Valentines day?' So I'm thinkin' to meself, what's this sap tryin' to get at? I was like, 'me and the girls are goin' to Galway for the weekend for Tracy's birthday.' And he was like, 'Oh, I just thought ya might have wanted to go for a drink or somethin'.' The cheek of him. I swear to god, I was ready to jump over the counter at the fucker. The neck of him to come into my shop and ask me out after tryin' to get into me best friend. Who does he think he is? I looked up at him anyway, a real sly grin on me face and I says, 'What about Bernie? I thought ya were into her.' Well his face dropped. He stood there with his mouth open, not able to think of anythin' to say so I was like, 'well you have a good Valentines day Paddy and I'm sure we'll see ya around when we get back from Galway.' It was gas. Julie Walsh was dyin' to know what was goin' on, the nosey cow. Ya know me, I didn't tell her anythin'. Sheila was kinda standin' near enough to me to kinda know what was happenin' so I kinda filled her in on everythin' coz I'd say even if she did hear everythin', she probably wouldn't have been able to understand it. I think she thought it was hilarious as well. The poor young-one nearly had a fit she was laughin' that much. Greg thought she was on somethin' when he heard her. Sayin' that now, she was a bit hyper today. If that Marie Daly one is givin' Sheila hash I'll kill her.

✳✳✳

I just realised somethin'. It's Friday the 13 and we're goin' on a train down to Galway. Now not that I'm supersticial or anythin' but I just thought I'd say. I mean, it doesn't bother me at all but I just thought about it when I looked at the calendar.

I'm all packed anyways. I have loads of stuff, a few nice things to wear goin' out and some nice stuff for durin' the day, comfortable stuff coz ya wanna be nice and comfortable when you're walkin' around durin' the day, ya know yourself. Jasmin Spi was goin' to bring a bikini but I told her it was Galway she was goin' to, not Benidorm. I got a suitcase down out of the attic so I'm goin' to bring that. Me ma says four pairs of shoes is too much for a weekend but the way I see it, ya can never have too many shoes and anyways, its only two pairs of shoes, a pair of runners and a pair of knee high boots and I'm the one carryin' them amn't I?

Miranda's not goin' now. Don't ask me why but she's not goin'. Tracy said it was somethin' to do with college and she has to go to some kind of meetin' tomorrow. I says to Tracy to tell Miranda to come down after the meetin' but she won't. I was dyin' to get to know her properly and all. I'll just have to wait now. So it's only the five of us. The girls. We were thinkin' of sayin' it to Bopper to come instead of Miranda but he thinks he's dyin' with this rash that he has. It's kind of spreadin' a bit. It's on his face now and our Bopper won't leave the house in case anyone sees him. He's like that, Bopper. He spends hours in the bathroom gettin' ready. He's worse than a young-one sometimes. I've never seen a young-fella with so many cosmetics. He's keepin' Boots in business he has that many.

Anyway, he says he's not comin' and we couldn't find anyone else so it's just the five of us. One of Jasmin's sisters wanted to come, Mandy I think it was, or maybe it was Sandy, or come to think of it, it could have been Andy. I can't remember who she said coz the names all sound the same when you're not really listenin' but whoever it was, the triplets are only 16 or whatever so there's no point really.

Bernie's da is givin' us a lift to the train station. Well me, Bernie and Jasmin. Tracy and Concepta are goin' with Concepta's ma. Can ya imagine tryin' to fit the five of us into a car? Whatever about me, Bernie, Jasmin and Tracy, but Concepta. She needs the back seat all to herself and that's without the luggage. She'll need her own carriage on the train, or better still, she could go in cargo!

✸✸✸

Mad. Just mad. That's all I can say. Galway doesn't know what hit them. It's been nothin' but madness since we left Dublin yesterday. We had such a laugh on the train down here. It was crazy. We got to the train station and ya know Concepta, she decides she's dyin' for somethin' to eat so we go to Supermacs in the train station. There we are just gettin' our food when Bernie turns around and says our train is about to pull out. Well ya wanna see us run. The five of us with our luggage in one hand and our Supermacs in the other, runnin' through Houston Station so we wouldn't miss our train. Ya wanna see the state of us. So we get to the place where ya give your man the tickets and he says to us 'I don't know what you're rushin' for girls, the trains not pullin' out for another ten minutes.' I tell ya, we could have battered Bernie until we hear another announcement about the train to Galway and it was only then that we realised we were at the wrong platform so we were off again. Even Concepta Cooney was runnin'. I think she was more concerned about droppin' her Supermacs than catchin' the train but that's Concepta for ya. She has her own priorities. I tell ya, try runnin' through Houston Station with a suitcase and you'll soon know all about it. I was only lucky that I had wheels although I don't know how many people lost ankles as I flew by them, not that I give a flyin' fuck. Thanks be to Jayzis though we got to the train and it wasn't even that packed. We were sittin' together and all – meself and Concepta on one side of the aisle and Bernie, Jasmin and Tracy on the other and the laugh we had. It was mad.

The hotel we're stayin' in is lovely as well and its not even that dear. It's right in Eyre Square and that's kind of right in the centre of Galway. It's a mafis hotel. Really nice. Meself and Concepta got thrown into a room together but the thing is, because there's only the two of us, we have a double bed each. The minute we got here I had to stop Concepta

Cooney from goin' near the minibar so she went up to Supermacs to get somethin' to eat. That young-one thinks of nothin' but her stomach although she got as far as the Dunnes off license on the way back and ended up bringin' back two bottles of peach schnapps with her burger, which of course, meself and the girls lowered back in 20 minutes. We were locked by the time we were goin' out, the five of us. Well not locked but tipsy. On our way anyways.

We went to a place, I dunno what it was called, and then to Cuba afterwards, not the country, it's the name of the club. Packed isn't the word though. I think it took me 45 minutes to get from one side of the dancefloor to the other and they're all students and boggers although sayin' that I ended up snoggin' a lovely lookin' young-fella for half the night and he's from Galway and all. He offered to walk me back to the hotel and I said he could coz Concepta's 14 new Swedish friends were walkin' us back anyways. We kinda just left them there like spas though when we went in. The gobshites are probably still standin' outside.

***

I'm lovin' Valentines Day, now lovin' it. We were in a place last night called the GPO and the laugh we had.

We spent the whole day shoppin' first though. They have this big long street called Shop Street and they've loads of shops. It's a bit like Grafton Street but not as good. There's some lovely stuff though if you were lookin' and I definitely wasn't. I'd be lucky to get anythin' else into me suitcase, the amount of stuff I brought with me. I'm ragin' I didn't listen to me ma about the shoes. The weight of the case and me havin' to drag it through Houston Station and all. Never again.

It was lovely lookin' through the shops mind you and Jasmin even bought a lovely top in Dorothy Perkins, a kind of green halter neck. It's lovely. Well on Jasmin anyway. The shops in Galway aren't as good as Dublin. That's the only thing. Ya don't have the same choice. I mean I didn't even see a Miss Selfridges and I get a lot of me cloths there. When your shoppin' ya want loads of different places so ya can always find somethin' although in sayin' that, they've a lovely Dunnes and the thing is, ya can't go wrong with Dunnes.

We went to an Indian restaurant for somethin' to eat for a change and I have to say, it was lovely, the five of us sittin' down to a meal. It was gas though coz it was Valentines and there was couples on every table except ours. Five Dublin young-ones sittin' around this table in the middle of the restaurant, none of us with a clue about Indian food, although Concepta did find a few things she recognised, trust her. We ended up gettin' loads of different things and sharin' and I have to say, it was mafis. I've never eaten Indian food before so it was a bit of an experience for me. The mouth was burnt off me, I swear to jayzis. I must have drank about five Smirnoff Ices to cool meself down and I knew at the time that was a bad idea.

By the time we got to the pub I was drunk. Now I'll be honest, not locked or anything but merry. It was a great night and the laugh we had. Bein' Valentine's night, all the fellas were all over us. There was one stage where there was just me and Tracy. Concepta was off doin' her bit for international relations as Tracy says. I think it has somethin' to do with her makin' friends with loads of foreigners. Jasmin was off wanderin' as she does and Bernie was gettin' stuck into a young-fella who I'll be the first to admit, was a ride even if he did look about 16. So anyway there me and Tracy are and this young-fella comes up and starts chattin' to me. Now he was actually a bit of alright although he was a bit of a culchie now that I come to think of it. So Tracy goes to the toilet and I end up kissin' this fella, Alan his name was. So whatever happened anyway, I ended up back in his place. He lives with his mate in this lovely apartment near enough to Eyre Square and the two of us are kissin' and one thing is leadin' to another and we get to the bedroom and he takes off his top and I swear to god, ya wanna see me run. His back was like a carpet. He had more hair than a gorilla and it must have been the same colour. I was tempted to look outside to see if there was a full moon he was that bad. I just left without sayin' anythin'. Ya thought I was runnin' in the train station the other day, that was nothin' compared to last night and me in six inch heels and all. I had to take a detour down loads of side streets and all in case he was followin' me. I mean, thank fuck I didn't tell him what hotel I was stayin' in. Now normally I wouldn't be that quick to judge but it turned me stomach. It'd be like havin' sex with the Bear in the Big Blue House.

***

Ah we'd a great day for Tracy's birthday yesterday, lovely it was. We got up in the mornin', well about 12 anyway, and went for a walk around the shops. We found the Galway Shoppin' Centre and although there's fuck all in it, it's still somethin' a bit different. There's a retail park across the road and they have a big Elvery's. Jasmin was dyin' to buy a pair of shorts for some mad reason. I mean, it's still freezin' out. There was a picture-house as well and Tracy saw a poster for a film she wanted to see, that new one with Matt Damon, so we said we'd go to it with her seein' as its her birthday and all. Well I tell ya, I don't think I've ever seen a cinema as small in me life. It was like someone's extension. It was like somebody got a dodgy DVD in Malaysia and put it on their plasma screen in their sittin' room like, I swear to jayzis and I wouldn't mind but me seat didn't even have one of them holders for ya to put your drink into. I had to leave it on the floor and Jasmin kicked it over when she was crossin' her legs. I would have drowned the bitch in Fanta if there had of been any left in it. I enjoyed the film though and more importantly, so did Tracy. After all, it is her day and once she's happy, we're happy.

We went for a meal in a lovely restaurant down at a place called the Spanish Arch. Why it's called that, I couldn't tell ya. I've been here since Friday and I still can't find an arch, Spanish, Irish or any other type of arch. The meal was lovely. I had the lasagne and it was only mafis. We were sittin' there and next minute, Tracy's phone rang and who was it only me Uncle Dessie to say happy birthday to her. Ya wanna see her, she was only delighted. I have to say, he's great when it comes to me mates, Dessie. He'd do anything for them. She's talkin' to him for a minute anyway and then another call starts comin' through on the call waitin' and who is it only Bopper and Paulo havin' one of them threesome callin's with Tracy. I wouldn't know how to do it but Paulo's always doin' it from the house phone. So ya know us anyway, the phone gets passed around the table and we all have a chat with the lads and tell them about what's happenin'. I nearly killed Bernie Boland for tellin' them about your man with the hairy back, or King Kong as the girls are callin' him. I mean, there's just some things ya don't tell your brother and his Bosnian mate. The lads were tellin' Jasmin somethin' really juicy coz she was there goin' 'Go way,' 'Jayzis,' 'I don't believe ya,' and all the rest of it and she wouldn't tell us what it was and then Tracy took the phone off her and it was all the same thing and she wouldn't tell us either. Meself, Bernie and Concepta were thinkin' of beatin' it out of them.

There was a lovely sweet in the restaurant as well. I had the Black Forest gateux and ice cream, and it was the nicest I've had this long time. I do like me Black Forest. Lovely after the bit of dinner, now I must say. I could have eaten two of them it was that nice. Concepta Cooney did eat two of them but trust her.

We went to a pub called the Livin' Room after and it was lovely. Really nice with a kind of chilled out atmosphere and not as full of kids as most of the other places we've been. That's the one thing about Galway. Half the people that live here are students. I know I'm only a young-one but I'm talkin' about kids that are 17 and 18 all over the place. The Livin' Room wasn't like that though. We had a lovely drink in there and its great, ya go to the toilet and ya wash your hands and whatever way they have it, ya can see the fellas washin' their hands on the other side. Some bloke grabbed Concepta's hand at one stage and she nearly broke his arm she pulled it that hard. I'm convinced I heard his face bangin' against the wall on the other side. I had to hold her back from goin' into the men's toilets to get him.

We decided to go back to Cuba after that. Well Tracy decided and we just followed her. I think Bernie is a bit spaced out of it this weekend coz she's never been to Galway and doesn't know anywhere so she can organise us to go to. She's probably after takin' notes for the next time we come. She probably has one of her itinerants written out and all for us. We had a good laugh in Cuba though. We nearly got squashed to death again. It was like one of them smelly rocker gigs. It did calm down a good bit by about one o'clock. We just got locked and had a good laugh. I even ended up kissin' one of Concepta's Swedish friends from the first night. He told me his name but I'm fucked if I can remember how to pronounce it. He was lovely though, real Swedish lookin', blonde hair and blue eyes, like that band Bros from years ago. He gave me his number too and I'm sure I put it into me phone. Only thing is, I can't remember his name to find it. I'm sure if I look through me phone book I'll spot it. It's probably somethin' real Swedish like Volvo or Bjorn or Francis.

I have to say though, it was an excellent weekend. We all had a blast, especially Tracy and I'm delighted coz I love her to bits. I'm delighted we all got on as well, even with me sharin' a room with Concepta although give credit where its due, she's very easy to live with even if she does fart a lot when she's asleep.

✳︎✳︎*✳︎*

Back in work today after the weekend and I just wasn't in the mood. I was exhausted as well and the fuckers had me in at nine o'clock this mornin' wouldn't ya know. All I wanted to do was sleep and I don't know if I've ever been happier seein' Julie Walsh coz it meant she'd spend the mornin' on the till while I could pretend to stock out the crisps or some shite like that. Greg was in at nine o'clock as well but he had to go off somewhere so it was only me and Julie Walsh until Dymphna came in at 12 o'clock so I spent half the mornin' asleep in the stockroom, flaked out on a box of Flakes. Julie Walsh kept tryin' to make conversation with me but I just wasn't in the mood although when am in ever in the mood to talk to Julie Walsh? She was askin' all about the weekend and I was tellin' her fuck all. The last thing I need is for that nosey cow to know all me business. Everyone on the Northside of Dublin would know in a few days, the mouth on her. I told Sheila when she started. 'Sheila,' I said, 'Tell her nothin'.' She'd only be short of ringin' the Adrian Kennedy Phone Show or takin' out an ad in the *Herald*.

I was on the hot food counter with Dymphna for a while although after about 20 minutes I felt that sick that I didn't think I'd be able to last. The bang off that woman is unreal. I don't think I've ever seen anyone sweat as much as Dymphna. I don't think she washes herself and I mean, there's no excuse for an auld-one that age. The bang off her does be absolutely woeful and we're tryin' to work with that. I mean, the thoughts of bein' stuck in between her and Julie Walsh on a normal day is bad enough but today above all days. Good jayzis. Now she's lovely, Dymphna, a real nice auld-one, the type of person ya can have a chat with and that's hard where I work coz durin' the day there does be me, Julie Walsh, Marie, and lets face it, she's always stoned off her box, I've seen her talkin' to a Toffee Crisp, Sheila who hardly has a word of English and Greg who's, well he's the boss and ya can't really have chats with him and Boris the Ukrainian fella never really stops workin' to chat so that just leaves smelly Dymphna. I mean, it's grand if she's at one end of the shop and you're at the other but if ya have to stand up close to her. That's why I don't mind doin' the Saturdays and Sundays that much coz it means I get to talk to the kids that do the part time or whatever. They're only 14 or 15 but at least they're not Chinese, smelly, stoned, Julie Walsh or a Toffee Crisp.

✳✳✳

Ski-Jumpin'. Now what a mad sport. I went to look for a bit of bobsleddin' or curlin' and the ski-jumpin' was on. Now I was about to turn it off but I ended up watchin' it for ages. It's only deadly.

If ya've never seen ski-jumpin' before, and I'm sure ya must have, I mean, ya'd know if ya have but anyway, I'll explain what it is. Remember now, I'm not the best at explainin' things like this but I'll try and as Jasmin's ma says all the time, the lord loves a trier.

What happens right, is there's this big slope, real steep with a kind of a ramp at the end and what happens is the skier sits on this bench yoke up the top and lets himself go and he goes flyin' down the slope thing and flies off the ramp and leans forward and at the same time, he kind of turns his feet upwards so the ski's are goin' the same way as his body so its like he's flyin' through the air and then they land at the bottom of the hill and they're given points for how far they flew and how good the jump was. It's only great it is.

I'd say ya have to have balls to do that, not literally like coz I'm sure ya could do it without balls no problem. Actually I'm convinced one of the commentators said the women do it too but what I meant is that ya'd have to be very brave to do it. Like to just fly down that slope and then jump down a mountain. I'd be shittin' meself.

The thing I noticed as well is the skimpy little things they wear. It's the same as the bobsleddin'. I mean, ya'd be freezin' in a bit of Lycra on the side of a ski slope. At least the curlers have the right idea. They're all wearin' big heavy jumpers and jackets and everythin' and they're inside even.

The Japanese are very good at the ski-jumpin'. One fella, only a tiny bloke he was, he flew really far. Ya wanna see him. Or maybe it just looked further than the others coz he's so small. Ya do see Norway and Finland doin' very well as well. I'd say there's fuck all else to do in these cold countries when it's snowin' so they all just ski-jump and play curlin'. I remember it snowed here one night about two year ago and it was a fucker gettin' home. Three hours we waited in town for a taxi coz the Nitelinks weren't runnin'. Its like that every night in these cold countries. The Norwegians and the Finlanders are lucky they don't have Dublin Bus.

✲✲✲

Our Bopper eventually ventured out of the house for the first time since before I went to Galway. I swear to jayzis, there's somethin' wrong with that young-fella. I wouldn't mind but the rash is only on one of his legs and it has been since he got it. I think he got a spot there last week and he was convinced the rash was spreadin' to his face but ya can't tell him. I swear to god, he's unreal.

He's always been like that, Bopper. He spends hours gettin' ready. There'd be nights when we're goin' out, this is no word of a lie, and Bopper will start gettin' ready before me and be finished an hour after me and he doesn't even have any hair to wash and try to straighten although that's never stopped him. I've caught him once or twice usin' me hair straightener on his hair and I wouldn't mind but he puts gel in it straight away anyway. I've never seen a young-fella so into the way he looks and I'll be honest, our Bopper is a good lookin' fella as it is. I mean, he is related to me after all. It's gettin' to a stage now where I do be takin' a lend of stuff on him. Like there the week before last I couldn't find me tweezers so he gave me a lend of his. I don't think I've ever met anyone, young-fella or young-one, who spends as much time fixin' their eyebrows. I even get him to do mine sometimes he's that good. He always gets a good arch on them and he makes it look really natural. Where he learned to do it, I haven't a clue but he's great at it. Ya don't really ask questions with our Bopper. I mean, I told ya before, he is a bit weird.

I caught him usin' me concealer there last week and I wouldn't mind, it was the Touché D'Eclat by Yves Saint Loraine and that's dear enough. He was usin' it to cover the bags under his eyes or so he says. I mean, would ya be well? And then he has the cheek to turn around to me and tell me I never put it on right and starts showin' me how to do it.

Then another time he used me hair removal cream to wax his chest and stomach, the gobshite. I wouldn't even mind but I've seen more hair on a frog. He still does it though although I told him there was no way he was usin' mine so he went out and got his own. I dread the day I come in and find Bopper waxin' his bikini line.

✳✳✳

That Marie Daly one from work is a mad yoke. She's off her rocker. She came into work today stoned, which, let the truth be told, is nothin' strange for Marie. I'd be surprised if she came into work not stoned but she was just really out of it today. Thank god Greg wasn't around coz he would have killed her.

She comes in and its all, 'Howaya Joanna, howaya Julie Walsh, howaya Sheila, howaya Joanna, howaya Sheila, howaya Joanna, howaya Joanna.' How many Joanna's she thought were in there I don't know so we were all like, 'Howaya Marie.' Except Sheila. She just said somethin' else that nobody understood but Marie must have said hello to me about 45 times. Now I'm sayin' to meself, what the fuck is goin' on here like and next minute she starts sayin' howaya to everythin' in the shop. She was like, 'Howaya fridge, howaya till, howaya Joanna, howaya packets of Starburst, howaya packets of Starburst Sours, howaya packets of Fruit Pastilles, howaya Joanna.' So there was a customer starin' her out of it, this auld-fella with a head like a turnip and he's givin' Marie mad looks although can ya blame him? So I'm terrified he'd say somethin' to Greg coz I'm kinda the supervisor when he's not around and I'd get a bollickin' if anythin' went wrong so I grabbed a hold of Marie and dragged her into the stockroom and when I say dragged I mean it. The poor auld-one nearly had whiplash when I was finished with her. 'What the fuck is wrong with ya?' I shouts. In the height of it at this stage I was but can ya blame me? If the customer didn't say anythin' to Greg I'm sure Julie Walsh would. That cow is always tryin' to get me into trouble. She knows she can't lie though coz of the security cameras. I don't have to worry about Sheila sayin' anythin' coz Greg understands her less than I do and he doesn't ever wait for her to try to explain.

Anyway there was me and Marie in the stockroom, her sittin' on a box of Tayto, not by her own choice I may add so I says to her again 'What the fuck is wrong with ya?' And she says 'Yogurt.' Now I was in no mood let me tell ya. So she says 'yogurt' again and I was about to beat an explanation out of her when I realised Marie bought five of them natural yogurts that are on special on the way home yesterday and she has a bit of a habit of addin' a few of her own flavours, mostly hash. I swear to god, she even told me and Julie Walsh how to make hash yogurts one day.

I didn't know what to do with her. I mean, I couldn't rat her out to Greg coz I'm not like that. Julie Walsh is but I'm not so I had to think of how to sober her up or come down or whatever it is ya do after the hash, I don't know, I think I've only ever done it about three times in me life. So I was about to make her a cup of coffee when I thought to meself, hold on, what if the caffeine makes it worse. At this stage she was havin' a conversation with a tub of McDonnell's Curry Sauce about an episode of ER she'd seen the other day and I wouldn't mind but there was no way the curry sauce saw it. So I started fillin' her full of water. Litres of it. At one stage I was even thinkin' about shovin' a hose down her throat so I left her in the jaxx and went back to work. Can ya imagine the surprise I got two hours later when I was goin' the toilet and she was gone. The silly cow had only gone and fallen asleep in the stockroom with the curry sauce in her hand. I'm tellin' ya, that's it. I'm hidin' the fuckin' yogurts!

***

Spare tit is not the word. Yeah it's two words I know but ya know what I'm tryin' to say. Just pretend its one word for fuck sake. I'm goin' to tell ya what I'm talkin' about anyway. Jayzis.

I came home from work yesterday, gaspin' for a drink after all that madness with stoned Marie so I'm havin' me dinner watchin' the telly and I decide to ring the others to see what they were up to. Dyin' for a drink at this stage I was.

Bernie wasn't feelin' the best so she wouldn't come out. I tried to guilt trip her but she was havin' none of it and I wouldn't mind but she always does it to me. I'll be honest though, she hasn't been the best since Galway. I think she got a bit of a cold but ya will do if ya wear a skirt up to your belly button and no jacket. I told her.

Jasmin was doin' somethin' again with the triplets, well the girls anyways. I think she said she was goin' late night shoppin' with them in Blanchardstown. Her phone is fucked so I couldn't really catch what she was sayin' but then again it is Jasmin and she's very hard to understand anyways.

Concepta said she was stayin' in to watch a film with her ma coz it was only the two of them in the house. Her brothers and sister are in her aunts house and her da's away for the weekend so she said there was no way she was goin' out and leavin' her ma on her own.

Bopper and Paulo were goin' to somethin' in the Pod but it was ticket only so I couldn't go with them and Bopper said it wouldn't be my scene anyways. They said they'd give me a ring if they were goin' to somewhere else, which they didn't. Well as far as I know. Bopper didn't come home again last night.

I even rang me Uncle Dessie but he had a date with some young-one about half his age. He even said date. Whatever about Tracy but me Uncle Dessie usin' that word. Jayzis.

So it was just me and Tracy headin' out then or so I thought. We got to the Q-Bar and who's sittin' there only Lance and some bloke called Pietro from France who was about as interestin' as Marie's tub of curry sauce. So Tracy and Lance are there all lovey dovey and havin' a laugh and I'm tryin' to have a conversation with this gobshite who's talkin' about paintin's and all this other shite and next minute Tracy and Lance hear a song that they like and get up to dance. So Tracy and Lance are havin' a dance, while I'm in a trance, listenin' to this spa from France, when he takes a chance and puts his hand up me skirt and inside me pants. Well ya wanna see me jump. I don't think I've got up that quickly in me life. So he starts sayin' somethin' to me in French and I go off to the toilet and come back and he's gone so I ended up sittin' there half the night on me own and even when Tracy and Lance came back I was still left on me own. As I said, spare fuckin' tit. Now it's three words.

✷✷✷

I actually stayed in on a Saturday night can ya believe it? Well when I say stay in, I went around to Bernie's to watch Muriel's Weddin' with her coz the poor cow is dyin' with the flu. Bernie this is, not Muriel although sayin' that, Muriel could be. I don't know, do I? I don't know the young-one. I offered to bring around a few cans but she said she wouldn't have been up to it so I brought her around a bottle of the Calpol so that should keep her happy for a while. I know meself I'd prefer a bottle of Calpol to six Dutch any day. That Dutch tastes like piss but at six for a fiver ya can't really complain can ya? It gets ya locked doesn't it and that's all that matters. Jasmin mixes it with 7UP but ya know what Jasmin's like.

Poor Bernie is in an awful state though, an awful state. I can't remember seein' her look that bad in a long time. Her skin is all pasty kinda. She's very pale, very pale now. She looks like a ghost. I got the fright of me life when I walked in, because she was so pale, not because she looked like a ghost. Her eyes are all puffy as well, all kinda inflamed like she has hayfever, well she does have hayfever but I'd say her eyes are puffy from the flu coz there's no flowers around at the moment and if there was, they'd be blown to pieces. Me ma's geraniums still haven't recovered from bein' blown off the wall in the hangin' basket that time.

Bernie's nose is all stuffed as well. Ya wanna hear her tryin' to talk. Its gas. She went through half a roll of tissue paper in the time I was there, half a roll and that was just from blowin' her nose. We couldn't even do the songs from Muriel's Weddin' coz she can hardly talk let alone sing and there wasn't a hope of her gettin' up to do the dance, the poor thing.

I wouldn't mind but she's doped out of her face on the Uniflu and with the Calpol as well. Jayzis, she'll be walkin' around like a zombie and it doesn't suit Bernie bein' sick. It's not her. She's kinda, what's the word I'm lookin' for? Glamorous. Yeah she's kinda glamorous. Like your woman Claudia Schiffer but nowhere near as good lookin'. If I catch it off her I'll kill her.

✳✳✳

Me ma was tellin me, now I don't know how true this is coz she heard it from Petulia next door and we all know that ones a bit of a spacer but Petulia was tellin' me ma that Misses O'Driscoll from up the road told her that she was in mass there yesterday and just as Father

Mulhern is finished wafflin' the ears off everyone, before he blesses the bread and wine I think it is, someone started a Mexican wave. I swear to god. This is what Misses O'Driscoll told Petulia, but as I said, I don't know how true it is. Can ya imagine though? Me ma said that Petulia said that Misses O'Driscoll said that she was sittin' there half way down the church, and it's a big church, they do fit loads in of a mass, and someone about five rows from the front stands up really quickly, then the person beside them and then the next person. What had happened, Misses O'Driscoll told Petulia, is that a little kid was goin' along behind the people stickin' a pen into their arse cheeks and that's why they stood up so quickly and these young-ones, they can't have been older than 10, Misses O'Driscoll was tellin' Petulia, thought it would be hilarious if they did it too, stood up quickly that is, not stabbin' people with pens. So everyone thinks they're meant to be standin' up and so people are gettin' up all over the place and the young-ones, who were in the 7th row I believe, start a Mexican wave. Nobody was doin' it at first but then it kinda started to spread until the whole church was doin' it like they were at an Ireland match. Now can ya imagine it? All the auld-ones there doin' the Mexican wave in mass. I'm ragin' coz I'd say it would have been hilarious although in sayin' that I haven't been to mass since Christmas Eve, let the truth be told and I only went then coz the girls were goin'.

Can ya imagine what must have been goin' through poor Father Mulhern's head? Wonderin' what was goin' on. He probably tried to exorcise the front row although knowin' the auld-ones around here, they need all the exercise they can get but as I said, me ma heard this off Petulia who heard it off Misses O'Driscoll so I'm not sure how true it is. Why the fuck is it called a Mexican wave anyways? I've never seen anyone from Mexico doin' it although then again, I've never seen anyone from Mexico.

※※

Ya'll never believe this. No seriously, ya won't. 'Member I was sayin' about the rash that everyone was gettin' was like that film

Outbreak? Well ya wont believe it but Tracy has it now but not only Tracy but Lance too and her friend Miranda, the one from college that was meant to be comin' to Galway but didn't. The three of them have the exact same thing that everyone else had. It's unreal at this stage. There was me first, or maybe Paulo. Now personally I think I caught it off him but he thinks he caught it off me although it's about a month ago now so we'll never really know but anyway, then Jasmin got it and then Bopper and Bernie around the same time. Bernie has the cold on top of it as well, although the rash wasn't that bad in Galway. Now Tracy, Lance and Miranda. The only one of us who hasn't caught it at this stage is Concepta believe it or not. She rang me there earlier on sayin' she wont be out with any of us until it's all gone. I mean, the cheek of her. What does she think it is? Bionic plague? It's not like anyone's died from it or anythin'. Well not yet anyway. There could always be a chance but I've been to the doctor, Paulo's been to a doctor and an STP Clinic, don't bleedin' ask by the way. Let's just say he got prescribed a different medicine there. I knew by the way Bopper was talkin' that Paulo had crabs or somethin' as well as the other rash. Bernie's been to the doctor too, so has Jasmin and Bopper would have if he wasn't takin' a mixture of the stuff me and Paulo were told to take so I'd say the chances of someone dyin' from it are slim.

Concepta Cooney is still havin' none of it. She even sponged herself down with Dettol she was tellin' me, although the last thing I needed to hear about on me lunch break was Concepta tryin' to reach her toes with a sponge and I wouldn't mind but I was halfway through a packet of salt and vinegar Hunky Dory's at the time. I'm goin' to tell the bitch I still have the rash for weeks now just out of spite. We might not see her for months. Now there's an idea.

✳✳✳

Meself and Jasmin were bored out of our tits last night so we decided to go see a film. It was the usual stuff; Get the bus into town, get off in O'Connell Street and walk to the Cineworld on Parnell

Street. I love the Cineworld, I have to say. It's the best picture-house I've ever been to and I mean, especially compared to that one in Galway and its mad classy as well, the Cineworld. Its always spotless and they have a bar on the second floor although I've never been to it let the truth be told. I mean, it's in town so we do just go to somewhere else for a drink, a pub like. I must try it sometime to see what its like. It looks nice and ya can only go to it if you're goin' to a film like. Ya can't just wander in off the street to go for a drink. I think Bopper and Paulo have been there a few times and Bopper says it's nice as far as I remember, although maybe it was somewhere else.

Anyway, meself and Jasmin get our tickets, go the toilet and get our food. I had medium popcorn and Diet Coke and Jasmin had a big bag of the Skittles and Coke although I was nearly not lettin' Jasmin get the Skittles. Not after the last time when her and Bopper thought it would be only hilarious to start throwin' them at people and I have to admit, it was hilarious until we all got thrown out of Miss Selfridges. The staff didn't know what was goin' on at the time. It was like Iraq with all these Skittles flyin' around.

Anyway I said nothin' to Jasmin about the Skittles coz the dizzy cow has probably forgotten about Miss Selfridges already. The two us start to walk towards the screen we were meant to be in and I had a look at the tickets to make sure coz the last time we let Jasmin find the screen, we ended up in this French shite with subtitles instead of the one with George Clooney we were meant to see, although to be honest, I'd say the French film would have been better after all. So we get to the screen and pick our seats and we're sittin' there before the ads or the trailers or anythin' comes on, eatin' away, when next minute, who do we see walkin' in only Phillip with some young-one. Now as I said before, I haven't heard from Phillip since that time I asked him out a few weeks ago and he told me we were gonna be mates and all the rest of it, which, I have to be honest, would have been grand by me. I'm not one of these people that gets bitter or anythin'. I get on with Phillip and I'm sure I'd get on with him as a mate just the same as I did before I asked him out but as I said, I've text him a few times since and he's just ignored me, the fucker.

So anyway, the film starts and Phillip and this young-one, disgraceful lookin' thing she was, are sittin' about six or seven rows in front of us and Jasmin offers me a Skittle. Well an idea came to me, a flash of inspiration. I got one of the Skittles, took aim and walloped it off the side of his head. So he doesn't know what's happenin' and when he gets back to lookin' at the film, I throw another one and hit the young-one in the head. So she's there wonderin' what's goin' on now at this stage so I throw another one and hit Phillip again. So he's turnin' around to see if he can see who it is and me and Jasmin can't really be seen that well because this auld-one with hair that should have been left in the 80's is sittin' in front of us and the two of us are there tryin' not to break our shites laughin' and I have to say, it was very hard. So we spend the whole film hittin' them with Skittles and at the end we leg it out before he can recognise us. So we're standin' there at the end of the escalator while Jasmin's puttin' on her jacket and I see him comin' towards us and I say to Jasmin 'Will ya look who it is?' and he goes kinda scarlet but he has nowhere to go coz he's on the escalator comin' towards us. So he's like, 'What's the story girls? How's things?' and I'm like, 'Grand, Phillip. Couldn't be better.' And he smiles and says, 'What film were ya at?' and I looked at Jasmin and back at him and I says, 'The same one as you Phillip. We were sittin' right down the front. Jasmin's blind, aren't ya Jasmin?' So she nods at him and he's like, 'I didn't see ya.' So I was just like, 'Ah well, see ya later anyways. Jasmin, giz a Skittle.' And the two of us walk off makin' sure he can see the bag and he turns and starts walkin' away from us with the young-one, walkin' towards the men's jaxx and he's just about to go inside when a Skittle flies through the air and hits him in the head.

✲✲✲

I've actually found a winter sport that's better than bobsleddin', curlin' and ski-jumpin' — speed skatin'. Or short course speed skatin' to be exact. There's two types. Me da was tellin' me. I was askin' him about it there earlier. I mean, he's the best to ask. He knows what he's talkin' about although that's a very different thing to knowin' everythin', which he thinks he does but as long as he was able to tell me about the speed skatin' I was happy.

Ya see the long course speed skatin' is done on a longer track and for longer distances and there's only two people racin' against each other and they're in their own lanes and everythin'. In the short course though, the track is really small and tight and a few people race against each other. I have to say, it's only deadly. I mean, I couldn't stop watchin' it there today. The best bit though is when there's a few of them flyin' around a corner and they crash into each other and they all go flyin' into the wall at the side of the ice rink and land on top of each other and everythin'. I don't know how they don't lose fingers. Ya wanna see the blades on the skates. They're not your usual ice skate boots like the ones ya used to get when the ice rink used to be open down in Phibsboro. These things are so sharp they'd take the finger off ya like they're cuttin' a carrot. I'd say its like skatin' on the edge of a sword, although not that I know what the edge of a sword is like. I'm just guessin'.

Whatever happened to that ice rink in Phibsboro? We used to have great craic there, me and the girls. It's a furniture shop now. No wonder we don't have anyone in the speed skatin' or the figure skatin' for that matter. We don't have an ice rink. I mean, how the fuck do we have a curlin' team? They must practice in Smithfield at the outdoor rink at Christmas. Ya'd think in a city this size with so many Russians, Czechs, Canadians, Nigerians and all these other cold countries that we'd have an ice rink. It's a disgrace. Me and Tracy used to be deadly. Bernie was just into goin' really fast. She'd be more of a speed skater than anythin' but meself and Tracy could do all the tricks and the jumps and all and the fuckers came and turned it into a furniture showroom. I mean, that American one, the one that was in the Olympics a few years ago, she got kneecapped by some other young-one, I can't think of her name for the life of me but she would never have got a medal at the Winter Olympics if they came and turned the ice rink she trained at into a furniture showroom. As far as I'm concerned, the Olympics are far more important than a three-piece leather suite with matchin' display cabinet and side tables. Me and Tracy could be there trainin' for the next Olympics if they hadn't of closed it. We could have been the ones doin' the kneecappin' although sayin' that, given half a chance, me and Tracy would be the only ones left without broken kneecaps. That's one way to win a gold medal.

I was sayin' it to Jasmin today and she didn't even know there was such a thing as the Winter Olympics although let the truth be told, I don't think Jasmin realised there was such a thing as the Summer Olympics. There's things that happen that she doesn't even notice. I bet ya she still thinks the ice rink in Phibsboro is still open. She's the type of sap who'd go down and go ice skatin' on a dinner table.

✷✷✷

There's a rumour flyin' around, now it's only a rumour so I don't know how true it is and Julie Walsh told me and ya can't believe the angelus out of her mouth even if ya knew what the angelus was and its not just going 'dong' every couple of seconds. I thought it was but its not. Stupid havin' church bells on the telly if ya ask me.

Anyway, there's a rumour flyin' around and Julie Walsh wouldn't tell me how she knows, the dozy cow, but there's a rumour that Greg is leavin' to go back to South Africa. Now I was shocked to be honest coz I mean, as far as I know, Greg loves it here. He loves the job, loves the people, loves the city. He hates the weather mind you but then again, don't we all. If you were to come from somewhere like South Africa to Ireland wouldn't you hate the weather, swappin' sunshine and heat for pissin' rain and freezin' cold and clouds all the time. Ya'd have to be crazy. But other than the weather, he loves it as far as I know so that's why I was a bit surprised when I heard he might be leavin'. I was thinkin' of askin' him meself but he went off somewhere before I got a chance to. The only one that was able to tell me anythin' was Julie Walsh and even then she knew fuck all even though she pretended she did and just wouldn't tell me, the sap. Dymphna wasn't in and she'd usually be great with the gossip as long as ya don't stand too close to her although sometimes ya have to bare the bang off her to get all the juicy bits of gossip. Sheila and Marie were in but as I said before, Sheila speaks hardly any English and Marie's always stoned so they usually know nothing more than what Julie Walsh knows. We even had some of the customers talkin' about it. The regulars like. Petulia that lives next door to me is mad about him. She thinks he's a ride. I mean, the state of him. He's like a baldy lanky gorilla.

I wonder why he might be leavin' though. I know he used to be married in South Africa so I'm thinkin' maybe that has somethin' to do with it, like it has somethin' to do with his ex-wife maybe, or maybe his ma or da are sick or somethin' and he has to go home. Or maybe, just like the rest of us, Julie Walsh gives him a pain in the hole or he has to get away from the smell of Dymphna.

※

I was just home from work last night and the phone rings and who is it only Concepta askin' me was I goin' out, which I have to say, made me laugh after her goin' mad about Tracy gettin' the rash and how she wasn't comin' near any of us until it was gone and all the rest of it. I knew that come the weekend, Concepta Cooney would be the first one to ring me. So ya know me, I seldom pass up the opportunity for a night out. Needless to say, Bernie was the one that rang Concepta with a night already organised. She'd been ringin' me in work, Bernie, and I forgot all about ringin' her back. So I get meself ready and knock around to Bernie and the two of us go to meet Tracy and Concepta at the bus stop. Jasmin was goin' out with Bopper and we asked them to come with us but they wouldn't. It wasn't anythin' serious or anythin'. I mean, as I said before, before Paulo came along, Bopper and Jasmin used to always hang around together. The best of mates they were, the best of mates.

So anyway, Bernie is all up for goin' to Bad Bobs but Tracy wanted to go to Q-bar and the one thing I have to say about Bernie is, she doesn't really like when ya don't go along with her plan but I was thinkin' about the night I was left sittin' in the Q-bar like a sap that night with Tracy, Lance and the French fella so I try to get them to go to Fitzsimons. I could see things gettin' a bit tense with Tracy and Bernie so I says to meself, I better not get involved. So I agreed with Tracy, hopin' Bernie would listen to both of us instead of causin' a row until Concepta turns around and suggests goin' to Coyote. Well Bernie nearly snapped 'I thought we said we were goin' to Bad Bobs.' She says. 'No. YOU said we were goin' to Bad Bobs.' Tracy says really smart like so the two of them start goin' at it in the middle of Temple Bar. They're the last two people ya wanna see arguin'. Bernie is as loud as fuck and Tracy uses all her psychology shite and it does be headwreckin' at times so while this is happenin', I give Jasmin a ring to see where she is but she says she can't tell me for some reason and then hangs up. So I look at Concepta who, I have to say, doesn't look in the mood for this at all so she walks in between them and tells them to shut up. So she says to Bernie, 'Are you meetin' someone in Bad Bobs?' and Bernie says, 'No' and she says to Tracy, 'Are you meetin' anyone in Q-bar?' and Tracy says, 'No' and Concepta goes, 'Right, we're goin' to Coyote then.' And she starts walkin' off and without thinkin', I start to follow her and after walkin' for about 30 seconds, we look back and there's Bernie and Tracy followin' us, still arguin' though but followin' us all the same. Fair play to Concepta. I have to say.

    We had a great night in Coyote anyway. I got talkin' to this fella, a ride I have to say but he was as borin' as fuck. He was tellin' me about his dog for 45 minutes. Thank god Tracy came to find me when she did coz he'd just started about the dog gettin' neutered as if I give a fuck. It should have been him gettin' neutered, the gobshite.

March

I tell ya, I'm lucky to be alive. Well okay, that's a bit of an exaggeration but it was a mad night, I swear to Jayzis and I wouldn't mind because at one stage things were lookin' very good if ya know what I mean.

There was only the three of us that went out: Meself, Concepta and Sheila from work and I have to say now, we had a bit of buzz. We went up to Farley's for a few drinks first and then we went into Fitzsimons coz as I said before, I do enjoy a night in Fitzsimons. They play good music, kinda mixed so everyone's happy.

Bernie didn't come coz she wasn't feelin' the best. Her cold isn't really gone yet and she was out the other night in a skimpy little jacket. I said it to her at the time but do ya think she'd listen to me? No. Bernie just wants to look nice . I mean, I was the one sittin' in with her last week when she was sick. Its her own fault is all I'll say.

Tracy was goin' out with Lance so that's why she didn't come with us. I think she was doin' somethin' with a few of her friends from college and she said it to me to come but I didn't want to be left on me own like a spa again. I don't think her and Bernie are on the best of terms after that argument the last time we were out and the last thing I want to do is get dragged into the middle of it.

Jasmin was headin' out with Bopper and Paulo and wouldn't tell us where they were goin'. I tell ya, there's somethin' funny goin' on there. Jasmin and Bopper are all best mates again and they're all secrets and talkin' about things really quietly. She's goin' to some cabaret show with them tonight. I mean, Jasmin can't even say cabaret.

So it was only me, Concepta and Sheila anyway. Farley's was packed enough when we went down. We were lucky to get a seat even. These two young-ones Concepta knew, I hadn't a clue who they were but as I said, Concepta knows everyone, they moved over to let us sit in beside them so it was grand. We left about 11 to go to Fitzsimons and it was packed enough in there as well. We had a few shots to get ourselves goin'. Well me and Concepta did. We don't let Sheila have shots. She gets drunk too easily. I've seen her get locked on two bottles of Smirnoff Ice. She's better now but we still have to watch her just to make sure she doesn't get too hammered. I was delighted when I saw her talkin' to some fella. He seemed to be mad into her and I even saw the two of them kissin' which I have to say, is the first time I've seen her with anyone.

Concepta went off doin' her meet the nightclub again. This time there was a group of about five young-ones from Bristol in England and two blokes from Sweden she was tryin' to impress by speakin' Swedish to them. I didn't even know she could speak Swedish but she said them young-fellas in Galway thought her a bit. She's mad.

I got talkin' to this lovely fella. He was from Leeds in England and he had a lovely accent. A real good lookin' fella he was too. A bit like Hugh Jackman only with better hair. He was layin' all the moves on me so we started kissin' and the rest of it so I'm thinkin' to meself, this is great. He asks me back to his hotel and I go and find Concepta and tell her to look after Sheila who, at this stage, is locked. Palatic isn't the word. She's in the middle of Concepta's new friends from Bristol and Sweden speakin' a mixture of Chinese and English and everyone thinks she's only great.

So I leave with your man from Leeds, Paul his name is, and the two of us are walkin' up towards Grafton Street and where's he stayin' only the Westbury so I was only delighted with meself. Its only gorgeous. Ya wanna see the rooms in it. It was like a palace although in sayin' that, I wouldn't know what a palace looks like. They even put chocolates on the pillows. It's far from the Westbury I was reared I can assure ya. I was lucky they even let me in. I've been kicked out of worse!

So anyway, meself and this Paul fella are there kissin' and one thing is leadin' to another and the clothes are comin' off and I'm there in me knickers and bra, a matchin' pair from Dunnes only €24 and they're mafis. I mean, where would ya get it? Ya can't go wrong. He's there in just his boxers and next minute he jumps off the bed, searches in his bag on the floor and takes out this leather thing with a handle and loads of these floppy things on it. So I was like, 'What the fuck is that?' and he says, 'I want you to spank me.' Well I just broke me shite laughin'. So he says, 'I'd say you do it rough Joanna.' And he pulls these leather handcuffs from the suitcase and then these things that look like them things ya use to start a car. Jump-leads I think they're called. I was like 'Will ya fuck off.' So the fucker jumps on top of me and before I know what's happenin', me left hand is handcuffed to the headboard. So now, I have to admit, I was freaked out at this stage so he starts tryin' to take off me knickers and I knee the fucker into the chin and he starts gettin' a bit angry and goes to grab me knickers off. Needless to say I was havin' none of it so I grabbed the jump-lead thing and lunged it towards his mickey. Well the screams off him. I says, 'Take these fuckin' handcuffs off now or I'll attach the other end of this wire to the telly and turn it on and then fuck it out the window.' He's still in agony and he puts his hand into the side pocket of the suitcase and pulls out the key, unlocks it and I'm still holdin' this clamp thing tightly. So I try the best I can to get dressed with me free hand, give the fucker one last almighty squeeze and clamp the other end to one of his nipples and just walked out, the dirty pervert. I wouldn't mind but I was dyin' to stay in the Westbury and all.

***

There's somethin' goin' on with Jasmin and our Bopper. I'm convinced of it. She was around in the house there earlier and all she was talkin' about was the cabaret they were at last night. She loved it she said although I'm sure Jasmin's been to one of them cabaret things before with our Bopper. Ya wanna see the two of them talkin' about it. I was gonna hit one of them at one stage and they're still bein' all secretive about things. I asked Jasmin where it was and she went all blank and looked at Bopper and he said Vicar Street which is strange coz Tracy said her Lance was goin' to see some shite band there last night and there definitely was no cabaret on. I said nothin' to Jasmin and Bopper though. There's definitely somethin' goin' on.

Jasmin was sayin' somethin' about fellas dressed up as girls doin' the songs as well. Now I don't really know what the fuck a cabaret is but then again, I don't think Jasmin does either. As far as I know, a fella that dresses up as a young-one is a transvestism or whatever ya call them but Bopper tells me that when they dress up to do a show they're called drag queens like in that film Priscilla, Queen of the Dessert. I have to say, I wouldn't have known the difference but Bopper knows everythin' about it. I think it was the only thing they weren't tryin' to hide. I'm wonderin' why Bopper knows so much about drag queens. I'm tellin' ya, if I catch him in my hotpants I'll reef him. I mean, if they don't fit me, they won't go anywhere near him!

※※※

Me Uncle Dessie rang today for a chat and I mean, that's nothin' strange. Me Uncle Dessie is always on the phone to me tryin' to find out all the latest scandal. Who else is he gonna ring like? Bopper? I know what its like tryin' to have a conversation with our Bopper. He tells ya nothin'. I think he thinks ya'll take him away from the mirror for too long or somethin' and ya know the way he is about talkin' about stuff. He's a mouth as long as its about him so Dessie does just rings me and I fill him in on everythin'. I mean, I couldn't give a shite.

So we're there talkin' away and he says 'Joanna, where would ya like someone to take ya for a night out?' so I'm thinkin' to meself what sort of question is that to ask someone and I wouldn't mind but at the time we were talkin' about the chances of Concepta gettin' that rash. So I ask him why he's askin' me and he tells me to just answer the question and I'm thinkin' and thinkin' and all of a sudden it dawns on me. 'Who are you goin' on a night out with?' says I and he goes all quiet. So I'm laughin' to meself and asks him again who it is and he says 'Some young-one. Ya don't know her.' 'Young-one!' I says, soundin' a bit more shocked than I should have and he says 'Woman, it's a woman.'

The thing is, me Uncle Dessie is mad for the young-ones, mad for the young-ones he is and I suppose ya can't really blame him after what happened with me Aunt Doris. He was in bits after that for ages. What happened was, the two of them were livin' in England, near enough to London as far as I remember. The last time I was there I was about seven. Anyway, Dessie came home from work one day and me Aunt Doris had left him a note sayin' she was runnin' away with a 17 year old young-fella from up the road who was best friends with me cousin Nigel. The last anyone heard from her, she was livin' in a flat in Amsterdam with this young-fella. Me Uncle Dessie was in bits after it and so was Nigel. This was about five years ago now. It would be coz Nigel's three years older than me sister Wanda and she's only two years older than me. Me Uncle Dessie moved back here when Nigel went off to college. He's great Nigel. We have such a laugh. Him and Bopper get on great. He does always stay in our Bopper's room when he comes over and the noise of the two of them. Me Uncle Dessie's daughter Jacinta is a looper. She's one of these hippies that's mad into the feminist shite. Her and her boyfriend live in Birmingham and are tryin' to stop a motorway bein' built, or at least that's the last Dessie heard.

Anyway as I was sayin', Dessie is mad into the young-ones. He's always flirtin' away when we're out and all the rest of it so I'm tryin' to think of somewhere he can go for his 'date' and suddenly I think of somethin'. 'Ring Tracy and ask her.' I tell him and he thinks about it and says 'I can't really ask her.' 'It's not Tracy is it?' I ask, half jokin'. 'No its not.' he says, startin' to laugh. It better not be, although Tracy has taste!

✳✳✳

I can't believe it. Me boss Greg really is goin' back to South Africa. Now as I said, rumours were flyin' around all week but he came around to all of us and told us although that was pointless coz he told Julie Walsh first and she told everyone else straight away. He didn't even give a reason. He just said he was leavin'. It'll be in about two weeks he said, just after Paddy's day. He never said why he was goin' or anythin', just that he was. Ya know us, we were all dyin' to find out why, guessin' all day. I even asked him at one stage and he wouldn't tell me and that's not like him coz me and him do usually have a good chat.

Julie Walsh is convinced it has somethin' to do with his ex-wife although that ones always lookin' for a bit of scandal. That's what happens when ya spend all your time on your hole watchin' Ricki Lake and Jerry Springer although when its about her it's a different story altogether. She's still goin' on about that fight a few weeks ago believe it or not. She still has me driven mad with it. I feel like batterin' her sometimes.

I'm ragin' Greg is leavin' though to tell ya the truth coz I like him. I mean, there's worse bosses ya can have. He's usually a good bit of laugh and to be honest, I think I'm his favourite. He's never said anythin' but I can tell by the way he goes on. He's always lettin' me have days off when I ask him and as I said, me and him are always havin' chats and havin' a bit of buzz.

The other thing I'm wonderin' is who they're gonna get to replace him. It could be some fucker that's all like 'do this,' and 'do that.' Greg isn't like that at all. Better the divil ya know as they say, well me ma does anyway. I can imagine us gettin' some new manager and Julie Walsh lickin' up and all the rest of it. Her tongue will turn brown, the dirty bitch.

We'll definitely have to have a night out before he leaves. Maybe we can forget Julie Walsh accidentally on purpose so she doesn't show up. Ah well, at least I'll have somewhere to stay if I ever go to South Africa on me holidays, whether Greg likes it or not. I'll just turn up.

✳✳✳

I can't believe it. Like seriously, I'm in an awful state. Remember I was tellin' ya about that winter sports channel? The one with the bobsleddin', curlin', ski-jumpin' and speed skatin'? Well its gone. It just disappeared. I went to turn it on there today coz I was watchin' the curlin' last night live all the way from Innsbruck wherever the fuck that is. I think it might be in Norway although I don't even know where Norway is, let the truth be told. I couldn't believe it though. The channel had just disappeared. I thought at first it might have been moved to a different number but I went through every single one about four times and I couldn't find it. I was disgusted. I was tempted to ring NTL and all to find out what was goin' on and I would have and all except I couldn't find the number and when I did it was the wrong one. I mean, ya'd think they'd warn ya before they just take a channel away and I'd say I wasn't the only one goin' mad. I had Paulo watchin' it as well, although Bosnia are a lot better at the winter sports than us. They held the Winter Olympics there in the 80's, Paulo tells me, although I don't know if he was born at the time. I think it was before the war anyway coz I mean, ya can't really hold the Winter Olympics if you're in the middle of a war or maybe they stopped the war, let them have the Winter Olympics and then started again. I don't know but then again, I know fuck all about Bosnia, although in sayin' that, either does Paulo.

I rang him straight away and I got him to check if it was still on his telly but its gone in his house too. He has the NTL too. He was goin' mad as well coz there's a Bosnian fella doin' great in the slalom ski-in' lately. Well I mean fair play to them. Anytime I've seen Ireland at anythin' they've been shite although the curlin' and the bobsleddin' is the only things we've been in, but as I told Paulo, we don't have any snow. We don't even have the winter sports channel now so we're totally fucked.

✻✻✻

Well ya'd never guess who text me today? I was in work at the time and me phone beeped and I looked at it expectin' it to be one of the girls askin' me to go out tonight or Paulo tellin' me the winter sports channel is back, although its unlikely, or me Uncle Dessie askin' for more advice about his night out tonight with your woman. We still don't know who she is and even Tracy tried to get it out of him and couldn't and she's good at that sort of thing, what with her studyin' psychology and all. But it was none of the girls or Paulo or Dessie, it was your man Phillip. I swear to god. I couldn't believe it so I was thinkin' to meself, what does this tool want? It's probably after takin' him this long to realise it was me hittin' him in the head with Skittles, the stupid fucker. So I look at the message and it says, 'HEY BABE WOT U UP 2? U WNT 2 DO SUMTIN L8R?' So I nearly died like. The cheek of him textin' me after all this time wantin' me to go out. I was in the height of it I was and I was tellin' Sheila all about it and she thinks I shouldn't text him back or at least that's what I think she was tryin' to say. Julie Walsh and Marie were in as well and as I said before, never tell Julie Walsh anythin' unless you want the whole world to find out and Marie was down the other end of the shop havin' a chat with a box of Cheerios as far as I could see although you'd never know what that auld-one does be up to. I decided to give Tracy a ring coz she'd know what to do. So I rang her and told her about the message and she nearly hit the roof. She said there was no way I was to text him back and the cheek of him not replyin' to me for weeks and then askin' me out all of a sudden and who does he think he is and it's a pity me and Jasmin weren't throwin' anythin' bigger than Skittles at him that time and the neck of him textin' me at all. So she went on for another quarter of an hour before I said I had to go make sure Marie was still alive, which, thank fuck, she was although not by much let the truth be told. So I was goin' to take Tracy's advice when I had a thought. I got me phone and wrote back, 'WUD LUV 2 DO SUMTIN L8R,' and he writes back, 'KOOL. WOT U WNT 2 DO?' And I says, 'ANYTIN THAT DOESNT INVOLVE U!' Then I laughed.

***

There was killin's tonight. Killin's. It was like the Royal Rumble in the middle of Temple Bar and that's no exaggeration. I thought the United Nations would have had to be called in at one stage to keep the peace it got that bad.

We were all headin' out for the night. By we I mean there was was loads of us there, all walkin' through Temple Bar, havin' just come in from Farley's, all of us except Bernie who went out for dinner with someone although the cow won't tell us who it is. She met us after it. Jasmin and Bopper were walkin' with us but they were goin' to some place up on George's Street and there was me, Tracy, her fella Lance, Sheila, Concepta and Paulo. He was comin' out with us coz he didn't want to go with Jasmin and Bopper, although can ya blame him? I mean, they'd wreck my head bein' left alone with them and he's more than welcome to hang out with us, Paulo. At least ya can look at him, not that I fancy him or anythin'.

So there we all were walkin' through Temple Bar lookin' like S Club 7 only there was nine of us and I was kinda walkin' a little bit behind the others with Concepta havin' a chat about Paulo's arse when Bernie turns to Tracy and shouts 'What's that meant to mean?' and Tracy looks back and goes 'Ya know what its supposed to mean.' So the two of them start shoutin' the heads off each other. Now what it's over, I don't know but Lance tries to stop it and Bernie starts shoutin' at him and then the same thing happens with Jasmin and soon everybody is roarin' the heads off each other in the middle of Temple Bar and Bopper is tryin' to separate Tracy and Bernie and they're tryin' to bash each other and Jasmin is helpin' Lance stop it and they're roarin' at her too and Sheila is roarin' too, just for the sake of roarin' as far as I can tell and Concepta is roarin' at Bopper and Jasmin and Jasmin's tellin' her to keep out of it and then Concepta turns on Lance and he hardly can understand a word of what they're shoutin', him bein' from Cork and all and Sheila is still roarin'. I think she's tellin' everyone to shut up but its comin' out 'slut up' and Concepta asks her who she's callin' a slut and then Jasmin and Lance have to jump to save Sheila from Concepta and Bernie swings her handbag, tell a lie, it was my handbag I lent her, 35 quid in River Island, the bitch. Anyway she tries to hit Tracy with it but misses and hits our Bopper with it across the back of the head by accident instead so Jasmin runs over and starts givin' Bernie loads of abuse Tracy's still roarin' and Lance tries to calm her down but Tracy turns on him, and he's still tryin' to keep Concepta and Sheila apart and while all this is happenin', meself and Paulo are just standin' there lookin' at it all along with half of Temple Bar and all the tourists think its some kind of street entertainment and they're takin' pictures and clappin' and all the rest of it. Some yank even threw a few coins at them although that only got Concepta angrier, a bit like the Incredible Hulk only smaller, only a bit smaller mind. It was crazy though. I still don't know what it was over.

✳✳✳

I'm not able for it, I'm tellin' ya. I'm not able for it. My phone has been ringin' all day. I swear to god, its like the RTE complaints line in my house. I mean, who do they think I am? Do they not think I have me own problems to deal with without theirs as well? All I've been listenin' to today is them bitchin' about each other and at this stage I've had enough. I'm seriously thinkin' of turnin' me phone off or just fuckin' it out the window. With the blessin's of Jesus, it'll hit one of the fuckers and knock them out. They think I'm Oprah or Adrian Kennedy.

  I wouldn't mind but after me gettin' dressed and goin' into town and all I didn't even get a night out. Jayzis, could ya imagine all of us after a few more drinks and that happenin'? God only knows how I didn't get involved. I think it just all happened too quickly and it was over before I realised. I mean, it all happened in a flash. Meself and Paulo were just standin' there lookin' at them. They all just ended up runnin' off eventually. Bopper and Jasmin still went out for their drink and all. Unbelievable the pair of them. Tracy and Lance ran off somewhere, oh back to his place she was sayin'. Bernie ran off and then Concepta ran after her and then I sent Paulo after the two of them just in case anythin' else happened. Sheila ran off at the same time so I had to chase her, the bitch. I could have killed her. All the way through Temple Bar, across O'Connell Bridge, up O'Connell Street, up Parnell Square and halfway down Dorset Street but at that stage I'd had enough. I wouldn't mind but she kept shoutin' at me in Chinese as if I had a clue what she was sayin' to me. I'm goin' to have to learn Chinese coz its ridiculous at this stage but in sayin' that if its as hard as the Spanish is for Jasmin then ya can fuck off. Shanghai me arse.

Ya wanna hear them all on the phone today though. Paulo was the first one to ring, which, I have to say, surprised me a bit. He was givin' out stink about Bernie and Concepta. He said they got as far as Parliament Street and the two of them turned on each other and started batterin' each other and poor Paulo was just left standin' there. They were separated by two waiters workin' in one of the restaurants along there. I mean, scarlet.

Bopper is wreckin' me buzz all day. I was sittin' in the sittin' room this mornin' watchin' Murder She Wrote and havin' a bowl of Special K when he walks in and starts goin' on about everyone. He's not impressed with Paulo at all for some reason. I think he's just jealous coz Paulo was meant to come out with us last night instead of him. Our Bopper is like that. He gets as jealous sometimes. Every time anyone rang today he kept askin' me who it was and when I'd tell him he'd start bitchin' about them. I felt like stranglin' him.

Me Uncle Dessie was on as well, although he had just rang to tell me how his night out went. He knew nothin' about the fight. His night went grand he said. He brought her to some posh restaurant on the Quays but then she had to run off to meet her mates in Temple Bar and she said she'd ring him. The bastard still won't tell me who she is. He couldn't believe it about the fight when I told him. He was shocked. He went all quiet. I thought he was dead or somethin' for a minute. I do be afraid to tell him things sometimes. I'd be afraid I'd shock him so much he'd have a heart attack. I thought it happened once before. I told him me period was late about a year ago and he just went all quiet and I was ready to ring the ambulance for him and all when he rang me back and told me he pulled the phone out of the wall reachin' for a packet of Jaffa Cakes. He says he'll sort a few of them out for me, the others, not the Jaffa Cakes, coz at this stage I am not listenin' to any more shite, Chinese or English!

✱✱✱

Guess who's gonna be the new manager of the Spar when Greg leaves? Me! Okay nothing's definite or anything but it's more than likely. Greg said and he'd know coz I mean, he's been the manager here for a while and they get told things that we don't. I nearly died when I came in this mornin'. I couldn't remember if Sheila was meant to be in or not so I was kinda hopin' she wasn't coz the last thing I need is for her to be tellin' Julie Walsh what happened. That bitch would think it was great, she'd have a right laugh, the dopey cow.

It was only Julie Walsh and Dymphna there when I went in and I was tempted to tell Dymphna what had happened but Julie Walsh was up off her stool so I knew she was tryin' to earwig so I said nothin'. Seriously, the only time that cow gets up off that stool is to listen to someone else's conversation.

I was standin' there anyway sortin' out the newspapers, well readin' them anyway, when Greg walks in and asks me to follow him into the office. So I'm thinkin' to meself, I'm in trouble here. Either that or he wanted his way with me, I don't know which I thought would be worse. I thought he might have caught me readin' the papers or whatever, although in sayin' that, I'm usually great at pretendin' to work. Needless to say, Julie Walsh hears what Greg says and has a smug grin on her face coz she thinks I'm about to get a bollockin'.

So I knock on the door of Greg's office and he tells me to sit down so I plonk meself down on the chair in front of his desk and I'm still thinkin' I'm in shit over somethin' when he tells me I'm a great worker and I was like 'What?' and he says he was asked to pick someone to replace him and he picked me. Now I have to say, I nearly hit the ceilin' I was that excited. Me a manager in a shop! Can ya imagine? Now, the only thing is, there's an interview this Friday but Greg says there shouldn't be any trouble and I'll probably sail through that. I felt like huggin' him though, I really did. I was speechless and ya know me, I could talk for Ireland. So I ran outside straight away and told Dymphna and Julie Walsh's mouth dropped and I was delighted as well. The first thing I'm goin' to do when I'm the manager is make that cow get up off that stool, that's unless the thing isn't superglued to her arse, although it probably isn't coz that would require effort.

✳✳✳

Of all the people ya don't wanna see in the middle of Penney's, who do I see only your man Phillip. Whether he saw me or not is a different matter altogether coz I did me best to hide but ya'd never know really. If he did see me he kept quiet about it. I thought he might have text me or something if he did but he didn't. Maybe he was tryin' to hide from me but I don't think so coz I was kinda followin' him and he didn't look like he was tryin' to hide from someone.

I was in town shoppin' with Concepta coz we both had the day off and I have to say, I do like shoppin' with Concepta, mainly coz she doesn't fit into anythin' I want to buy. I don't know how many times I've seen something and Bernie, Tracy or Jasmin end up gettin' it instead, the cows. Concepta's been very quiet since the argument the other night, not herself at all, although in sayin' that, none of them have and because none of them are talkin' to each other, I have to do stuff with everyone on their own. I don't have a problem with anyone except Bopper coz he's wreckin' me head talkin' shite but I have to live with him.

Anyway as I was sayin', meself and Concepta were in town and we decided to pop into Penney's on Henry Street coz ya always find a few nice bits in Penney's, especially the handbags. I bought a lovely clutch bag in a black PVC for only €4. So we were there lookin' around and Concepta nudges me, although when I say nudge, I nearly ended up in a rail of ponchos. Anyway she nudges me and says 'Isn't that your man Phillip over there?' So I'm tryin' to get a better look and true enough, it is Phillip. 'Who's that with him?' I ask Concepta although she's as blind as me. So the two of us try to get a little closer, kinda duckin' down behind the rails of cloths and behind pillars, like somethin' from James Bond. So we see that he's with some woman and they're lookin' at skirts so meself and Concepta run behind a rail of coats and poke our heads over the top to have a better look and we still can't see who she is. Now it's a wonder he didn't see us coz I mean, as yiz know, Concepta's a big girl and there's not much of her ya'd fit behind a rail of coats. So we make another run for it and end up about 20 feet in front of Phillip behind a table with shoes on it, lovely strap sandals for only €10. So we're kneelin' on the ground behind this thing and realise that the woman he's with is an auld-one, probably his ma or somethin'. So there we are on the ground and we look around and there's a security guard standin' over us and he asks us what were doin'. I have to say, I was fucked for an answer but Concepta says, and I have to be honest, it was brilliant, I wouldn't have thought of it. She says 'I'm lookin' for me contact lens.' I thought we were goin' to get fucked out but your man gets down on his hands and knees and starts helpin' to look for this contact lens that doesn't exist. So Concepta says 'I have it' and stands up and starts walkin' off and I run after her and look back to see if Phillip saw us but he's walkin' off in the opposite direction. If only I had a packet of Skittles.

✳✳✳

Ya should see the stuff I got for me interview in town yesterday. It's only mafis. They better gimme a job now coz I'm goin' to look like a ride on Friday. Seriously like, there better be a fella askin' the questions coz the stuff I'm wearin' is goin' to make me look gorgeous and intelligent as well, and that's sayin' somethin'.

Meself and Concepta spent ages lookin' for stuff after we left Penney's yesterday and I got some mafis gear. I must have tried on half the cloths in Henry Street. I even wanted Concepta to come over to Grafton Street with me but the lazy cow wanted to get a taxi so I said to just leave it. Even thinkin' about a five minute walk and that one breaks out in a sweat. I swear to god, the young-ones unreal.

So we're in Arnotts and they had some lovely stuff but a lot of it is very dear, ya know all the designer stuff, all the Mango and Tommy Hilfinger and that. I'd be the business. So eventually we went into Dunnes in the Ilac Centre and Concepta tells me that she thinks I should go for a business woman look so I says right. So first of all I see this skirt. Now ya wanna see it. Its kind of a beige down past the knee in a cord kind of material, mafis for only €30 and I normally wouldn't wear a skirt lower than me knee but Concepta said it'd make me look important. So I got that and then I saw a lovely top, on sale and all. A black, off the shoulder with a plungin' neck line so I'm showin' off loads of tit and I can wear a push up bra so your man will think it's Janet Jackson he's interviewin'. The top was only €12 so it was a bargain as well. €12 like, where would ya get it? Ya can't pass it. So all I needed was shoes and I'd seen this gorgeous pair in Barretts in Blanchardstown so I went into the one in Henry Street and there was an even nicer pair there. €50, six inch heel, up to me knee, gorgeous and they go mafis with skirt and top I got. I'm goin' to be the business for this interview and as Concepta says, if I don't get the job, at least I have new cloths.

✷✷✷

Bernie's actin' very strange. I tried to ring her there today and it was ringin' and ringin' and ringin' and she didn't answer and I know she wasn't workin' coz me ma saw her goin' into her house about 12-ish and normally if I ring her, she'd ring me back but I still haven't heard a thing from her and I mean, it can't have anythin' to do with the argument. Well at least I don't think it does coz I've been over to her house since, talkin' to her and tellin' her about the job interview and that and she's been grand although I have to say, she hasn't really been herself, but in sayin' that, none of them have, even Paulo and he had fuck all to do with it and he should be used to worse than that bein' from Bosnia, although tanks and missiles are nothin' compared to my mates fightin' in the middle of Temple Bar.

I'm just thinkin' though, I was in her gaff the night before last, the night I had been in town with Concepta, and she was very snappy with me. I knocked in on the way home to show her me bits that I got and she didn't really want to know and usually she's dyin' to try on me stuff even if she doesn't like it. Mad for the cloths is Bernie. I was talkin' to her about the fight and every time I mentioned someone's name she started goin' mad about them. She has an awful bruise on her cheek from where Concepta hit her a dig. She must have got some punch coz its still swollen since last week. She says she hates Tracy, can't stand Jasmin, Lance is a prick, Paulo's a fucker, Sheila's a cow and Boppers an annoyin' little bollix, which I have to agree with her about. Lets not lie, he is. She says she never wants to see any of them again. My only concern is that St Patrick's Day is next week and we all usually have a great bit of buzz for that. All of us like. Goin' mad and goin' to the parade, gettin' on all the the things at the carnival, gettin' locked. I mean its not the same if its not all of us but Bernie's determined she's not talkin' to the others. She wants nothin' to do with them and I've tried everythin' to get them to talk to each other. I'm like Ricki Lake at this stage but its not workin'. The whole thing has me head melted. I mean it had nothin' to do with me and now Bernie's in a mood with me for some reason. I wouldn't mind but she started the whole thing.

✳✳✳

Typical that me interview would be on Friday the 13. We only had a Friday the 13 last month and now there's another one as if me nerves weren't bad enough as it is. I'm shittin' meself. Not literally like coz it'd show through in this beige skirt and I wouldn't want to be ruinin' it only me first time wearin' it. I mean, ya can't exactly bring it back to the shop just coz ya've had a bad dose of the Pamela Scott's, even if ya have washed it twice, believe me, I've tried, and I had a receipt and all!

Me nerves really are in bits but. Tracy's just after ringin' to give me some advice. She says to try not to be nervous coz its one thing ya notice about someone straight away and the shakin' and the sweaty palms don't really help. She said to sit up straight coz it makes me look confident but I says to her what if I'm sittin' up too straight and your man can't see down me top? She thought I was messin'. I mean, I'm deadly serious. I'm not wearin' a Wonderbra for nothin'. The way I see it, if ya have it, flaunt it, especially when you're goin' for a job and ya need somethin' to wear to the interview.

I'm just hopin' that this Friday the thirteenth doesn't affect me. I mean, I'm not superficial or anythin' but I was walkin' down the stairs this mornin' and I was near the bottom and I tripped and fell about four steps and luckily enough me ma had the bed cloths she was about to wash at the bottom, otherwise I would have broken me neck although to tell ya the truth, I'd say me fallin' has more to do with six inch heels than Friday the thirteenth. Like, there's not a bother on me walkin' in them on flat ground but even the best of us would have a bit of trouble on stairs.

There was no milk either for me cornflakes and I wouldn't mind but I don't often eat a breakfast but I said I'd have one today and I poured the cornflakes into the bowl and all and it was only when I went to get the milk from the fridge that I realised there was none. I was goin' to get our Bopper to go and get some but that would have meant wakin' the fucker up first and I hadn't the time. If Jasmin had of been there, she would have told me to put Coke on me cornflakes. I've seen her do it before but then again, nothin' surprises me with Jasmin.

Anyway, fingers crossed for me interview. Me ma said a few prayers for me last night and Petulia from next door got Misses O'Driscoll to pray to Saint Francis of a see-saw so I'll be grand.

✳✳✳

I was only great, now I have to say. I'm not bein' big headed or anythin' but I was only deadly in the interview. I was flyin' through the answers to all the questions and all. Ya wanna see me. I mean, I know I can talk and all but I was only amazin' and ya know me, I'm modest.

I have to say, I got a bit of a fright when I walked in. This place was on Baggot Street and I hadn't a clue where I was goin' but I found it. I was sittin' there in this waitin' room and I was the only one there and I eventually got called and I walked into the office and I nearly died coz it was a woman sittin' behind the desk. That kinda threw me off a bit coz I was expectin' a fella. What was the point of wearin' a Wonderbra and the low cut top but I tried not to think about it coz I thought to meself, it means I can sit up straight and look confident like Tracy said. So there I was and your woman starts lookin' through me CV and she's there for a good five minutes without sayin' anythin'. Ya'd swear she was readin' Harry Potter. I was kinda gettin' a bit worried coz she wasn't talkin' to me or anythin'. So all of a sudden she turns and tells me that I come highly recommended or whatever and Greg thinks I should be the manager and that they're expectin' a lot from me. So I start wafflin' on about how I want to be the new manager and that Greg thinks I'm great and about Julie Walsh bein' a horrible cow, not in so many words but in a roundabout way, and about Dymphna bein' a bit smelly and Sheila not speakin' any English and all the rest of it and I'm tellin' her what I'd do to the shop to make it different and all the rest of it and she's only delighted listenin' to me and writin' down all her notes and noddin' at me and smilin' and thinkin' I'm only deadly, I could see by the look on her face. She was even kinda laughin' at some of the things I was sayin'. I mean, ya have to have a sense of humour even if you're bein' interviewed. It helps everyone relax or so Tracy says. Once I don't tell me joke about the vampire and the tampon.

 I was delighted with meself comin' out. It looks certain that I'm goin' to get the job now. Your woman almost said it to me on me way out. Not in as many words but she was hintin' at it.

 I rang everyone in me phone to tell them it went deadly and I tried to get all the others to come out for a drink but Bernie wouldn't come if any of the others were comin'. Tracy wouldn't come if Bernie and Jasmin were comin'. Jasmin didn't know what was goin' on. She wanted to do somethin' with Bopper but I didn't. He's not talkin' to Paulo but Paulo's not talkin' to Concepta and Sheila doesn't speak English. So I went for a drink with me Uncle Dessie. His Nigel, me cousin, is comin' over in the summer for a few months after he's finished college kinda thing. As long as me mad cousin Jacinta doesn't come, we'll be grand but she probably won't be able to untie herself from her tree long enough to get the flight anyway.

✳︎✳︎✳︎

I'm sick of the fuckers at this stage. They're wreckin' me head all of them. I mean, Saturday night last night and ya'd think we'd be able to go out for a drink and then to a club. No! They're still not talkin' to each other and at this stage, I'm fed up with all of them. Bernie's hardly talkin' to me for some reason. What I did on her, I don't know. I bet ya its coz I'm not payin' her more attention than the others but ya have to be fair. I'm not treatin' anyone any differently except our Bopper coz hes a wreck the head but all the others I'm the exact same with. I told every single one of them what I thought of the argument and Bernie knew well that I said she'd started it all. I said it to her face. I mean, lets call a spade a spade and Bernie needs a bang of a spade at this stage. I wouldn't mind but out of them all, she was the only one I rang to see what was up last night. All the others rang me; every single one of them, even Bopper, the sap and he lives with me. I wouldn't mind but I was in the next room at the time. The young-fellas a gobshite. He's gettin' a smack off me very soon. Him and Jasmin are sickenin' at the moment with their little private jokes and thinkin' everythin' is hilarious. I feel like bangin' their heads together sometimes. Bopper and Paulo are in the height of it with each other over somethin' and I still don't know if he meant to ask me out or anythin' or just as friends coz we all know he fancies but he said I better not bring Bopper which, I have to say, would be the last thing on me mind. Lance rang me to ask me did I want to go out with Tracy, him and the lads from college but I'll never forget that time him and Tracy left me sittin' there like a spare tit. Why Lance was ringin' me and not Tracy, I don't know. I didn't even have Lances number until he rang me. I didn't know it was him for a good five minutes after he rang coz he was speakin' to me in his mad Cork accent. I thought it was a wrong number from Slovakia or one of them mad countries.

Concepta and Jasmin seem to be talkin' anyway, thank god. They bumped into each other in town, Concepta tells me, and they had a bit of a chat to clear the air and the two of them seem to be grand now. Well at least it's a start.

I had all of them askin' me to go out tonight and I was afraid to say yes to any of them in case I piss someone else off. Its gettin' to that stage. Ya'd think they'd all be grown up enough. So in the end I rang Sheila and Dymphna from work and Dymphna rang Marie and the four of us went up to Heaven in Blanchardstown for a few drinks. I hope all the rest of them stayed in coz they might realise what fuckin' eejits they are. I had a great night without them.

✳✳✳

I'm scarlet. No really I am. Ya'll never guess what happened me. Now this is no word of a lie. I was down in Phibsboro today droppin' a thing in for me da's car insurance, some buildin' there beside McDonalds. I dropped in for a Big Mac and McFlurry and one of them Shamrock Shakes. I tell ya, I'm gettin' worse than Concepta. Anyway, that was grand. I walked to the bus stop there beside the shopping centre and I was standin' there waitin' and not a sign of a bus and it was a good 10 minutes at this stage so I says to meself, I'm sittin' down. So there was this wall kinda thing about a foot off the ground with just about enough room for me arse to fit on so I sit down and I'm still waitin' and waitin' and eventually the bus comes, actually tell a lie, two buses come together. I mean, typical isn't it. Me waitin' for ages and then two come. So I stand up and suddenly I realise me arse is all wet and I look down and ya'd never guess what I'd been sittin' on. No seriously, ya'd never guess. It was disgustin'. I felt like throwin' up outside Tescos. I look down and what do I see? This big, ugly, manky, scruffy, filthy dogshite. No word of a lie, it was disgustin'. There was no way I was gettin' on that bus though, or one of them busses anyway. Can ya imagine? Scarlet isn't the word. I was as red as a sunburnt nipple. I didn't really know what to do and I took off me jacket and it was all on the back of it and it ended up goin' in me hair and everythin' and the smell of it was disgraceful. Honestly now. It was atrocious and I was there hopin' to Jayzis that nobody could see or that nobody knew what was goin' on. So I ran towards this side door of the shopping centre and there's this kinda community area and I ran in there and some woman behind a desk stares me out of it and I run up to her and say 'Sorry love, where's the toilet?' and she looks at me real smart, a miserable lookin' cow, and she says 'I'm sorry, the toilets are for the use of the people who use the centre only.' So I'm not in the mood for this cow and at that stage, she was lucky I didn't jump over the counter and tear lumps out of her. So I give her this filthy look and I says 'Look love, I'm covered in shite and I don't think anyone will mind me usin' your toilet for two minutes to let me wash it off. Do you?' The miserable cow didn't know what to say and points me off in the direction of the toilet and I go in and I'm up on the sink sprayin' meself with water and all the rest of it and then when I'm finished, I stand on me tippy toes, bend over and point me arse up towards the hand dryer and next minute, some auld-one comes in. She must have been about 75 this one, the blue rinse and all in her hair and she nearly dies when she sees me and she says 'What are ya doin'?' Real angry like. So I look up at her and I says 'I had to wash the shite off me arse' so she's still disgusted and she says 'Can ya not just use toilet paper like everyone else?' Well I laughed for about an hour.

※

When Joanna Ryde means business, Joanna Ryde means business! With it bein' St Patrick's day and all today, I says to meself yesterday that somethin' had to be done about the gang. It was ridiculous nobody talkin' to each other and the biggest day of the drinkin' year comin' up and all so I says to meself, right, its time for action. I'd been thinkin' of an idea for a while, just somethin' that was in me head kinda. So I rang Bernie and I says, 'Bernie love, I need to talk to ya. Can ya meet me in Farley's at half seven?' She was askin' me was anythin' wrong and all the rest of it but still bein' a snotty cow let the truth be told and eventually she just says she'll be there. Next I rang Tracy and I was like, 'Tracy love I need to talk to ya. Can ya meet me in Farley's at half seven?' She was the same so I just told her to be there. I do the same thing to

Concepta, Jasmin and Paulo and about seven o'clock I go into Bopper's room. He was watchin' Bridget Jones on the DVD and I says to him, 'We're goin' to Farley's' and he's like, 'What for?' and I says, 'Just get ready.' Now I'd made sure I'd told everyone not to tell anyone else if they saw them or whatever so they all thought it would be just them and me instead of the whole lot of them. It wasn't a lie or anythin', it was just the only way I could get them all to the one place at the one time.

So it's quarter past seven and Bopper is takin' ages to get ready as usual and I wanted to be there before any of them show up just in case a riot starts. Eventually Boppers ready and I'm power-walkin' up the road and Bopper wants to know why I'm in such a rush and I look at me watch and its 25 to eight and I walk into Farley's and who's sittin' there only Jasmin and Concepta, which I have to say isn't too bad coz Concepta, Jasmin and Bopper are all talkin' to each other. Concepta's there with a pint in front of her and Jasmin has a glass of Guinness and Cranberry juice and I tell our Bopper to get the drinks in for the two of us as I sit in beside the girls. He's at the bar anyway and turns around and sees Paulo walkin' towards him and Concepta and Jasmin are lookin' the other way at Bernie comin' in the door and next minute, the whole place just erupts. The pub didn't know what the fuck had hit them and if that wasn't bad enough, who walks in behind Paulo, it couldn't have been more than a minute, only Tracy and there's war in the middle of Farley's. It was like somethin' out of the Jerry Springer show and there's people just starin' at us like we're some sort of freaks and its like that night in Temple Bar all over again and let the truth be told, it wasn't really what I imagined was gonna happen. Paulo and Bopper are goin' at it up at the bar. Apparently our Bopper isn't impressed about some chap called Jason and what happened with him and Paulo. I'm tellin' ya, I don't know what them young-fellas do be talkin' about half the time. Concepta and Bernie were nearly batterin' the heads off each other and probably would have if meself and Joe, the barman, weren't standin' in between them and Tracy and Jasmin, well that was a non-starter, what with Tracy and all her psychology and well, Jasmin. She was fucked before she even opened her mouth, the poor young-one.

Anyway I'd had enough at that stage. Seriously, it was beyond a joke so as loud as I could, I shouted, 'Shut the fuck up' and they all did believe it or not and turned around to look at me. So I says, 'Right, I've had enough of this shite. I want yiz all to shut the fuck up and listen.' The whole pub was listenin' at this stage, 'Now I've had it up to me tits listenin' to yiz all bitchin' about each other and all the rest of it and its gone beyond a joke at this stage. Now its St Patrick's day tomorrow and we always have a great laugh of a Paddy's day so none of us is leavin' this pub until this shit is sorted.' It was quarter past three in the mornin' when we left. I wouldn't mind, it closed at 12.

***

I have to say, I'm delira everyone's talkin' again. It's not the same as it was or anythin' but at least we all spent St Patrick's day together which was nice. The laugh we had. Everyone's grand except for Bernie really. She's still kinda a bit moody but she'll be grand in a few days. Well at least she better be coz I'm not puttin' up with her and I know the others won't. I don't know whats wrong with her. I've never seen her like this before and as ya know, I know Bernie forever.

We all headed into town for the parade yesterday, the lot of us; Meself, Bernie, Tracy, Concepta, Jasmin, Bopper, Paulo, Lance and me Uncle Dessie. It was early enough when we got in coz we wanted a good spot for the parade. I was ragin' the fuckers weren't talkin' on Saturday night coz I believe the Skyfest was the best in years. I do love the fireworks and we usually have a great bit of the buzz in town of a night for the Skyfest.

Anyway, ya wanna see the spot we got for the parade, right across from Trinity College and near enough to the TV cameras although your man Joe Duffy wouldn't come near us and Tracy's a big fan of his. She was dyin' to get his autograph. Not once were we on telly, not once. So I have to say, the parade was as borin' as fuck. I hate them American marchin' bands from mad places like Nebraska and Idaho. What the fuck is the story with them? With their big drums and their walkin' like they're in the army. Get the boat will yiz. There wasn't half as many floats as last year either and after about an hour I turned to the others and I said 'Come on, this is a load of me arse. Lets go the carnival.' Well it was a nightmare tryin' to get to the Customs House. I don't know how many times we lost Jasmin. We had to get Bopper to hold her hand it got that bad and then we all tried to get across the road at O'Connell Bridge, right in front of the parade and all of us get across grand except Concepta who's still on the other side waitin' for a big vikin' float to pass and she's runnin' across the road and this big vikin' on stilts bends down in front of her and says hello and Concepta tells him to fuck off and pushes him on the ground and he knocks over another fella on stilts and second fella knocks down a third fella and they were like dominos. Six vikin's on stilts lyin' there on O'Connell Bridge and there's one of them American marchin' bands comin' behind and they all have to stop real quickly and they're crashin' into each other and there's young-fellas gettin' trombones stuck into their backs and there's people from the first aid runnin' around to make sure everyone's alright and its mayhem and Concepta just casually walks across the road and walks through the crowd to us havin' just caused madness behind her.

 The carnival was gas. We got me Uncle Dessie to go on everythin' and I'm not jokin' ya, he was green. Our Bopper got on this thing with Dessie that goes upside down and ya wanna hear the screams of them. Joe Duffy could probably hear them all the way back at Trinity College. I got on this other thing with Jasmin. It spins ya round really fast and she was holdin' onto me hands that tight that she left nail marks in the back of me hand. I nearly killed her over it later. That's after we lost her another three or four times. We left Concepta mindin' the bags while we all went on this thing and came back and she was chattin' to these three American young-ones, two South African fellas and a young one from Finland who's name was Saddle. Her real name like. I wouldn't mind, but we can't have left Concepta for more than three minutes. How she does it, I'll never know. Arrangin' to meet up with them after and all she was.

After the carnival, we all headed back to Farley's for a drink. We were goin' to stay in town but there was too many tourists around although Farley's wasn't short of a few either let the truth be told. We had a great bit of craic in there anyway and then we all headed home for an hour and met up again to go back into town. Everywhere was jammed as ya'd expect so we eventually got into Fitzsimons and had a great night. I even ended up kissin' a fella from Romania, a lovely lookin' chap he was, livin' in Templeogue although after that everythin' started to become a blur.

✷✷✷

Bernie rang me today full of the joys of spring which I have to say, I found a bit strange after the way she's been lately but I was delighted she's back to her old self. She was in a mood with me since just after the argument and I hadn't a clue what I had done on her. The way I see it is, Bernie's me best mate and it was strange seein' her like that. I mean, usually the two of us can't be kept apart but in the last week or so she's been a bit off with me. I was thrilled when she rang today though and although I couldn't really talk for long coz I was in work and Julie Walsh was in the height of it coz she had a hangover, as if that was my fault, the slimy cow. Sheila was on the deli and that's just a disaster. I don't think the poor young-one knows the difference between tuna and coleslaw. I had about six rolls back because of her. Dymphna called in sick coz she has a fungal infection on her right eyebrow, although let the truth be told, I'm surprised its taken this long. She probably used soap or somethin' for the first time and Marie was off somewhere tryin' to talk to a packet of Findus Crispy Pancakes. Greg was in his office for the day so I barely saw him. So it was left to me to make sure the shop wasn't fallin' apart. It was only a quick chat to Bernie but I told her I'd knock around to her after work.

She was still in great form when I knocked around to her house. I'd been home and had me dinner and got changed and that so we decided to go into town to watch a film and we're on the bus and she says, 'Joanna, I've somethin' to tell ya.' So I'm thinkin' the worst and she says, 'It was me who went out with your Uncle Dessie that night.' I nearly hit the roof of the bus. I went spare. She says, 'Hold on, it wasn't like me and him were doin' anythin' weird. I just did him a favour and he brought me for a meal to say thank you.' Now I have to say, I was very conspicious, especially coz she hadn't told me since then. Normally Bernie would tell me everythin' but she still wouldn't tell me what favour she had done for him no matter what I asked and when I rang him later he wouldn't tell me either. Now I'm convinced there's somethin' strange goin' on. There has to be. For starters, its not like me Uncle Dessie to bring anyone out to dinner to say thanks for doin' him a favour, although credit where its due, he's very good to me friends. I wouldn't let it be said. I'm dyin' to find out what this favour was. I'm tellin' ya one thing though, it better not have been a sexual favour. That's just wrong.

✱✱

I can't believe it. Seriously, I'm in shock. I got a phone call today off your woman that interviewed me. What her name was, I can't remember but it doesn't matter now. She rang me and she was sayin' she was very pleased with the interview and I was a great candidate for the job and I had a lot of potential but that they had found someone better for the job. Well I have to tell ya, I felt sick. I was gonna hang up on the bitch and all. I really hadn't a clue what to say so I says 'Who could be better than me?' I have to admit, it was a bit big-headed but I had to ask. So your woman tells me I'll find out soon enough. She was kinda snotty at this stage and I was only short of headin' down to Baggot Street and reefin' the head off this woman. The cheek of her, whatever her name was.

    I have to say, I was convinced I had the job, convinced. I mean, when Greg's not there I practically run the shop. The place wouldn't be standin' if it wasn't for me. Could ya imagine leavin' it to the others? Fair enough, Dymphna would be grand but Julie Walsh. She wouldn't have a clue. She'd have half the food eaten. Sheila hardly speaks a word of English and the less said about Marie the better. I have all the experience and Greg was convinced I had it as well. It was his idea to begin with. He was even more shocked than I was when I told him. By the way your woman was talkin' in the interview, I thought I had it, really I did. I had myself all built up for it so I'm not gonna lie, I am disappointed, angry even and I'm seriously thinkin' of leavin' now and goin' somewhere else. At least then I might be appreciated.

***

Why do I keep bumpin' into freaks? Seriously now, it's become a joke. We went out last night. There was myself, Bernie, Concepta and Paulo. Jasmin was off with Bopper goin' to some thing up in the Pod and Tracy was at some college thing with Lance and said they might follow us into town if they weren't too locked.

We started off with a few drinks in Farley's although how we're still allowed in there is a mystery after the other night. I could see the look of fear on the bar staff's faces when Concepta Cooney walked in the door although she has that affect on a lot of people.

We decided to go to Boomerangs, tell a lie, Bernie decided we were goin' to Boomerangs although none of us were about to argue with her coz Tracy did that last time and look where we ended up and anyway, as I said before, Bernie usually picks a good place to go and we'd be lost without her.

It was packed enough inside although nowhere near as bad as Fitzsimons on Paddy's night. We got a table easy enough and all. Well we got Concepta to make friends with these two young-fellas sittin' on their own and we sat in with them. It worked well enough for Concepta coz she ended up kissin' one of them towards the end of the night. That's after she had brought Paulo over to meet these young-fellas from Croatia, which I believe is very near to Bosnia where Paulo comes from. We didn't see him for the rest of the night. Tell a lie, he came back towards the end of the night to tell us he was goin' home with one of the fellas to have a few drinks. I saw Bernie gettin' stuck into one of them and I wouldn't mind but she never even heard of Croatia until then. He was a bit of a ride as well, I have to say. I got talkin' to this bloke called Dan. He was from Wicklow I believe and he was stayin' in some flat in Rathmines with his friend that was with him, John. Now this Dan fella was a bit of a ride; Tall, dark hair, kinda tanned and I was delighted with meself so when he asked me back to his place with him I was delighted. So we left and me and him and this John fella get a taxi up to Rathmines and we're in his sittin' room, meself and Dan, and we're snoggin' and gettin' it on on the sofa, a great kisser he was, and one thing is leadin' to another and I turn around and your man John is standin' at the door naked. Now when I say naked, I mean stark bollock naked. Not a scrap of cloths on him. So I get a bit of a fright and he's walkin' towards us and I look up at your man Dan and he has this big grin on his face and he says 'two for the price of one Joanna, you got a bargain.' as if it was an offer on chicken kievs in Dunnes. Well I jumped up as quick. I'm not into them threesomes or anythin'. Lookin' back now, it would have been a nice experience or whatever but at the time I got the fright of me life. Ya wanna see me run. I'd say I was in the taxi and all before your man John had his knickers back on. Jayzis.

※

I love wakin' up on a Sunday mornin' without a hangover. It's great. Ya kinda think to yourself, this is deadly and ya pull the duvet up and roll over coz ya have fuck all to do. Well that's unless you're workin' and I wasn't today, thank fuck.

No, a very relaxin' day. I got up, had a shower, made a fry. A lovely fry it was. Sausages, rashers, a bit of white puddin' and a few slices of toast. I never have egg. I think its disgustin'. Then I watched the replay of the formula one with me da. Malaysia it was in at six o'clock this mornin' although why they have it on at that time is beyond me. Malaysia like. I can't even spell Malaysia let alone know where it is. I'd say Concepta knows a few Malaysians. I must ask her. I'll ask Tracy where the fuck it is at the same time.

We did fuck all last night. None of us as far as I know although Tracy did her fuck all over in Lances and Jasmin and Bernie did their fuck all in our gaff coz me ma and da were out. I didn't think our Bopper was gonna be in coz lets face it, he's like meself of a Saturday night, very seldom in. So I says to Bernie to come over to watch a bit of telly and get a curry and Boppers in his room, Cher blarin' out of the stereo. The noise of her and I hate the bitch anyways and meself and Bernie are about to order a curry and the knock comes to the door and who is it only Jasmin. So Bopper turns off the shite and comes down and the four of us end up gettin' loads from the Chinese, havin' a few drinks although we didn't go as far as lettin' Jasmin make the cocktails, not when theres bleach and olive oil in the house. We tried to watch Findin' Nemo again but we were too busy talkin', ya know yourself. I'm thinkin' though, I mustn't have had much to drink at all coz I was grand this mornin'. We should stay in more often.

***

Mad night last night, mad. It was Greg's leavin' do in work and we all went to TGI Fridays up on Stephens Green for a meal and then to Club M. When I say we all, I mean me, Greg, Dymphna, Marie, Sheila, Julie Walsh and Jason, one of the young-fellas that works the weekends. He's a pain in the arse if ever I met one. I wouldn't mind but he's only gone 16 and he uses his older brothers passport so he can get in. Thank god I don't work with him too much coz the young-fella wrecks me head. He thinks he knows everythin'. I know I'm only 18 and all but he's a kid. Him and Julie Walsh are the best of mates. The two of them are all over each other when they're together, wouldn't ya know. A pair of irritatin' fannies. Like thrush only twice. I wouldn't mind but Jason was up for school and all this mornin'. He's in 5th year and all although he doesn't think he has to go to school coz he thinks he's the smartest person since some other smart fucker, ya know the type of young-fella. He talks some shite at times, tellin' ya all these interestin' facts like if we're in work and he picks up a can of Pepsi Max and says, 'Did ya know that Pepsi Max is the same as Diet Pepsi but with a different name to appeal more to male drinkers.' As if I give two fucks. The young-fella is unreal. We were standin' there in Club M and he gets a Baileys. A Baileys in a nightclub, would ya be able, and he says, 'Did ya know that a third of all Irish milk is used to make Baileys.' I was only short of fuckin' the thing over him.

The meal in TGI's was lovely. Mafis it was. I had barbeque ribs and chips and I very nearly didn't finish them. We all had a few cocktails as well. I had a long island ice tea first, then a tequila sunrise, a margarita, a blue lagoon and an orgasm. The first orgasm I've had this long time let the truth be told.

We were all well locked by the time we got to Club M. I had visions of the last time we were out with Julie Walsh, the night she got kicked out of Club M but she was too busy with Jason this time to be too drunk and we made sure she went nowhere near the podium. Greg on the other hand was palatic. Locked is not the word. We wanted to get him as pissed as we could. His last day kinda thing. Somethin' to remember us by, d'ya know what I mean? Although in sayin' that, I'll be surprised if he remembers anythin' he was that locked. I ended up snoggin' him and all at one stage although it was only for a couple of seconds. I always had a feelin' that he kinda fancied me though. He was always kinda lookin' at me and as ya know, I was always his favourite. I'll miss him loads though. It just won't be the same without him and he gave me his address in South Africa and his e-mail address although I wouldn't have a clue how to send an e-mail. He said I could come and stay with him whenever I want. Jayzis, South Africa wouldn't know what hit them.

✳✳✳

The new boss started today and I can't stand the bitch already. Leandra her name is and she's a spa, the biggest dope I've ever met in me life and I'm includin' Julie Walsh in that. We were all dyin' to find out who it was goin' to be coz we'd all been told fuck all about it. All we knew was that it wasn't gonna be me although I'm not gonna be bitter, the pack of stupid fuckers in their offices in Baggot Street thinkin' they're all that and a Kinder Bueno, fuckin' spas, who do they think they are, don't know a good thing when they see it, gobshites, not givin' me a job, arseholes, don't know what they're doin', I wish I could get me hands on them and break every bone in their bodies and don't get me started on that fuckin' ugly, smelly, skanky, disgustin', snobby, bitchy, dirty, rotten sap that interviewed me, whatever the fuckers name was, she better hope I never bump into her again. But I'm not gonna be bitter.

Anyway where was I before I got sidetracked. I told ya I have an awful habit of doin' that. I could be talkin' about one thing and next minute I go off talkin' about somethin' else and forget what the thing was that I was talkin' about in the first place and somebody has to remind me but at that stage its not as important anymore or I'll have forgotten what the point was.

Now where was I? Fuck I can't remember. Oh yeah, the new manager. What was I sayin'? Yeah we were there waitin' to see who it was goin' to be and your woman swans in through the door like she's arrivin' at a film premiere and she's wearin' a suit and she's carryin' a briefcase and she stops at the door and looks around and then looks at us and I have to say, she was grand at first but as the day went on, she became more and more of a pain in the hole, tellin' us what to do and dishin' out the orders and tellin' us she was in charge and things were gonna be done very differently and all the rest of it, although Julie Walsh had her hole stuck to the stool at the tills for the day so there's nothin' different there. She was lickin' up to Leandra all day. Leandra this and Leandra that and Leandra you're only great. Pain in the hole. I bet ya she never told Leandra that she beat up a customer in January or that she's still thinkin' of suin' over it. I tell ya, if your one Leandra keeps up the shit she was goin' on with today, she'll be in for an education soon enough. She hasn't even met Marie yet.

✶✶✶

Tracy told me the funniest thing today. I have to say I laughed for a good five minutes and then I had to ring Bernie, Concepta and me Uncle Dessie and tell them so I was laughin' again and then I had to tell Dymphna, Marie and Sheila and I even told Julie Walsh although Leandra came out of her office and gave out to us for laughin', the sap.

Now Tracy told me it was Lance's birthday yesterday and as a surprise, his ma came up to Dublin from Cork and they were off shoppin' and the rest of it in town first and then they're headin' back to his apartment and his ma tells him to put on a blindfold, well a scarf around his face, so Tracy tells me, and she leads him into his apartment and sits him down on the couch and he can't see a thing and he doesn't know what's goin' on so just as his ma's about to take the scarf off his face, her phone rings so she tells him not to take off the scarf and not to peek and runs into the bedroom and shuts the door behind her to take the call. So Lance is sittin' there with this scarf coverin' his face, not knowin' what's goin' on and thinkin' his ma can't hear him, he lets off this huge fart and then starts fannin' the air with his hand then does it again about 20 seconds later although this time its louder. Then he puts his hand down the front of his trousers and scratches himself for about a minute, farts again, then picks his nose and wipes it in the back of the sofa. His ma comes back and he still can't see anythin' and she asks if he was peekin' and he says no and she comes over and takes the blindfold off and what does he see only Tracy and half his family sittin' in the room disgusted. Tracy says the look on his face was priceless.

✳✳✳

Bernie got a new job and as much as I'm delighted for her, I am now, I really am, I can't help be devastated coz she has to move to London and its not as if it's a while away or anythin'. It's Sunday week and I've only got nine days left with her before she goes and I really don't think that's enough. I'm happy for her and all but at the same time, I don't want her to go coz she's me best mate and I can't really deal with the thought of losin' her. I mean, I know its only London but to me, that's like her goin' to the moon. Without havin' Bernie here I'm fucked. Who's gonna do the dance out of *Muriel's Weddin'* with me? Who's gonna pretend to be Dory when I'm pretendin' to be Marlin from *Findin' Nemo*? Who's cloths am I gonna rob, sorry, borrow? And she has the best GHD hair straightener and all. I'll be lost without her but at the same time, she's me best friend and she wants to do this and I'd never dream of stoppin' her. All I can do is wish her the best and hope she doesn't forget me.

Ryanair it is she got the job with. An air hostess. I'd say Bernie would be deadly doin' that. It's what she wanted to do since we were in school. I remember even when Tracy first came to the school, I'd want to be a singer, Tracy wanted to be a teacher and Bernie wanted to be an air hostess. I remember one time she went to Majorca with her ma and came back with loads of sick bags and magazines and shite that she robbed from the plane so we could play air hostess with her, like saps. I remember me and Tracy and two or three other little fuckers sittin' on chairs out Bernie's back garden while Bernie and our Bopper pretended to be the cabin crew, doin' safety demonstrations and handin' out magazines and all. Scarlet for us!

I'm delighted she got it though, even if it does mean she's movin' to London. I can't believe she never told us she was goin' for an interview or anythin'. Its not like her. She said with the argument and all goin' on she didn't bother. The only one she told was me Uncle Dessie and he didn't open his mouth.

The trainin' course she has to do is costin' her about a grand and a half and I asked her where she was goin' to get that much money but I nearly died when she told me how much she had saved in the Credit Union. Nearly six grand, most of it her nanny left to her when she died last year. Her nanny would have wanted her to spend it on somethin' she wanted to do. Bernie's nanny was mad. A looper. Me and Bernie used to always stay in her house and she'd make us watch horror films to scare the shite out of us for the laugh.

I couldn't believe Bernie had that much money though although she wouldn't be one to go mad with her wages although she does always have lovely gear. At least she won't have to worry about money and she even paid off the holiday to the Canaries already. Ah no, I'm delighted for her. I just wish she didn't have to move.

***

Leandra is still wreckin' me head. I feel like kickin' her head in at this stage. I hate the woman with a passion and I only know her a few days. There we were today and I was readin' this great article in one of the papers about botox and she comes out of her office and she says 'Joanna, have ya nothin' to do?' and I says 'Yeah, I'm readin' this article about botox,' and she gives me this filthy look and she says 'I don't pay you to stand around and read newspapers,' and I'm thinkin' to meself, who does this gobshite think she is. So I say 'You don't pay me at all love, the company does and I always read the papers in the mornin'' and she says to me 'Greg's not here anymore Joanna. I'm in charge and you'll do what I say and if you're not happy with that ya know where the door is.' The cheek of her talkin' to me like that. I mean, she's lucky I didn't put her head through the door. I was tempted, believe me, I was very tempted.

Julie Walsh is still lickin' her arse. Ya wanna see her. The two of them have these private jokes and all already and they're the best of friends and ya wanna see the two of them laughin' today like the whole world is only hilarious. I don't know how longer I can take it. I really don't.

It's gas coz that Leandra bitch hasn't a clue what Sheila does be sayin' to her. She has to keep askin' Julie Walsh to tell her what Sheila's tryin' to say to her and Sheila is gettin' pissed off with her. She told her to fuck off today and me, Julie Walsh and Dymphna thought it was hilarious but Leandra just smiled and nodded and then walked off, obviously she hadn't a clue what Sheila had said. I'm lovin' Sheila though. She's gettin' more Irish by the day and its gas. She told me today she had a pain in her hoop with Leandra. I swear to god, she didn't get that from me.

***

We went out last night for a few drinks for Lance's birthday and I have to say, it was the biggest load of shite. There was me, Bernie, Concepta, Paulo, Dessie, Tracy, Lance and some of his mates includin' that fella from France who tried to touch me up in Q-bar one night and where does Lance decide to go only The Pod. As I said before, The Pod does be a bit of a laugh even though I'm not into all that pumpy pumpy dance music shite. It's just not my scene. I'm more into RnB and the chart stuff.

First of all, we're standin' in the queue on the way in and some fella comes up to me and says 'Here young-ones. Have yiz any yokes?' Total skanger this fella was, although that's probably the pot callin' the kettle black, and I turn to look at him and I says 'Do I look like the type of young-one that does ecstasy?' and he looks at me, starin' me out of it he was, thinks about it for a couple of seconds and says 'Yeah, ya do love.' Well I had to be held back. Me Uncle Dessie and Bernie grabbed an arm each and Concepta threw herself in front of me so I couldn't get to the little bastard. I would have left him for dead there on Harcourt Street. Thank god the bouncers didn't see anythin' and we had no trouble gettin' in.

The place got packed very quickly and I started losin' everyone. I spent half the night runnin' around lookin' for everyone. Me Uncle Dessie was locked on the dance floor and I'm convinced someone gave him somethin' but he never said anythin'. He had his top off at one stage and was there gyratin' on a podium. I had to send Bernie up to get him down and he dragged her up with him and she was only scarlet.

Tracy and Lance disappeared into a corner for the night and nobody saw them til we were leavin' and Concepta met these three fellas from Bulgaria and was tryin' to show them how to dance. To me, it looked more like an epileptic fit though she's not the best at the auld dancin' is Concepta.

Paulo was down about somethin' and I tried chattin' to him to cheer him up but he didn't seem to want to know. He just sat lookin' over the balcony for the night and I'm gettin' a little bit worried about him. Maybe theres somethin' goin' on between him and Bopper and Jasmin. They were off somewhere else although d'ya think they'd tell us where? Fuck no. I just wasn't in the mood though. I don't know why. Maybe it was because I was worried about Paulo or maybe I'm just sad coz I know Bernie's goin' soon. Whatever it is, I had a shite night.

✳✳✳

I actually got me hole last night. Can ya believe it? It's been ages so I enjoyed every minute of it, twice.

    I have to admit, I wasn't even in the mood for goin' out last night but Sheila had been askin' me all day in work so I didn't want to say no to her coz I do feel terrible coz she doesn't really have any Irish friends so if she wants me to do somethin' I will coz she's a lovely young-one and I do have a laugh with her.

    I gave all the others a ring to come out too but only Concepta and Bernie came. Tracy was over in Lance's, Jasmin was comin' over to my gaff to watch a DVD with our Bopper and Paulo wasn't in the mood and as much as I tried to persuade him to come out, a good 20 minutes it was, he said he just wanted to stay in. I tell ya, I'm very worried about him. He's just not himself lately and I don't like the idea of him bein' upset. Its not like him at all. Usually he'd even have a chat with me and let me know what was goin' on but he's been very quiet. I might get Tracy on the case to see if she can do her psychoanalysis shit on him to see what's goin' on. I'm very worried about him as I said, very worried.

    We went to Coyote for the night. Just meself, Sheila, Concepta and Bernie as I said and it was black. Ya couldn't move in it to scratch your arse. But we had a laugh. We kept stoppin' these mingin' fellas and tellin' them Sheila was into them and she was goin' mad. One of them even tried to kiss her and she laughed into his face, the mad bitch. I tell ya she's gettin' more like us everyday.

Concepta Cooney did one of her disappearin' acts again and I found her talkin' to a fella from Malta which I have to say, fair play to her, is probably the smallest country she's ever met someone from. I'm convinced that young-one has some kind of 5th sense that she uses to find foreigners and then writes them all down in a little book or in an atlas she keeps under her bed. It wouldn't surprise me with that young-one. Nothin' would.

The fella that I was with was a ride. Dave his name is and he's from Crumlin originally but he's livin' in an apartment up at Christchurch, a lovely place it is and all. It wasn't even me that got talkin' to him. It was Bernie, outside when we were havin' a smoke and she asked him for a light and got talkin' to him and then she went inside and I was left talkin' and we were talkin' for ages. I must have gone through three or four smokes outside talkin' to him, we were there that long. So we went back inside and we were there dancin' and doin' all the moves and all the rest of it and we started kissin' on the dance floor and then we went back to where I had been sittin' and we kissed more and talked more and it was great and then at the end of the night we were all leavin' and he asked me if I wanted to walk him home so I told the girls I was goin' and we walked up to his place. When he asked me I was a bit weary to be honest. I was waitin' for him to have a hairy back or to take out a whip or to bring his friend in but he didn't. He was lovely and its about time I got me hole, twice.

✼✼✼

Bernie eventually told me all about why me Uncle Dessie brought her out to dinner. I think she just gave in coz I've been goin' on about it ever since she told me about it. She hasn't said anythin' til now and after she told me, I nearly killed her coz its not as if its as huge a deal as they were makin' it out to be. I was just happy that the two of them didn't have some sort of relationship goin' on. I mean, me Uncle Dessie is old and his kids are older than Bernie. Its just wrong. I'm disgusted just thinkin' about it.

Bernie knocked around here last night dyin' for all the details on me and Dave and I was dyin' to tell her let the truth be told so we decided to go on a walk, only to the chipper mind, but we got out of the house for a bit of air and a battered sausage, chips and garlic sauce. So we were walkin' along and I says to Bernie, 'So are ya ever goin' to tell me why me Uncle Dessie brought ya out to dinner?' Now he hadn't said a word and I was the one the fucker he had come runnin' to for a bit of advice. I know I sent him off to Tracy instead but still, he came to me first. Eventually she told me. Not everythin' coz she says its up to Dessie to tell me some of it but she told me a bit.

What happened was Bernie was gettin' me Uncle Dessie to help her get the job with Ryanair and he found out how much money the cow had stored up in the Credit Union that nobody knew about and he asked her for a loan of €4000 for somethin' that she wouldn't tell me. It wasn't her place to tell, she said. I've to ask me Uncle Dessie. What he wanted four grand for, I don't know. I mean, what do ya do with four grand? He's payin' her back over a few months so it means she can't spend it when she goes to England and she'll always have a few quid comin' in every month and she's delighted. So that's why he took her out to dinner anyways. To say thanks for a loan of four grand. I have to say, I thought it was lovely when I heard it. Although I think I was more delighted that they weren't shaggin' each other!

✷✷✷

I'm in work yesterday and the phone rings, me mobile, not the shop phone, and I got a bit of a fright coz I thought it was on silent. Leandra has this new rule that we're not allowed use our phones in work which I think is a stupid rule. What if someone's lookin' for us? How are they meant to get in touch with us? Obviously we've just been keepin' them in our pockets but just puttin' them on silent so she doesn't know. She had a go at me the other day for readin' a text message that Bernie sent me. I swear to god, I'll kill her if she keeps up this shite with all the new rules. Its like bein' in school and I left a long time ago.

So I'd seen Leandra leavin' a few minutes earlier so I says to meself, fuck it, I'll answer it and see who it is. The number didn't come up on the caller ID so I wasn't too sure. It's a fella and he says 'Heya Joanna,' and I'm like 'Who's this?' and he says 'Dave,' and I have to think for a minute and when I realised I nearly died. I hadn't heard from him since, well ya know. So he asks me do I want to go the pictures with him so I was only delighted with meself. A date as Tracy would say if she was around.

So I met him in town at the Central Bank and he was there and all when I arrived and I was a good ten minutes early and we walked over to the Cineworld on Parnell Street to watch a film, the new one with Tom Hanks in it. Dave bought me popcorn and a bag of Skittles which I thought was only hilarious but I never told him why.

I have to say though, the whole thing was lovely and he's a lovely fella, treats me really well and he has such a beautiful smile. I feel like just kissin' him then and there every time he smiles at me. He walked me to me bus stop and all after and he lives the other way and we were standin' there waitin' for the bus and he was holdin' me hand while we were talkin' and it just felt really nice. I have to say, I really like him. I just hope he doesn't turn out to be another Paddy or Phillip, the bastards.

April

I woke up this mornin' and walked into the bathroom, still half asleep at this stage. I mean, I was awake about 20 seconds and I was absolutely dyin' for a piss so I sit down on the toilet bowl and start to go me toilet and it splashes all back up on me and I'm soakin' and I look down and some fucker has put clingfilm over the toilet bowl as a joke and I hear Bopper Ryde and me da outside the bathroom breakin' their shites laughin' and I have to say, I didn't find it one bit funny. So I dry meself off and go outside and they're both gone and I go into me room and nearly died. I was kinda confused at first coz all me furniture was moved. The bed was facin' a different way and all and I'm tryin' to think if I was dreamin' or somethin' coz it was just weird. So I open the wardrobe to get me dressin' gown, a lovely one I got in Dunnes last week for only a tenner. Where would ya get it? Ya can't go wrong. When I open the door though, this life size plastic skeleton falls on me and I get the fright of me life. They must have heard me in Cork I was that loud. Screamed the house down I did. At this stage, I'd had enough and I'm about to walk downstairs when I spot a letter with me name on it and I open it and read it as I'm goin' down the stairs and it says 'Dear Miss Ryde. You are the lucky winner of a round the world trip. Thank you for enterin' the competition.' And all the rest of it and theres details and whatever and I scream the place down again and walk into the kitchen and me ma, me da and Bopper are sittin' there which they never do but at the time I didn't think anythin' of it and I show them the letter and next thing, Bopper breaks his shite laughin' and then me ma and da do too and I'm wonderin' what's goin' on and Bopper says 'April fool.' I have to say, I nearly killed the three of them. All I could think of was that skeleton all day. I could have had a heart attack, the bastards! And I wouldn't mind, I'd have been well of a round the world trip.

***

Meself and Concepta went into town today to get Bernie's goin' away present. We both had the day off and I have to say, I was in bits gettin' her stuff. I just don't want to believe she's goin' and I can't believe it's so soon. I mean, she's goin' on Sunday and today is Thursday. Its just weird.

Concepta, fair play to her, went around to everyone and got 20 quid off them. She probably threatened to beat it out of a few of them but she got it off them none the less. Jasmin, Tracy, Bopper, Paulo, Dessie and even Sheila gave a few quid so we had a good bit of money and we got her perfume, the Glow by Jennifer Lopez coz she loves that. The smell of it always reminds me of Bernie. We got her a lovely pyjama set in Dunnes as well, only €15, I mean, ya can't go wrong. Concepta wanted to go to Ann Summers to get her a vibrator but I said no way. I mean, imagine if she got stopped in customs on the way over.

We got her a few CDs as well. Stuff she wanted like and at the same time I got Paulo Kylie's Greatest Hits for his birthday coz he was tellin' me somebody robbed his, although I have a funny feelin' Concepta Cooney had somethin' to do with that. The young-one's a bitch for takin' peoples CDs.

My favourite present that we got for her though is this picture of us all the night of my birthday. We're all in it and I have to say, it's a deadly photo and we got it blown up and put it in a frame and I have to say, I was so upset when I saw it that I nearly started cryin'. Things aren't gonna be like that now with Bernie gone although they haven't been like that much lately with Jasmin and Bopper off doin' their own thing all the time and Tracy bein' with Lance. Things are just different now and they'll be even more different when Bernie goes. At least she'll have somethin' nice to remember us all by and she can just look at it when she thinks of us and she'll remember all the good times and even the bad times we've had. The gang just won't be the same with one of us missin'. It won't be the same without Bernie.

✳✳✳

I knocked around to Bernie's last night for a bit of a chat and to help her do a bit of packin' coz as I said, she's leavin' this Sunday and she has to have all her bits ready. Ya know Bernie though, she had it all done by the time I got there so we just made sure she has everythin' she needs. She's tryin' to bring over as little as she can coz she doesn't want all the hassle of bringin' loads of stuff with her the first time and she has a trainin' course to do for the first six weeks anyways. I was dyin' to tell her about the stuff we got for her but I promised the others I wouldn't give it to her until they're all there coz it's kinda a group thing.

I have to say, I got very emotional helpin' her pack but I was tryin' not to let her see that coz she'd just be in bits then. I want her to enjoy it as much as she can and she wouldn't be able to if she saw me cryin'. I mean, it wouldn't be fair on her. This is her big move and I want it to all go right for her and me cryin' would just put a dampener on it and we couldn't have that.

She handed me the *Muriel's Weddin'* DVD and I swear to god, it was very hard tryin' not to break into tears. I told her that she should have it but she insisted that I take it coz she probably won't have a DVD player when she moves to England. *Muriel's Weddin'* just reminds me of Bernie every time I think about it. Its our film. The film we watch all the time and know all the words off. She told me I'll have to teach Concepta or Tracy how to do *Waterloo* but it just won't be the same, as much as I love the two of them. Bernie is still me best mate in the world and nobody could replace her. It was pointless givin' me that DVD though coz there's no way I'll be able to watch it. I'll be in a state every time an Abba song comes on. At this stage, I'd even go with her. Anythin' other than the two of us bein' separated. She's been with me all me life. 19 years is a long time. What am I gonna do without her?

✳✳✳

I was hopin' to spend last night with Bernie but she was out with her family instead, not that I mind or anythin'. Even though I am her best mate, her family are her family if ya know what I mean. They went to some Chinese restaurant in Glassnevin, Bernie was tellin' me after. A lovely place she said and the food was only mafis. She said she enjoyed it anyway so I suppose that's all that matters really isn't it?

Concepta gave me a ring last night and said that her and Tracy were goin' up to Farley's for a drink and then headin' into town to meet up with Lance and his mates and asked if I wanted to go but I wasn't really in the mood. I'm not really feelin' up to anythin'. Even when Dave asked me to go to see the new Brad Pitt film I said no. I don't think these people realise that me best mate is movin' away. I'm unconsolable here and they're askin' me to go into town or the pictures or whatever. They might be able to push it to the back of their minds but I can't. None of them are losin' their best mate are they? It's a much bigger deal for me than it is for them. I really don't know what I'll do without her. I'm lost without her already and she hasn't even gone yet. I don't think I'll be able to bare it. Life just wont be worth livin' without Bernie. She's me rock, me oyster or lobster or whatever it is. She's like the sister I never had and she's leavin'. I need a moment. Actually I have a sister but she lives in Australia. That reminds me I must ring Wanda.

✳︎✳︎✳︎

Great night last night, now a great night. Fair play to whoever came up with the idea to have Paulo's birthday the same night as Bernie's leavin' do. There was two things to celebrate so we got twice as locked, except for poor Paulo who got three or four times as locked. The poor young-fella thought it was New Years Eve at one stage. He kept sayin' happy New Year to everyone and when we were singin' happy birthday to him, Bopper had to remind him it was him we were singin' to.

Bernie and Paulo had a chat between them about where to go and after much deliberation, which means they talked loads Tracy tells me, Bernie decided we were goin' to Fitzsimons, upstairs first and then downstairs to the nightclub although Concepta and Tracy weren't too keen on the idea because that's where they ended up the night before and where they ended up gettin' fucked out of the night before. Concepta said there was no way she had hit that fella with the glass on purpose, just like the fella had said he hadn't stuck his tongue in her ear on purpose. I swear to god, ya can't bring the young-one anywhere. Ya wanna see them hidin' from the bouncers and all on the way in. Concepta was only short of wearin' a disguise. Thank god they weren't recognised coz it would have meant the whole lot of us troupin' off somewhere else and there was far too many of us for that.

There was the usual gang. Meself, Paulo and Bernie obviously. It was their party. It'd be a bit poxy if they weren't there. Then there was Tracy and Lance, Concepta, Jasmin, Bopper, me Uncle Dessie and then there was Sheila and Dymphna from work, a few young-ones Bernie used to work with and two young-ones and a young-fella that Paulo works with, not much of a looker your man. Oh and a Turkish young-one called Yenta that Concepta got talkin' to on the bus. How she ended up in the club with us I couldn't tell ya but ya know Concepta! I asked Dave to come too but he was babysittin' his sister's kids and couldn't get out of it although he promised to take me to that Brad Pitt film soon, although I'm not pushed now coz Paulo said its muck.

Anyway, we were all twisted by the time we got down to the nightclub. Your woman Yenta started talkin' to me in the toilet and half an hour later I was still there. She's a lot better at the English than Sheila thank god. She's even better than Jasmin but that's not hard. I only met the young-one and she was tellin' me her life story and I didn't even know where Turkey was until then although I was meant to go a few year ago on me holidays but we went to Torremolinos instead. I have to say now, it sounds like a nice place and she told me I can stay with her family anytime I go to Turkey which I have to say, was weird and nice at the same time. That's Turkey and South Africa I can stay in now and London when Bernie goes. I must ask Bernie do Ryanair do cheap flights to Turkey. I have to say though, she sounds like a nice enough girl. A bit mad but nice.

We tried to give Paulo the bumps but the first time we threw him up, he kicked Jasmin in the face by accident and we all turned to look at her and didn't catch him and he landed on top of Bopper and me Uncle Dessie and the three of them collapsed on the floor and Jasmin, still in pain after bein' kicked in the face, stepped backwards and tripped over them and Bernie and Concepta tried to stop her and she pulled them down on top of her. Ya wanna see them all lyin' in a heap in the middle of Fitzsimons. It was gas. The last thing ya want when you're locked is Concepta Cooney on top of ya.

The rest of the night is a bit of a blank to tell ya the truth but I do remember us all singin' in a big circle at the end and a bouncer turnin' around to Concepta and sayin' 'I know you.'

Anyway, I'm off out to the airport to say goodbye to Bernie although if she has a hangover like mine, she's goin' to be fucked on that plane!

∗∗

Ah Jayzis now, I'm in an awful state. I don't think I've cried this much since Ireland were beaten by Spain a few years ago in the world cup. We all went out to say goodbye to Bernie in the airport and there wasn't a dry eye between us. Even Concepta cried and that's sayin' somethin'. She didn't even cry durin' *All Dogs Go To Heaven*. It was real sad. Bernie leavin', not *All Dogs Go To Heaven*, although that was sad too. There was me, Jasmin, Concepta, Tracy and Bopper. Paulo was in too much of a state to move and Dessie couldn't get there on time. Her ma and da were there and her little sister. I got the taxi out to the airport with our Bopper and Tracy and we didn't speak one word in the whole time. I just couldn't get me mind away from the fact that Bernie was goin', try as I might. We all got to the airport and it was like we were at a funeral and not a good funeral either, ya know the ones ya go to coz there'll be a bit of craic at the wake and a lovely spread.

Bernie was doin' her baggage drop thing and there was about 15 of us standin' in the queue with her. Your woman from Ryanair nearly died when she saw us comin' towards her and then she had a fit when she realised it was only Bernie gettin' on the flight. Needless to say, Concepta was havin' none of it and nearly went through your woman for a short cut for gettin' smart. The look on your woman's face was comical.

Then we all followed Bernie to that doorway thing where they check your boardin' card and ya go through the metal detectors and we all started sayin' goodbye to her. I was the last one and the two of us just stood there with our arms around each other for a good five minutes. I just didn't want to let her go but I knew I had to, especially coz we were blockin' the doorway and people couldn't get passed. She turned around as she was passin' through the door and waved and I swear to god, we all just broke down. As we were walkin' away, who runs towards me only me Uncle Dessie and he was distraught when he realised he was late, although it did mean he could give us a lift home. I was in no more of a humour for a taxi driver complainin' about the M50. If they don't like the traffic, what they fuck are they doin' drivin' taxis? It's like a prostitute not likin' ridin'.

***

I'm still distraught. How I'm goin' to get over this I'll never know. I mean, she's only been gone since Sunday and I already miss her terribly. I just feel lost without her. I was tellin' Mrs O'Leary next door about it and she said that if you're lost, ya should try Harry Krishna which at first I thought was a fish and chip restaurant but then I realised that was Harry Ramsden's. I asked Tracy and she said Harry Krishna is a kind of religious cult, although I didn't hear her right when I was talkin' to her on the phone and was goin' around tellin' everyone that Harry Krishna was a religious cunt. Anyway, that's beside the point. As traumatised as I am over Bernie leavin', I don't think I'll be turnin' to religion, be it me own or Harry Krishna's. No amount of prayin' is goin' to bring her back home. The thing is, she's gone now and I'm just goin' to have to come to terms with it and although it might be hard, I'll just have to soldier on because I know that it was Bernie's choice and she's me best mate and I want nothin' more in the world than for her to be happy because she deserves it coz she's a lovely young-one and she's got a heart of gold and everyone likes her and even though she's gone and abandoned me and the others to move to England, I know deep in her heart she would have stayed if she could have and fair play to her anyways for followin' her dream. If its what she really wants, then I hope she's happy.

✳✳✳

I can't take anymore. I've had enough. The final straw. No more. I can't take it. I'm distraught. I'm devastated. I'm traumatised. I'm upset. I'm angry. I'm annoyed. I'm tired. In fact, I'm very fuckin' tired. Knackered even. I'm sad. I'm temperamental. I think I am anyway. I don't know if that means what I think it does. Most of all though, I'm lonely. It might sound totally ridiculous or whatever but I miss Bernie so much and I never thought I'd end up bein' this bad but she is me best friend and we've been apart before but this time its for good. I talked to her on the phone last night and I just burst into tears. Its just not the same without her bein' here. I need a moment again. And a vodka.

✳✳✳

I went back to work today coz I'd just been sittin' around the house lettin' the whole thing get to me and I thought the best thing to do would be to go and do somethin' so it was either go back to work or join that Harry Krishna thing and I very nearly would have if I could have found one of their churches or somethin'. Instead, I just went back to work. Just the usual shite. Leandra is still bein' a bit of a spa although she tried to be nice today. Now when I say try to be nice, I mean she didn't try very hard but the way I see it, anythin' is better than nothin' with that moany cow.

While I was out 'sick', she moved Boris back to the daytime shifts. I'm sure I mentioned Boris before. He's the fella from Ukrainia. Tall, blonde, ugly, like that fella out of Rocky, the big Russian fella, not Arnold Scwarznegger. I don't think it was the first Rocky. It was one of the others. Two, three, four or five. Don't ask me which. Anyway, Boris is back on the day shifts so that means we now have him and Sheila to try to understand. I mean, it's bad enough havin' to understand Marie when she's stoned and Julie Walsh full stop without them as well. I'll need subtitles or somethin'. Talkin' of Sheila, she's in great form. She's discovered rap music thanks to me Uncle Dessie. He gave her the latest Lil Kim CD so she keeps rappin' in this kind of strange English-Chinese mix that sounds like she's havin' a nervous breakdown, not that I'd know what that sounds like. I've never tried one. She was goin' around all day sayin' 'Whassuup motherfucker' in a Chinese accent and I think one or two of the customers got a bit of a shock when she said it to them.

Julie Walsh was bein' a pain in the arse as usual. She kept askin' questions about Bernie and at one stage, I was ready to go over and push the cow off her stool only I was afraid the tremor might be picked up on the richter scale. The young-one just doesn't know when to shut up. I swear to god, one day she'll piss me off so much that she'll cause me to shut her up meself, probably by dislocatin' her jaw with me fist.

Dymphna was off today so I couldn't get any of the gossip I missed when I was off although Marie was in. I tried to talk to her but she seemed more interested in a pot plant in the staff room, although I have to admit, it's a nice pot plant.

✳✳✳

Good Friday. By that I mean the religion thing and not that it was a good Friday even though it was. Me ma told me today that I had to reflect on life because our Lord died on the cross for us. I have to say now, I did try. I wouldn't be what ya'd call a religious person but I do try to be a nice person. What me ma said was freakin' me out a little bit, I'll be honest with ya. I was tryin' to think of the 10 commandments but I could hardly think of one, let alone 10 so I spent the whole day thinkin' and I think I have a few.

Thou shalt not kill. Well that's me fucked for a start although I'm wonderin' does it count when its goldfish or does it have to be like killin' another person? Murder like? God, I'll never forget that time. The poor little goldfish swimmin' around and next minute it starts shakin' really fast and goin' silver and then starts to kind of break up. Jasmin's little sisters were in an awful state after it. How was I meant to know ya can't clean the tank with Domestos?

Thou shalt not steal. I borrow things on the girls and Bopper all the time. Borrow and don't give them back kinda thing but I don't think that's stealin'. I do always pick up Mars Bars and Kit Kats and eat them in work but I don't think that counts. I don't think I've ever stolen anythin', well really stolen, that's one commandment I passed. I don't think shopliftin' from Boots counts. Or Miss Selfridges. Actually we'll ignore this one.

Thou shalt not take the lords name in vain. I didn't know what that meant so I rang Tracy. I says, 'Tracy, what does it mean to take your name in vain?'

'Who's goin' to Spain?' she says. I'm tellin' ya, her phone is fucked so I tell her what I want to know and she says its like usin' the lords name as a curse and I says, 'Jayzis,' and she says, 'exactly,' so I'm fucked there as well.

Another one is thou shalt not covet thy neighbours wife. Now Petulia on one side of us lives on her own and on the other side, Mr Daly lives on his own, an elderly man, his wife long dead, god rest her soul. That means me neighbours don't have wives and even if they did, I wouldn't know how to covet them.

Another one is that ya can't have adultery. I know what that means but I'm not married and I've never been with anyone who is married. At least I hope not. Jayzis, I'll kill Dave if he is. If I'm livin' in sin because of him, he'll be the next fucker spread eagled on a cross and by that, I mean Harold's Cross!

**

Holy Saturday, although what's so different about it, I don't know. To me its just the same as every other Saturday except for the fact that nobody has hangovers coz we all stayed in last night. Not by choice of course but because that's what you're meant to do of a Good Friday. It doesn't matter if you're Catholic or Muslim or Bosnian or whatever, if ya live in Ireland, ya can't go to the pub on Good Friday. Now as I said, I wouldn't be the most religious person in the world. I mean, I didn't even know who Harry Krishna was but I do believe that everyone should have a choice to do what they want. Last night I had no choice but to sit at home and watch the *Late Late Show* with me ma and da even though I didn't want to. I mean, I know the whole story of Jesus and the cross and all the rest of it but he was meant to die for all our sins, not so we could sit in of a Friday. It's the same with not eatin' meat. I wouldn't say that when Jesus was up on the cross that he said 'In 2000 years, people can't eat meat or go the pub on me anniversary.' That wouldn't be like Jesus. He would have wanted us to celebrate. I still feel kinda guilty over the whole religion thing so I've been tryin' to be a bit of a better person. I went the shop for Petulia next door although what she wanted Sellotape, pipe cleaners, some crepe paper and yogurt for, I'll never know. I cleaned the house for me ma when she was in town, not very well I'll admit but the lord loves a trier. I made me da a cup of tea and a sambwhich when he was watchin' the match and cleaned it up when he threw it across the room when Chelsea scored. I went for a walk with Concepta coz she's back on her diet and didn't even slag her over it and then I helped me Uncle Dessie sort out his DVDs and then went over to Jasmin for a chat. I know its not savin' lives or anythin' but I feel a little bit better about meself. I even gave a few quid to charity. Jasmin tells me that just €2 a month could help them build wells so I gave them a tenner so they could build five wells.

***

I'm sittin' at home last night havin' only come back from Jasmin's. I think I was watchin' somethin' good on the telly but maybe I wasn't, I can't really remember. Anyway I'm sittin' there and next minute the phone rings and first I thought it might be Bernie coz she said she was gonna gimme a ring but I answered it and it was Dave askin' me did I want to go to the pictures and at first I thought to meself to say no, that I'd rather just stay in and wait for Bernie to ring but I hadn't been out with him for a few days and the last thing I'd want is for him to think I don't like him coz I do. So I thought to meself that Bernie has me mobile number and if she tries to call me, I'll know. So I got ready, ya know the usual — shower, dry hair, straighten hair, make-up, cloths and the rest of it and I was just about to leave when me da shouts that he'll gimme a lift in. He was in a great mood after United winnin' so it worked out well for me coz I was runnin' dead late and I was in no more of a humour for that bus. The worst thing is gettin' on a bus when you're not in the humour, d'ya know that kinda way and the journey does take ages and your head does be melted gettin' off. Fair play to me da though and Dave was outside the pictures and all when we pulled up. Me da was askin' me which one he was and when I pointed him out, he looked him up and down, told me to be safe and drove off. It was only then that I realised the fucker only gave me a lift so he could see what Dave looked like, tryin' to suss him out, makin' sure he doesn't mess his daughter around and all that shite. Me da's gas like that sometimes. Poor Dave looked terrified though. He kinda guessed who it was givin' me a lift so I told him to relax and we go inside the cinema. Cineworld it was. I don't like goin' anywhere else for a film. We met a friend of his and I was introduced as Joanna, his girlfriend, which I thought was lovely I have to say, even though I was never informed I was anyone's girlfriend but how and ever. So we saw the film, shite, don't even get me started, and then walked back over to his place and well ya can imagine the rest. I'd say me da was goin' spare that I didn't come home last night although do I look like I give a shite? Even though, lets not lie, ya can't see me right now. I'm gorgeous if that helps?

✷✷✷

Bernie rang last night and we must have been on the phone a good hour and a half if not more. It was more actually coz me ma had just started watchin' a film when she rang and it was over when we were finished talkin' and it was on RTE and they do even have ad breaks.

I was delighted she rang though coz I'd kinda calmed down a bit since she last rang. I was a little less hysterical. I wasn't cryin' so I'd say that made her feel a little bit better. I think the last time she rang it just upset her so the last thing I wanted was for her to be gettin' upset again and gettin' all homesick and as I said, it's kinda gettin' easier for me now. I think the shock of her leavin' got to me at first and I was devastated, although don't get me wrong, I still am, but I learned I had to deal with it.

She loves it though she says. She's only there a week and she's got a week of her trainin' course done and she says she's learnin' loads and the people doin' the course are lovely and she's livin' with a few of them and one of the young-ones likes all the same type of music. Dervla this girls name is and she's from Limerick and they're havin' a great bit of buzz and her room in the house is gorgeous. Its in a place called Bishops Stortford and its 45 minutes on the train from London although she said she's been really busy so far and hasn't had a chance to go to London but she's goin' to go when she gets a chance. She says she'll wait til I go over to her to do all the touristy things like goin' to the wax museum and on that big wheel yoke and all the rest of it. I can't wait for that now. It should be a great laugh.

Ah I'm delighted she's enjoyin' it and I hope it all works out for the best. Really now, I do. Her phone bill will be through the fuckin' roof though.

✷✷✷

Thank god that Easter shite is over. I'm done feelin' religious. For a few days there I felt meself goin' all holy. I had visions of me goin' to become a nun. Can ya imagine me as a nun? Although in sayin' that, stranger things have happened. I mean, only the other day I saw Jasmin Spi speakin' Spanish. No word of a lie. I told ya before that she was goin' to learn how to speak Spanish. Well fair play to her, she's givin' it a go. I wouldn't be able to. As I've said before, I struggle with English. Maybe it wasn't Spanish. It could have been anythin' and I wouldn't have a clue. Ya know what I'll do, the next time we're out, which better be soon may I add, I'll get Concepta to go and find me someone that speaks Spanish for Jasmin to talk to. It should be no problem for Concepta. That girl can spot a foreigner from half a mile. I wonder what language that young-one Yenta speaks, ya know Concepta's new mate from Turkey. Do they speak Spanish in Turkey I wonder? I wouldn't know meself coz I've never been there. I'll ask Tracy when I see her.

It'll be great if Jasmin can speak Spanish properly coz it'd be handy to have her around for when we go the Canaries, the only thing the young-one would be useful for, let the truth be told. Ah I'm jokin'. That's not nice. True, but not nice. I might even get her to teach me a bit. Ya know the usual stuff like hello, thank you, you're welcome, 20 John Player Blue and a naggin of vodka, that sort of thing. Stuff ya'd use every day. I'd be the business.

✳︎✳︎✳︎

I was in work today and it was the usual shite. Leandra, I have to give it to her, is bein' really nice lately. She was askin' me all about Bernie today and she was tellin' me a young-one she knows works for Ryanair but in Stockholm or some other place in Norway and that she said she loves it and she's always home and she's doin' real well and all the rest of it so not to worry about Bernie coz she'll be grand. I have to say now, the more I'm workin' with her, the more I like her. I think she's comin' down off her high horse a little bit and realised that its only a Spar she's managin' and not Harods although maybe its just after takin' her time to get to know everyone and she realises now that with most of us, she doesn't have to tell us what to do. We just get on and do it. I mean, we're like that most of us. Even Julie Walsh. It suits her to just sit on her hole on the till all day and that suits us coz it means we don't have to do it.

  I think Leandra is startin' to realise now as well the way me and Greg used to work and by that I mean she can leave the shop or whatever and leave me in charge and it'll be grand when she gets back. She knows now that I know what I'm doin' and at first she didn't. I have to say though, I'm startin' to enjoy me job again.

  Anyway, there I was today helpin' Dymphna on the hot food counter. Leandra had gone to the back and I looked around and Boris and Sheila are puttin' out trays of Coke, not a word of English between the pair of them, Julie Walsh was on tills havin' a chat with one of the customers about the time she got her belly button pierced and it got infected. The thoughts of it turned me stomach. Julie Walsh's belly button, never mind the infection. Anyway, Marie wasn't anywhere to be seen so I went to the back lookin' for her and no word of a lie, there she was in the toilet, kneelin' up on the toilet bowl talkin' to the pot plant on the window ledge. She didn't spot me at first and I could hear her talkin' to it about Coronation Street. That auld-one has to be smokin' a serious amount of hash.

✳✳✳

I'm very confused. Ya might say that's not very hard, we know what Joanna's like, she gets confused very easily and all the rest of it but really, ya would be too. I mean, I still don't know what's goin' on and believe me, I know its not just me bein' stupid or whatever and don't even think of callin' me stupid. Normally ya know yourself, I'd ask Tracy if theres somethin' I don't understand or if I'm confused about somethin' but she's the reason I'm confused so what chance do I have?

  It all happened when I was in work today. Just the usual shite. I was havin' a chat with Sheila, Boris was pretendin' to listen, Dymphna was makin' the rolls and the Julie Walsh one had her arse stuck to the stool as usual.

Anyway, me phone vibrates in me pocket and at first I thought it was the way I was standin' til I copped on and I took me phone out and theres a message from Tracy and it says 'hat time u finish ork at?' and I was lookin' at it askin' meself what the fuck the young-one is talkin' about and I send her one back sayin' 'Wot?' and a minute later, the phone vibrates again and she's after replyin' 'hat do u mean ot? hat time ou finish ork at?' I'm lookin' at the message wonderin' what's goin' on, whether its just her tryin' to be funny or whatever and I send her a message back sayin' 'Wot u send? Cant read msg!' and she replies, quick as fuck I might add, 'Sent ou text message. hy? Can u not read the ords?' So I'm sayin' to meself, this is some sort of joke and I read it out again and again and I still don't know what the fuck the young-ones tryin' to say to me and I even show it to Sheila and Boris, although in fairness, if I can't read it, there's not a hope they can. So then I show it to Dymphna and even Julie Walsh and none of us can make it out and Dymphna even tries to spell the original message backwards coz she was readin' that *Da Vinci Code* but it just says 'Ta kro hsinif uu emit tah' which isn't even Ukrainian Boris tells me. So I send Tracy another message and its like 'Wot u tryin to say?' and she replies 'hat time ou finish ork at? hat time does ork end? tonight? Ork?' So at this stage, ya can imagine I was in the height of it so and I ended up just ringin' her and I say, 'Tracy love, come 'ere, stop actin' the spa. What ya askin' me?' and she says 'I was askin' ya what time ya finish work at.' It's a pity the stupid cow couldn't have just said that in the first place.

※※※

I think we have Tracy's messages sussed at this stage all thanks to Jasmin would ya believe it. She popped in to me today in work and I was talkin' to her when I got a message off Tracy and I have to say, I was dreadin' readin' it after that shite yesterday and I read it out loud to Jasmin and it says 'hats the stor ith tonight? e going to anibar?' and the same as yesterday, I was lost. I mean, I thought it was even less English than it was before but Jasmin took it off me and read and well ya know the way Jasmin has a lisp? Well when she read out the text message, it sounded like 'What's the story with tonight? We going to Zanzibar?' and I says to Jasmin 'How did ya read that?' and she says 'I haven't a fuckin' clue what it means' although that dizzy bitch wouldn't even know what it meant even if it was spelt properly and I took the phone off her and look at the message and its only then that I realise what's goin' on, fair play to me. So I text Tracy and I say 'Don't think ur W and Z are workin' and a minute later I get a reply sayin' 'Shite. Nine not orking,' which I have to say, I thought was gas. I went around and showed Dymphna, Boris, Julie Walsh and Sheila and they all thought it was gas as well. I mean, imagine your number nine not workin'? Did ya ever hear the likes of it? We were laughin' for ages over it and we even had a look at the messages from yesterday and laughed at them and at Dymphna tryin' to write the letters backwards and all thinkin' it was a clue and Julie Walsh bein' adamant that it was Danish although the only Danish that one knows is the one she get in the bakery with apple and cinnamon on them, the hungry cow. I have to say, we had a good laugh over it although Jasmin still hadn't a clue what was goin' on. I wouldn't mind, but Zanzibar is closed ages.

✱✱

Well the madness last night. I swear to god, I'm still shakin' over it. I've never been through an ordeal like it. The fright I got is somethin' else. My poor heart nearly gave up at one stage. I have to say, it'll probably be a few days til I recover from the whole thing.

We went out last night, a few of us like. There was meself, Tracy and her fella Lance, Concepta, Sheila and Dave, me fella. I did tell ya about me fella Dave. He's me fella. Like as in boyfriend. As in we're goin' out together. He's me fella like. Anyway, I have to say, we're kinda lost without Bernie of a night out coz she's the one that always has us organised; What time we're gettin' the bus at, who's meetin' who where, where we're goin' and all the rest of it. All I'll say is, thank god we all have mobiles or we'd be fucked.

I think it was Concepta that suggested Bad Bobs and Sheila was agreein' with her, well at least I think she was although I must say, her English is gettin' better. The rest of us just went along with it coz they're the two single ones coz Lance was there with Tracy and my fella Dave was there with me. I'm sure I told ya about me fella Dave. He's me fella like.

So there we all are in Purty Kitchen havin' a great night, dancin' away, havin' a few drinks and a bit of a laugh and all of a sudden, I need to go me toilet so I'm goin' down the stairs to the middle floor and I get this horrible smell, worse than Dymphna from work even and I notice that me eyes are waterin' and there's smoke everywhere and next minute theres screamin' and shoutin' and madness everywhere and people are rushin' for the door and some spa of a young-one, if I ever get me hands on her I'll reef her, she shouts 'Chemical attack' and that just makes it worse and theres people runnin' for the door and pushin' each other out of the way and I just get taken along with the crowd and some how end up on the street without me jacket and I find Concepta and she looks at me and says 'Before ya say anythin', that has fuck all to do with me' and I have to say, I believe her.

Anyway, it turns out, so the bouncer told me, that it was tear gas and some gobshite let it off as a joke. I mean, would ya be well in this day and age with all the terrorist attacks and all goin' on. And I believe three girls pissed themselves and all with the fright. I just hope they weren't wearin' tights.

✳︎✳︎✳︎

We were out again last night although we weren't evacuated from the pub thank fuck. Me nerves are still gone over the other night. It was on the news and everythin'. Bopper was ragin' he missed it, or so he says anyways. I know him though, he'd be the first one out the door if he was there. He was just ragin' he missed bein' on the telly. Concepta's convinced she saw her hand on RTE, although with the size of her, how could ya miss her?

I have to say, Bopper was wreckin' me head a bit last night. We were in Break For The Border — meself, himself, Jasmin, Concepta and that Turkish young-one, Yenta, the one Concepta met on the bus last week. Now whatever about Concepta makin' all her foreign friends or whatever, but she doesn't usually see them ever again. This Yenta one seems to have latched onto us. Not that she's not a nice young-one or anythin' coz she is, but she could talk for Turkey. I mean, I told ya about the first night I met her in Fitzsimons and she had me talkin' in the toilet for a half an hour. Well last night I got planted beside her and no word of a lie, she must have told me not only her own life story but her ma's and da's as well and her brother Marvin or Martian or somethin' and one of her cousins in Syria as well, wherever the fuck that is. I'm sure she told me but I probably stopped listenin' again. I must ask Tracy. I was tellin' her about us gettin' evacuated from the place the night before and she was able to tell me all about chemical attacks and all the rest of it. She told me everythin' like how they're made and how they get them into the country and I know this might sound a little bit strange or whatever but I think she might be part of one of them terrorist groups. El Al or somethin' like that. I know it might sound a bit over the top but ya can't be too careful these days. She's just a little bit conspicious, that's all. I mean, they don't tell ya how to make chemical bombs on the Discovery Channel do they? She has to be a terrorist. How else would she know? I don't even think she has the Discovery Channel.

❋❋❋

Me Uncle Dessie came around to the gaff today for dinner and he was in an awful state although d'ya think he'd tell us what's goin' on? No. This is big. I can feel it and it has somethin' to do with the money that Bernie gave him a lend of although tryin' to get it out of him is like tryin' to get that stool off Julie Walsh. I have to say, I'm very worried. Me Uncle Dessie looks after me and I'd be afraid I won't be able to look after him if theres anythin' wrong like.

He did tell us though that me cousin Jacinta rang. His daughter like and I have to say, she's a nut job. She's a few cards short of a full deck if ya know what I mean. I'm sure I was tellin' ya before that she's one of these hippies who worships the sun and all the rest of that mad shit. Well she rang me Uncle Dessie today, even though she doesn't agree with usin' phones coz she doesn't want to see the money goin' to the telephone companies but she said she had to ring to tell him she's changin' her name to Pussy-willow. No word of a lie. As true as I'm sittin' here, Jacinta's new name is Pussy-willow. Well I couldn't keep a straight face when he told me and either could our Bopper although me ma and da did. Even Dessie saw the funny side of it.

Anyway, he said that she might see him later in the year and that she loves him and she's goin' back to tie herself to her tree in the path of a motorway somewhere outside Birmingham with her boyfriend Fudge. Its worse that Jacinta one is gettin'. Sorry, I meant Pussy-willow. What sort of a name is that?

※

Right, I'm just lettin' ya know that Jasmin can speak Spanish. Really like coz remember I was sayin' before that she probably couldn't but she can and fair play to her and she even proved it last night.

We were at the pictures — meself, herself and Concepta. We were in the Cineworld coz I do like seein' a picture in there and Jasmin was dyin' to see that new chick flick with Hugh Grant in it and we said we'd go with her. I can't stand him meself but she was lookin' forward to seein' it and I had nothin' better to do anyways. It wasn't really that bad to be honest although Concepta wasn't mad about it. She loves superhero films. I don't know how many times we've been dragged along to *X-men* or *Spiderman* or *The Hulk* or somethin' else like that. She even dressed up as Wonder Woman there last Halloween. Can ya imagine someone the size of Concepta in a Wonder Woman outfit? And where she got one to fit her, I'll never know. And she thought she was only great and all, swingin' her lasso and everything. It was even worse than when she dressed up as Storm from the X-men the year before. Me as Jean Grey! Gas.

Anyway, meself and Jasmin went into the toilet on the way out and when we came back out, Concepta was talkin' to this young-one and young-fella and she introduces them to us although what there names were, I couldn't tell ya. I couldn't even pronounce them. She says they're from Guatemala, wherever the fuck that is. I must ask Tracy. Guatemala and Syria that is now. I should just buy an atlas. Anyway, Jasmin turns around and starts havin' a full blown conversation with these two in Spanish which must be the language they speak in their country. I mean, fair play to her, she's only been doin' it a few months. I have to say, I was well impressed with her and they were as well, ya could see by the looks on their faces although in sayin' that, maybe they couldn't understand a word she was sayin' and were just smilin' to be nice. Well that's what everyone else does with Jasmin.

✻✻✻

The bang off Dymphna is unacceptable. I'm bein' serious. I've never met a woman that smells as bad as she does and its always there. Always. Whatever about us, how her husband puts up with it I'll never know. I mean, we can only smell it through her cloths but he has to sleep beside her at night. Can ya imagine havin' to sleep beside someone that smells as bad as Dymphna? Its just not natural and especially in a woman of her age who should know better. Theres no excuse for it really. How hard could it be to hop into the shower before comin' to work? I do it every mornin' and it only takes me five minutes although that doesn't count blow-dryin' me hair or straightenin' it or whatever but she wouldn't have to do that. She doesn't have enough hair to straighten in the first place.

She definitely has an electric shower coz I asked her straight out. I said, 'Dymphna,' I can't remember what it was we were talkin' about at the time but anyways I says, 'Dymphna, do you have a shower?' and she doesn't get the hint though and starts tellin' me about her electric shower she got a month or two earlier, a Triton T90, whatever the fuck that is and how great it is and all the rest of it and she says how she doesn't really like usin' it much and I say, 'Really', tryin' to be real sarcastic like.

Imagine this, right. You're standin' there makin' a sambwhich for a customer and on one side of ya there's a smell of, I don't know, sewerage and rotten cabbage and gone off milk and an ash tray all mixed together and on the other side of ya is Julie Walsh we're talkin' about and who, in fairness, doesn't smell much better. Well that's what it's like for me sometimes and its gettin' too often for my likin'. I asked Sheila to swap with me earlier but she just smiled back at me and went back to sortin' out the magazines, the sly bitch, although she knew exactly why I wanted to swap. I wouldn't mind but she doesn't know what half the magazines are. I found *Nasty Housewives* down on the second last shelf between *Soaps Weekly* and *Hello*.

No, I'll have to try and give Dymphna a few subtle hints about the smell like tyin' her down and sprayin' her with Right Guard or some other shite. As I said, the smell of her is unacceptable. And as if Dymphnas not bad enough, Marie took the pot plant out of the toilet and put it in the staff room and spent her whole lunch hour talkin' to it. I swear to god, I'm not able.

✳✳✳

Bernie rang last night and she was in flyin' form. Flyin' form, d'ya get it? She's goin' to be an air hostess and she's in flyin' form. Why is there never anyone else around when I say somethin' funny? She seems to be really gettin' on well over there and havin' a ball and fair play to her. I mean, I'm finally gettin' used to the idea that she's gone. It was hard but I think I'm adjustin' to life without her here, hard and all as it was.

Anyway, I was givin' her all the gossip about me fella Dave and about Jasmin really bein' able to speak Spanish and us gettin' evacuated from Bad Bob's and all the rest of it and she's delighted to be hearin' all the latest from home so I tell her about Jacinta changin' her name to Pussy-willow and she says that she knows and I'm wonderin' has she been talkin' to any of the others although I never said it to any of them although our Bopper could have. Ya know what he's like. He couldn't hold his piss. So I ask her how she knows and she said she was talkin' to Nigel. Well I couldn't believe it. Nigel's me cousin. Dessie's son. Jacinta's, sorry, Pussy-willow's brother and he lives in London. I'm sure I've mentioned him before. He's a few years older than me and he'd kinda remind ya of our Bopper. What happened anyway was that me Uncle Dessie gave Bernie Nigel's number before she went and she got a day off from the trainin' course yesterday so she rang him and arranged to meet him in London. She said they had a great day and he brought her to see all the sights, her and this Dervla young-one from Limerick she keeps tellin' me about. He even brought her to Oxford Street to go shoppin' and she says H&M over there is only deadly and I'd love it. She says Nigel is a great laugh and he's gonna drive up to Bishops Stortford where she lives on the weekend to go to the pub with her and she was tellin' him that I'm goin' over and he said he can't wait and he'll look after me and all so that should be a great bit of laugh. I wonder if Bernie and Nigel are gettin' it on. I should have asked her. Shite.

*※※

I was in the bath there, ya know yourself, I was just home from work and I said I'd have a bath to relax meself a bit before goin' out. So there I am lyin' in the bath covered in bubbles and theres a lovely smell of Radox and all the rest of it and I'm really chilled out and next minute there's a ringin' noise and I got such a fright that I nearly drowned. I really panicked. I could have died. Anyway, I'm listenin' and I realise it's me phone so I just say fuck it, whoever it is will send me a text message and their name will come up as a missed call so I just ignore it and wait for it to stop but then just as it does, it starts again and I'm thinkin' to meself it must be important so I get up and shake meself a bit and grab a towel and throw the door open and run down the landin' towards me room and I let go of the towel as I jump for the phone. There was no one in the house at the time thank fuck coz ya wanna see the mess I made. If me ma had of seen it she would have battered me. I tried to dry the carpet with the hairdryer and all after. Seriously like, although the cable wasn't nearly long enough.

Anyway, I picked up the phone and said hello and there was no one on it. They had hung up or whatever and I looked at the screen and whoever it was had been ringin' off a private number so there I am standin' in me bedroom stark bollock naked, the carpet on the landin' destroyed, me drippin' wet all over the bedroom floor and me phone in me hand and I look out me window and there's Mr O'Toole from across the road starin' over at me and I think, although I'm not a hundred percent, but I think he has a pair of binoculars in his hand, the dirty prevert.

✳︎✳︎✳︎

I hadn't seen me fella Dave in a few days so I was delighted when he rang me yesterday and asked me to go for a meal with him. I mean, he is me fella after all. I was thrilled coz I was in work when he rang and I was in a bit of a mood at the time coz Julie Walsh was wreckin' me head. She keeps goin' on about her belly button piercin' and I don't know what's worse — the thoughts of Julie Walsh's belly button or the thoughts of it bein' infected. Either way, it's disgustin' and she had me stomach turnin' when she was goin' on about it. There really isn't any need for it, especially when you're tryin' to have your lunch. Me Cuppa Soup nearly ended up comin' up again and whatever about Julie Walsh's belly button, the bang off Dymphna is enough to make anyone sick. I swear to god, its like someone killed a cat and put it in her knickers. It wouldn't be the only smelly pussy she has in there I'd say. Oh that's disgustin'. There's no talkin' to Marie either. She's walkin' around with that pot plant now, still talkin' to the thing and all. I just try and hang around with Sheila and Boris coz even though they don't speak English, at least they don't smell or have a septic belly button. I can't believe that. How can someone as big as Julie Walsh have their belly button pierced? That's a disgrace.

    Anyway, as I was sayin', Dave rang and asked me did I want to go out with him so I says lovely, thinkin' we'd be goin' to the pictures or the pub or somethin' and he tells me to meet him at the Central Bank at half eight. So I go home, have a sambwhich, and hopped into the bath. I made sure me phone was off before I got in this time, just in case someone was tryin' to ring me. I get the bus into town and I arrive at the Central Bank at 25 to nine and there's Dave standin' there with a big smile on his face and I ask him where we're goin' and he says it's a surprise and starts walkin' towards the north side and I just think to meself that we're goin' to the Cineworld to watch a film but we get to that Millennium Bridge and he stops and goes into this fancy restaurant just beside Fitzsimons and I was delighted with meself.

    So we're sittin' there, table for two, candles and all the rest of it and he orders a bottle of wine and he asks what type of wine I like and I tell him I'm fond of a South African Sauvignon Blanc and he just smiles, thinkin' how someone like me knows what a Sauvignon Blanc is, let alone know how to say it but not realisin' that I work in a shop that sells wine and that me old manager was South African. That and the fact that me and Bernie have been locked on it many a night watchin' *Muriel's Weddin'*.

    I had a look at the menu and I have to say, I was fucked. There was nothin' on it I recognised at all, all this salmon and date and posh people food. I mean, my favourite meal would be a Big Mac and large chips so I said fuck it and got the potato skins covered in a sauce of olive and almond and topped with the finest Austrian goats cheese, mainly coz I kinda had an idea of what it was goin' to be like. That was me starter and for me main course I got the linguini with fresh Sicilian olives, chillies and tomatoes coz I was convinced linguini was a type of pasta. I'd seen it on one of them Dolmio ads. The food was gorgeous anyway and I demolished it, along with a bottle of that wine. Dave had to order another one and that was gone by the time desert came. Now whatever about the dinner, the desert was only mafis. I got a cherry tart with fresh cream and it was only amazin'. I could have eaten two or three more of them. I would have.

It was a lovely night I have to say and I really could get used to this posh restaurant thing. Well as long as Dave pays for it. If we've to rely on me, we'll be stickin' to the Big Macs.

✳︎✳︎✳︎

Yenta says she knows how to fly a plane. She says she learned in Turkey. Now I don't know about you, but to me that says one thing. She's a terrorist. I mean, there's no other explanation for it. The young-one knows how to make chemical bombs and how to fly a plane and its not as if its part of her job because she works in a bank and not even a Turkish one. Its not like it'd be somethin' they'd learn in school or maybe it is, I wouldn't know. While we're all studyin' the poems of Emily Dickinson and Irish, they're studyin' how to blow up buildin's, which in fairness, is a lot more interestin'. They probably have a terrorism exam in the leavin' cert. Can ya imagine? Question one — describe the best method of blowin' up a yacht usin' examples. Question two — draw and label a diagram of an ideal aircraft hostage situation. I'm just afraid she's plannin' to kill us all.

I said it to Tracy, ya know me. We were in the toilet in Fitzsimons and I told Tracy about Yenta knowin' how to make chemical bombs and how to fly a plane and that she might be a terrorist and Tracy says she'll have a chat with her and see what she can suss out, use her psychology on her and all the rest of it. So I'm standin' there with Sheila and Concepta, lookin' over. Paulo was talkin' to someone and Jasmin and Bopper weren't with us. So Tracy and Yenta are there havin' a great chat and Yenta eventually goes to the toilet and I say to Tracy, 'Well?' And she goes, 'Well what?' And I says, 'Did ya suss her out?' And Tracy says, 'Ah yeah, she's a lovely young-one.'

'But is she a terrorist?' says I.

'I don't think so,' Tracy tells me and just walks off to the bar. So she was fuck-all use to me. We have to sort out a plan or somethin'. Maybe we could follow her or get her to take a lie detector test or somethin' although I don't know if they work. I wouldn't know, I've only ever seen them in films or on *CSI*.

She is very strange though. Kinda conspicious even. Weird ya could say. I mean, she is a lovely young-one and a great bit of laugh and the best dancer I've seen this long time but that doesn't mean that she's not just tryin' to get close to us. It takes all sorts and she could be just puttin' up a front while she's plannin' to kill us or even worse, while she's plannin' to blow up the Jervis Street Shoppin' Centre or somethin'. I'd be devastated if that happened. There's a lovely Champion Sports in there. I have a funny feelin' about this so I'm not lettin' it rest. Not yet anyways. I couldn't live with meself if she did somethin' and I could have stopped it. Especially to Champion Sports.

✳✳✳

That Jason spa was in the shop today for what must have been well over an hour talkin' to Julie Walsh and I swear to god, I was only short of stranglin' the fucker. I told ya about Jason before. He was out with us the night of Greg's leavin' do. He's the young-fella that works in the shop at the weekends and thinks he knows everythin'. He has his leavin' cert comin' up and he's convinced that because he's in school, that he's smarter than everyone else. There's times when I feel like puttin' me fist through his face, although in sayin' that, that's most of the time.

So anyway, he comes into the shop today on his way home from school, his uniform still on and all and Julie Walsh sees him and nearly has a seizure. I was convinced she was for a minute. I was only short of ringin' the ambulance. Now Leandra wasn't in so I was keepin' an eye on the place but ya know me, I don't like tellin' people what to do so her and Jason are standin' there in the middle of the shop and Sheila took over the till from Julie Walsh and Marie and her pot plant were on the other one so ya can imagine what the queues were like. I have to give it to Julie Walsh, credit where it's due, but she's not bad on the till as long as she doesn't have to get up off the stool for anythin' although that wouldn't be very often. She has everythin' laid out so all she has to do is swivel to get to it.

Anyway, me head was melted with the queues and Sheila and Marie callin' me to help them and Dymphna was run off her feet doin' the rolls and Boris was on his break so it got to the stage where I'd had enough so I told Julie Walsh to hurry the fuck up and get back on the tills but she ignored me, the cheeky cow. So I went over to them and I says to Jason, 'Are ya gettin' paid to be here today?' And he says, 'no,' and I says, 'Are ya buyin' anythin'?' And he says, 'No,' so I says, 'Right. Get the fuck out and stop disturbin' the staff,' and they both look me up and down and I just say, 'Well I could just show the tape from the security camera to Leandra tomorrow.' So he just said goodbye real smartly to Julie Walsh and left. That fucker better watch himself or he'll be doin' his leavin' from six feet under the ground in Glasnevin Cemetery.

✳✳✳

Bernie rang me today and I have to say, she sounds in great form, she really does and I'd know with Bernie. If there's somethin' wrong, ya can pick it up from the way she's talkin' but on the phone today she sounded great.

She was tellin' me she's gettin' on great in the course. She's three weeks of it done already. Three weeks can ya believe it? It doesn't seem she's gone that long although in a way it does. I have to say, I miss her and all the rest of it but I'm after gettin' used to it I think. I know now that we can still keep in contact and I still get all the gossip off her and she does get all the gossip off me so neither of us are missin' out really. I do be the same with me sister Wanda in Australia.

I was tellin' her all about Yenta who may or may not be a terrorist and Bernie thinks we should just ask her. I mean, is she well in the head? Ya can't go up to a young-one, and especially not a young-one who's your mate that ya only know a few weeks and say 'Come 'ere love, d'ya mind me askin' but are ya a terrorist or what?' Its just not done. I told

Bernie as much. We have to do it in a roundabout way. Subtle I think the word is. I told her we tried to get Tracy to suss it out for us but she was as much use as a naggin of vodka and 20 John Player Blue to a Mormon and Tracy's meant to be the one studyin' psychology. Bernie met Yenta the night of her leavin' do but she says she didn't get much of a terrorist vibe off her but then again, they were only talkin' for a few minutes, definitely not long enough for Bernie to be able to judge her properly. Fair play to Bernie, she was able to tell me what to do if I was ever in a hostage situation. She learned it on her course. It is a good to know though, d'ya know that kinda way, coz like, ya never know what's gonna happen these days. Bernie had to learn all about it coz planes are always gettin' hijacked although it hasn't been as bad since the September 11 thing.

Anyway, Bernie was tellin' me that herself and this Dervla young-one, who she seems to be gettin' very pally with, were out on Saturday night in this place called Chicago's and had a great night. The two of them were locked and had to be carried home, she says. Dervla's mad, Bernie says. Up on the table dancin', swingin' around the poles on the way home, runnin' over cars, Bernie says. Chattin' up the fellas, Bernie says. Dervla's a great bit of laugh, Bernie says. I have to meet her, she says. I feel like I already know her. I mean, Bernie went on enough about her on the phone. Dervla this and Dervla that and Dervla is deadly. Why doesn't she just go and ride Dervla if she's that great? Not that I'm jealous or anythin'. Bernie's me best mate and this Dervla young-one and no one else will ever come between us. Or else!

✳✳✳

I had the day off work today so Dave asked me did I want to stay over at his place last night and I'm no position to turn down an offer of sex so I was on the bus within a half an hour and met him in town. Now to be honest, I was kinda in the humour for goin' out but he said he was tired after workin' all day so we went to Dunnes in Stephen's Green to get a few bits of shoppin' for his apartment and then the two of us walked to his place. He was holdin' me hand and all and I have to say, it felt lovely.

So anyway, we got to his place and there was no one else there. His flat mate is gone to Japan with the company for some convention. Dave and this room mate fella work together in the bank although he never told me the name of it. Sayin' that, he probably didn't think I'd have heard of it but then in sayin' that, I probably wouldn't have. They send him all over the world for different things. He was in Buenos Aires there just after Christmas he was sayin'. I'd love that. I've always wanted to go to Brazil.

Anyway, back to last night. So we went into his apartment and I sat meself down on the sofa and was there watchin' an episode of *Friends* I'd seen at least 20 times while he was makin' the dinner so out he comes with the plates, a lovely sweet and sour chicken with rice he made and it was only mafis and we had a bottle of the South African Sauvignon Blanc. If he was tryin' to impress me, I have to say, it was workin'. I was goin' weak at the knees because of it. It was only mafis, although I was sittin' down so if I was goin' weak at the knees, I didn't really notice it. It happened me on a plane once. I was on me way back from the toilet and all of a sudden, me legs just went from under me and I fell in front of half the plane. Needless to say, I was mortified. I was standin' waitin' for me bag later and I was convinced I could hear all the fuckers sayin' 'There's that young-one that fell on her ear.' Me da thinks it could have been that STD or DDT or whatever ya call it. The deep vein trombone. The thing ya get when your arse goes numb from sittin' in the same position for so long but thank the lord nothin' came of it. Jayzis, Julie Walsh must have that all the time.

We watched a film as well last night. He asked me to pick one out of his collection so I went for the *Lion King* straight away, mainly coz it's funny and romantic but not too serious. Tracy told me somethin' about cartoon films bein' the best for couples to watch although I can't remember why. It was nice, the two of us lyin' there watchin' the *Lion King*, him rubbin' me ear and playin' with me hair and all the rest of it. It really got me in the mood for the sex.

✽✽✽

The pot plant has a name. I swear to god. No word of a lie, I heard Marie today callin' it Cliff. Really. I'm not lyin'. There she was today sittin' in the canteen, although why we call it a canteen I'll never know. I've seen bigger en suites. Anyway, she was sittin' in the canteen, the pot plant on the table in front of her, a Toffee Crisp in her hand and just as I walk by the door, she says, 'So what d'ya think about that Cliff?' I'm wonderin' if there's anyone in there with her and poke me head in the doorway tryin' not to let her see me and there's no one there only Marie and the pot plant and I'm wonderin' if she might be on one of them hands-free phone things. Ya know the ones that makes it look like you're talkin' to yourself but it doesn't really look like she is and then she says, 'It looks like its only me and you now Cliff.' At this stage, I'm thinkin' I'm goin' mad, never mind Marie. I mean, there was definitely no one else in the room and she really can't have been on one of them phone things and as I said, we've seen her talkin' to the pot plant before. She's started bringin' it places with her like if she's on tills, she'll have it beside her or she'll bring it to the toilet with her and when she hasn't got it, its on the window ledge in the canteen. What's funny is though is that she doesn't think we notice, although how could we not?

Why did she call it Cliff I wonder? Maybe its after Cliff Richard. I wonder does she like Cliff Richard. She never really said although she never really says much to us anyways. She's usually too stoned to talk. Maybe its Jimmy Cliff? Who's he? I've heard the name. I think he's a reggae singer. Was one of the fellas in *Cool Runnin's* called Cliff? No that was Sanka I'm thinkin' about. Maybe she called it after cliff, ya know, like the side of a mountain like the cliffs of Moher or whatever. I was there on a school tour. It was shite.

May

Mayday! Mayday! That's what they always say in them films. Ya know the ones from the war when the planes about to crash. I mean, what's the deal with that? Would they not shout, 'The planes about to crash!' or 'I'm crashin'!' or even, 'Ah shite!' What's the point in shoutin' mayday? What use will that do ya?

Its Mayday today. The first of May already, can ya believe it? I don't know where the time is goin'. It doesn't seem that long ago that it was Easter although that was only three weeks ago but Paddy's day and even Christmas and the New Year don't seem long gone but here we are in the middle of summer already although ya know what it's like in Ireland — pissin' rain and not a ray of sunshine in sight. The only thing keepin' me goin' is the fact that we don't have long left til we go to Gran Canaria. I can't wait. Its goin' to be only deadly. Only two months to go and that's not really that long when ya think about it.

Yeah. Mayday. Why do they call it that? Why is it so special like? It's the start of the month. Big fuckin' deal. They don't have special names for the start of the other months. Like back in the old days, me da says they had loads of traditions and all coz it was somethin' to do with the start of summer but they don't do it anymore. Now they just have riots. Our Bopper was convinced he was goin' to see a riot. Convinced of it. He was ragin' he missed the one last year with all them countries joining the European Union and all the rioters were marchin' down the Navan Road to that government place in the Phoenix Park where all the foreign presidents and all stay and I wouldn't even mind but we don't live too far from that. Well it's walking distance from Finglas if ya walk fast. I remember the next day seein' all the bus shelters and all, smashed to pieces, I'm not jokin' ya. Concepta was on her way home and couldn't get passed coz the riot was goin' on. So ya know her. She just pushes her way through everyone, sendin' hippies and communists flyin', givin' a few sly digs to anyone lookin' at her funny. A police woman in all the riot gear grabbed her and Concepta turned around and told her she couldn't give a shite about the European Union, that all she wanted to do was get home in time for Coronation Street. The police woman helped her and all.

There was a riot a year or two before that in town as well. I know coz I was in town at the time and d'ya think the 39 could get down Dame Street? The traffic was a nightmare. I just got out and walked up Manor Street and rang me da to come and collect me but he wouldn't coz he was afraid the car would get hopped on by a bunch of hippies, not that he gave a fuck about his only daughter bein' hopped on by a bunch of hippies.

That time they had the riot on the Navan Road, the year of the EU thing, it was all over the news that the Wombles were comin' over and Jasmin was real excited. She couldn't sleep for three days 'til Tracy told her that it wasn't the Wombles from the telly but a group that's always at riots. Me cousin Jacinta, sorry, I mean Pussywillow, Jayzis, I'll never be able to say that with a straight face, she was meant to be comin' over for the riot that year but she doesn't believe in airplanes coz they pollute the air, use oil and they're owned by companies that don't respect the environment. We told her to get the boat but she said the same thing about the ferry companies. I don't think she realized I actually meant fuck off. I told me Uncle Dessie to tell her to swim but I don't think he did and even if he did, she wouldn't.

Yeah so there was no riot today. Not even a small argument outside McDonalds on Grafton Street so our Bopper wasn't impressed, although he's just sayin' that. He'd be runnin' away. He's not really one for violence our Bopper but he does love a bit of drama.

✷✷✷

Yenta can speak Spanish. I swear to god. Her and Jasmin were there last night havin' a conversation in Spanish. I mean, can ya believe it? There the two of them were laughin' and jokin' and talkin' in Spanish. Spanish. I even asked Tracy and they speak Turkish in Turkey, not Spanish and not only that but Tracy says Yenta can speak not only Turkish, English and Spanish but Arabic and a bit of French and German as well. Six languages. I struggle with English and she speaks six languages. What is she? A machine? I'll tell ya what she is. She's a terrorist. There's no other explanation for it. The girl can make bombs, fly planes and speak six languages. Now if that doesn't mean she's a terrorist, I don't know what does. I spent the whole night lookin' for little clues but all the others kept talkin' to her all the time so it was very hard coz I was thinkin' to meself that she wouldn't do anythin' with us around. I even followed her into the toilet two or three times but she did nothin' suspicious or unusual. She did offer me some lip gloss but I didn't take it because I was thinkin' there might be poison on it. Ya can't be too careful. One minute I could be puttin' Cherry Tube on me lips and the next, I could be dead on the floor of the toilet in Break For The Border. Its been known to happen. Well it hasn't but ya know what I'm tryin' to get at.

✳✳✳

Lance is in an awful state. Ya know Tracy's fella Lance. Ya wanna see the bruises on him. Purple and yellow and everythin'. I was horrified, I really was. Now fair play to him, he gave as good as he got and let the truth be told, it was a deadly fight. Even our Bopper said and he's not usually one for violence.

Anyway, what happened was, we were out last night, a good few of us — meself, Bopper, Jasmin, Tracy, Lance, me fella Dave, Sheila, Concepta and the terrorist, sorry, I mean Yenta. Paulo was out with us for a bit too but he had a headache and went home early. Paulo's worryin' me again. He's been very quiet lately. Maybe he's distraught coz I'm goin' out with someone now and he can't have me. He always had a soft spot for me. I'll give him a ring later and see what's goin' on.

So there we were in Bad Bobs not gettin' evacuated and havin' a great night. ya know all the usual crack. Gettin' drunk, dancin', followin' Yenta to make sure she's not up to anythin'. I'm convinced she had somethin' to do with that tear gas a few weeks ago. Jasmin and Bopper were givin' it loads to Girls Aloud. Ya know what the two of them are like. They're mad with all the moves although whatever about Bopper, Jasmin looks a bit spasticated doin' it. That Yenta one can dance rings around everyone. She'd put Janet Jackson to shame. I wonder would it have anythin' to do with her bein' a terrorist.

So we left Bad Bobs anyway, well we had to, it was closed, and we went to that Charlie's Chinese place for somethin' to eat. Nothin' like a nice Chinese after a night out, especially when there's a gang of yiz and ya can get a few different things. I do miss Bernie coz we used to go halves on a chicken balls, curry sauce, chips and fried rice. Concepta asked me to go halves with her last night. She must be fuckin' jokin'. I'd have a chicken ball and a bit of rice and she'd have the rest of it finished.

So there we were havin' our Chinese. I made Dave get a few things with me in the end. Even the Singapore noodles that Sheila has us all eatin'. Lance was comin' back from the toilet and this gobshite, a big thick ugly fucker, bumps into him and Lance turns around and says sorry even though he shouldn't have and your man starts callin' him a prick and all the rest of it and Lance, fair play to him, just says sorry and walks back to us, ignorin' your man.

So we had the food finished and went outside. I mean, we had to coz it was closin' and we needed to get the Nitelink and we're walkin' and next minute, your man from the Chinese runs up behind Lance and pushes him. Now, strangely enough, this happens in the same place in Temple Bar that the big argument happened that time before Paddy's day. The night that Bernie and Tracy nearly battered each other. So your man from the Chinese comes up and pushes Lance. The one that he bumped into, not the one from behind the counter. Jayzis. Can ya imagine Bruce Lee comin' up and pushin' Lance in the middle of Temple Bar? He'd shit his kacks and run away. Anyway, the other bloke pushes

Lance and he turns around and your man asks him is he lookin' for a fight and Lance says 'No. I'm lookin' for Westmoreland Street.' But your man doesn't even answer and just punches Lance and starts layin' into him and we're all speechless and Dave is tryin' to join in to help Lance but I won't let him until your mans mate joins in and the two of them are batterin' Lance and Dave and Tracy is screamin' and I'm tryin' to get our Bopper to join in but he's screamin' more than Tracy. So eventually, we can't hold Concepta back any longer and she barges in, fists flyin', batterin' the two young-fellas and next minute, Yenta runs up and this does flyin' kick and hit's the first fella in the face with her six inch heels. I'm not jokin' ya, it was like somethin' out of the X-men films. It must be somethin' she learned in the terrorist trainin' camp.

Anyway, the two young-fellas hadn't a chance with Yenta and Concepta and they just left them on the ground and we all walked off to get the bus, Concepta callin' them bastards and Yenta shoutin' at them in whatever language it was, one of the six she speaks. We thought it best to walk in case the guards came along. Ya know yourself. We didn't run or anything. We walked. Very quickly now, but we walked. I wouldn't have been able to run in them strapless stilettos anyway. I could hardly walk let alone run but we eventually got on the Nitelink and apart from Lance endin' up lookin' like he'd fallen off the side of a mountain, everyone was grand. Yenta is definitely a terrorist though.

✳✳✳

Me Uncle Dessie was around yesterday and was in an awful state. I haven't seen him lookin' this bad since he came back to live here from England and that was a good while ago. A few years at this stage. He came around for dinner and we were sittin' there. Meself, himself, me ma and da and our Bopper and he didn't even make one joke about me ma's cookin' and the last time he was around, she was only short of fuckin' him out. She wasn't impressed at all but what he said about her meatballs that time was true. They were a little rubbery but I think she's started puttin' jellies into everythin' coz Concepta gave us that many that the press is startin' to bend in the middle coz of the weight of them and every time we think we're gettin' through them, she gives us more. Me ma's doin' everythin' she can to get rid of them without wastin' them. She has herself convinced that they're not fattenin' so she has an excuse to eat them. Bopper told her the other day that he thinks she's puttin' on weight to annoy her. She nearly fucked him out of the house.

Yeah, me Uncle Dessie just wasn't himself at all yesterday. He seems kinda different although he wouldn't tell us. Well at least me or Bopper anyway. He could have told me ma but she wouldn't tell us. He's startin' to worry me a bit coz he's startin' to act his age and that's not like me Uncle Dessie. For a long time he was goin' through his hip hop phase, thinkin' he was a 19 year old black kid. Him and Jasmin were gas although then her and Bopper started gettin' all pally again. I think Dessie misses Bernie a little bit as well. They're very close, especially coz she's me best mate and then with her lendin' him that money and all. I still never found out what that was for and I must coz it might have somethin' to do with why he's not himself. Maybe its somethin' to do with Jacinta/Pussywillow and her tree in the path of a motorway outside Birmingham or maybe he found out where Doris is, although at this stage, I'd say it would be easier to find a virgin in Finglas.

※

I was in the shop today, the one I work in like, working like, and I was tryin' to sort out a delivery of magazines we just got. I would have got Sheila to do it but there was war after the last time. She got all the subscriptions wrong and Mrs O'Driscoll got *Hard Hot Husbands* instead of *Christian Fortnightly* and ya can imagine the reaction, although let the truth be told, I would have paid to see the look on Mrs O'Driscolls face when she saw the cover of *Hard Hot Husbands*.

There I was anyway, standin' there beside the ice cream fridge tryin' to sort out the magazines and tryin' to figure out the balls they had made of the last delivery and I look up and notice Mister O'Toole that lives across the road from me walkin' into the shop so I just smiled at him, said hello and went back to the magazines. I got a bit side tracked by an article in the *Economist* about terrorism in some place called Yemen, wherever that is, but I thought it might be helpful with the whole Yenta situation.

So the next time I look up, there's Mister O'Toole with a Yop in his hand, holdin' it at head height and starin' at me behind it so I just kinda moved out of his view, kinda like I was gettin' somethin'. So then a couple of minutes pass and Dymphna comes over to me and says, 'Joanna, I think that auld-fella is starin' at ya,' and I look up and as obvious as I don't know what, he's pretendin' to be readin' the back of a Cornflakes box but he's kinda peekin' around the side of it and at this stage, I was gettin' a little bit freaked out. So real loud so he hears me I says, 'I'm goin' into the staffroom for me break,' and go to leave and Julie Walsh shouts after me, 'You were just on your break,' the dizzy cow. So I go in the back and go into the office and look at Mister O'Toole on the cameras and he kinda waits a minute starin' at the door I've just gone through, waitin' to see if I'll come back out and then he walks up to the till, picks up a Toffee Crisp, pays for it and leaves. Now if that's not weird then tell me what is.

✳✳✳

Dessie is in trouble. I know he is coz I rang him today and all he said was, 'Joanna this isn't the right time.' And I know Dessie and he would never talk to me like that. Ever. Its just not like him. He's not himself at all and I'd notice coz not only am I his niece but I feel like I'm his mate as well, if ya get me?

I rang our Bopper to see if he knew anythin' but he didn't. He said he hadn't talked to Dessie since he was around in our house there on Sunday. At this stage, I'm gettin' worried, mainly because I don't know what's goin' on. Ya know me, I don't like bein' kept in the dark about anythin'.

I wonder what it is though. He better not have got some young-one pregnant. I mean, it's the type of thing he'd do. Not on purpose or anythin' but by accident. Everyone would be callin' him Georgie Burgess! Can ya imagine?

For some reason I think it might have somethin' to do with me Aunt Doris. Its just this feelin' I have in me waters. Call it woman's instituation or whatever but I don't know what it is. Its just the way he's actin'. Maybe Pussy-willow told him where Doris was or maybe Nigel told Bernie and she told Dessie although I'd say she would have told me. She said she'd ring tonight so she better spill all the gossip or I'll go all the way over there and reef her.

∗∗∗

I'm goin' to London next week. No really I am. Bernie rang me last night and said she had a ticket for me and I'm delighted coz it's her birthday and her graduation from her course while I'm goin' to be there. I'm leavin' here on the Friday afternoon and get back here on the followin' Tuesday night so I'm there for a few days and it means I have ages to hang out with Bernie. I was goin' to get her a birthday present and send it over but now I can give it to her meself.

She says Dervla is dyin' to meet me and that I'm goin' to love Dervla coz she's a sound young-one and ya can have a great laugh with Dervla and Dervla loves dancin' and havin' a few drinks of a night out and Dervla's mad into the Abba songs and loves *Muriel's Weddin'*. I'm sure Dervla's lovely, especially the way Bernie's been goin' on about her. The two of them are the best of mates at the moment and only for she rang me last night with the tickets to go see her, I'd have thought she was startin' to forget who I am, startin' to forget who always watched *Muriel's Weddin'* with her, who her best friend is. I'm sure Dervla's lovely.

She says she had two invitations to her graduation thing so straight up I'm wonderin' where this is goin' and I'm thinkin' to myself that her ma is comin' with me but then she's goin' on about not wantin' to hurt anyone's feelin's and that she didn't wanna ask Tracy coz she has exams soon and about Jasmin not bein' able to get off work and all the rest of it so I forgot to ask her who else is comin' coz somehow the conversation changes to me Uncle Dessie but she doesn't have a clue what's wrong and Nigel hasn't said anythin' to her and I told her not to tell Nigel in that case coz he's me Uncle Dessie's son and he'd just worry but Bernie's very worried and she says she has to go coz Dervla is callin' her for pizza and she just says she'll talk to me soon and hangs up.

Half an hour later, I'm sittin' there wonderin' who else is comin' to London and I get a phone call off Concepta and I answer and I don't even get a chance to say hello before she shouts, 'Guess who's goin' to London next week!' Fuck that.

※

I picked up a piece of paper in work today and no word of a lie, it had 'Marie loves Cliff' written on it. Now I can't remember if I said it before but that pot plant that Marie has been carryin' around is called Cliff. She even says good mornin' to it when she walks in and good night when she's leavin' and when she's in the shop she carries it around with her and at this stage, she won't even talk to anyone else unless she has to. Leandra tried tellin' her the other day that it was only a pot plant but she just gave her a dirty look and walked off.

I have to say, the hash has definitely done somethin' to her brain at this stage. Like a few months ago she was grand, havin' the bit of laugh with us, slaggin' off Julie Walsh, tryin' to take the piss out of that Jason spa if he was in and all the rest of it but now she just walks around in this kinda trance like she's so stoned she doesn't know what's goin' on although to be honest, maybe she is but there's no way someone can be stoned that much and surely her family have noticed. I mean, she has kids and grand kids and all and she can't be walkin' around like a zombie talkin' to pot plants and packets of Cheese Strings around them, although I've met her son and he's even more of a hash head than his ma and that's sayin' somethin'.

I was thinkin' maybe it was some sort of hash plant, Cliff this is, but Leandra tells me all hash plants have them leaves that ya do see on the Bob Marley tee-shirts and Cliff doesn't look like that at all. I can't believe I'm callin' a pot plant Cliff. To be honest, I think its gettin' a bit weird at this stage. Poor Leandra doesn't know what she walked into. I bet she's ragin' she took the job what with mad Marie, smelly Dymphna, lazy hole Julie Walsh, up his own hole Jason and Boris and Sheila. I think I'm the only one that's any way normal, although Sheila and Boris aren't too bad, just that they're hard to understand. I think that's why Leandra isn't a bitch to me anymore. Coz she knows I have to put up with it all as well. If its bad for us, can ya imagine what poor Cliff has to go through?

✳✳✳

Dave is really startin' to spoil me now. Really. Not that I'm complainin' or anythin'. Jayzis no. He can spoil me as much as he likes. To be honest with ya, I think its deadly. Its been a long time since a fella treated me this well and sometimes I can't really believe its real. I don't mean to sound soppy or anythin' but he is a really great fella and he's mad about me and I'll be honest and say I'm mad about him.

He rings me yesterday when I was in work and he asks me if he can meet me later and I says no problem. The girls hadn't got in touch with me about doin' anythin' so I had nothin' better to do, although Concepta had been talkin' about headin' up to Farley's for a few drinks but at that stage, I'd heard nothin' from her and she ended up goin' up with Tracy, Lance and Paulo anyways.

I met Dave at the Central Bank as usual. Its kind of a thing we have. I'm not overly fond of the Central Bank to be honest but its handy. He made me meet him there one Saturday afternoon and I was sayin' never again. I was sittin' there and these mosher gothic spas were all sittin' around me and this fella on a skateboard nearly goes over me foot and next time he goes past, I just pushed the fucker off his skateboard. Ya wanna see the blood. Now I wasn't expectin' that and ya wanna see the looks I was gettin' off all the others. I told Dave he tripped over a rock when he eventually turned up. Never again of a Saturday afternoon I told him.

So I met him there last night and it was all the usual stuff. I ask where we're going and he says it's a surprise. I think he just does that to annoy me and then the two of us just walk through Temple Bar and we cross that Millennium Bridge yoke. It bounces as ya walk across it. I would have kept goin' across it all night only Dave would have thought I was mad. I never noticed that before. The homeless fella sleepin' in the middle of it must feel awful sea sick.

We went to a lovely Italian restaurant just through the gap in the building's there that I didn't even know existed and what the name of it was, I can't remember but it was a lovely place with the reddish kinda lights and the table cloths with the candle in the middle of the table and the Italian music in the background and all the rest of it. They even had lasagne and that was only mafis, the nicest lasagne I've had this long time. Even better than me ma's.

Dave wanted to sit beside the window so we could watch everyone pass by and I would have said he only wanted to perve at the young-ones passin' by but he was payin' for the meal and I didn't want to cause an argument so we got a table by the window in the end and we're sittin' there eatin' our food, drinkin' our Sauvignon Blanc from Tuscany, wherever the fuck that is, and I look up and who's walkin' by starin' me out of it only Mister O'Toole that lives across the road from me, no word of a lie, walkin' really slow and just starin' me out of it. I got such a fright that I nearly dropped me wine. Nearly. Can ya imagine me droppin' good alcohol?

Anyway, I just put the whole thing down to coincidence or somethin'. I was thinkin', just because he passed by the restaurant I was eatin' in, starin' me out of it, doesn't mean he's stalkin' me despite what happened in the shop the other day and that day he had the binoculars when I had to get out of the bath that time to get the phone so I just forgot about it and said nothin' but then five minutes later, I look up and there he is again, only this time he's walkin' slower and still starin' me out of it. It was at that stage that I started gettin' freaked out but I said nothin' to Dave. Maybe it was just a coincidence or then again, maybe Mister O'Toole was followin' me, although ya can't blame him. He's a only a man after all and I'm a very good lookin' young-one.

※※※

Yenta was tellin' me all about Black November last night or Black September or Black October or whatever it is. Some black month anyway and I think that might be the terrorist group she's in coz she knows loads about them. Loads! Too much ya could say. We were around in Concepta's for a few drinks, just a girlie night in although we felt sorry for Paulo coz Jasmin and Bopper never rang him to go out with them so we made him come with us. There was just me, Concepta, well obviously she was there, it was her house, Tracy, Sheila, Yenta and Concepta's sister with the weird name, Veronica, although she's only 15 so she doesn't really count. 15 years old, not stone, although she must be more. Anyway, we're sittin' there and Concepta has us all locked on the cocktails. The blender was goin' all night and fair play to her, she bought all the drink herself and we're all stuffin' our faces on the 40 million jellies she has on the table in front of us and somehow, don't ask me how coz I can't remember coz I was fairly locked at this stage but someone says somethin' about god knows what and Yenta and Tracy start havin' a chat about that Munich film and Tracy says somethin' about Black November or whatever they're called and Yenta starts goin' into mad detail about them, tellin' us all about the places they get people to join them from and she even mentioned Turkey and I think she was givin' us some kind of hint although at the time I was a bit too drunk to notice and she knows all the terrorist attacks they did and all the rest of it. I mean, if that's not her tryin' to tell us somethin' then I don't know what is. I'm thinkin' is there some kind of place ya can ring to report terrorists although I'd feel dreadful doin' it coz she's such a lovely young-one and she's a great bit of laugh and as I said before, she's the best dancer I've seen this long time but the thing is, would I be able to live with meself if somethin' happened and I could have stopped it? If she is a member of Black August then who knows what she's plannin'!

✳︎✳︎✳︎

I'm fuckin' knackered. Wrecked I am. I hardly got a wink of sleep all night. Not for want of tryin' mind you. I lay there half the night tryin' to get to sleep but no matter how hard I tried I just couldn't. I even went downstairs and got meself a glass of whiskey but that did fuck all. It must have been around six when I eventually dozed off and I had to be up and all at half eight coz I was in work at ten. I mean, its just a disgrace.

Ya see, Petulia next door got a new dog and the little fucker barked the whole night. The dog this is, not Petulia although she has been known to bark on a few occasions herself. Me ma will tell ya. Ya mightn't believe me but nothin' would surprise ya with Petulia. Nothin'. The woman is a bit of a nutter. I mean, nobody hides it or anythin'. It's a well known fact and the older she gets, the more of a nutter she becomes.

Her new dog is a little shit of a thing. A jack russell I think he is and he's as ugly as fuck, although he'd be nothin' to his owner if he wasn't. Petulia is more lassie than lass if the truth be told. I've often heard people shout 'Here girl' when she walks down the road and I wouldn't mind but I've seen her turn to look. No word of a lie.

The dog for the size of the yoke, has the loudest bark I've ever heard in me life. Its like somethin' out of Jurassic Park and I wouldn't mind but Petulia put it out the back all night and wouldn't take it in and she lives on her own and all, the miserable cow. No wonder the poor thing was barkin' all night, although it just better stay the fuck away from me coz I'll drown the little bollix.

✳︎✳︎✳︎

Bernie rang today askin' was I all set for London, although the real reason she was ringin' was to make sure I was still goin' after hearin' about Concepta comin' but to be a hundred percent honest with ya, I'm only delighted that Concepta is comin' coz I wasn't really lookin' forward to the idea of gettin' on a plane on me own, even if it is only to London. I'd be fuckin' hopeless anyway. I'd end up gettin' on the wrong plane and endin' up in Cairo or one of these other mad places in Saudi Irania and me luggage would be in the Canaries. I'm no good at that sort of thing although in fairness, I'd say Bernie knew that and thought I'd be grand with Concepta goin'.

Me and Concepta are the best of mates lately anyways. She's been great since Bernie left, I have to say. She's goin' out of her way to make sure I'm okay and she's comin' out with me all the time and when we do go out we have a good laugh. Not that we didn't before but I feel a lot closer to her now than I did before Bernie left and if anythin', I thought it would have been Tracy I would have got closer to but she spends a lot of her time with Lance. A lot more than I spend with my Dave although they're in college together and me and Dave both have full time jobs so we're a lot busier.

She was talkin' about Dervla again, Bernie was. Dervla's after doin' up her room, Bernie says. A lovely light purple colour and a bright pink. She said its gorgeous, that we'd love it when we see it and that Dervla is goin' to share with Bernie so me and Concepta can have her room, fair play to her. Bernie and Dervla have great craic livin' together Bernie tells me, great craic. To me, this Dervla young-one is startin' to sound like a pain in the hole but Bernie seems to like her so I won't say anythin'. Obviously I told Concepta all about her and although we haven't met her, she agrees.

※

That fuckin' dog. I swear to god, I'm goin' to cut the little fucker's voice box out when I get it. Petulia only loves it, or so she says. How much can she love it if she's leavin' the poor thing out the back for the whole night barkin' and keepin' half of Dublin awake. Me ma gave me these things to put in me ears that she got on a flight goin' to New York there the year before last and they worked grand there the night before last but then I couldn't hear the alarm goin' off in the mornin' and I was late for work so they ended up bein' fuck all use. Petulia must be deaf or somethin' coz I said it to her this mornin' goin' out that the dog barks a lot and she said she hadn't noticed, although to be honest, Petulia wouldn't notice a rhino if it had its horn shoved up her arse.

The dog's name is Disco. I swear to god. Disco. That's what she called him. I wonder does it have anythin' to do with it bein' as loud as a disco out our back every night? She only has him a few days and already I'm on the verge of murder and not even the dog coz I'd be barkin' like mad if Petulia was my owner. If it goes on much longer I'll have to sneak in some night and let him go free, although Petulia says he can get onto the wall in the back garden already. I wouldn't mind but I can't even got on that wall. Its seven foot high.

Maybe there's somewhere I can ring just to scare the shite out of her although I'll give it a few days to see if Disco calms down a bit. He's probably still sufferin' with shock after realisin' he's gonna be livin' with Petulia.

✳✳✳

I'm just out of the shower and I'm standin' there in the nip lookin' in the mirror pluckin' me eyebrows. I had a towel around me as well but other than that I was starkers. Anyway there I was pluckin' away. Me eyebrows were a state coz I hadn't done them in ages but next minute I hear a sound so stop and listen for a few seconds and its gone so I start pluckin' again and next thing I hear the doorbell so I walk down the stairs and answer the door coz there was no one else in. Don't ask me where they were but they weren't in the house.

Anyway, I get downstairs and open the door, me standin' there in a towel with a tweezers in me hand and I look around and there's no one there. So I wait a few seconds and have a good look around to make sure there definitely isn't anyone there and shut the door. So I go back up the stairs thinkin' to meself that I'm hearin' things and I just start pluckin' me eyebrows again when the doorbell rings again. So I go back down the stairs to see who it is and just as I swing open the door, Mister O'Tooles door across the road slams closed and then a couple of seconds later, I see him tryin' to peek out behind the net curtains in his livin' room and I have to say, I'm freaked out over it. I'm wonderin' should I tell someone about him coz he is bein' a bit weird at this stage. I mean, he's a grown man and I'm only a young-one.

✱✱✱

There was madness this mornin'. Madness. I woke up to a commotion out the back garden and at first I thought the gaff was bein' broken into or somethin'. I mean, the noise was unreal and that fuckin' dog was goin' ballistic. It was the worst I've heard him. So I manage to drag meself out of bed and go to the window, pull back the curtain and look out and there's me ma standin' there with her arms folded and me da with a big bit of bamboo in his hand and Petulia from next door is out her own back up a ladder lookin' down into the gap between our shed and the wall and the dog is still barkin' like mad even though I can't see the little shite.

I'm wonderin' what's goin' on, thinkin' maybe someone lost somethin' down the side of the shed so I grab me housecoat and go downstairs and go out the back and me ma and da and Petulia all turn to look at the same time and I just says 'What's goin' on?' and Petulia, now this is as true as god, she was as serious as I don't know what. Petulia says 'Disco was walkin' on the wall and fell down between the shed and the wall.' I couldn't help it, I know its terrible, but I just had to laugh and all I could do was try to keep it in long enough to tell Petulia that it was dreadful and go back inside.

Now in fairness, it was fuckin' hilarious although the poor little thing must have been terrified although it was its own fault for climbin' on the wall, the stupid mutt of a dog. They had to knock a bit of the wall down to get him out in the end and all, although it was only a little bit. Me ma said Petulia's in an awful state. I asked over the dog or just in general. She didn't answer.

***

Meself and Concepta got to London, or should I say, the arse end of nowhere miles and miles away from London, and we were just too tired to do anythin' but chill out. I mean, we had all the flyin' and the airport shit yesterday and then we had a nice relaxin' night and tonight we're goin' mad coz its Bernie's birthday and all of us are real excited.

Me Uncle Dessie insisted on leavin' me and Concepta out to the airport yesterday although we were both delighted of the offer coz we were just goin' to get a taxi and that would have cost us a good few quid. I mean, its ridiculous the price of taxis these days and ya wouldn't mind but ya get into the taxi and the driver complains about everythin' else.

Dessie still isn't in the best of form but he was delighted that we were goin' to see Bernie and Nigel as well, especially coz he hasn't seen Nigel since Christmas and I'd say its hard for me Uncle Dessie with his two kids livin' in England and his wife havin' run off with a young-fella.

Anyway, we get to the airport and Dessie gives meself and Concepta a big hug and tells us to enjoy ourselves which we were both plannin' on doin' anyway so we go and do all the usual check-in shite. All I had off Bernie was a number, no tickets or anythin' but the girl with no eyebrows caked in 14 layers of foundation behind the counter seemed to know what it was.

Concepta wanted to go to McDonalds, ya know what she's like but I'd just had somethin' before I left so I told her to just forget it and we went through to the departure gate and we're goin' through the x-ray things and the thing didn't beep or anythin' but one of the security young-ones told Concepta to spread her arms out to be checked and ya wanna see the look Concepta gave her. I mean, just because we have a friend that's a terrorist doesn't mean we are too.

We tried to get duty free vodka as well but we nearly got arrested over that too. Concepta said all we had to do is name somewhere outside the European Union when they were askin' us where we were flyin' to so we got two litre bottles of the Smirnoff and true enough, your woman behind the till asks where we're flyin' to and Concepta says Nairobi and your woman looks her up and down and tells her there's no flights from Dublin to Nairobi, wherever the fuck that is anyway and the two of them start arguin' and Concepta is tellin' her that Aer Lingus just started flyin' to Nairobi and that's when your woman threatened to have us arrested so we just left the vodka and go to the gate to get the flight.

I have to say, it was a grand flight. Only 50 minutes and ya know Ryanair, its like gettin' on a bus. Officiant I think the word is although Dessie hates them, although can ya blame him when his cloths ended up in Sydney and him only flyin' Stansted to Dublin.

Bernie was there at the airport to meet us as well and I was delighted to see her. We were all there givin' each other hugs and all the rest of it and Dervla was with her and we got introduced to her and she seems nice enough although Tracy says that's what they say about some fella called Mussolini, or maybe it was Ravioli, I can't remember, some fella that owns a chipper anyway. Dervla seemed delighted to meet us and Bernie was only thrilled to see us and all the rest of it and dyin' to find out all the gossip so I didn't know where to start. I have to say, its only deadly seein' her.

***

Oh good God. I have to have the worst hangover in history. I'm in a fuckin' state and I wouldn't mind but Bernie wants us to go to London. All I can say is they better have a toilet on the train coz I won't be leavin' it.

We got up yesterday mornin' and thought it'd be a good idea to see this town she lives in. Bishops Stortford its called. She made us walk the half hour walk to get to the town centre. Now when I say town, its more like a little village. I mean, we were around all the shops in half an hour and there was fuck all we wanted to buy. I mean, Next in England sells the same stuff as Next in Dublin. Meself and Concepta went to KFC to get a bite to eat, ya know Concepta, a large meal and a box of popcorn chicken and an ice cream, not a bother to her. Then the three of us went to the off-licence to get a bit of booze for before goin' out tonight, just two bottles of the sauvignon blanc, a bottle of the Ernest and Julio rosé for Concepta, a big bottle of West Coast Cooler for Dervla and a bottle of vodka between all of us. We walked all the way back to the house and got stuck into the drink and by the time we were ready and goin' out, we were hammered. Yenta text Concepta to ask how we were gettin' on and Concepta told her we were locked and Yenta said we better not get on the London Eye, ya know that big wheel thing. Concepta says Yenta meant it as a joke coz we'd get sick bein' locked but I'm thinkin' she's tellin' us not to get on the London Eye coz her terrorist mates are gonna blow it up. Ya'd never know with Yenta. Dervla laughed and said there's no way Yenta is a terrorist but Dervla doesn't know her and anyways, Dervla's a sap. She is. I'll be honest now and say I don't like the young-one. I know her and Bernie are great mates but she wouldn't be my cup of tea.

 I made Bernie ring a taxi to take us back into the town coz me hole was I walkin', not in the shoes I was wearin'. We went to that Chicago's place that Bernie was tellin' me about and it kinda reminds me of Bondi back home. I had a deadly night. Brilliant it was. Bernie and Dervla introduced me to a few of the people they were doin' the trainin' course with. The young-ones all seemed nice enough and the fellas were all a good laugh although most of them were mingin' and more than half of them were gay so my Dave had nothin' to worry about.

 Concepta was everyone's best mate by the end of the night, ya know what she's like, impressin' all the Swedish people doin' the course with her little bit of Swedish she learned in Galway and she brought some young-one over to say hello to me that was from St Lucia, wherever the fuck that is. I've never heard of it. Things started goin' blank after that but Bernie tells me I was up on the dance floor in the middle of everyone pretendin' to be Britney Spears with a straw hangin' out of me ear like one of them microphones she wears when she's dancin'. Bernie says she wouldn't mind but they were playin' U2 at the time. The thoughts of gettin' on that train!

***

London is deadly. I have to say, I fuckin' love the place. We had such a crazy day yesterday. Bernie made meself and Concepta get up real early to get the train and I was in a state by the time we got to Liverpool Street Station but I started to forget about it with the excitement of goin' on the Underground. I have to say, it's only deadly. The trains go under the ground like. Amazin'.

 Concepta was starvin' so we decided to go to McDonalds so we went to the one in Leicester Square and it was deadly seein' it for real after seein' it so many times at all them premieres on the telly, Leicester Square this is, not McDonalds, although I think Concepta was more impressed with her BigMac than anythin' else and then we went to Picadilly Circus and looked around Gap and Lilywhites and all, although I said I wouldn't do any shoppin' yet coz we'd be goin' back and Bernie and Concepta wanted to go on the London Eye and I didn't want to be carryin' bags onto it.

 We got the tube to Tower Bridge, the mad lookin' one ya do see when ya see London on the telly, and we walked down the river and it was a lovely walk coz there was only the three of us and it was a nice enough day. Ya can't really see the London Eye for ages but then its just huge. There wasn't a queue or anythin' but I thought there was goin' to be. I wasn't too mad to get on it let the truth be told, mainly coz of what Yenta had said but I'd always wanted to so I said I may as well just risk it and I have to say, I'm glad we did. It was deadly. It takes ya about half an hour to get around and ya see loads of things like all the tall buildin's and all the rest of it. It was brilliant. They should have one in Dublin although there's fuck all to see in Dublin and the thing didn't even blow up. I was delighted gettin' off. I was ragin' havin' to go back to that Bishops Stortford shithole.

***

We went back to London yesterday to do our shoppin' and I'm terrified to translate what I spent back into euros coz Jayzis, was it a lot! I would have spent a whole lot more only we spent half the day lookin' for a dress for Bernie and I wouldn't mind but she bought the first one she had tried on.

We got the train from Bishops Stortford early in the mornin', too fuckin' early for my likin', and went straight to Oxford Street to meet Nigel. I was only delighted to see him and he's lookin' great, real kinda healthy lookin' and dressin' really well and all the rest of it. He was delighted to see me as well and we had a big hug although the last time he'd seen Concepta, she had been mad into him so he was a little weary of her but she was too busy thinkin' of gettin' somethin' to eat.

We went to Starbucks and I have to say, it was only mafis. I'm not one for coffee normally but I love Starbucks. I got a white chocolate mocha and a cherry Danish and I wanted more when I was finished but Bernie was dyin' to get her dress so she dragged meself, Concepta and Nigel up and down Oxford Street and she even wanted to go down Bond Street and at first I was like deadly, thinkin' it's the place that James Bond and all the secret agents are but Nigel told me its where all the designer shops are. I told Bernie she can't even afford to shop in A-wear never mind Armani so eventually she went back to Debenhams and bought a beautiful lilac dress and matchin' shoes and she looked only gorgeous in them. It meant though that meself and Concepta could start lookin' for things. Well we went crazy. H&M is only deadly in London and they have a huge Gap as well. Ya wanna see the things I picked up and we even went to the Disney Store and I got Dave a big Animal from the Muppets and I picked up our Bopper a few things coz he loves Disney films. I'm tellin' ya, London is great for the shoppin'.

Nigel dropped us all back to Bishops Stortford, although he did a bit of a tour of London showin' us Buckingham Palace and where Chelsea play and all the rest of it and we had a great laugh in the car but he couldn't stay for Bernie's wings party so we said goodbye and he said he'd be over to Dublin as soon as he can and I hope he is coz we have such a laugh.

We spent ages gettin' ready for the wings party and meself and Concepta wore some of our new cloths. Dervla's ma and da came over for it but they were stayin' at a hotel at Stansted airport where the ceremony thing was on. Ya wanna see us all sittin' there and all the people on the course up the front. It was deadly and I was really proud of Bernie, really proud of her. I was nearly cryin' and all. Concepta offered me a tissue but it looked used so I didn't take it. There was a free bar after so ya know what we're like. Meself, Concepta and Bernie got hammered and were dancin' around the place and all and we got Dervla's ma and da locked as well and it was just mental. They were up on the tables and all and Dervla's ma did the splits at one stage. Free bars and me just don't mix though so I ended up gettin' sick half the night. Bernie enjoyed it though so I suppose that's the main thing and at least I know she's happy in England now. I'll definitely be comin' back.

✱✱✱

I came home yesterday only to find me Uncle Dessie has moved into me room. No word of a lie. All me stuff was moved in with Bopper's and loads of me Uncle Dessie's stuff was in my room and ya can imagine, I nearly had a canary, not knowin' what was goin' on and I was just about to ring me ma when the front door opens and in walks me Uncle Dessie and I was in the height of it. 'What the fuck is goin' on?' I shouts at him. So he starts tellin' me that there's loads of shit goin' on over the divorce and me Aunt Doris wants half of everythin' and he has to rent out the house to four Filipino nurses for some reason and that its only goin' to be until he finds the bitch and has her shot, his words not mine, and the face on him, I'm wonderin' just how serious he is, although me Uncle Dessie wouldn't be like that, but the bitch did run off with our Nigel's best friend so who could blame him?

I felt kinda guilty then for shoutin' at him so I said sorry and gave him a big hug and then I gave him his Mickey Mouse mug and the new

Eminem CD I bought him in London and then the two of us sat down and had a cup of tea and told him all about London and what we got up to and about how Bernie was gettin' on and about me not likin' that Dervla young-one all that much and about Nigel and he told me about the Filipino nurses livin' in his house and I have to say, it was lovely. I think I might enjoy me Uncle Dessie livin' with us. I'd swap him for our Bopper any day. I wonder can we send Bopper to live with the Filipino nurses?

**

Me Uncle Dessie thinks we should drown Petulia's dog or feed him somethin' to poison him and I know what its like coz I had that room until I went to London but now that me and Bopper are at the front of the house, I can't really hear him and its not really that bad sleepin' in the same room as Bopper, even if I am on a mattress on the floor but I'll make him gimme the bed next time he needs a lend of money.

Now from what me ma and da tells me, Disco, Petulia's dog, has calmed down a lot since the day he fell down the side of the shed and they told me Uncle Dessie that he's only a pup and needs to settle into his new surroundin's, just like me Uncle Dessie has to settle into his new surroundin's and I've to settle into my new surroundin's but me Uncle Dessie said he doesn't bark and me ma says he snores loud enough which I have to agree with but he said he'd suggest a few things to Petulia to help the dog settle in better. He's only in a few days and he's already havin' problems with the neighbours. I can see him and me ma killin' each other before long. I wouldn't mind but now that he's not keepin' me awake anymore, I'm startin' to like Disco.

**

Somebody stole Cliff. I swear to god, no word of a lie. I walked into the shop this mornin' and Marie was in an awful state.

At first I thought she'd had too much hash or somethin' again but then Dymphna told me that when Marie came in this mornin', Cliff was gone. Now I know its only a pot plant but that's not on. Whatever about Marie bein' in love with it or whatever but it kept her out of trouble and kept her happy. She was very upset over it and ya normally wouldn't see Marie upset over anythin'. Its just not like her.

We're tryin' to work out who it could have been though. It was definitely one of the staff coz the last place she says she saw it was the staff room coz she says she said goodbye to it. The fact that a grown woman is admittin' that she said goodbye to a pot plant goes to show ya just how much the hash has affected her brain.

Meself and Dymphna were tryin' to think of who it could have been. It definitely wasn't me or her coz both of us left before Marie yesterday, Sheila wasn't in, Leandra left just after Marie and Julie Walsh, Boris and that Jason spa were on 'til the end of the night so that kinda narrows it down to four. I doubt Leandra would have taken it in fairness although ya never know. She's bein' givin' out about Marie doin' fuck all coz of the pot plant lately. It could easily have been Jason or Julie Walsh coz it wouldn't surprise me for them to do somethin' like that. Boris wouldn't really be that type and anyways, I think he's quite fond of Cliff himself although maybe he took it coz he wanted it for himself. I'll find out though. Miss Maple hasn't a patch on me!

❋❋❋

Dave and Yenta work together. No word of a lie, and they only realised when they were talkin' to each other last night and they must know each other well over a month at this stage.

There we all were on a night out in Bondi, the usual craic, the few drinks, the bit of dancin', Concepta talkin' to half the pub. I wasn't even mad on goin' out only me Uncle Dessie wanted to. I was just home from work and was sittin' down watchin' *Cribs* on MTV and he comes in and asks are we headin' out for the night and I says no, that I'm a bit wrecked after London still and he says he was lookin' forward to goin' out coz its his first weekend livin' in the house so I couldn't really disappoint him after all that's happened so I rang Concepta but she was just about to ring me coz she already had organised Tracy, Paulo and Yenta for goin' into town and was ringin' to try to get me to change me mind so she was delighted me and Dessie were goin'.

We had a great night, now I have to say. I like Bondi. It's a nice spot and never too crowded but I think that's coz it seems so big. They play great music as well and I'm always up and down to the dance floor all night.

We were there anyway and Dave had said to me earlier in the night that Yenta looked familiar and I thought maybe he'd seen her in the paper or somethin' coz of a terrorist attack she did or somethin' and Tracy told him that they've met each other on a few nights out but he said he knows her from somewhere else. So I was in the toilet with Concepta and Tracy and when I came back, Dave and Yenta were talkin' and they only realised that the two of them work in the same buildin'. How mad is that? The two of them were havin' a great chat. I'm wonderin' can I get him to suss her out in work for me, see if anyone else thinks she's a bit suss. Maybe he could even try and read some of the stuff on her computer. Tracy tells me ya can learn a lot about someone from their computer. We'll see what happens though.

The only thing about havin' me Uncle Dessie livin' with us is that I have to go home with him. Like I mean, I was dyin' to go back to Dave's for a bit of you know what but me Uncle Dessie was a bit locked so me ma would have battered me if I had of let him go home on his own, despite the fact that he's a grown man. I think she's afraid he'd go back to his own gaff and walk in on the Fillipino nurses. They wouldn't know what hit them, although in sayin' that, either would he.

✻✻✻

Dessie was in a bit of a state last night over somethin', very upset he was, so I told him I'd stay in with him coz me ma and da were goin' to a 50th and Bopper was doin' somethin' with Jasmin as per usual so I didn't really want me Uncle Dessie sittin' in on his own. So I was talkin' to Concepta and tellin' her why I was stayin' in and she said it was grand. Meself and Dessie are just about to order a curry an hour or so later and next minute, a knock comes to the door and who is it only Concepta and Paulo with a curry. I was delighted coz I was only starvin' and Dessie was glad of the company. The four of us sat down and watched the *Eurovision Song Contest* and ate our Chinese and we had a great night. I love watchin' the *Eurovision*. Ireland were shite the other night so weren't even in it but that's what ya expect these days. Greece won, fair play to them but I don't even think half these places do be in Europe.

The votin' does be great. Paulo was goin' mad coz Bosnia were doin' great up towards the end when they slipped back a bit. The screams out of him were unreal. He made all of us vote for them on our phones and from the gaff phone and all. I wouldn't even mind but Bosnia's song was worse than ours and ours was total shite.

***

I was havin' a bit of a lie in this mornin' coz I was on a late shift in work and next minute I hear this buzzin' noise and I thought I was havin' mad dreams but it was wakin' me up and I opened me eyes and I could still hear it and I realised it was the doorbell but I thought Dessie would be in to get it or somethin' so I closed me eyes again but then it started ringin' again and I was in the height of it coz it meant I had to get up out of bed, find a housecoat that I ended up puttin' on inside out and then go all the way downstairs to answer the door and when I opened it, there was no one there and at this stage I was goin' mad. So I was just about to close the door when I noticed a bouquet of flowers in the middle of the garden and I went to get them, a lovely bunch of flowers they were, a lovely arrangement, I have to say. There was a card with them that had Joanna written on the envelope and I took the card out and it said, 'To my darling, hope you like the flowers.' I'm wonderin' are they from Dave but it's definitely not Dave's writin'. I look around before I close the door and I can see the outline of Mister O'Toole from across the road lookin' out from behind his net curtains, not realisin' I can see him starin' me out of it and it kind of freaks me out a bit, especially when I ring Dave and he tells me that he didn't send me any flowers. And then when I was goin' to work, Petulia from next door was walkin' Disco and she asked me why Mister O'Toole was bringin' flowers to the house. I wish I fuckin' knew.

✳✳✳

Meself and Dymphna are still tryin' to work out who stole Cliff. It definitely wasn't Leandra coz we did everythin' short of torturin' her to get the information out of her. I don't think it was Boris either coz he was a bit down over the pot plant goin' missin' as well so that leaves Jason and Julie Walsh but as Dymphna says, we can't prove nothin' yet. We just have to try and get them to speak. It wouldn't surprise me in the least if it was one of them. They're like that. I'd say the two of them did it together. They probably had the whole thing planned and thought it would be great craic. If I find out it was them, they'll know all about craic coz that's the noise their noses will make when I break them.

Poor Marie is still in an awful state. She's hardly said a word all week and she's mopin' around the place actin' kinda normal but really depressed and its not like her at all. She's usually in great form, even if she is always stoned, but always in great form. We were tryin' to cheer her up and tellin' her we'd get her a new plant, a lovely ivy or somethin', maybe an aloe vera plant or a bonsai tree but all she wants is Cliff back. I feel kinda sorry for her though. I wanna do somethin' to help her but I don't know what. Maybe I'll get her a bonsai tree. Where the fuck d'ya buy bonsai trees?

✳✳✳

Me Uncle Dessie was tellin' me that he was havin' a chat with Petulia next door and he found out, god only knows how, that her real name isn't Petulia at all but Mary. I swear to god. We've been livin' next door to her for years and I've never in the whole time heard anyone callin' her Mary. Me Uncle Dessie said he got all the gossip there today when he was talkin' to her about Disco. The two of them even brought the dog to the park for a walk and he said they had a great chat.

What happened, Dessie tells me, is that when she was a young-one, back in the 60's or whatever, her friends used to say that she looked like Petulia Clarke so that's where she got the name from. Now in case ya don't know, Petulia Clarke is this singer from the 60's that sang that song *Downtown*, ya know the one — 'Downtown, things will be great when you're downtown, everythin's waitin' for you.' Me and Bernie have sung it once or twice in karaoke but I can't see how Petulia next door looks anythin' like Petulia Clarke. I mean, I look more like Mariah Carey than she looks like Petulia Clarke and I don't look anythin' like Mariah as much as I wish I did.

I wonder why she tells everyone her name is Petulia though. I mean, why not just tell people that her name is Mary. Maybe she has somethin' to hide. Maybe she's hidin' from the tax people or maybe she's a terrorist.

✳✳✳

Meself, Concepta and Tracy went into town today for a bit of shoppin'. We met Tracy after college coz she had an English exam. The poor young-one is stressed so meself and Concepta said seein' as we have the day off we'll meet her and do a bit of shoppin'. So there we were buzzin' around the shops lookin' at loads of stuff when Tracy decided she wants to go to Arnotts to look at the perfumes. I was thinkin' of hintin' at Dave to get me a new one so we went up to one of the counters and Concepta picks up one of the sample bottles and sprays it onto her wrist and has a good sniff of it and holds her wrist out for us to smell. 'That's lovely, isn't it girls?' she says as meself and Tracy have a sniff and I have to admit, its lovely so I say, 'What's it called?' and she says, really posh, or at least she was tryin' to be.

'*Viens A Moi.*'

'*Viens A Moi?*' says I. 'What the fuck does that mean?'

'*Viens A Moi* means 'come to me' in French,' Tracy tells us.

Concepta takes another sniff of her wrist and shoves it back in me face and says, 'That doesn't smell like come to me. Does that smell like come to you Joanna?'

✳✳✳

Where the fuck do ya get bonsai trees? I spent half the day in town yesterday lookin' for one and I couldn't find one although in sayin' that, it was a bit obvious that we wouldn't get one in Top Shop or Miss Selfridge's but there was no harm in tryin'. I mean, ya'd never know when ya'd get lucky and I got some lovely bits without even havin' gone in lookin' for anythin'. I got this fabulous pair of boots in Office and they were less than half price, lovely they are and I've been lookin' at them for ages and never got them. I even saw somethin' similar in London when we were there but I didn't get them then coz I thought the suitcase would be too heavy with them.

Concepta's delighted with herself coz she's a dress size smaller. I mean, its only taken her five months since her diet started all the way back in January but fair play to her. She did it even if it took ages. She was thrilled with herself and went to that Australian ice-cream place to celebrate and she bought herself a lovely top in H&M.

So we were lookin' everywhere for a bonsai tree and couldn't get one anywhere. We did see some lovely fake flowers in Dunnes but I don't think Marie would be that mad into the fake ones. I might ask Sheila where ya'd get a bonsai coz she's Chinese and that's where the bonsai's come from. I have to get one soon though coz poor Marie is in an awful state. If worse comes to worse though, I'll just have to get her a geranium.

✳✳✳

Meself and Dave had our first row last night and I wouldn't mind, it was over somethin' stupid. Ya'd hardly even call it a row. It was only small and we made up before we left but I know for a fact he's still not happy. I even text him today and he was a bit snappy with me. I wouldn't mind but it was all over Yenta, not that it was her fault or anythin' but it was over her if ya know what I mean?

We were in Fitzsimon's at the time. There was meself, Concepta, Yenta, me Uncle Dessie, Paulo, Sheila and Dave. Tracy couldn't come out coz she still has exams to do and don't even get me started on Jasmin and Bopper. They haven't been out with us in weeks, ever since Lance was in that fight. That was weeks ago.

So we were havin' a great night and even Dessie was gettin' back to his old form. Him, Paulo and Sheila were havin' a great laugh about somethin' and Concepta had made a new friend from El Salvador which Dessie tells me is near enough to Mexico, although I haven't a fuckin' clue where that is either. So I was talkin' to Dave and I asked him had he sussed Yenta out yet and he said no and I asked him why not and he said that I was actin' over the top. I mean, the cheek of him. Over the top? At the end of the day, I'm only concerned about him and the others and if Yenta is a terrorist and I wouldn't mind but he works with her as well but if she is a terrorist, we have a right to know and he said that I shouldn't be so ridiculous, that there's no way Yenta is a terrorist and that she's meant to be me friend and I should trust her and stop bein' so suspicious of her and I says, 'Why are ya stickin' up for her?' and he says, 'Coz she thinks you're really nice and she likes ya and you think she's a terrorist.' As much as I was in the height of it, I have to say I started to feel a little bit guilty although I didn't show him that. I just got up, grabbed Concepta and went to the toilet leavin' Dave there talkin' to the person from Elador or whatever the fuck it's called. I was in the height of it but we both said sorry and made up by the end of the night. I still had to go home because Dessie was with us and I wouldn't mind but Paulo and Sheila were locked as well. Palatic isn't the word. I tell ya, if Dessie keeps comin' out with us all the time, I'll have no sex life at all.

✳✳✳

I asked Dave over to the house last night coz I was there on me own. Me ma and da were in Kilkenny for some do, god only knows what it was for or when they'll be back or anythin' but they just got into the car and went yesterday afternoon, tellin' me, Bopper and Dessie to be good, not really givin' a fuck if we are or not once they had a good time. So Dessie had arranged to go out with someone, he wouldn't tell me who but he said it wasn't one of me friends. He'd be terrified coz of the way I reacted over him and Bernie goin' for meal that time and that was only coz he was sayin' thank you to her for givin' him a loan. I still never found out what that was for after all this time. I must try and get it out of him.

Bopper was out for the night with Jasmin although don't even ask me where. Bopper and Jasmin are keepin' to themselves lately and whether one of us has done somethin' on them or what, I don't know but they're actin' very strange. I must see what's happenin' there. I'm like your woman Jessica Fletcher or somethin' lately. Did ya ever notice that everywhere that Jessica Fletcher went, someone died. She was like the grim reaper only worse. Ya'd shit yourself if ya answered the door and she was standin' there.

Anyway, Dave came over and we ordered a curry and sat down to watch a DVD and after it, we were sittin' there on the couch and we started kissin' and we turned off the telly and the lights and we're there kissin' more and one thing is leadin' to another and there's cloths comin' off and all the rest of it. So to cut a long story short, the two of us were there ridin' on the couch in the front room and next minute, the door of the front room opens, the light goes on, I scream and who's standin' there only me Uncle Dessie and he hardly notices. He just says 'Don't mind me,' turns off the light and walks back out. So obviously, we couldn't finish what we started and then Bopper came in. Dave had to take my bed on Boppers floor in the end and I slept in me ma and da's room. I don't give a shite, the next time we're out, Dessie can go home on his own. I need a ride.

June

Me ma and da are still not back and none of us have heard anything from them since they left on Saturday and it's Monday now. Me Uncle Dessie tried to phone their mobiles there today but they were both off. We were all under the impression that they'd only be gone for one night so we got a bit worried when they didn't turn up last night. Not that we weren't grand or anything. We actually had a bit of a laugh, meself, Dessie and Bopper. We ordered a big curry and laid it out on the table in the livin' room and sat down to watch *The Incredibles* with a few drinks. So we had a bit of a laugh and had a nice night in. It was great to be able to just chill out coz it's a bank holiday today and none of us had to be up for work so we stayed up late and got fairly locked and after the film, the three of us just sat in the sittin' room talkin' about everything. We're gettin' on grand without me ma and da around. Had we known they wouldn't be back we would have arranged a bit of a party. That would have been a great laugh. Ya do only ever think of these things when its too late.

✳✳✳

Cliff is back. No word of a lie. Marie walked into the staffroom today and there he was on the window sill lookin' better than ever, or so she tells me. We all had a good look at it, and I mean a really good look at it and we all agree that it definitely is the same pot plant as before and not a new one. Marie was thrilled as ya'd imagine. She was in great form all day and it was good to see. Boris was over the moon as well coz, as I was sayin', he liked the pot plant a lot as well. He wasn't in love with it or anything like Marie but then again, he's not always stoned like she is.

Meself and Dymphna were tryin' to find out how it just turned up again and we're convinced that whoever was in late last night must have put it back coz Dymphna opened the shop this mornin' with Marie and there was no one here before them. Leandra was workin' til close last night with Julie Walsh so it has to have been one of them and we already know it wasn't Leandra so that leaves that other cow. I knew it was Julie Walsh. I did. I just knew it and Dymphna did as well. She's the only one of us cruel enough to do something like that apart from that Jason spa and the two of them are as bad as each other. Meself and Dymphna kinda kept it to ourselves today coz its not really our place to go round accusin' people coz we don't really have any evidence despite the fact we know she stole it. I bet ya she put it back coz she knew we had an idea she took it and thought we'd forget about it if she put it back but believe me, we won't. Not after the way Marie was while it was gone. Whatever about havin' a joke or whatever but that's goin' too far. Julie Walsh will get her comeuppance though. I know for a fact coz me and Dymphna are already plannin' it.

***

Mad night last night, now it really was, even though it was only a Tuesday and all but it was a mad night. What happened was, me ma rang, at last I might add, and told us she wouldn't be home til today so I told me Uncle Dessie and he just smiled and said he'd go to Tescos and pick up a few bits for the party and I says 'What party?' and he says 'The one we're havin' tonight' and just walks out of the house. So I ring our Bopper and he's all for it so it was two against one and that meant I couldn't do anything about it, even though I thought it wasn't a good idea coz I was afraid of the gaff gettin' destroyed and me havin' to clean it. Dessie and Bopper wouldn't get up off their holes to give the place a bit of a hooverin'. I know what they're like but as I said, it was two against one so I had to go along with it whether I wanted to or not.

The first thing I did though was ring Dessie and tell him that he better get the Dyson out after the party coz there was no way I'd be doin' the cleanin'.

So I went to work, did the same shite as usual and came back to the gaff, cleaned up a bit, hid anything that looked expensive, ornaments like, put out the few tortillas and dips and boxes of Pringles that Dessie got in Tesco and went up to get ready, mad as it was with the three of us rushin' about and ya know what our Bopper is like with the bathroom. I had to batter him out of it.

So anyway, I was just ready when a knock comes to the door and who was it only Concepta, two bags full of drink with her, askin' did I want a hand with anything. Typical of that bitch showin' up when everything's done but fair play to her anyway for the offer. So they all start comin' then and for a Tuesday night there was a great turnout. There was us for a start, as in meself, Dessie and Bopper, then there was Concepta, Jasmin, Tracy, Tracy's friend Miranda that's comin' on the holiday with us, Paulo, Sheila, Yenta, me fella Dave, Tracy's fella Lance, three or four young-ones Dessie knew from somewhere, the Filipino nurses, Boppers mates Niall, Niall and Niall, no word of a lie. We were callin' them the three Nialls. Who else was there? Oh Dymphna and Marie showed up for an hour with Cliff. Marie is takin' him home with her after work now. Leandra wasn't in so I said she could. A few more of Boppers mates showed up at some stage, about 10 I think. I didn't want to say anything but I think a few of Boppers friends are gay. Now I don't know if he knows or anything so I kept it quiet. Not that I have a problem with gay people or anything. Jayzis no. I think they're great.

Jasmin was a bit off with us but maybe I was pickin' it up wrong but Concepta said she never went near her all night either. It was like she was ignorin' us. Paulo was stayin' away from Bopper and his mates although him and Bopper don't really talk much anymore anyway. Paulo and Sheila kinda sat in the kitchen all night gettin' locked.

Tracy's friend Miranda is a pain in the hole. Really she is and shes comin' on holiday with us. She's as up her own hole and she better not think she can act like that around me coz I'll have no problem puttin' her in her place and whatever about me, Concepta Cooney is worse. I've never met anyone as into themselves in me life as that Miranda young-one and fair enough, she's a good lookin' young-one but she'd be no Jennifer Lopez. I can see a few rows with her on the holiday already.

The party was a good laugh anyway and the gaff wasn't too bad and fair play to Concepta, she was doin' a bit of tidyin' all night, sortin' the rubbish and all so Dessie could bring the bottles and cans to be recycled. She even got out a cloth and a bit of Flash after everyone was gone coz she was stayin' over. I don't know how everyone fit. I made Dessie sleep in me ma's bed coz I didn't want any strangers sleepin' in it. Ya'd never know what me ma and da might catch. Me and Dave and Tracy and Lance stayed in me and Boppers room, Bopper stayed in Dessie's room with Jasmin and the three Nialls on the floor or somethin' but there's a king size bed in there so ya'd fit three of them on that. Concepta had the fold out sofa in the sittin' room with Yenta and everyone else went home, even Paulo and Sheila and they were meant to be stayin'. It must have been after six when we goin' to bed. I don't think anyone went to work although I had told Leandra about the party and she told me to take today off. Fair play to her. She said she'd come as well but never did, now that I come to think of it.

The place was spotless after. Not even a bottle cap was left and I'd made Dessie check out the back garden two or three times coz that's where we made everyone go for a smoke. I have me own little ash tray and all out there coz me ma doesn't let me smoke in the gaff and I made sure all the ornaments were put back in the right place and all but me ma walked in this evenin' and the first thing she says is 'You'se had a party.' Now how she knew I'll never know but mas always can tell things like that. I mean, the house was cleaner than when she left. Dessie just told her we had Paulo, Concepta and Tracy over on Sunday night for a film but she didn't look convinced but at the same time, she said nothing and she can't complain. She fucked off for days on end with me da and hadn't even told us when she'd be back, the bitch.

✲✲

Me ma found a bonsai tree in Kilkenny. God knows where but she brought it back for me to give to Marie, not knowin' that Cliff had returned since she left. She said I should give it to Marie anyway coz she'd be delighted with it so I said I would and brought it into work today and Dymphna told me she was in the staff room and I went in and gave it to her and she was only delighted. The only problem though was that Sheila and Dymphna had the same idea about buyin' Marie a pot plant to replace Cliff so now she not only has a whatever the fuck Cliff is but the bonsai tree I gave her, the aloe vera Dymphna gave her and a lovely little conifer that Sheila bought her. The staffroom is startin' to look a little bit like the Phoenix Park and Marie is only thrilled. The only thing is, she keeps bringin' all four of the plants with her when she's on the till and they're gettin' in the way a bit and we can't really complain coz we bought them for her, apart from Cliff and she had a tough time when he was robbed on her.

I have to say, I think Marie must be puttin' hash into our tea or something coz I think I'm goin' a little bit mad. I mean, here we are makin' all this fuss over a pot plant. Really. Its got to a stage now where we're talkin' about them like they're real people, although try tellin' Marie that Cliff's only a pot plant and see how she reacts.

***

Julie Walsh got knocked down. Not a word of a lie. She was crossin' the road this mornin' and got hit by a van. She broke her arm and has a few bruises and all but she's grand although knowin' her, we'll hear about it for months. I mean, I don't mean to be bad or anything but I'd say bein' that big kinda stopped her bein' hurt more.

I think its just comeuppance for robbin' Cliff. I do, although me and Dymphna were plannin' a few things but we don't need to do them now. I mean, she'll learn from that now. Karma its called. What goes around comes around. Me ma always says that.

The funny thing is, I know I shouldn't laugh but it was a Diet Coke van. Tracy says its ironic that someone like Julie Walsh was hit by a Diet Coke van. 'Ironic,' says I, 'Not even Alanis Morrisette would find that ironic.'

***

I went downstairs this mornin' after just wakin' up and I notice an envelope on the floor in front of the door and went to pick it up before I thought to meself that today is Saturday and there doesn't be any post of a Saturday so I thought it might have been an invitation to something that someone put through the door themselves or one of them charities that asks ya to put anything ya don't want in the porch and they'll take it. I wonder if I got our Bopper to sit out there would they take him. It'd be worth a try anyway.

I pick up this envelope and on the front it just says 'Joanna' which I have to admit, I found a little bit strange but I still thought it might have been an invitation to something, a 21st or a 50th or something, but I open it and take out the letter from inside and I get the fright of me life. I'd have pissed meself only I'd just gone before I came down the stairs. It was a white piece of paper with letters from a newspaper cut out and stuck on and all it said was: 'Her face at first just ghostly turned a whiter shade of pale.' What the fuck that means I didn't know but from the sounds of it, it didn't sound too nice. My first thought was that someone was havin' a laugh but then I said to meself that nobody would go to all that trouble just for a laugh and I've seen enough films to know about letters like that.

I was thinkin' should I ring the police or something coz I mean, it sounded a bit like a threat but instead I rang Tracy and I didn't mention anything about the letter just in case but I asked her what it meant and she said its from a song that was out in the 60's called *Whiter Shade Of Pale* and I went to look through me da's CDs and found it on a compilation and had a listen just in case someone was sendin' me riddles like in *Batman Forever*, the one with your man Val Kilmer as Batman and Jim Carey as the Riddler but I couldn't really get any clues from listenin' to it. Maybe it really is a threat. Maybe someone does want me dead or whatever they meant by whiter shade of pale. If I find it was someone messin' I'll batter them coz as I said, I got an awful fright. Never mind me heart, my bladder doesn't be able for it.

✻✻✻

I'm lost. Not really coz I'm not that bad with directions. Tell a lie. I am but I mean lost as in confused, not as in I'm in the middle of Tallaght with no phone or money and haven't a clue how to get home.

The reason I'm confused is coz we were out last night and there was war and I don't even have a clue what it was over or what happened and I was there for the whole thing.

It all started, surprise surprise, in Temple Bar Square, the same place Lance was in that fight a few weeks back and where Bernie and Tracy had that huge row a few months ago. What happened was, meself, Concepta, Yenta, Sheila and Paulo had been in Farley's for a drink and we were on our way up to meet Tracy, my Dave and Lance in Bobs and we're walkin' through Temple Bar and who do we spot only Bopper, Jasmin and one of the three Nialls comin' towards us and I was like 'Ah howayiz,' but Sheila said something to Paulo that I didn't hear and I could see Jasmin and whichever one of the three Nialls it was sayin' something to Bopper and then all of a sudden our Bopper says to Paulo 'Who the fuck do ya think you are?' and Paulo says, 'Who d'ya think you are?'

'What d'ya mean who do I think I am? Who d'ya think you are?' our Bopper says real bitchy like. So Paulo says, just as bitchy, 'I know who I am but who d'ya think you are?' Now I was as confused at this stage and by the look on Concepta and Yenta's faces, they were too. So Bopper and Paulo start havin' this kind of bitch fight in the middle of Temple Bar and its like something off *Ricki Lake* with the two of them and whichever one of the three Nialls it was, not that it matters, but he says something to Paulo which I missed coz Yenta was sayin' something to me. So this Niall fella and Paulo start shoutin' at each other and then

Sheila starts shoutin' and I can't really understand a word of it. I mean, its hard enough to understand Paulo and Sheila at the best of times. So Jasmin says something to Concepta and Yenta has to hold Concepta back and all of a sudden, its just madness and I don't know why but I haven't a clue what's goin' on, not a clue and I'm just standin' there like a sap lookin' at it all and there's all the American and Japanese tourists takin' pictures, thinkin' its some sort of street entertainment or whatever and ya can't really blame them to be honest. So I'm wonderin' to meself what to do so I take out me phone and ring Tracy and tell her to get her arse down to where I am as quick as she can and she asks what's wrong and I just tell her to run. In the meantime, Bopper, Jasmin and the Niall fella run off one way in the height of it and Paulo walks the other way with Sheila behind him and Concepta walks over towards the bank machine with Yenta and Concepta shouts 'What the fuck are yiz lookin' at?' and everyone turns away and goes back to what they were doin' and then I can hear her sayin' 'I'm grand Yenta' as she skips the whole ATM queue and walks straight up to the machine although, fair play to her, the mad cow. So Tracy arrives a minute or two later in a panic with Dave and she says 'What's wrong Joanna?' and I look at her and say 'I haven't a clue, but if ya find out, will ya let me know?'

✷✷✷

I was on me way out to work this mornin' and I see an envelope just in front of the door, the same as the last one and true enough, I pick it up and it just has Joanna written on it like the last one so straight away I get a little bit of a fright but nowhere near as bad as the first time and I take it with me on the way to work and open it and it says, 'You'd better hope and pray that you wake one day in your own world.' Which straight out I know is from that song *Stay* by Shakespeare's Aunt or Ma or Sister or something. Great song it is as well but I'm thinkin' that it doesn't really sound that nice and is kind of, in a roundabout way, like the first one, talkin' about death and I'm thinkin' to meself who'd go to all that trouble and more importantly, who'd want to kill me.

Oh good Jayzis! I'm just after thinkin'. What if its Yenta? What if she's givin' me some kind of warnin'? Maybe the next letter she sends me is goin' to have that white powder stuff in it that kills ya when ya breath it in. Traintrax or something its called. I mean, she'd be well capable of it, bein' a terrorist and all.

I'm wonderin' should I tell anyone about the letters though coz maybe it is kinda serious. I'd be afraid tellin' some people though coz they'd probably go mad over it, especially me ma and da. They wouldn't let me out or anything in case something happened me. Maybe I'll say it to me Uncle Dessie although then again, maybe not. Tracy would probably know what to do. See, ya do miss Bernie for things like this.

✳✳✳

Julie Walsh is goin' to be off work til the end of the month, I swear to god, she brought her doctors note into Leandra today. I knew what she'd be like. She's playin' this gettin' knocked down thing for everything its worth. I mean, it was only Friday that she got knocked down and its Tuesday now and apart from the broken arm, there's nothing wrong with her, not even a bruise and I was talkin' to Amy, one of the young-ones that does a couple of hours at the weekend and she said that by the way Jason had been goin' on, ya'd swear Julie Walsh was on her last legs. I had visions of her in a wheelchair the way Amy said Jason was talkin' about it although maybe thinkin' of Julie Walsh bein' seriously injured was just wishful thinkin' on my behalf. I suppose I should be happy that she won't be in work for three weeks. It means we don't have to look at her or listen to her and somebody else can use the stool for a change although instead of sittin' on it yesterday, Marie had Cliff and Tinky Winky on it. Did I tell ya about Marie namin' the new pot plants. She said she'd call them after the Tellytubbies so the one I got her, the bonsai, is Tinky Winky, the aloe vera is Dipsy, the conifer is Lala and then theres Cliff. See she already named Cliff so she was gonna change it to Po but we told her she couldn't just change the name like that and she agreed. So now its Tinky Winky, Dipsy, Lala and Cliff.

Anyway, Leandra thinks we should find some proof of Julie Walsh gettin' knocked down just in case she's fakin' it all to get an extra three weeks off work to go to Santa Ponsa or something. I don't know, maybe there was a witness or better still, a video. Oh please let there be a video. I'd pay to see that.

✳✳✳

I got a phone call today. I was just on me way home from work and it was a mad day what with us bein' someone down with Julie Walsh out sick although not that she does anything when she's there but at least it means I don't have to do the till when she's in coz she doesn't really like doin' anything other than tills, mainly coz anything else would involve her gettin' her hole off the stool and we all know how that thing is superglued to her arse.

Anyway, I got a phone call as I was walkin' home and it was from a number that I didn't recognise and I'm tryin' to think did anyone say they were gettin' a new mobile. So I answer anyway and I just say hello and this mad accent come back at me and its like 'Oo-ara Joa-na' and I was lost. I thought Sheila had givin' me number to one of her Chinese friends or something. So I was like 'What?' and the voice says 'Howarya Joanna?' and its still a mad accent but I understand it better the second time around. So I say 'Who is this?' and the voice says – I think this person is from Kerry or something or Peru, wherever the fuck that is – 'Tis Dermot, Joanna, you remember me?' and of course I don't. So I'm like 'Dermot who?' and he's like, 'Dermot from Kerry. I met ya in Dublin a few weeks back. Sure you told me to ring ya if I'm ever in Dublin again.' And true as I'm here, I haven't a breeze who this chap is, not a breeze. So I thought to meself, I'd play along. So I was like 'Really? When are ya goin' to be in Dublin?' And he's like, 'This weekend,' and I was thinkin' to meself to get out of this mad situation with this mad stranger I don't know so I was like, 'Ah that's a pity. I'm goin' to Turkey tomorrow.' Why I said Turkey I'll never know but it just kinda came out, probably coz I know Yenta and she's from Turkey. So your man says

'Ah Joanna that's an awful pity. I was dying to see you.' In the end I just said goodbye and hung up, still wonderin' who the fuck Dermot is.

✱✱✱

Oh good Jesus. I can't believe it. I told Concepta about me phone call from Dermot from Kerry and she actually wet herself laughin' and I'm wonderin' have I missed something coz that often happens to me. I mean, I'm still not sure what that argument in Temple Bar was over the other night but I think it has something to do with Paulo thinkin' Bopper snuck off on him with Jasmin and then the three Nialls, which, I have to say, I agree with Paulo about coz Jasmin's the exact same and I know what they're like Jasmin and Bopper. They'll both come crawlin' back. They always do. Ya have to remember they're a year younger than us so we're obviously goin' to be more maturer than they are but the way they're actin' ya'd swear they were in 3rd class. They're like kids. I don't know why they can't just sort it out and be friends but who I am I to interfere? Not that I would, even if I did have a clue what was goin' on?

So anyway, I was tellin' Concepta about Dermot and as I said, she laughed a lot but then laughed a lot more when I told her I didn't remember him and eventually I get her to calm down enough to tell me who he is. Well remember that night a few months ago, January I think it might have been, and we met these fellas from Kerry in Bobs that said they were stayin' in a hotel out in Ballsbridge but Concepta said they were travellers? Well your man Dermot was the bloke I was with that night. Jayzis. The state of him now that I think back on it. Why I give people my real number I'll never know. I'll give them Jasmin's in future.

✱✱✱

Bernie rang me today to find out what the story is with Paulo, Bopper and Jasmin although I was the worst person to ring about that coz I haven't a clue what's goin' on meself. Bopper is startin' to ignore me a bit, even in the gaff like, and what I did on anyone, I don't know but if he keeps it up, I'll kick him so far up the hole, he'll be able to tie me shoe laces when he opens his mouth and don't even start me on Jasmin. She was in the house last night and I was there tryin' to strike up a conversation and she kept givin' me these really short answers like she didn't really want to talk to me and as I said, I haven't a clue what I did on anyone.

I was actually surprised to hear Bernie ringin' about something happenin' here. Usually she rings to tell me something that Dervla did or what her and Dervla got up to or something to do with Dervla or else it has something to do with her job like some new airport she's flyin' to or about one of the other air hostesses. She says I should call them cabin crew coz theres fellas too, as if I really give a shite, and at the end of the day, I can call them what I like coz I don't know any of these losers although Bernie thinks they're all great although as far as she's concerned, nothing is better than Dervla coz Dervla's great and Dervla does such a thing better than anyone else and Dervla likes such a thing and Dervla watches such a thing on the telly and listens to such a thing on the radio. Well I've met Dervla and I think she's a sap. I don't care what Bernie thinks about her.

Anyway, Bernie just wanted all the gossip on Paulo and Bopper but she'll probably end up tellin' me all about it and she lives in England. She said I should help make peace. I asked her what the fuck she thought I was. The Unitin' Nations?

✷✷✷

Dave rang me yesterday, ya know the usual thing of a Friday, ringin' to tell me to meet him at the Central Bank and all the rest of it so I was like 'grand'. I enjoy when we go out for a meal, especially coz I don't pay for it.

Anyway, Leandra pulls the phone off me and starts askin' him all these mad questions like what's his favourite Indian dish, who's his favourite Muppet, does he prefer chicken or beef curry, what's his favourite sexual position and I was there goin' scarlet and tryin' to grab the phone back off her but Dymphna was holdin' me back and the two of them are breakin' their shites laughin' and Leandra eventually just hands the phone back to me and says, 'No phones on the shop floor Joanna,' and laughs coz we do always slag her about how much of a bitch she was when she started and now she's grand, worse than us even.

Anyway, I met Dave at the Central Bank last night and he tells me he's goin' to show me what his favourite Indian dish is, seein' as me manager was askin' him earlier so he brings me to this place in Temple Bar and I'm lookin' at the menu and I haven't a clue what half the stuff is so I just pick the Korma and pilau rice. We're sittin' there eatin', havin' a few bottles of wine and all the rest of it and Dave tells me he's been gettin' threatenin' phone calls off some man sayin' 'leave Joanna alone or I'll slit your throat,' or something so I got the fright of me life and I tell him about the letters I got and he goes mental, tellin' me I should have told him earlier and that I should have told someone. So he asks me is there anything else I should tell him and I'm wonderin' is he tryin' to ask am I pregnant which I definitely amn't coz I just had me period but I think he's askin' has anything else happened and I'm thinkin' of sayin' it might be Yenta seein' as she's a terrorist but then I think of Mister O'Toole and him leavin' me flowers and passin' by the restaurant and starin' at me in work and knick-knackin' at me door and all the rest of it but I don't tell Dave about all this coz I don't want any trouble although he wants to see the letters even though I'm not certain that it was Mister O'Toole that sent them. Then again, how many stalkers could I have? I know I'm a ride but I'm no Catherine Zeta Jones. Although I'm close.

✷✷✷

The laugh we had last night. Really. It was mad. There was just meself, Concepta, Tracy and Paulo and we had a mad night. It was crazy. It was great with just the four of us and we helped cheer Paulo up coz he's been a bit down since his big argument with Bopper. Yenta couldn't come out coz she had other plans. She probably had a terrorist meetin' or somethin'. Don't ask me where Sheila was coz me phone was breakin' up when she rang and she's bad enough to understand at the best of times. Tracy's fella Lance took my Dave to see some rock band in the Temple Bar Music Centre and they brought Jasmin's little brother Andy coz he's a little bit of a mosher and they promised they'd bring him sometime, although I told Dave to keep an eye on him coz he's only 16 or somethin' and not to let him take any drugs or anything. Jayzis, if Jasmin ever finds out our fellas are takin' her little brother to a mosher gig, she'll kill us. Just lets hope she doesn't find out coz she's not talkin' to us as it is.

Anyway, meself, Tracy, Concepta and Paulo went to Farley's for a few drinks but then we were dyin' to go dancin' so we went into Bondi in town and it was a great night and we got locked. The laugh we had though coz the four of us were standin' just at the stairs on the middle floor and next minute I hear someone callin' me, hard enough as it was with the noise of the music and I turn around and theres this youngfella in what I believe was an Aran knit jumper, or so Tracy was tellin' me. He was with three or four other fellas and ya wanna see the state of them and the dirt of one of them. How they let him in, I don't know. He even had Irish teeth. I'm not jokin' ya, they were green, white and orange and he was an ugly lookin' yoke.

The fella that had called me in the first place, the one in the Aran knit jumper looked kinda familiar and it only dawned on me who it was when he said 'I thought you were goin' to Turkey.' Who was it only your mad Dermot and I swear to Jayzis, I nearly died. After me tellin' the fucker I wasn't goin' to be in Dublin to avoid him and then I bump into him in the pub and I wouldn't mind if he was half decent lookin' but he's not although I'm sure back in January before I met Dave me standards were a lot lower coz I was a bit more desperate then. I mean, lookin' at him I felt a bit sick thinkin' that he had his tongue in me mouth and then his dirty lookin' friend came and stood beside me and I was close to vomitin'. He smelt worse than Dymphna after a hot day wearin' nylon.

We just made our excuses and got away from them and the laugh we had tryin' to avoid them all night. We were goin' up one stairs and down the other and Concepta was goin' mad until I told her to think of all the weight she'd be losin'. Paulo even snorted Smirnoff Ice out of his nose from laughin' at one stage and by the amount of it, it must have been half a bottle. We didn't see Dermot and his mates after about quarter to two so they probably left or were more than likely fucked out.

✷✷✷

Jasmin's in the height of it. Well so I believe seein' as she won't talk to me for some reason but she told Bopper, although he won't talk to me either for whatever reason. What I did on either of them, I don't know but Bopper told me Uncle Dessie and he told me although he told me not to say that I know. He said that Bopper said that Jasmin was in the height of it coz Dave and Lance brought Andy to that Mosher gig the other night although how she found out, I don't know. I'd say Bopper told her. He's a fucker like that. He can't hold his piss and I wouldn't mind but it was me Uncle Dessie that told him by accident, or at least he says it was an accident. I think me Uncle Dessie does be stirin' shit sometimes for a bit of drama, just to get some kind of kick out of it. Maybe I'm wrong but ya'd never know.

Anyway, Dessie said that Bopper said that Jasmin said that Lance and Dave had no right to bring Andy anywhere and they should have even asked her first. We would have if the dizzy bitch was talkin' to us. Fuck her. She can say what she like but Dave and Lance were bein' nice by bringin' her brother with them. I mean, they didn't have to bring him anywhere and they did and not only that but they wouldn't let him spend a penny. They even paid for his drink for the night and all. When they told me that I nearly killed them meself until they told me it was only Coke and that only made it worse coz I had visions of Jasmin's 15 year old brother, or however old he is, doin' lines of coke in the toilet of the Temple Bar Music Centre til they told me it was Pepsi. I was that age meself not too long ago. The bastards got him drunk I'd say.

Jasmin can fuck right off coz I'm not in the mood for her, the way she's been actin' lately and I wouldn't mind but Jasmin gave him a few quid goin' out and all although Dave told him there was no way he could buy hash, even if it was his own money and it wasn't, it was Jasmin's.

✳✳✳

I got another one of them letters today and I said nothing to anyone, especially Dave coz he'd only just have a heart attack. He wants me to ring the police over the first two but I don't want to cause a load of trouble and then for it to be only a joke coz I'm still convinced its someone messin' coz the one I got today made me laugh more than anything else. It was the exact same as the first two, just a white envelope with Joanna written on it and then inside, a white piece of paper with words and letters from a newspaper stuck on it and this time it said 'No more carefree laughter, silence ever after, walking through an empty house, tears in my eyes, this is where the story ends, this is goodbye.' And I know straight away that it was an Abba sing. Don't ask me how but watchin' *Muriel's Weddin'* four million times is startin' to pay off.

I put on the ABBA *Gold* CD and skipped straight to the second song coz I know the words definitely weren't from *Dancin' Queen* and that's the first song on the album and then there it was — number two. The same words on the letter in me hand from *Knowin' me Knowin' you*. Whatever about the first two but this one is mad. I mean, if you were tryin' to frighten someone would ya send them an ABBA song unless its someone like Jasmin's little brother Andy. He's terrified of ABBA although he's mad into Megadeath and Marilyn Manson so it wouldn't really be his type of thing.

The letters are definitely someone havin' a laugh although I'm goin' to wear rubber gloves pickin' up the post from now on just in case theres that powder in it that kills ya if ya inhale it. Arsenal or something it is that Tracy says its called.

***

Dessie is very hard to live with sometimes. Really he is. There's times when I feel like killin' him. I love him to bits, I really do but sometimes he just does me head in.

Theres little things he does that annoys me. Nothin' big but they annoy me. Like when we're watchin' telly or a film and you're really into it and Dessie will keep tryin' to guess what's goin' to happen next and it annoys the fuck out of me. Everything will be quiet and the scary music is on and he'll just say, really loud and all, he'll say 'Your mans goin' to get killed here' and I wouldn't mind but most of time he gets it wrong, even if he's seen it before. It's not a big thing or anything but it just annoys me tryin' to watch anything with him in the room and its only lately I've started noticin' it.

And then there's times when he just walks into me and Boppers room without knockin' and even we don't do that. He even did it to me when I was in the bathroom the day before yesterday and thank Christ I was only doin' me hair coz if I had of been in the bath or havin' a piss or something, I would have killed him.

I don't know. I think the house is just startin' to feel a bit crowded or something and it's bad enough sharin' a room with Bopper but it's worse with him ignorin' me. I love me Uncle Dessie to bits but I think I'd love to have me own room more. At least me bedroom doesn't try tell ya the end of *Romeo and Juliet*.

***

That Miranda young-one is a sap. How I'm goin' to spend two weeks in the Canaries with her without killin' her, I don't know. I know she's Tracy's mate and all but that really doesn't take away from the fact that the girl is nothing but a stuck up, mad into herself, snotty bitch.

Tracy had this thing on last night with a few of her friends from college in Traffic in town and asked meself, Concepta, Yenta and Paulo to go with her so I wasn't goin' because I had work this mornin' but I said I may as well when I heard all the rest of them were goin'. So we all headed in and we were sittin' with Tracy and some of her mates and Lance was there and that Miranda young-one sat herself down in between me and Yenta and she was askin' me what I do and I told her about me job in the Spar and she looked disgusted. I was only short of plantin' her. She was talkin' about how great UCD was and how she doesn't like people from the north side usually but Tracy's lovely and I told her I was from the north side and she looks me up and down and says, really sarcastically and all, she says 'It shows' and turns to start talkin' to Yenta like I'm a piece of dirt. Two weeks in the Canaries? I'll have the bitch drownded after two hours.

***

I got me fourth letter today so I thought it was time to tell someone coz I wasn't really sure what the song was or who sang it or anything so I rang Tracy and asked her to come round to the gaff and within 15 minutes, there she was at the door.

The letter was just the same as the first three, only this time it said 'Tonight's the night, its gonna be alright because I love you girl' and I hand this to Tracy and she takes it and she looks at it, then looks back at me and then looks at it again for a good two minutes without sayin' anything, then hands it back to me and just says 'Rod Stewart' and I was like 'What?' and she says 'Its *Tonight's The Night* by Rod Stewart, although Janet Jackson did a version of it on her *Velvet Rope* album' and I think for a minute and remember the Janet version coz I have that CD. Tell a lie, Concepta has that CD coz she robbed it on me. So I take out the first letter and show it to Tracy and she says '*Whiter Shade Of Pale* by Procal Harem although Sarah Brightman did a version of it as well.' As if I give a fuck. Then I show her the second letter and she takes about 10 seconds and then says '*Stay* by Shakespeare's Sister' and then I give her the third and straight off she says '*The Winner Takes It All*' and I say '*Knowin' me, Knowin' you.*' And she says 'Aha' whether on purpose or by accident but the two of us just laugh. So I ask her what they are and she tells me they're song lyrics as if I didn't know, the sap. I end up tellin' her about the way that I got them and she tells me I should go to the guards over it and starts goin' into a big psychology thing about the type of people that send death threats and I ask her is she sure they're death threats and she says 'more than likely' and that I should take them seriously just in case but I tell her I'll sleep on and that she can't tell anyone and she promises and then she says, 'I wonder why they sent that one sayin' "*Tonight's The Night*"?' So do I!

✲✲✲

I am traumatised for life. Really I am. I'm still shakin' over the fright of it all and I'm knackered coz I was up half the night and I was talkin' to the guards and all for hours and I was cryin' for ages and I just couldn't stop. Every time I close me eyes I think about it and that even makes me cry more and I have to close me eyes coz I'm knackered but I can't coz every time I do, I see it and start cryin' and I'm still terrified. Not like as in the terrified ya get when ya watch Scream, I mean real terrified, more than just scared or afraid, real terrified and I wouldn't mind but I was goin' to stay in Dave's and all.

Meself and Dave were goin' to go for a meal with Tracy and Lance last night but Concepta found out about it, not that it was a secret or anything, but she invited herself along as well as Paulo, Yenta and Sheila so we went to TGI Fridays on Stephen's Green and had a lovely meal and stayed there for the night and when we were leavin' to go home, Dave asked me to go to his but thinkin' I'd have to be up for work, I said I'd leave it coz it's not every Saturday I have to work so I don't really mind.

Anyway, I went home and went straight to bed coz I was a bit tired and I was delighted to have the room to meself coz Bopper was stayin in one of the three Nialls houses in Greystones for the weekend. I even put the mattress back under the bed out of the way so I'd have loads of room.

There I was asleep anyway and I get this kinda feelin' in me sleep, don't ask me what it was, but I opened me eyes and there was someone standin' over the bed with their back to me, a man like, and at first I thought it was Bopper or maybe me da or Dessie but he turned around and he had a big knife in his hand and he got a bit of a fright when he realised me eyes were open but that was fuckin' nothing compared to the fright I got at seein' a man with a knife standin' over me bed. I screamed the house down and your man looks at me for a second before runnin' out of the room and its only then that I realise that its Mister O'Toole from across the road and I'm still screamin' the house down and me Uncle Dessie is the first one to run into the room to see what's wrong, as naked as the day he was born and that's frightenin' in itself and he asks what's wrong and grabs me house coat and puts it on and me ma and da run in and I'm still screamin' and they're all a bit freaked out and I can't do anything but scream and they're askin' me what's wrong and eventually I say 'He tried to kill me' and they think I'm dreamin' and I shout 'He tried to kill me' and then start cryin' and I'm hysterical and I shout 'He tried to fuckin' kill me' again and me ma comes over and says its only a dream and I tell her it wasn't and Dessie leaves the room in me pink housecoat I got in Penneys and goes down the stairs and shouts that the front door is open and me ma and da's faces just drop coz they realise I'm tellin' the truth and Dessie is already out on the road lookin' around, or at least I think he is coz I'm still in bed with me ma huggin' me to calm me down and me da keeps shoutin', 'What happened Joanna?' And all I say is, 'I woke up and Mister O'Toole was standin' over me with a knife,' and he doesn't know whether to believe me or not and says nothing and I hear someone comin' up the stairs and I'm a bit frightened 'til I hear me Uncle Dessie's voice and me da tells me I have to tell him everything so I tell him what happened and then he runs out of the room and Dessie follows him and they both went over to Mister O'Tooles house, I didn't see it but Dessie told me after, and banged on the door but there was no answer so they came back and rang the police and by this stage, me ma had brought me down stairs for a cup of tea and I'm still cryin' and shakin' and me da asks why do I think Mister

O'Toole would try to kill me so I tell him about the letters and the one sayin' 'Tonight's the Night' and Dave gettin' the phone calls about me and about Mister O'Toole leavin' flowers and Petulia next door seein' him that time and about him knick-knackin', walkin' past the restaurant and starin' at me in the Spar and about him ringin' me when I'm in the bath or whatever and starin' at me from his window and me ma, da and Dessie can't believe what I'm tellin' them and me da asks why I didn't tell anyone and I tell him coz I thought it was only a joke and he asks me how much of a joke can it be when someone's tryin' to kill me and I just start bawlin' again and I can tell that the three of them are ready to kill Mister O'Toole but are tryin' to hide their anger coz they don't want to upset me anymore but they're tryin' to stay as quiet as they can and me da gets up and runs out again and Dessie follows him and I can hear him bangin' on Mister O'Toole's door and shoutin' 'Come out O'Toole ya bastard,' and me and me ma are still huggin' and they come back with two guards and I say nothing for a good five minutes coz me ma and Dessie are tellin' them everything and the girl guard is takin' down notes and the fella is standin' there with his hands on his hip lookin' at me, kinda lookin' a bit disgusted at the whole thing and when me ma and Dessie finish the story, the girl asks me have I still got the letters and I tell Dessie where they are and he goes up and gets them and everyone has a look at them and can't really believe it. So the fella guard asks me why I didn't report the letters – in a bit of a culchie accent – and I'm still cryin' but I say, 'Coz I thought it was a joke. If you were sendin' death threats, would ya use songs by ABBA and Rod Stewart?' And the gobshite actually thinks about it for a second and goes, 'Probably not.' The fuckin' sap. So it seems hours that I'm sittin' there talkin' to these two and then they say they're goin' to try to see if Mister O'Toole is home so they go to his house and knock! Fuckin' knock, believe it or not. If you're after tryin' to kill a young-one that lives across the road from ya, would ya go back to your house and if ya did, would ya answer the door to the cops and here the two of these are knockin' like Jehovah's Witnesses. No wonder there's crime in this country.

Anyway, I tried to get asleep but I couldn't so I just lay in me mas bed beside her for a while and Dessie tells me that the cops got a warrant and searched Mister O'Toole's house and found loads of evidence and they were shocked. There was pictures of me and me work roster and a calendar with places I'd been to on it and Dessie tellin' me this makes it all worse but the police told him that when they catch him, they'll have no problem havin' him charged coz of all the evidence they have against him but the thing is, they have to catch him first. I mean, he's still out there somewhere and he's tried to kill me once already so what's to stop him doin' it to me again or what about me ma and da or Dessie or Bopper or Dave or the girls, Concepta, Tracy, Yenta, Jasmin, Sheila and even Paulo. How can I do anything on me own until they catch him? I'm scared shit-less. As I said, I'm afraid to close me eyes coz I just keep seein' it in me mind and all I can think of is him standin' there with the knife in his hand and the look on his face when he realised me eyes were open and then when I screamed and thinkin' back on it, it seems like he was standin' there for ages but it was only a couple of seconds. I mean, it had to have been.

How did he get into our house anyway? The guards say there's no evidence of a forced entry which I think means that he didn't try to break in so how he got up to me bedroom is a mystery to everyone coz the alarm was on and everything. The thoughts of the whole thing makes me sick. The police say they think they're dealin' with a stalker. Now I wonder what gave them that idea!

✳✳✳

I'm still in a state. I couldn't even watch the telly coz I couldn't concentrate on anything. I just keep thinkin' about it over and over again and every time I shut me eyes, all I see is Mister O'Toole standin' over me with a knife. I managed to get to sleep last night after a few sleepin' tablets but I just had a horrible dream where I was runnin' away from Mister O'Toole and he was chasin' after me with a knife and all I could do was run and scream and I just kept on runnin' and he keeps following me and no matter what I did in the dream, I can't get away from him.

What did I do to deserve all this? I keep thinkin' about little things from the past. Like did I do anything to annoy him but all me memories of Mister O'Toole are good ones like when he used to give us cool pops when it was a hot day out and stuff like that. Its only in the last few months that he started gettin' weird and I'm wonderin' how he got me number to ring me coz I'm convinced it was him them times I was in the toilet or in the bath and he was lookin' over when I got to the phone and I was even convinced I'd seen binoculars one time. And then there was that time outside the restaurant and in the shop and everything and all along I just played it down, thinkin' he was just goin' a bit crazy in his old age, not knowin' how crazy. I mean, I never thought he'd try and kill me and I wouldn't mind, I only thought famous people have stalkers. At least they can afford bodyguards. I can't even afford *The Bodyguard* on DVD.

✷✷✷

Half of Dublin seems to know what happened at this stage. Me phones been ringin' non-stop with people askin' me am I okay. I mean, for fuck sake, someone tried to kill me. D'ya think I'd be okay?

Me nerves are still in shite, I swear to god. I'm not leavin' the house and I won't stay in on me own so someone has to be here all the time and fair play to me ma and da and Dessie and Bopper coz they've been great and Concepta took today and tomorrow off work so she could stay with me. She's been tryin' to get me mind off it by talkin' about the holiday and all the rest of it. She's been great, I have to say.

The rest of them have all been in to see me. Tracy has been around about six times and she's feelin' a bit guilty coz she was the one I told about it and she didn't make me do anything about the letters but I told her not to be so stupid. The main thing is that I'm still alive. Bernie rang from London so she's tryin' to get home a little earlier but they mightn't let her coz she has two weeks off for the holiday. Jasmin sent me around a big box of Celebrations, which Concepta has half eaten already, and a big teddy bear even though she hasn't talked to me in ages, although it's nice to know she still cares. Paulo rang Concepta to make sure Bopper wasn't here before droppin' around and then when Bopper came in, Paulo gave him a dirty look, said goodbye to me, Concepta and Dessie and left. Even Petulia next door sent in grapes and a big bottle of Lucozade, the stupid bitch. I was nearly murdered and she sends in presents that ya get when ya have the flu and I wouldn't mind but I don't even like grapes. Obviously Concepta ate them.

✳︎

Leandra rang me today and asked me to come back to work and at first I thought she was serious but it turns out she was only jokin'. She says she's makin' the company pay full sick pay even though I'm not really sick coz there's nothing in the staff handbook about takin' time off after someone's tried to kill ya. She says the company are very sympathetic to me situation, which means that they haven't a fuckin' clue what to do so they'll pay me anyway to cover themselves.

I felt a bit guilty for takin' time off coz Julie Walsh is out too but Leandra said she has that spa Jason and Amy and some of the other kids that do the weekends to do extra hours coz they're off school and have nothing else to do. Julie Walsh will be back within a week anyway so they'll be grand. Dymphna is trained to do all the stuff that I do anyway so they won't miss me too much and they better get used to it anyway coz I'll be in Spain for two weeks soon enough.

Leandra was sayin' that Marie was goin' to bring the pot plants around to see me but she told her not to coz I was still too upset to have visitors. I couldn't thank Leandra enough. The thoughts of havin' to talk to Marie and Tinky Winky, Dipsy, LaLa and Cliff are too much although I might get her to send around a bit of hash to help me sleep a bit better. She says it's great for when ya can't sleep although I've never really tried it before, well without knowin' anyway. I'm convinced she's been slippin' it into me tea for years.

✳︎

Dave came around to visit today. My Dave. Me fella. It was just my luck though coz me ma and da were here and they haven't met him yet so it was all forget about Joanna and the fact that some nut job tried to stick a knife in her when she was asleep and instead ask her boyfriend who we never met loads of questions and embarrass him.

I was more embarrassed than he was. Me ma and da made a show of me, ya know what they're like. Me ma was tryin' to force feed the young-fella, offerin' him everything from tea to the jellies that we get off Concepta and even a full dinner and me da was doin' all his best pal shite and tellin' all his jokes about one handed Arabs and all the rest of it and then me ma was tellin' stories about me when I was kid and I was just sittin' there mortified and in walks Dessie and says hello to Dave and then says, 'Jayzis, I didn't recognise ya with your clothes on. The springs on that sofa haven't been the same since the time you and Joanna were on it.' And everything just goes quiet and then Dessie starts tellin' us about one of the Filipino nurses that lives in his house and me ma and da forget what he says about the sofa.

I was still scarleh though coz they were askin' him loads of questions about his job, about his apartment, about his family and all the rest of it and me da made a joke about hopin' that Dave didn't turn out to be a crazy stalker that tries to kill people when they're in bed and no one laughed although me da thought it was hilarious, although he thought the joke about the one handed Arab was funny too and believe me, it wasn't.

It was nice for Dave to meet me ma and da anyway, even if they did make a holy show of me. I told him that I want to meet his ma and da now but he tried to ignore me and told me they lived all the way away in Kildare but I told him I don't mind but he seems like he doesn't want me to. Maybe he has an embarrassin' Uncle as well, although nothing, and I mean nothing, can be as bad as Dessie, not even a bad dose of crabs. Not that I'd know.

※※※

I left the house today for the first time since I was nearly killed, although in sayin' that, when I say I left the house, I went out the back garden with Concepta and Paulo for a couple of hours because it was a gorgeous day out and it was roastin' and we were thinkin' we might be able to get a bit of a base tan for the holiday, ya know yourself, so we won't be burnin' when we're there.

Paulo is sallow enough so he doesn't burn that much or so he says anyway. Concepta does burn a little bit and then it turns into a lovely colour and she gets a nice tan all over as well and its surprisin' because there's so much of her. I always seem to get sunburnt no matter what I do. Even today. I put loads of suncream on and it was a high factor and all, a 25 I think, and I still got burned on me shoulders and on the back of me knees and that's always a horrible place to get burned coz ya can't sit down properly for a day or two. I lashed on loads of aloe vera though so it shouldn't be that bad.

It was great to get a nice day like that, ya know, really sunny and hot and ya do have to make the most of it coz it doesn't happen very often in Ireland. It was lovely just sittin' out the back, meself, Concepta and Paulo, listenin' to the radio and havin' a few drinks. We kept sayin' that in a week and a half we'll be sittin' by the pool in Playa Del Ingles and Petulia's dog won't be there barkin' to wreck our heads either. If he was I'd drown the fucker in the pool

***

Believe it or not, the police still have no idea where Mister O'Toole is. Seriously. Not a clue and its nearly a week since he tried to kill me and disappeared. The last place he was seen was in my bedroom and nothing since then. They raided his house and have been in and out tryin' to get clues about where he is. They've traced his relatives and nobody has heard from him. They even checked his credit card bills and phone bills and all but nothing came up except that he took a few thousand out of his bank account in the two weeks before he tried to kill me so they think he might have used the money to skip the country but they checked the airlines and his name doesn't match anything out of Dublin since then so it's still all a mystery although in fairness, I don't think they're really all that pushed about findin' him. They even told me themselves that attempted murder isn't something worth followin' someone half way across the world for. The main thing is that I'm still alive. I don't think they realise though that I'm terrified to leave me house in case some nut job tries to stab me. All I want to know is that they know where he is. Anywhere once it's nowhere near me.

✳✳✳

I got a phone call yesterday off some fella claimin' to be from the *Herald* and at first I thought it was someone messin' but he said he'd heard about me ordeal and would I be interested in givin' an interview for the paper so at first I was thinkin' there was no way but then I thought why not, sure it might help the police find Mister O'Toole. So your man on the phone asked me would I like to meet him somewhere but I said I'd prefer if he could come to the house coz I'm still not really pushed on the idea of leavin' the house on me own and I'm still havin' the nightmares as well. I had one last night that I was runnin' through a lane with Mister O'Toole chasin' me and Petulia, or Mary as she's really called, was chasin' him and Disco her dog was chasin' her. Thank god I never took the hash to help me sleep if that's what the sleepin' tablets do.

Anyway, about an hour later, your man knocks at the door and I answer, lookin' only gorgeous havin' spent ages gettin' ready. Christina Aguilera wouldn't have a patch on me. Your man comes into the livin' room and me mas with me and he starts askin' all these questions so I go into the whole story tellin' him about everything like the letters, the stalkin' and everything and your mans writin' it down and he starts askin' me questions and then the photographer that's with him asks to get a few pictures so he takes a few of me on me own and then a few with me and me ma and then he says thanks a million and that he hopes Mister O'Toole gets caught and all the rest of it and to look out for the next paper.

So I got up today havin' forgot all about it and next minute the phone rings and I realise its nearly in the afternoon and its Leandra and she just says I look lovely in the paper and it's a very interestin' story and I should be proud of meself for bein' so brave and that she's sendin' Sheila to me house with a copy of the paper. So five minutes later, the doorbell rings and believe it or not, it's the first time I'm in the house on me own since it happened. I don't know where everyone is so I go to the front door and look through the little hole in the door and see Sheila. So I open the door and tell her to come in and she's real excited and she hands me the *Herald* and I open it and start lookin' through it to see me picture but Sheila stops me, takes the paper from me, closes it and hands it back to me and there I am on the front page of the newspaper underneath the headline 'My neighbour tried to kill me,' and it's only then that I think about many people read that paper and how I really need to use a better concealer.

✷✷✷

I'm goin' to batter Concepta Cooney when I get her. She rang me three times today. The first time she was pretendin' to be from TV3 news and was askin' me could they do an interview with me in the Phoenix Park with the pope's cross in the background. The second time she was pretendin' to be from FM104 and was akin' me did I want to go into the studio to be on the Adrian Kennedy show coz Adrian saw me picture on the front page of the *Herald* and thought I was a lovely lookin' young-one and wanted me as a guest on his show. The third time she rang she was pretendin' to be from the Order of Saint Martin of Orlando wonderin' would I be interested in joinin' a convent. I have to give it to her though, she's gas and with Concepta, she knows when a joke is a joke. She would never take it too far. The laugh the two of us had though.

I'm still only scarlet after bein' on the front page of the *Herald*. I think every person I know must have rang me or text me. Me ma said she was in Dunnes grabbin' a few bits for the dinner and she was stopped by a good few people askin' her all sorts of questions. One of them asked her was it true I was writin' a book about me ordeal. I can hardly write me own name, let alone a book. 'What would I call it?' I asked Concepta. 'How about, "My neighbour tried to kill me,"' she says. I'm never goin' to live that headline down.

※※※

I picked up the post off the floor in the hall today and nearly died when I saw a letter for me, mainly coz the name and address on the front were written by hand and the only letters I've got since the death threats were from Vodafone and the bank and I know what they were coz there was logos on the envelopes. This one gave me a bit of a fright. I was expectin' it to be full of anthrax or something but Dessie told me that they can tell in the place that sorts the post if a letter has anthrax in it or not so I shouldn't really be too worried about it and anthrax is really hard to get hold of anyway.

 I open this letter anyway and slowly take the piece of paper out from inside and it was like, 'Dear Joanna, we would like to thank you for expressing an interest in becoming a member of Trainspotting Ireland. In order to become a member you will need to send a cheque or postal order for €30, payable to Trainspotting Ireland to PO box 710, Dublin 2 or alternatively you can now join on the internet at www.traincrazy.ie/newmembers. We look forward to hearing from you. Should you require any further information, please check out the website. Kindest regards, John Rogan, Chairman, Trainspotting Ireland.'

 I haven't a clue what that's all about. I can't remember wantin' to join anything and I don't even know what trainspottin' is. I haven't even seen that film.

※※※

Yenta text me today askin' did I want to go to her apartment with Concepta for a meal so I text her tellin' her that I still wasn't too pushed on the idea of leavin' the house but then a few minutes later, Concepta rang sayin' Yenta was a bit upset coz she'd gone to a lot of effort and she just wants to do something nice to cheer me up. So I tell her I'll think about it and I'm tellin' Dessie and he says he'll drive me to Yenta's and pick me up when I want to come home so I think to meself, 'fuck it, I can't stay in the house all the time.' So Concepta knocks over and the two of us get a lift to Yenta's and we knock on the door and she opens it and we walk in and who's sittin' there only Tracy, Lance, my Dave, Paulo and Sheila and I'm not jokin' ya, I nearly died. I was shocked. Yenta was after organisin' for everyone to go to her place so we could do something coz I haven't been out and I have to be honest, I was a bit shocked by it all, Tracy will tell ya. I was nearly cryin'. Yenta even made a big meal and we had Turkish meatballs and all and they were only mafis. Really now. They were gorgeous and we even had Turkish delight for desert that she made herself. I swear to Jayzis, she made her own Turkish delight. That was only mafis as well and I have to give it to Yenta, she can cook as good as she dances.

It was lovely seein' everyone as the same time though although Yenta tells me she asked Jasmin and Bopper but they're still not talkin' to Paulo and all the rest of it. I wouldn't mind but we have to go on holidays together in a few days. Jayzis, I just realised it's in a few days and I haven't even got a bikini. I wonder would it be safe for me to go shoppin' in town with Concepta and Tracy. Maybe I should bring Yenta as well. She'd know what to do if someone attacked me, although I'm startin' to doubt she's a terrorist at this stage. I don't think terrorists can make Angel Delight let alone Turkish delight!

July

Bernie rang today in a panic coz she might not be able to get home til Friday although what she was panicking for I don't know coz we're not goin' the Canaries til Sunday so she'll have loads of time. She was tellin' me that Dervla was mad jealous that we're goin' the Canaries and she said Dervla, or Derv as she's callin' her now, was in the Canaries last year and had a great time and that Derv told her all the best places to go and that Derv knows how to have a good time and about how much she's goin' to miss Derv coz she won't see her for two and a half weeks.

I told her all about us goin' to Yenta's just to annoy her. She hates havin' to miss things like that but as I said to her, really smartly I might add, but I says to her that she has Derv and Derv's mad. I told her about how great everyone's been to me since I was nearly murdered especially Concepta. I know Bernie's in England and all but she hasn't really bothered her hole much to make an effort since it happened. I mean, she's meant to be me best mate and this is only the 2nd call I got off her since and I rang her a few times although most of the time when I ring she's not there, probably out havin' a great time with Derv coz Derv's mad.

Bernie was askin' all about Paulo, Bopper and Jasmin as well but I told her it wasn't my place to get involved. She was askin' what we're gonna do about it on the holiday and I said just ignore them and then Bernie told me to remember how I made everyone become friends again before, back before Paddy's day after Bernie and Tracy had that big argument and she says that I'm the only one who can sort out this mess. Who the fuck does she think I am? Judge Judy?

**

*Yenta knocked around to me this mornin' and the young-*one nearly dragged me out of the house kickin' and screamin'. She said she'd taken the day off work to bring me shoppin' so I was goin' whether I wanted to or not and as much as I didn't want to leave the house, I knew I'd have to get a few bits for the holidays. I mean, only a few days to go and I hadn't even a bikini bought. Yenta told me not to worry about Mr O'Toole, that if he came near us while we were out shoppin', she'd give him a swingin' roundhouse kick into the side of the head. I thought that was nice of her.

We went into town and it was packed. Ya see them Spanish students. I don't know how many of them I nearly pushed under a bus, not that I was tryin' or anything coz if I was, Temple Street Hospital would be full of the little fuckers. They all just seem to hang around in crowds in the middle of O'Connell Street. I think they must wear them illuminous backpacks so the traffic will see them if they get pushed onto the road. Its so the driver will know to speed up to hit one of the bastards. Ah I'm only jokin'. I had a Spanish student. He wasn't stayin' in the house or anything, I just had him in a lane near the gaff, just kissin' and a bit of heavy pettin'. Years ago it was. What his name was I can't remember. Something foreign anyway.

So meself and Yenta were in town and I got meself all me cosmetics and all the rest of it and got a bikini and a beach towel in Dunnes. The bikini was only €12. €12! I mean, where would ya get it? Ya can't go wrong. I picked up a lovely sarong and swimsuit in Top Shop and they're a lovely army green colour. I'll only look the business in it in Playa Del Ingles. Yenta thinks its mafis as well. It's an awful pity she's not comin' with us. I've taken to Yenta and especially the way she's been lately. She's made a real effort. Maybe we can pretend that Yenta is Jasmin so she can come on the holiday instead, although in sayin' that, Yenta looks about as Irish as Bob Marley.

**

Mrs O'Driscoll is convinced that Sister Mary Immaculate Conception is seein' some man. Intimate relations is what Petulia next door is callin' it, well so me ma says anyways. I don't know why me ma does be listenin' to Petulia anyway. I mean, the woman's real name is Mary for a start. There's one lie to begin with and don't get me started on your woman Mrs O'Driscoll. I swear to Jayzis, I've never met anyone like her. She does come into the Spar and she knows everyone's business and she's always sayin' that such a person at mass told her such a thing. I mean, do they go to pray or just to have a gossip about who's shaggin' who. At least now that Sister Mary Immaculate Conception has found herself a fella they'll all stop talkin' about me. Just when I thought they had all got bored with the story, I have me face plastered all over the front of the *Herald* and I'm the talk of mass and the bingo hall again. Petulia said that Mrs O'Driscoll had even been pluggin' her for information about me although Petulia says she never opened her mouth. My arse she didn't. I bet ya she was lovin' the attention. I bet ya it was her that started the rumour about Mister O'Toole and my Dave havin' an affair.

Does it really matter that Sister Mary Immaculate Conception has a fella? I know she's a nun and all but at the end of the day, all that matters is that she's happy. As far as I'm concerned, she's done her bit for god and deserves to enjoy her life although me ma said that Petulia said that Mrs O'Driscoll said that Sister Mary Immaculate Conception is goin' to hell.

✳✳✳

Bernie's back. She knocked around late last night. We were watchin' the *Late Late Show* at the time, meself, me ma and Dessie and when she came in it was all hugs and kisses and all the rest of it and it must have been a whole 25 seconds before she mentioned Dervla or Derv as she's known now. How she managed to get her into the conversation I don't know but she managed it and me ma and Dessie were dyin' to know all about her new job and about her new home and her new friends and all the rest of it so I was made go in and make the tea while the three of them had a chat and I could hear them laughin' and jokin' from the livin' room while I was in the kitchen.

I don't really know why I felt angry at Bernie. I think it was because we've drifted so much since she left. Believe it or not, it's already been three months. It doesn't seem that long at all. Maybe I just felt she wasn't there for me when I needed her although she couldn't be, she was in a different country.

Anyway, I went back in with the tea and within a few minutes it was as if she hadn't left. We were fillin' her in on all the gossip and Dessie was tellin' her all about the Filipino nurses and she says to him, 'So how long will ya be livin' here?' and he just says, 'Til that thing I told ya about is sorted.' Now if he told Bernie, I don't see why he can't tell me. I mean, just because she lent him thousands of euros. I gave him me fuckin' room.

**

Independence Day my arse. It's a load of bollix if ya ask me. It's grand if you're American but we're not. Just coz they want to take St Patrick's Day from the Irish doesn't mean they have to give us Independence Day. Sayin' that now, I liked the film and I've always liked Will Smith.

Ya'd know Bernie was back coz we were all organised goin' out. She made us all go to Heaven in Blanchardstown coz they were havin' an American night, surprise, surprise. There was loads of us coz it's our last night before goin' away. There was me, Bernie, Concepta, Paulo, Sheila, Yenta, my Dave, Tracy and her Lance and me Uncle Dessie.

We're all sittin' there havin' the few drinks, sittin' at the door we were, and who walks in only Jasmin and our Bopper and we all just go quiet for some reason and Bernie goes over and hugs them and brings them over to sit with us and as Concepta says, she had a cheek coz they haven't been anywhere near us in weeks. I look at Paulo and he just stands up and him and Sheila go out to the smokin' area and stay there for ages. For a good hour it was Jasmin, Bopper and Bernie on one side and the rest of us on the other so I says to Concepta and Yenta to come out with me for a smoke coz I wanted to see where Paulo and Sheila were anyway and we were there havin' our smoke, a lovely night it was as well, and we when went back in, Paulo and Sheila had gone back in to the others and for some reason they're all sittin' there with real angry faces and me Uncle Dessie was nowhere to be seen. So meself, Concepta and Yenta go to sit down and Concepta says 'Jayzis, what's wrong with yiz? Ya'd swear someone was after tryin' to kill yiz in your sleep.' And for some reason, I'm the only one that laughs coz I know she's tryin' to make a joke of things and isn't bein' serious or anything and Bernie says to her 'I don't think that's very funny Concepta' and poor Concepta looks at me like she's about to start cryin'. I was really pissed off with Bernie over it although it probably had something to do with the fact that she's been annoyin' me lately anyway but I turned to her and says 'I thought it was gas. Sure what would you know?' And she looks back at me and says 'Well I haven't been here.' And at this stage, I lose it. I says, 'You're right Bernie. Ya haven't been here but ya have a phone and if ya do bother your hole to ring me, it's all just about you. You're meant to be me best mate and ya just don't bother your arse anymore. Concepta, Tracy, Paulo and Yenta were all there for me when I needed them.' And I stand up and am about to walk off and I turn to her and say, 'And they reply to me text messages.' Then I storm off and Dave runs after me, although I'm not upset, just kinda glad I got it off me chest. How we're all gonna spend two weeks together in the Canaries I don't know. I'm wonderin' should I ring Jerry Springer now or when I get back.

***

What an ordeal to get to the Canaries but we got here in the end, nearly 12 hours late I might add but we got here. Trust us to be goin' away the day that there's a big storm. It was like a hurricane it was that bad.

Me ma and da dropped me and our Bopper out to the airport and they kept tellin' me to keep an eye on him in Spain and make sure he doesn't get in to trouble and all and the rest of it. I mean, who do they think I am? I didn't spend all this money on a holiday just to babysit our Bopper. It's bad enough me havin' to share a room with him in Dublin.

Me ma insisted on comin' into the airport with us and all the others had already been there ages when we met them but I blame Bopper for us bein' late. He took ages to do his hair. Me ma even brought us all up to the check-in and was tryin' to organise us and all. I was only scarlet and we were all pretendin' to like each other and all in case she said anythin'. She even walked us all to the customs thing and was nearly cryin' when we went through. I swear to god, I was mortified.

We were able to get the bit of duty free coz Tracy tells me that the Canaries is exempt from European Union duty free laws, whatever the fuck she means by that. We were gettin' a bit worried coz as we were walkin' around they kept cancellin' flights coz of the wind. All we could hear was, 'Flight whatever to Luxembourg has been cancelled due to high winds at the airport,' and then they cancelled all the Ryanair flights and then all the Aer Lingus flights and our flight was one of the only ones left. I had gone into the book shop with Concepta and Paulo and the rest of them went on to the gate and when we got there, there was an announcement sayin', 'Could all passengers on Futura flight FUA2052 to Las Palmas please collect your baggage from the baggage reclaim and make your way to the front of the arrivals hall where a bus will transfer you to Belfast where your plane is waiting.' We all looked at each other in shock. Concepta was in the height of it, cursin' everyone she was. Ya wanna see her flyin' down that movin' walkway with meself and Paulo behind her. Our bags were already out when we got there so Concepta reefed her suitcase off the yoke and nearly broke about 15 peoples ankles as she ran to the front of the airport and then she started givin' out to some woman sortin' out all the mess from the airlines so ya know Concepta, she asks would we have enough time to go to McDonalds before gettin' on the bus and off she walks with Bopper and Jasmin and the rest of us are standin' there waitin' on them and by the time they come back, the first lot of buses are gone and we have to sit there on the ground waitin' for the bus and it was two hours, no word of a lie, two hours before it came and Concepta was starvin' again already.

We were like kids gettin' onto the bus and meself, Concepta, Paulo, Tracy and Miranda ran straight to the back and Bernie gets on, gives us a kind of dirty look and sits about halfway down, tryin' to make a point kinda thing and Jasmin and Bopper sit beside her. We just leave them to it and had a bit of a chat and Miranda and Concepta fell asleep eventually and Tracy takes out a packet of Wine Gums and I take one and lick it and stick it to Concepta's head and me, Tracy and Paulo are breakin' our shites laughin' coz she ends up with more than half the packet stuck to her face and Bopper looks back, probably thinkin' we're laughin' at them and Miranda wakes up, looks at Concepta, shakes her head and goes back to sleep, the stuck up bitch.

Two hours it took us to get to Belfast and then we had to check-in again and your woman behind the desk, the state of her as well, make up plastered onto her, and she tells us that the plane won't be leavin' for another five and a half hours coz the pilots have to sleep. Something to do with European flyin' laws Tracy told us. Needless to say, Concepta was havin' none of it but they gave us 10 pounds in vouchers for food so that calmed her down a bit and apart from Burger King, there is fuck all to do in Belfast airport. Concepta made one of the pubs take euros although how she did it, I don't know but everyone on our flight was delighted.

By the time we got on the plane, it was half 12 at night, half 12! And then it was four hours to Las Palmas, then half an hour to the apartments and at that stage I was so knackered that I didn't know what was happenin'. I just walked into the apartment and fell straight asleep. I think I might have been a little bit drunk as well. That'd explain a lot.

***

I woke up this mornin' and got a bit of a fright coz I wasn't really that sure of where I was until I turned around and saw a fella's arse just before he pulled up his shorts and it definitely wasn't my Dave coz this arse was a bit darker and I panicked for a second, not knowin' what had happened until he turned around and I realised it was only Paulo. He smiles at me and says, 'Ah you're awake. We were goin' to go to the pool without ya.' And its only then that I remember that I'm in Spain and I must have drank a lot more than I thought.

Tracy had arranged the rooms when we arrived so I was in with Concepta and Paulo, Tracy was in with Miranda and Bernie two floors down and Jasmin and Bopper were next door to them. I think Tracy did it like that to keep us all apart in case we all start big rows.

Fair play to Concepta and Paulo, they had even got up and went out to the supermarket to get a few bits while I was asleep so there was even Pepsi there for me when I woke up.

I threw me bikini on and put me sarong on and me, Paulo and Concepta went down to the pool and the others were there already. Paulo had kept me a sun lounger beside his and I went to put me book and suncream on it and suddenly I realize that Jasmin, Tracy, Miranda and Bernie were all wearin' the same bikini as me. I swear to god, the four of them were standin' there arguin'' about it and needless to say, I was only mortified. The five of us looked like spas in our army green bikinis. I felt like killin' Yenta coz she was the one that picked it out. I could see other people around the pool starin' at us, thinkin' we were gobshites who all went out and bought the same army green bikini. Concepta was the only one of the girls not to have one and that's only coz it wouldn't have fit her. She was wearing a red swimsuit with a white stripe down the side. All she needed was Coca Cola written on it and she'd be the image of a can of coke.

None of us wanted to get changed except Miranda so we all sat there for the day like saps although Bernie, Jasmin and Bopper were lyin' a bit away from us.

We went to the welcome meetin' and our rep, Jessica, was givin' us all the beef about what to do and all the rest of it. She seems a lovely young-one but she's a bit dizzy, one of these airhead types, kinda like Jasmin without the lisp.

Concepta was starvin' after the welcome meetin', although what's new, and she was dyin' for something to eat so me, her and Paulo went to find Burger King and I have to say, it was gorgeous, even though we'd just had it the day before in Belfast airport. Even though Concepta's lost a bit of weight and is meant to be on a diet, she's still diggin' into the Whoppers, the hungry cow.

When we got back to the pool, all the others were gone so we got in and ended up playin' a game of chasin'. It was gas when Concepta was on coz she can't swim near as fast as me and Paulo. We didn't even realise the time because by the time we got out, it was nearly six. I was a bit knackered and I went up to lie down for a while. I had a bit of sunburn on me shoulders but I'm glad we tried to get a base coz it would have been worse. That Miranda one did the sunbeds, I'm convinced of it, although she was sayin' sunbeds are for skangers.

***

The laugh we had last night, I'm tellin' ya. Gran Canaria is mad. We all went out together which I have to say, is a miracle considerin' the way everyone is actin' at the moment but the travel company we came with laid on a night in one of the pubs down the road.

Locked isn't the word. I swear to Jayzis, I don't know where all the drink was comin' from and meself, Paulo and Concepta had a few glasses of peach schnapps and orange juice before we left the apartment. They gave us a glass of champagne as we walked in and then there was shots of peach schnapps on the table when we walked in. I think they were tryin' to get us locked and it worked coz we were all palatic after an hour.

They had these games and one of them was all the lads against the girls and the lads lost and they had to go into the audience and get things like a lipstick, a bra, a pair of women's shoes and a handbag and then the rep that was doin' the thing told them they'd just entered the miss Gran Canaria contest. Well the face on poor Paulo but when they did him up he was lovely. Well to be honest, he just looked like a man in a dress. He told them his name was Jacinta when they asked him and Concepta shouted up 'But ya've changed it to Pussy-Willow.' Although no one laughed at that except us. He didn't win though. Some auld-fella did. A right ugly fucker.

We were sittin' beside this auld-one and auld-fella from Cork and I swear to god, they were mental. The man kept tryin' to kiss all the young-ones and the woman drank half the bar and was fallin' around the place. The man was tellin' our Bopper that he'd love him to be his son. They were crazy. I felt a hand on me arse at one stage and I turned around thinkin' it was your man and it was your woman and she smiles at me and says, 'Are ya right there Joanna?' The mental cow.

Great night though. I don't think I'll be able to handle two weeks of this cheap drink, although I'll give it a try.

※※※

We went on one of them booze cruise things yesterday and I swear I amn't able for it. Well me stomach isn't. Normally we'd all be delighted with a boat full of free booze but we were in the Hippodrome down the Plaza Centre the night before and we were all locked. One of the waiters loves us and he keeps givin' us free drink all the time. Martin his name is and he's a lovely lookin' fella from Argentina. It was gas. Bernie asked him where he was from and he said 'BA' and she was like, 'The airline? Like British Airways?' and he was like, 'Buenos Aires.' And Bernie says, 'Funny that, I always thought Buenos Aires was Spanish for hello!'

'And ya thought Rio De Janeiro played for Man Utd as well,' Concepta says to her. Not that we're all back talkin' or anything. God no. There's nearly after bein' murder on this holiday a few times. We've all bein' doin' stuff together and goin' out together and all but Jasmin, Bernie and Bopper sit on one side, me, Concepta and Paulo on the other and Tracy and that Miranda gobshite in the middle. That one's lucky I haven't smacked her one yet. She deserves it. She told me there yesterday that only skangers wear tracksuit tops. The day before she said only skangers have Sky Digital. I'll drown the stuck up bitch if I get her into the pool.

Anyway, the boat we were on yesterday was a disaster. The state of the thing. I was convinced that if anyone farted on it, it was goin' to fall apart. Then it started rockin' and we were all in bits with hangovers and we stopped in a little bay, a lovely place it was mind you, and everyone was swimmin' in the sea. Well only Bopper and Bernie out of our group were, and Concepta Cooney went to get sick over the side and got it all over some German young-one swimmin' underneath. Well the laughs out of us and the young-one was in the height of it. She came over to Concepta later and starts eatin' the head off her in German and Concepta just smiles at her, shrugs her shoulders and says, 'Vorsrpung Durk Technik,' which she heard on an Audi ad or something. Miranda wasn't impressed but then again, nothing impresses her, the snobby cow.

It's a pity we were all so hungover coz we would have enjoyed it a lot better I'm sure. Our Bopper got a bad bit of sunburn as well and I told him to put more cream on when he had finished swimmin'. Three nights since we came here, that fucker has gone off and not come home 'til all hours or the next mornin'. I wouldn't give a shite but me ma would batter me if anything happened him. Apparently, Jasmin and Bernie have got their hole twice each, Miranda once, Concepta once, although I saw your man she was with and he was mingin', Danish he was, and me, Tracy and Paulo haven't although me and Tracy have fellas and Paulo's not really that pushed, although in sayin' that, I could easily have got a bit. The fellas are all over me over here. It's not my fault I'm so good lookin'.

✳✳✳

There was killin's last night in the middle of Playa Del Ingles and when I say it, I mean it. Half the island knows about it at this stage. These young-fellas we met from Cabra, some of them know that spa Paddy I was into a while back, they all know and the young-ones from Ballyfermot and even Kevin, a fella that's here with his ma and da that Concepta made friends with and made come out with us last night.

We were up in the Irish Centre and we were all up doin' the karaoke and we had met up with the lads from Cabra; Anto, Padjo, Whacko, Micko and Git. Miranda can't stand them. She says their all workin' class hoodlums, whatever that means. She's a snotty cow and she's comin' very close to gettin' a dig.

The young-ones from Ballyfermot came out as well so we had a bit of laugh. They're lovely. There's Asho, Tasha, Natalie and Kylie. We were all locked, up singin' the Spice Girls and all the rest of it and Concepta got up and did *Like A Virgin*, surprise, surprise. She's done it every night since we got here and let me tell ya, Concepta Cooney is far from bein' like a virgin! Your man Padjo is always all over me but I told him I have a fella. I don't know how many times one of them had an argument with Miranda coz she said Celtic Jerseys are for skangers. Only for Tracy stepped in to stop them from killin' each other. That Miranda one is the biggest bitch I've ever met. She even told Natalie that workin' as a hairdresser was a job for gay men and skangers and Natalie told her that she might be a skanger, but there was no way she was a gay man.

Anyway, none of us met up with anyone so the girls left to go on to a club and the fellas said they were goin' back to their apartments to get something to eat so it was only our own group of eight and your man Kevin walkin' home. He's a bit of alright Kevin, and a lovely bloke and he's from Blanchardstown too so it's not too far from us.

We were on our way home and Miranda says something to Concepta. I didn't hear coz I was talkin' to Paulo and Kevin and Concepta goes to hit her a dig but Miranda ducks and gives Concepta an uppercut into the face. An uppercut! It was like something out of Street Fighter! Well all hell broke loose and Concepta and Miranda are goin' at it and I have to give it to Miranda, despite the fact she's a snobby, stuck up, two-faced, posh cow, she knows how to fight but meself, Paulo, Tracy and Jasmin are in the middle tryin' to break it up and Tracy starts shoutin' at Miranda and Bernie shouts at Tracy and that fight from back before

Paddy's day is brought back up and then the fight between Paulo and Bopper and Jasmin and even the fight between me and Concepta and Bernie the night before we left and there's madness and we're all shoutin' at each other and theres people passin' by wonderin' what's goin' on and poor Kevin is standin' there thinkin' we're all mental, although can ya blame him?

To cut a long story short, Tracy brought the cushions from the sofa bed in her apartment down to ours and all her stuff as well so now she's sleepin' on our floor and won't talk to Bernie or Miranda. I wonder will Kevin come out with us again after that.

✳✳✳

We were robbed. I swear to god, it was a disgrace. There we were walkin' down the road mindin' our own business, this was meself, Tracy, the Concepta one, Paulo and Kevin, who I'd say is only hangin' around with us coz he has no friends here and he gets on with Paulo better than anyone else so that's why he does be with us instead of Bopper, Miranda, Jasmin and Bernie, or the saps as we're callin' them. In fairness though, that's what they are!

So we're walkin' down the road comin' back from the beach, sand everywhere I might add, I'll never get it out of me arse, and about eight of these big African women start comin' towards us. Now before ya start callin' me a racialist, let me remind ya I have a friend from Bosnia, a friend from China and a friend from Turkey and I work with a fella from Ukrainia so I'm far from a racialist. I'm just tellin' ya that these were big mammas, like it wouldn't have mattered if they were black, white or pink with green stripes, they were fuckers after what they did.

We're walkin' towards them anyways and they kind of try block us and put their hands out to shake and I put both me hands behind me back coz the rep warned us about it at the meetin' and Concepta is havin' none of it but Paulo, Kevin and Tracy shake hands and the women tie these pieces of string around their wrists and there's two in front of me and two in front of Concepta and I go to move and one of them grabs me arm and ties one of these things around it and I can see the others all arguin' and Paulo hands over €20 and your woman walks off and they have us all separated so one of them goes for me wallet and I move again and start strugglin' and get meself free from your woman's grip and grab Kevin by the arm and pull him away. Next minute, Concepta goes berserk and punches one of them, kicks another, punches another two and turns and one of them has a knife on her and tells her to hand over her wallet so they're all around Concepta now and I was terrified but ya know Concepta, she pushes the knife out of your woman's hand, head butts her, struggles through them and tells us to run and there the five of us were runnin' down the road although they didn't follow us. Concepta's in the height of it although she said she's not gonna get worked up about it and let it spoil her holiday. We ended up laughin' about it at the pool later. It was gas coz we were on one side of the pool and the saps were on the other and they must have been convinced we were laughin' at them. I hope they were.

***

It's gas. We have half the people in the apartments playin' water polo. There's no entertainment or anything so durin' the day we all just sit around the pool gettin' a tan, or severely sunburned in some cases. One of the lads from Cabra told us that they heard our Bopper took the wrong bottle out of Jasmin's suitcase and ended up puttin' on Immac instead of aftersun and took off all the hair on his arms. I asked him was it true and he ignored me but I took a look and there's not a hair on his body from his neck to his waist, the stupid fucker.

None of the four of them, Bernie, Miranda, Bopper or Jasmin were at the pool the last two days so they haven't seen the water polo. It started off with me, Tracy, Paulo and Kevin and more and more people started joinin' in. Concepta's not a strong swimmer and she went down the deep end the first time she got in the pool and nearly drowned only Paulo saved her.

The water is freezin' when ya first get in. Me nipples do be so hard ya can hang keys from them and there's a horrible smell from the pool as well. I'm convinced there does be cats pissin' in it at night or the little German kids although we're makin' them stay in the baby pool when we're playin water polo. Half the people playin' don't speak a word of English but ya know Concepta, she seems to be able to communicate with them all, no problem to her. She sorts out the teams and everything. She's an awful dirty tackler as well. We made her cut her toe-nails after she made some poor Dutch girl bleed, although in fairness, it was an accident. Concepta was tryin' to swim away and didn't see your woman and there's nothing worse than a kick in the fanny.

✼✼✼

It was another mad locked night last night. That Concepta one is a dirty bitch. She had sex on the beach last night and I'm not talkin' about the cocktail although she had plenty of them as well and I wouldn't mind but it was with two of the fellas from Cabra. Two of them. Whacko and Git. I was disgusted with her at first but she said she was really careful and it was only great, so once she knows what she's doin'. She gave us all the details about it and all and I have to say, fair play to her. Whacko and Git are nice enough lookin' fellas as well. She was sayin' Git has both his nipples pierced and a really big willy, the dirty slapper.

Meself and Tracy were bein' chatted up by these two fellas from Waterford and they had to have been the stupidest fuckers I've met in me life. Jasmin wouldn't have a patch on them and that's sayin' something. Me and Tracy got a great laugh out of confusin' them.

Concepta Cooney nearly fell off the podium at one stage. Now can ya imagine Concepta fallin' on top of someone? She'd crush them. It'd be like an elephant fallin' on an ant. I told her not to be on that podium when she's drunk coz she has no balance. She'll end up hurtin' some poor unsuspectin' fucker.

I'm still shocked about her and her sex on the beach. It kinda makes me think about my Dave and I have to be honest, I've come close to cheatin' on him more than once since we got to the Canaries but meself and Tracy are lookin' out for each other to make sure we're bein' good. This fella was all over her there last night. The state of him. He looked like your man that plays football for Holland with the sunglasses, Ruud Gullit or something, only this fella has huge lips. Huge! Your man Pete Burns wouldn't have a patch on him but had he been any better lookin', I'm sure Tracy would have ended up snoggin' him and we promised each other we'd be faithful to our boyfriends, although as I said, its gettin' harder everyday especially with Concepta tellin' us what she's gettin' up to.

***

Oh good god. The scandal here in Gran Canaria. I'm not able. It's like an episode of *Eastenders* on this holiday only worse.

We were in that Hippodrome place last night, meself, Concepta, Tracy, Paulo and that Kevin fella and it was all the usual, us gettin' locked, havin' a laugh and all the rest of it and some fella is chattin' up Tracy and I go to the toilet with Concepta and I nearly died. There was Tracy Murtagh with her tongue down this young-fellas throat. Needless to say, I reefed her away from him and told her she should have more sense but she wasn't really too pushed and said a little kiss wouldn't matter which is unbelievable comin' from her coz I said the exact same thing to her about your man Padjo from Cabra and she nearly had a conniption, the cheeky cow.

An hour or so later, I look around and I was convinced I saw Paulo kissin' someone only I didn't get a proper look and I got distracted by something Tracy was tellin' me and I forgot all about it and its not til I go to the toilet that I see Paulo again and true enough, there he was kissin' someone and at first I thought nothing of it til I realised the person he was kissin' was your man Kevin. So instead of goin' to the toilet, I go straight back to the girls and Concepta says to me, 'Jayzis

Joanna, are ya alright?' I look up at her and I says, 'I think Paulo is gay. I'm after seein' him kissin' that fella Kevin.' And Concepta smiles and says, 'Ah fuck off, Joanna,' but I tell them what I saw and Tracy says fellas are always doin' that on holidays. All the drink makes them horny and they get to a stage where it doesn't matter if they're kissin' a bird or a bloke but Concepta still wasn't convinced so the two of us go over to where I'd seen them and true enough, there they were still kissin' and ya know Concepta, she says Jayzis a little bit too loud and they hear her and turn to look and there's me and Concepta lookin' at them and they nearly died but nothing was said. Me and Concepta went back to Tracy and she wouldn't say a word about it for some reason. We didn't see Paulo and Kevin for the rest of the night. They must have gone somewhere else, probably scarlet although they needn't have been. I love Paulo to bits and once he's happy then that's all that matters. I don't care if he's gay. And here was me always convinced that he was into me. Maybe he was and became a gay when he realised he couldn't have me. I should have asked Tracy does that happen often. She'd know what with her studyin' psychology at UCD and all. Maybe he turned gay coz Concepta kept askin' him out that time, although maybe he was gay all along and we just never noticed. Usually ya can tell in a person, although in sayin' that, I was shocked when I found out about your man from Westlife.

✳✳✳

Paulo's a bisexual and not a gay. He told us this mornin'. Meself, Tracy and Concepta were asleep when he came in last night so he told us all about it this mornin' while we sat down to breakfast. It was actually the first mornin' we had breakfast since we got here. Proper breakfast like, not just a Cornetto or a Burger King. We actually sat down at the table in the apartment and ate. I think it was coz we were all after the gossip from Paulo. Meself, Concepta and Tracy were sittin' there when he woke up and he came and sat down and says he knows we saw what happened and that he's bisexual and me and Concepta are shocked but Tracy doesn't bat an eyelid and it turns out that she's known ages. She found out ages ago coz a fella in her college knows him and he told Bopper ages ago and Jasmin as well and even Sheila and me Uncle Dessie know and Yenta asked him straight out the first night we were out with her. The only ones that didn't know were meself, Concepta and Bernie. Can ya believe that? Bisexual though! He was tellin' us all about it. It means that he fancies girls and fellas and that he doesn't really have a preference. Concepeta told him he was just greedy but he said it's not really a choice. I'm delighted now coz I've never met a bisexual before and it turns out Paulo was one all along. So I still could have been right about him fancyin' me. I'm ragin' I never knew though.

✲✲✲

I don't think I've ever been in as much pain in me life. We went go-kartin' today and I've got bruises in places I never even knew I had places and they're huge bruises as well and bright blue and purple. There isn't a hope that I'll be able to wear a skirt tonight.

The lads from Cabra were all goin' to the go-kartin' and they said it to Paulo and Kevin to go as well and meself, Tracy and Concepta ended up invitin' ourselves along as well. I don't know where Bernie, Bopper, Jasmin and Miranda were. We haven't seen much of them the last few days. They don't even sit at the pool and even if we see them we just say hello and keep walkin' although if its Bopper I'll make sure he's alright coz as I said, me ma would batter me if anything happened to the little bollix.

The go-kartin' was a great laugh though. All the lads thought they were Michael Schumacher. We did this race kinda thing and we were all behind them little painted lines, the grid I think they call it, and the lads from Cabra made the three girls go at the back, the cheek of them. So then when the race started, I put me foot to the floor and started overtakin' them all and meself and Kevin are flyin' ahead of everyone and then Concepta spins in front of me when I'm tryin' to overtake her and how I didn't crash into a big wall of tyres, I don't know. I could have been killed over her. I ended up winnin' and all so I was delighted and I kept askin' the fellas from Cabra what it was like bein' beaten by a girl and they said credit where it's due, I'm a great driver. I should take it up professionally. I'd be deadly in Formula 1. I'd be only the image of mafis in a Ferrari.

※※※

I feel terrible, really I do. I couldn't even face ringin' Dave today to talk to him coz I'm kinda, what's the word? Ashamed over what I did.

We went to the Irish Centre last night. It was meself, Concepta, Tracy and the girls from Ballyfermot. Paulo and Kevin went up to the Yumbo Centre to watch a drag show and I was only dyin' to go with them but we'd already promised the Ballyfermot young-ones.

I feel a bit sorry for your man Kevin. Paulo was tellin' us all about him. The poor young-fella doesn't know what he is. Paulo was the first fella he's ever kissed and his mind is all over the place, god love him. He's only 16 as well so ya do have to think about that as well. Tracy says he might just be goin' through a bit of a phase and that it happens to most people at some stage and he's probably just a little bit curious. She says it happens all the time with fellas. Young-ones are worse she says, coz if two girls kiss its sexy and if two fellas kiss, everyone thinks they're gay. I suppose she's right. She's great for explainin' things like this. It's all that studyin' English and Psychology in UCD.

There was nearly killin's and us only after walkin' into the pub last night. This waiter pulled a stool out for Asho, one of the Ballyfermot young-ones, to sit down on and next minute, Natalie sits on it. Well the two of them started screamin' the heads off each other there in the middle of the bar and the poor waiter hadn't a clue where to look. Sayin' that now, either did meself, Concepta or Tracy. It was crazy, and all over a stool as well. Natalie ended up walkin' out in a huff and Kylie had to run after her. She's unreal is Kylie. She won't sip drinks. She just lowers them back in one go when she gets them. She had a bottle of Fanta there yesterday and just drank the whole thing straight away. The same in McDonalds the day before.

Anyway, after they left, we did what we usually do, which is just gettin' locked really. I was out of me bin. Seriously now. I don't think I've been as bad since I got here and this Austrian fella, well Concepta tells me he was Austrian, he comes over and starts chattin' me up and he was the image of Robbie Williams although I was that drink he was probably more like Venus Williams but what happens was, with me bein' so drunk and all, I ended up kissin' him and he starts askin' me to go back to his place and all the rest of it and I tell him I have a fella and he starts bein' real forceful, grabbin' me arm and that so I just told him to fuck off and he starts shoutin' something at me in Austrian and then disappears. I know it wasn't anything big but I still feel bad out on Dave. I kinda miss him to be honest, plus I haven't had sex in two weeks.

✳✳✳

Our apartment was raided last night. I swear to god. I didn't know what was goin' on at first. I thought it was Paulo or something but the door burst open and we eventually wake up, meself, Concepta in the bedroom and Paulo and Tracy in the livin' room on the fold out beds all fast asleep coz we came home early coz Concepta Cooney fell off the podium and twisted her ankle and managed to land on someone, although the poor young-fella wasn't squashed too much although he's probably traumatised for life. She would have been injured a lot worse if he wasn't there to break her fall.

Anyway, there we are all asleep and next minute, I hear a big bang and I wake up and there's these guards rushin' through the apartment and shoutin' in Spanish and to be honest, at first I thought it might have something to do with Tracy bunkin' into our apartment when there's only meant to be three of us and then I thought maybe it has something to do with Concepta breakin' that machine in the arcade. The bitch was so heavy that she broke this kids thing when she sat on it. But then I realise they all have machine guns and that it's something more serious than that and they open the balcony door, shine a torch onto the floor of it, shout something in Spanish and then all of them leave, five of them there were, and we're all still there wonderin' what's just after happenin'. Concepta Cooney's not impressed at all so she throws on a pair of shorts and a tee-shirt and hobbles down to the reception to give out yards and the ugly lookin' auld-one behind the desk tells her it's a drugs raid and Concepta tells her we don't have any drugs and that the strongest thing any of us has taken is a Nurofen Plus and your woman tells her that the police thought someone outside had thrown something onto our balcony and Concepta says to her, 'We're on the 8th floor, ya'd need a rocket to get something onto our balcony from down there.' We're gonna complain to the rep. Concepta wants compensation.

✳✳✳

I can hardly believe what happened last night. All of us are actually back talkin' again. No word of a lie. We all made up on the last night of the holiday and fair enough, there was a lot of drink involved, a hell of a lot of drink involved, but still, it's good that it happened coz it was just ridiculous that eight of us came on this holiday and we split into two groups of four although ours was five really coz Kevin's been with us the whole time. It was great to be a big group again, even if it was the last night.

Meself, Concepta, Tracy, Paulo and Kevin left our apartment last night, all of us lookin' forward to a good night, although I'll admit, I was knackered after the big game of water polo we'd played in the pool. Three and a half hours. We didn't even notice the time. We went to this bungee trampoline thing as well and it was great craic. What they do is put a harness around ya with bungee ropes attached to it and they're hangin' from big poles 50 foot in the air and you're on trampolines and when ya bounce, ya go up real high. Ya wanna see us doin' flips and all. Concepta couldn't get on coz of her sore ankle although I doubt they'd have found a harness big enough for her.

We did a bit of a pub crawl and eventually end up in the Hippodrome and who's sittin' there only Bernie, Jasmin, Bopper and Miranda so for the whole night, we're all there givin' each other filthy looks and at one stage, I'm dancin' with Paulo and I see Miranda and she's tryin' to get away from this fella but he's not takin' no for an answer and he's got his hands all over her and I can tell by her face that he's botherin' her and she goes to walk away and he grabs her and the strap off her top breaks and she's about to burst out cryin', I could tell by her face, so I run over, push your man and give him a dig into the face and his nose is bleedin' and Miranda can't believe what I've just done and everyone is just starin' and I say to her 'Don't let a prick like him treat ya like that.' And she breaks into tears and throws her arms around me, givin' me a big hug and she can't thank me enough so I eventually say to her, 'Look Miranda love, let's put all this shite behind us.' So I go up to Bernie, Bopper and Jasmin and I say, 'look lads, we've been mates for years so it'd be mad to keep carryin' on like this. Now I'm willin' to forget everything and whatever about everyone else, my problems with people are in the past and as far as I'm concerned, everything's forgiven and forgotten.' So ten minutes later and everyone's back talkin' and we're all havin' a laugh and it's by far the best night of the holiday and I'm just ragin' that I have to go home, that we couldn't have had a few good nights like that where we're all friends and where no ones fightin' coz the whole time I was lookin' forward to it bein' all eight of us havin' a great time together and it didn't happen until the last night, not that I haven't had a great time, just that it would have been nice.

※※

It was much less of an ordeal comin' home than goin' out, mainly coz we could fly directly from Las Palmas to Dublin and not have to go through Belfast or anywhere else although in sayin' that, we were very nearly not allowed leave Spain.

What happened was, Concepta found a little lizard on the balcony yesterday mornin' and decided she kinda liked him and wanted to keep him but we told her there was no way coz ya can't take things like that out of the country. The rep told me I couldn't even bring home a cactus for Marie from work so we told Concepta to let the lizard go and we all thought she did and that'd be the end of it but when we were goin' through customs in the airport, they stopped Concepta's bag when it went through the scanner yoke and opened it in front of all of us and pulled out this box and what's inside it only this lizard. At first Concepta pretended she knew nothing about it but it was kinda obvious she did and the customs people started goin' mad and nearly weren't lettin' us through but then they just took the lizard, which Concepta had named Usher, and she was in bits.

The plane home was grand only Tracy started tellin' me about blood clots ya do get in your legs on long flights. DDT or something it's called and they have these special socks ya wear for it and all. I made sure not to drink on the plane after me gettin' locked on the way over and anyways, I've had so much drink over the last two weeks that I wouldn't be too bothered if I never had vodka again, although in sayin' that.

***

Me uncle Dessie is gone. God knows where but he's gone. Me ma's the only one that knows but won't tell any of us, not even me da coz she says he could be in a lot of danger if we find out. I doubt he's gone off to spy on Russia or anything but it has to be a big enough deal if even me and Bopper aren't allowed know where he is. Bopper is convinced he's gonna be on Big Brother.

He has me ma lookin' after his house as well and she got to meet all the Filipino nurses and she said they're lovely. I wonder does him disappearin' have anything to do with the Filipino nurses. Or maybe it has something to do with the house and the thing about me Aunt Doris wantin' half of everything he owns. I bet ya it has something to do with that bitch. I never did like her.

Bopper seems to think that Dessie and Sister Mary Immaculate Conception are havin' some sort of relationship. I don't know whether he's just makin' that up or it's based on something Dessie told him but I'm sure if there was any chance of it, Petulia next door would have found out and told half the city. There'd be auld-ones ringin' Joe Duffy about me Uncle Dessie goin' out with a nun, but in sayin' that, who are we to judge? As far as I'm concerned, all that matters in life is that people are happy. She's still around though so maybe it's not true.

I have to admit, I'm kinda worried about him. I've gotten even closer to him since he moved in and it was his birthday while we were in Spain and I was dyin' to see him to give him his present. I got him a big bottle of Eternity by Calvin Klein. I hope he's alright. On the other hand, at least I can sleep in me own bed for a change, although I made sure I changed the covers first. Me Uncle Dessie is a single man after all. Well unless he's shaggin' the nun.

***

Bernie went back to London today and I'm kinda ragin' coz we weren't talkin' most of the time she was here and then in the Canaries and its only since the night we made up that everything seems to be back to normal between us. Even in the few days before she went it wasn't the same coz I was annoyed and all that stuff with Mister O'Toole had just happened so I wasn't too happy with her but now that she's goin', I don't really want her to. I'd like to have her here for a few more days so we can hang out together and have a laugh. Ya know all the usual stuff we do.

Yesterday we went into town, this was after I finished work. I left early coz Amy wanted to do a few extra hours and I don't really need the money. I'm kinda loaded at the moment coz I didn't spend half the money I brought to the Canaries with me and I even bought loads of perfume there and all. Anyway, meself and Bernie are in town yesterday and we caught the shops before they closed and she got herself a few bits for goin' back to England coz they don't have a Dunnes near where she lives, let alone a Sasha. We went to Eddie Rockets then and I even had the chicken tenders as well as a burger and chips. I felt like Concepta eatin' all that food but I was starvin'.

I'm in bits over Bernie goin' back to be honest but I've learned me lesson. She was the one that rang me and asked me to sort everyone else out and then I got involved, although in fairness, I was goin' through a very traumatic time in me life. I could have died.

✳✳✳

Concepta Cooney joined Weight Watchers. I swear to god. Her, me ma and Jasmin's ma went last night. I think Concepta got a bit of a fright when she saw some of the pictures of the holiday and realised what she looked like in a swimsuit. I didn't say anything when she told me about the pictures but when I saw them I had to agree. I know what they say about the camera addin' 10 pounds but let's call a spade a spade, Concepta is fat.

When she told me about the Weight Watchers, I wasn't holdin' me breath coz Concepta's always on a diet and has never lost any weight although she says she dropped a dress size there a while ago but I don't really believe her. She's tried every diet, the Atkins diet, the protein diet and all the rest of it but it never works, mainly because Concepta Cooney has problems walkin' past a McDonalds. At the end of the day, she eats too much and doesn't exercise enough.

She went the Weight Watchers last night and she said she was real nervous coz she's never done anything like that before and she nearly died when she went to be weighed and they told her she was 17 stone 2 pounds. She said what it was in Kilograms but I can't remember. 17 stone 2 pounds though. I'm only nine and a half so she's nearly two of me. She says she wants to get down to 10 stone by Christmas. I'll believe it when I see it. It's not that I have no faith in Concepta or anything, actually no, that's a lie, I don't have any faith in Concepta. Give it a few days and she'll be in Burdocks havin' a battered sausage and curry chips and that's about 50 Weight Watchers points.

✳✳✳

Paulo thinks Leandra is a lesbian. Ya know me manager Leandra? He says he's definitely seen her in gay places before but as I said to him, she just could have friends that are gay. I mean, just because she was drinkin' in a gay pub doesn't make her a lesbian does it? He said there was just something about her as well though although he couldn't really put his finger on it.

He came into the shop today all smiles coz him and your man Kevin from the holiday are goin' to the pictures tonight. They're kinda goin' out together and Paulo is only delighted. It's great though coz the two of them get on great together and I have to say, I like Kevin. He does have a bit of Westlife look off him, I'll admit, but he's still a good lookin' fella. I think he's finally comin' to terms with his sexuality. Tracy told me all about it. I'm still ragin' that bitch knew about Paulo bein' bisexual before me. She told me it was kind of obvious and she had set Paulo up with fellas when I was there. I must have been drunk when this happened coz I can't remember although in sayin' that, it's very likely I was.

He was talkin' to Leandra for a minute when he was in today and when she walked off, he asked me was she a lesbian and of course I'd never even thought about it and anyways, it's none of my business. I mean, she's never talked about a fella, or a young-one for that matter, so I don't really know although Paulo says ya can tell. Fair enough, some lesbians ya can kinda guess but to say all lesbians are butch is like sayin' everyone from Turkey is a terrorist.

No. I doubt Leandra is a lesbian. Not that it's any of my business. I'll still try to find out mind you. Trust me to get all the gossip on someone.

**

I finally got to see Dave last night for the first time since I got back from the Canaries and I'll be honest, I missed him terribly. He was in Tullamore all week on a conference and he only got back last night, although he's been ringin' me every night askin' how

I got on in Spain, what I got up to and all the rest of it. I kinda felt really bad over kissin' that fella in Spain last week, Padjo I think it was although it could have been Git. Jayzis isn't that dreadful? I don't even remember the fellas name although I was locked, don't forget that. It's not really an excuse for cheatin' on me fella though and it doesn't matter whether it was Padjo, Git or Gonzo from the Muppets.

Tracy says it was only a kiss and it's not really a big deal and that even if her fella Lance found out, he wouldn't mind too much but in sayin' that, she warned us not to tell him about her and that young-fella in the Hippodrome. I had no intention of tellin' anyone anything to be honest although Tracy wouldn't be the type to tell on me if I told on her kinda thing. Concepta would and Bernie definitely would but come to think of it, Concepta, Paulo, Kevin and Tracy are the only ones that know unless the Cabra lads told the others. The lads from Cabra even want to meet up with us for a drink. Can ya imagine? Whatever about introducin' them to me boyfriend, I can't even remember which of them I was kissin'.

✳✳✳

Most of us are broke after the holidays so no one wanted to go out, Saturday night or not. I'm not broke or anything but the others are so we had to stay in and I was havin' none of it so eventually Yenta asks us around to her place. I kinda missed Yenta when I was in Spain. I was ragin' she didn't come coz I'd say she would have been a deadly laugh and she would have been able to handle them women with the bracelets that pulled a knife on poor Concepta. If there's someone who knows how to handle herself, its Yenta.

We went to the offo first before goin' to Yenta's gaff, one of them apartments on the 6th floor in one of them new places flyin' up all over the place although not that far from us. We were dyin' for Kevin to meet her as well and she was dyin' to meet him coz Paulo had been talkin' to her durin' the week and told her about him. We made sure to bring the pictures as well to show her.

We got to Yenta's and bloody typical, the lift wasn't workin' so we had to walk up six flights of stairs to her apartment with all the drink and I have to be honest, I was wrecked after it and I thought I was fit, especially with all that dancin' and water polo on holidays. Whatever about me, Concepta Cooney nearly died twice on the way up. I told her it'd be great for her Weight Watchers. She told me to fuck off.

We'd a good night in the end and Tracy knocked up about one o'clock after bein' out with Lance and Jasmin and Bopper were goin' to but didn't in the end. Yenta was sayin' her brother is comin' over next week too. She told us his name but I'm fucked if I remember it, let alone be able to pronounce it.

✳︎✳︎✳︎

I got a phone call today and I'm still a bit confused over it. I was on me break in work today and the phone rings and at first I thought it was one of the girls or maybe Bopper or even me Uncle Dessie to let me know he's alright coz me nerves are in bits over him but its this auld-fella on the phone and he says, 'Hello am I speakin' to Joanna Ryde?' 'Yeah,' says I, wonderin' what this is about and he says, 'Hello Joanna, this is John Rogan from Trainspotting Ireland and I was just wondering if you were still interested in becoming a member.' So I'm thinkin' this is someone takin' the piss til I remember that letter I got before I went to Spain about transportin' or somethin'. So I says to him, 'Sorry I think ya have the wrong person.' And he says, 'Are you not interested in trainspotting?' And I says to him, I says 'I haven't even seen it. It was on Channel 4 there a few weeks ago and I was meant to watch it but I don't know what happened that I didn't. I think me mate Concepta has it on DVD although in sayin' that, she probably robbed it off one of me other mates. She does that, Concepta.' And your man on the other end of the phone goes all quiet and says he thinks he might have the wrong person and I ask him does he want me to watch *Transpottin'* and ring him back but he tells me that it has nothing to do with the film, that trainspottin' is lookin' at trains to see the numbers on them or some shite like that and I'm wonderin' is this fella for real so I say to him, 'That sounds like a load of bollix. Why the fuck would ya want to sit beside a train track lookin' at the trains passin' by. Ya'd have to be a bit of a sad bastard wouldn't ya?' But he just hung up. The cheek.

✷✷✷

I've been tryin' to get all the gossip on Leandra but she's not sayin' much. I was talkin' to her for ages today and I was tryin' to drop things into the conversation and she was talkin' about ex-boyfriends and all the rest of it but Paulo says she could have realised recently and that she could be a bisexual as well and that more people are bisexual than ya think coz most people think ya have to be straight or gay and that there's nothing in between. He'd know, I wouldn't.

    Leandra was talkin' about this girl called Samantha a lot and I was tryin' to get a bit of info on her and it turns out that Leandra actually lives with this Samantha one. Now whether they're shaggin' or not, she didn't say, although I very nearly asked. Ya think ya know someone though don't ya. I mean, I've been workin' with Leandra for god knows how long and it's only now that I find out who she lives with and ya think that's something that would have come up in conversation before. Paulo said it didn't coz she was hidin' it from us coz this Samantha one is actually her girlfriend. I told him that's stupid though. Just coz two young-ones live together doesn't make them lesbians does it? I mean, what about the Filipino nurses in Dessie's gaff? They're four young-ones, it doesn't mean they're lesbians. Paulo still thinks he's right though. I'm not too sure. I mean, if Leandra was a lesbian, she would have told us, mainly just to see the look on Julie Walsh's face.

✷✷✷

I got a letter today and straight away I got a fright coz I recognised the handwritin' as Mister O'Toole's. So I called our

Bopper and he comes down and I hand the letter to him and ask him to open it but I don't say anything about it bein' from Mister O'Toole or the fact that there might be anthrax in it and at first he looks at me and tells me to open it meself and I just say, 'Please Bopper, I'm afraid.' And he sighs and rips it open and takes two pieces of paper out of it. One of them is a note written on a piece of white paper and the other is a €500 note. I knew straight away coz it's purple and I can see Boppers face drop and he's about to read the note, the nosey fucker, only I grab it off him and it says, 'Dearest Joanna, my apologies for the hardship I've put you through. Please accept this as a sign of my remorse, with love.' And that's it. No name signed on the end of it. No nothing, although it was kinda obvious who it's from and our Bopper's examinin' the envelope and he says to me, 'Who do ya know in Brazil?' And I ask him what he's talkin' about and he says, 'This letter was sent from Rio De Janeiro in Brazil.' And I have to say, I nearly died. Mister O'Toole ran away to Brazil. That's how the police couldn't find him. He wasn't even in the country. At least now I know he's hundreds of miles away so he won't really be able to try and kill me again. Plus I'm €500 richer as well so good news all round.

∗∗

Fair play to Concepta, she lost five pounds this week and she was only delighted. She went to the Weight Watchers last night, dreadin' gettin' on the scales me ma was tellin' me and she nearly died when they told her she was only 16 stone 11, down from 17 stone 2 and she wasn't even tryin' that much. She was even eatin' pizza with the rest of us in Yenta's there on Saturday night and not just one slice, she ate nearly a whole pepperoni and extra cheese to herself. She has been goin' walkin' though so that's probably helpin'. Her and me ma went there on Monday night and ya wanna see the state of me ma. She was wearin' these grey leggin's that were bet on to her. I think she got them in Penneys about three years ago and has never worn them and these white runners that I'm sure she's never worn before even though she says she has. A good long walk they went on as well and I'd say poor Concepta was only in bits after it. Me ma's only over 12 stone so I'd say she can walk a good bit further than Concepta. They even walked to the Weight Watchers tonight. There was me ma, Jasmin's ma, Concepta and that Celine O'Reilly one, all of them with the leggin's and never been worn runners, even Concepta. The slaggin's I gave her over it. Me da thinks they're like a fat version of the Spice Girls.

✷✷✷

I was on the bus today with Yenta coz the two of us had a day off and we thought we'd go into town to get a bit of shoppin' coz her brother is comin' over tomorrow from Turkey and she wanted a few things for the apartment coz her old flat mate just moved out while we were in Spain and took loads of things with her and Yenta was in the height of it coz most of it was hers anyway coz it's her apartment. She owns it like and was rentin' the other room out to this one. Where she gets the money from I don't know but we think the bank are payin' her loads coz she speaks about 27 languages and all the rest of it. She doesn't even know how long her brother is comin' over for and she doubts that he even knows. She said that the way he was talkin' on the phone, he wants to stay here for a while, see how things go, get a job and all the rest of it. She thought he was comin' for a holiday for a week and then he rings her and tells her he's sorted out a work permit and all that shit.

Anyway, we're on the bus today, meself and Yenta and the traffic is dreadful. I haven't seen it as bad in a long time and we're about 40 minutes goin' past Glasnevin Cemetery and we look out the window and see what's holdin' up the traffic. There, in the middle of the road outside the petrol station, is an elephant. No word of a lie. An elephant. Where it came from, I don't know but the police were there and all although what did they think they were goin' to do? Arrest it? An elephant in the middle of Glasnevin! And it wasn't Julie Walsh before ya say it!

August

Dave wants me to go meet his ma and I told him there was no way. I mean, can ya imagine me? Scarlet like. I know where he's comin' from like coz we've been goin' out for four months and I still haven't met his parents but I'm not really that pushed. I wouldn't mind but he wants me to go all the way to Kildare with him next weekend to meet them so I've been beggin' Leandra to make me come into work but she thinks it's gas, the bitch. She thinks I should go coz it's only fair that I meet his ma and da after him meetin' mine but as I told her, I couldn't have cared if he had met me ma and da, the only reason he did was coz some nutcase who now happens to be in Brazil, thank god, tried to kill me and the only way he could see me was to come over to the gaff.

Talkin' about Leandra, I was tryin' to suss out whether she's a lezzer again and it turns out that her flat mate Samantha has a fella who does this mad job, something to do with the government and space. There was a word she said but I can't remember, not that it matters, whoever this chap is. It does prove though that Leandra and Samantha aren't lesbian lovers though, although in sayin' that, maybe they are and this spacey fella hasn't a clue what's goin' on.

Anyway, back to Dave. I don't really want to meet his ma and da but I bet ya he's goin' to guilt trip me into it and none of me mates will help me coz they all think I should go too, the bastards. I bet ya Dave was talkin' to them all already. I thought Yenta or Concepta would have helped but no. The pair of bitches are on his side. I'm wonderin' if I could try catch something before next weekend. Maybe the flu. Or better still, Syphilis!

✳✳✳

Yenta's brother is mad. I wouldn't mind but the chap can't speak a word of English and I thought Sheila from work was bad.

He arrived yesterday and ya know Yenta, she invites the whole lot of us over to her place for dinner and a few drinks so we can meet her brother. Marvin his name is and I'll be honest, he's a looker, real dark and handsome. We walk in and Yenta is introducin' all of us in Spanish or whatever language they speak in Turkey. There was me, Tracy, Concepta, Sheila, Paulo, Kevin and Jasmin, who, by the way is lickin' up to us so much since the holiday her tongue is startin' to go brown. Anyway we all say hello and Marvin just smiles and says 'Which is the coolest way to walk?' And Concepta says to him 'So what d'ya think of Dublin so far?' And he smiles and says 'Ah, which is the coolest way to walk?' And then Yenta says something to him in Istanbuli or whatever it is they speak and he says something back to her and then turns to Concepta and says, 'Which is the coolest way to walk?' and no word of a lie, Concepta starts struttin' around the apartment and says, 'probably like this.' She's the image of Beyonce only bigger and we all start crackin' our shites laughin' and Marvin smiles and says, 'Ah yes. Which is the coolest way to walk?' Then Yenta tells us that for some reason, that's the only thing he can say in English and she'd translate for him, which I have to admit, got to be a pain in the arse after half an hour. He's a great bit of laugh though, even if he hasn't a word of our language, although it doesn't really matter much when you're locked. Look at Jasmin. She's managed grand for years.

✳✳✳

I got up this mornin' early, got washed and dressed and went down stairs and I have to be honest, I was only exhausted after bein' in Farley's with Yenta, Marvin and Concepta last night and it wasn't til after two o'clock when we got home. God only knows how coz it was shut at half 12 and its only down the road but sayin' that, I was absolutely locked so we could have been chattin' to people or something and I just can't remember.

So I go down stairs this mornin' with a terrible hangover and not in the mood for work at all and me ma looks at me and goes 'What are ya doin' up so early?' And I tell her I'm goin' to work like I always do and she says to me 'But ya don't usually work bank holidays and it's only then that I realise that it's the August bank holiday and I amn't due in work so I grab a carton of orange juice, drink half of it back in one go and turn and go back upstairs without sayin' anything and manage to take me cloths off somehow before fallin' onto the bed and goin' back to sleep. I must have still been locked at that stage although maybe it was the fact that I'd only had four hours sleep.

Five hours later and I wake up again and I ended up spendin' the rest of the day sittin' out the back in the sun listenin' to the radio. Paulo dropped in for an hour and we had a good chat and it was lovely and relaxin'. Well until a big cloud came and it started rainin'. Me ma's sun lounger was destroyed.

***

Me Uncle Dessie rang today to tell us he's safe and well and that he has some good news although he wouldn't say exactly what it is and that he'll tell us when he gets back and I was only delighted coz I've been really worried about him ever since he disappeared. I thought something terrible had happened or that he was on the run from the police or something. I thought he might have crept in on some poor young-one while she was sleepin' and tried to kill her. We all know it can happen. I had visions of him and Mister O'Toole sittin' on a beach in Brazil. Me Uncle Dessie's not like that though. He wouldn't hurt anyone, although if he ever saw me Aunt Doris again, I'm sure he'd try.

I was thinkin' maybe he got some poor young-one pregnant and ran away coz everyone found out it was him. That'd be more like Dessie. It'd be the type of thing he'd do. It'd be like that film *The Snapper* and everyone would be callin' him Georgie Burgess.

I asked him straight out was there something goin' on with him and Sister Mary Immaculate Conception and he said there wasn't but

I amn't convinced. The rumours are still flyin' around about the two of them but I blame that Misses O'Driscoll one. She's a mouth. She's good friends with that Celine O'Reilly one that goes to the Weight Watchers with me ma and Concepta so I bet ya they're tryin' to get all the gossip, the pair of nosey cows. I warned me ma and Concepta to tell her nothing.

I nearly died when I asked him where he was and he told me he was in Amsterdam although he said he couldn't tell me why he was there. What in the name of Jayzis is he doin' in Amsterdam? I was sayin' it to our Bopper and I was wonderin' if he knew why me Uncle Dessie had gone all the way to Holland but he says he doesn't. I asked him what was in Holland and he says, 'Drugs, Tulips, The Vengaboys and the Philips factory and there's loads of dykes in Holland.' And I was a bit confused and I says, 'What? Like Leandra?'

✳✳✳

I was in work today on the till, Julie Walsh is in Tunisia on her holidays so someone else had to go on the till instead of her. I'm surprised she didn't take the stool with her seein' as she never gets her hole off it. Whatever about seein' Concepta in a bikini, can ya imagine Julie Walsh? I've been tryin' to drop her hints about joinin' the Weight Watchers ever since Concepta started goin' but ya know what Julie Walsh is like, ya'd have to spell it out for her before she knew what you were talkin' about. Hopefully she won't come back from Tunisia and we'll never see her again, or better still, that she goes into the sea and gets eaten by a shark. Jayzis. Theres enough of Julie Walsh to feed every shark in Tunisia for a year.

Anyway, there I was in work today and this young-one I used to go to school with comes in, Yvonne her name is, and I was convinced that Concepta had told me this young-one was pregnant sometime last week and it's been ages since I've seen her and I say, 'Ah howaya Yvonne. I heard the good news. Congratulations. How many months are ya gone?' And she looks at me, not a breeze about what I'm talkin' about and says to me, 'I'm not pregnant Joanna. I got a bad infection in me ovaries there a few months ago and I can't have kids.' Well I nearly died. I don't think I've ever been so scarlet in me life. Concepta Cooney is dead when I get her.

***

It's Boppers birthday today and none of us were too sure about what to get him so Concepta sorted out a bit of a collection for him and we just gave him the money so he can buy something out of it. He's broke at the moment so he needs every bit of money he can get his hands on. We were goin' to go out for a drink tonight but with it bein' Thursday, we said we'd leave it til tomorrow night instead so we could all get locked without havin' to worry about work the next mornin'. I was tryin' to get him to do something on Saturday night so I wouldn't have to go down to Dave's ma and da's house in Kildare but d'ya think he'd do what I asked him and him bein' me brother and all.

He was 17 today. Jayzis. I can remember bein' 17, although I should, it was only seven months ago. People do ask me what it's like havin' a brother a year and a half younger than me and I tell them to try live with our Bopper and then they'd know all about it. I'd much rather have me sister Wanda back from Australia. Ah no in fairness, he can be a pain in the hole at times but I love him to bits and at the end of the day, and even at the start of the day, he's me little brother and I have to look after him even if he doesn't want me to. Not that I did a very good job in the Canaries but he got back to Dublin in one piece and without any sexual diseases, well as far as I know anyway.

Concepta's only delighted today as well coz she lost seven pounds. I nearly died when she told me. I mean, fair play to her, she's doin' deadly. She's down to 16 stone 4 now so she's only 6 stone and 4 pounds away from her target weight and she was delighted as well coz that Celine O'Reilly one put on two pounds and ya'd think she's have lost a bit more coz her mouth has been gettin' enough exercise.

***

Mad night it was last night. Absolutely crazy. We all decided to go to Farley's to start off. This was meself, Concepta, Bopper, Sheila, Jasmin, Paulo and Kevin, my Dave, Tracy and her Lance and Yenta and her brother Marvin, who, fair play to him, has learned how to say 'how's it going?' now as well as 'which is the coolest way to walk?' which is at least a start. Yenta is goin' to start teachin' him English. I got stuck beside him at one stage in the night and it was like tryin' to have a conversation with a Mars Bar. Everytime I tried to say something to him, he'd just smile and either say 'which is the coolest way to walk?' or 'how's it going?' Although now he's tryin' to communicate with his hands. At one stage he was tellin' me he was goin' to the toilet and I thought he was doin' the *Macarena*. I was there joinin' in like a sap and all. In all fairness though, the poor young-fella should make the effort to learn the bit of English. He's here nearly a week and can only say two things, although as I said, Jasmin's been here most of her life and its more than she can manage.

We even brought a cake to Farley's with us and we got Jasmin to make sure Bopper stayed in the toilet for ages so we could put 19 candles on it, mainly coz he has false ID about a year at this stage, and we lit it and when he came back he nearly died coz he wasn't expectin' it, although from the look on Jasmin's face, I don't think she was either and I wouldn't mind but we told her about it and all. We cut the cake up and gave everyone a slice, although Concepta wouldn't have any coz of her diet. She said she didn't know how many Weight Watchers points were in it. I think it's the first time I've ever seen Concepta Cooney say no to a bit of cake but it shows she's serious about this diet. She used to make up diets to suit whatever she wanted to eat at the time.

After Farley's, we all headed into town on the bus like a pack of kids on a school tour. I even threw half a carton of Capri Sun at Sheila and it hit her in the head. The poor bitch thought it was rainin' on the bus. She just laughed. If it had of been Concepta, I would have had the Capri Sun shoved up me arse!

We went to TwentyOne which is what they're after changin' Coyote to and we ended up havin' a great night. We were locked although ya have to be on a birthday. Bopper Ryde was in an awful state and he fell down the stairs at one stage. I'm convinced I saw Concepta Cooney push him, the mad cow. The poor young-fella didn't know where he was but we weren't helpin' him by givin' him more drink. We were goin' to go around gettin' him 17 kisses but he was far too locked for that, and they would have fucked us out if they realised him and Jasmin were under age. He even got sick on the way home and then when we got to the gaff he must have spent a good hour and a half on the floor in the bathroom and I had to carry him to bed. Thank god Dave was stayin' over coz there was no way I'd have carried him up on me own, not that our Bopper is heavy or anything. I went down for a drink at half five this mornin' and there was Bopper asleep on the kitchen floor stark bollock naked. How he got from his bed to the kitchen without killin' himself I don't know. I had to go and wake Dave again to bring him back up although I made Dave put a pair of boxers on him first coz there was no way I was gonna carry our Bopper up the stairs with his willy hangin' out. It's not the type of thing ya want to see at half five on a Saturday mornin'. In fact, I'll be quite happy never to see our Bopper naked again.

※

Dave made me go to his parents' house and I could have killed him. There I was hopin' to enjoy a nice quiet Saturday in, watchin' the telly, maybe goin' over to Yenta's for a chat and a few Turkish meatballs and then probably out for a few drinks but no, Dave dragged me to his ma and da's gaff, kickin' and screamin'. I didn't want to go and I told him as much but then he starts gettin' into a huff and starts sayin' I have to start makin' sacrifices for him and I told him I sacrificed half me bed when he stayed over but he was in a mood over it and starts actin' like a child and askin' me do I still want to be his girlfriend because sometimes he doesn't think I love him and all this shite and I tell him not to be such a sap coz if I didn't want to be with him, then he'd be the first to know. Tell a lie, he wouldn't coz ya know me, I'd probably say it to Tracy, but he'd be second, although now that I think about it, if I told Tracy, I'd have to tell Concepta and probably Paulo and probably Jasmin, Yenta and even our Bopper and I'd have to ring Bernie in England and Wanda in Australia and me Aunty Linda twice and I'd probably tell Leandra, Sheila and Dymphna in work and me Uncle Dessie if he ever comes back from Holland. Anyway, the point is, if I didn't wanna be with Dave, he'd know about it and just because I cheated on him, it doesn't mean anything coz I was locked out of me tree and I was in a different country and it was only a little kiss.

I told Dave all of this of course but I had to give in in the end and go with him but I warned him that I wasn't lookin' forward to it but he was only delighted that he had got me to say yes.

Me da dropped us into town and then we had to go to that big bus station place, Bus R Us, or whatever it is ya call it, to get a bus to Kildare, one of them white buses ya do get to the country and it took us just over an hour to get there and we're walkin' to Dave's house from where the bus drops us off and he's tellin' me about places we're passin' and showin' me where he went to school and all the rest of it and next thing we come to these big gates and Dave presses a few buttons on the panel yoke beside it and start to open on their own and he walks in and there was his house, only huge! At first I thought it was a small hotel but no, it was his house. Seein' his gaff, I was scarlet after bringin' him to my three bedroom terraced house. Tell a lie, I wasn't. I'm happy with what I have. I'm proud of where I came from and I don't need a big house, a Mercedes, a Land Rover and a Ford Fusion to make me happy. Of course I didn't say this to Dave.

We walked up the driveway, me nearly breakin' the heel of me boot walkin' on the pebbles and he goes to the door and opens it and my heart is beatin' really fast as I go inside. I could feel it. Obviously not really feel it coz I'd have to put me hand down me throat to do that but ya know what I mean. Next minute, this huge fucker of a dog runs up and jumps on Dave and then tries to jump on me and I nearly shit meself. This thing was huge. One of them ones out of that film Beethoven, a Saint Brendan I think Dave told me later. Well he licked me face and I screamed, the dog this is, not Dave and he pins me against the wall and Dave had to pull him off me and I look up and there's Dave's ma and da standin' at the door smilin'. 'So this must be Joanna.' Dave's ma says, puttin' her hand out for me to shake and I'm convinced I was bright red at this stage and she gives me a kiss on the cheek right where the dog has just slobbered all over me and then she says, 'Call me Penelope and this is my husband Benjamin and I see you've met Rex.' And like a sap I say, 'Is that the dog?' and Dave's da smiles and gives me a kiss on the cheek and says, 'It's lovely to meet you at last Joanna. Dave told us so much about you.' The fucker. When I get him back to Dublin I'll batter him, don't think I won't!

    Dave brought me up to the room and I left me bag down and he showed me around his room. It was gas, it was still like a kids bedroom even though before we met he used to spend nearly every weekend at home. Its gas isn't it. Like Dave's really mature and all but yet he still has teddy bears on his bed.

    We kinda chilled out for about 40 minutes while Dave showed me a few pictures of when he was a kid and then we went downstairs for dinner and his ma had everything set up in the dinin' room, again, huge it was, 10 people could have fit around the table. She made a soup which I have to admit, was only mafis and then we had some kind of beef dish for the main course with a kind of pepper sauce which was nice enough despite the fact it was a bit nibbly and then the bit of homemade banoffi for desert. I do be well of a bit of banoffi.

    I was scarlet coz his ma and da were askin' me all sorts of questions about me family, what I do and all the rest of it and they were askin' me about Gran Canaria and all and we then moved into what they called the lounge, probably coz they have a sittin' room, a livin' room, a conservatory, a music room, an exercise room, a utility room, an entertainment room, the dinin' room and the kitchen all downstairs too and we had a few glasses of wine and they asked more questions about me and Dave tells them about how he works with me friend Yenta and how I thought she might have been a terrorist just because she's Turkish. The cheek of him. That wasn't the reason I thought she was a terrorist at all. It was a little bit to do with it but it wasn't the reason.

It was after one o'clock when we got to bed and I was a bit knackered anyway. I'm surprised I didn't get me own bedroom coz come on, lets face it, there's enough of them. His ma and da must get lost coz they're there on their own most of the time coz Dave's older brother lives in Canada and his sister is travellin' around South America for some mad reason. Even the dog has his own bedroom. I wonder if they'd be interested in takin' me Uncle Dessie and a few Filipino nurses in.

✳︎✳︎✳︎

She hates me. She absolutely hates me. Penelope I'm talkin' about. Dave's ma. She keeps makin' these smart arsed comments and I don't know if she's jokin' or just tryin' to put me down but it's really gettin' in on me, the same way Miranda got in on me on holiday before she was put in her place but I couldn't do that to Dave's ma and as I learned from Miranda, that's just the way certain people are brought up. People with money just sometimes think they're better than people without money, especially if they had no money to begin with and married into it.

I didn't want to say anything to Dave coz I wouldn't want to put him in an awkward situation and what do ya say anyway? 'Oh I think your ma hates me and by the way, she's a stuck up snob and her face lift is really obvious.'

Seriously like, Dave's brother is nearly 30 which means she has to be at least 50, maybe 55 and she's like a bad version of Cher except a bit smaller. I'd say she got a few things done. Definitely her tits. There is no 50 year old women with tits that perky. Most women that age that I know are lucky their tits aren't scrapin' along the ground as they walk. I don't know what it is though that makes me think she doesn't like me. She was definitely a lot worse today than she was yesterday. Maybe it was coz I was sharin' a bed with her son. We didn't do anything and anyway, even if we did, their bedroom is on the other side of the house.

I think there's a few mas out there who don't like their child's boyfriend or girlfriend, no matter what. In sayin' that now, his da thinks

I'm great. Thank god I go home tomorrow though, if even just to get away from that horrible dog. Rex I'm talkin' about, not Dave's ma.

※

Well thank the good Lord I'm back in Dublin. Seriously like. I miss it when I'm away from it for too long. Fair enough, I was only in Kildare but still, there's no place like home. Now all I have to do is get a pair of red shoes, click them together three times and I'll end up in Kansas. I always loved the *Wizard of Oz*. Me and Bopper used to love it when we were kids with Dorothy and the scarecrow and the tinman and the lion and little Toto the dog, although our Bopper used to be terrified of the munchkins. He's still a big Judy Garland fan to this day.

We got the bus back from Kildare there today. Dave's ma gave us a lift to the bus stop and was still actin' a bit snotty sayin' goodbye. I'm convinced she hates me, convinced of it, although would ya blame her, the things Dave was tellin' her about me. He made me out to be mad into the drink and ya know me, I wouldn't be one to get locked every night of the week. I'm not mad into the drink at all.

I was glad to be on the bus and on the way home to be honest and Dave was wonderin' why I was in a mood. He asked me did I enjoy meself and I just said yes even though I didn't. It was hardly a weekend in Mosney. Still, I went and I acted like I was delighted to be there meetin' his parents and all the rest of it and it's not my fault his ma doesn't like me. It'll be a while before I go back anyway. I know for a fact coz I'll have the flu next time he asks.

※

Yenta rang me today and asked me could I drop over to her apartment after work coz she bought me a little something in town and wanted to give it to me and she said not to have dinner either coz she was goin' to make something so I was thinkin' to meself, lovely, a present and a meal and Yenta's a great cook. Her meatballs are deadly.

Me ma once tried to make meatballs a while back but they were a bit rubbery. Thinkin' about it, I'd say they had a few of Concepta's jellies in them.

Anyway, I finished work, although I was a bit late coz Marie was out sick and Julie Walsh is still in Tunisia, probably lyin' on a beach. She better not fall asleep or she'll wake up with 16 members of Greenpeace tryin' to push her back out to sea. It's probably like watchin' Free Willy every time she gets in the pool.

I got to Yenta's just after seven and Marvin answered the door and said, 'Lovely jubbly. He who dares wins. This time next year we be millionaire.' Which my Dave must have thought him because he loves *Only Fools and Horses* and that's what Del Boy says. So I go in and he says to me, 'Joanna, you langer,' which Tracy's Lance must have taught him coz he's from Cork and that's what people from Cork say. At least he's learnin' a little bit of English and Yenta is teachin' him for a couple of hours every night.

She was all hugs when I saw her and the three of us sat down to dinner and I'm tellin' her all about goin' down to Dave's for the weekend and about his ma not likin' me and about that mutt of a dog Rex and the fact that he kept lickin' me. I wouldn't mind but he'd just been lickin' his hole two minutes before hand.

She was tellin' me all about her weekend and what they got up to and that I didn't miss much except Concepta gettin' off with some fella from Greece in Fitzsimons on Saturday night. Other than that though, she says she has no news and then she remembered the present she got for me in town and I'm wonderin' what it is and she goes into the kitchen and comes back with this little gift bag and hands it to me and I put me hand in and pull out a Tamagotchi. A Tamagotchi! I mean, how old does she think I am? I just smiled and said thank you and pretended I was delighted. Now what would I do with a Tamagotchi?

✳✳✳

The Tamagotchi is only deadly. I sat down last night and read through the instructions so I decided to give it a go to see if I can look after it. I called it Bob but I only found out a few minutes later that it was a girl and I didn't know how to change it then. Ya can only use five letters and there I was tryin' to call the thing Michael and wonderin' why it would only let me write Micha. In the end, I decided on Bob. Not after anyone or anything, just coz it was easy to write.

The poor thing nearly died after only an hour coz I forgot to feed it and it had gone the toilet all over the place and I hadn't cleaned and it was sick as well and this was all in the space of time it took me to go in and have a bath. She was very unhappy as well so I gave her a few sweets and played a game with her so she was grand after that and she fell asleep.

It's great though. I brought it into work today with me. I mean, I was hardly goin' to leave it at home was I? If Marie is allowed bring her four pot plants in with her, then there should be no problem with my Tamagotchi.

Marie didn't know what it was. She thought there was a little person inside it but then again, we all know what that ones like. Sheila spent half the day playin' with it so if I see one around I'll get it for her. She needs a friend. I do feel sorry for her. A Tamagotchi is just what she needs.

***

Concepta Cooney lost another seven pounds. That's nearly €10! I couldn't believe when me ma told me. Fifteen stone 11. She lost a stone in the last two weeks. Now whether that's safe or not, I don't know but she must be doin' something. I'd say she's takin' them slimmin' tablets coz I mean, she only started three weeks ago and she's already down to 15 stone 11 and me ma said she's been slimmer of the week two weeks runnin'. Me ma said she's only delighted with herself but there has to be something up there coz as I told ya before, Concepta Cooney's been on every diet ever invented and some she even invented herself and nothing ever worked for her. She never did the walkin' before but I doubt that's goin' to make a big difference, not as much as it has been. I mean, the first week she lost five pounds, seven the second week and seven this week. That's loads! I'd need a calculator to add that all up.

Maybe she's anorexic. I mean, ya don't have to be skinny to be anorexic, or so Tracy tells me. Most anorexic people start off like Concepta and end up lookin' like pencils with arms, and it's very bad for ya, the anorexia. That's what Karen Carpenter died of and she was only gorgeous and a deadly singer. I do love listenin' to their greatest hits. It's Boppers CD like but I do rob it on him.

Or maybe Concepta has Bulgaria. Ya know when ya eat something and then put your hands down your throat to make yourself sick. I mean, if ya don't want to get fat then don't eat the thing in the first place. That's only a waste of food. There's plenty of children in Ethiopia who'd be glad of a ham sambwhich and a Mars Delight.

***

Bernie rang me today askin' what the story was with me cousin Nigel. Now I have to be honest, I didn't know there was a story with me cousin Nigel and I told Bernie this and ask her what she's talkin' about and she tells me that he met her in Starbucks in Leicester Square in London for a cup of coffee and told her he was movin' away and I nearly died coz I mean, it's the first I'd heard of it. I thought maybe me ma would have known, or even Bopper but I said it to them and it was the first they'd heard of it as well. Bernie said he wouldn't even tell her where he was goin', that he had sold his car and loads of his other stuff and would only be in London a few more days. There has to be something fishy there though, especially after me Uncle Dessie runnin' off to Amsterdam as well. Don't they smuggle all the drugs through Amsterdam? Maybe that's what me Uncle Dessie is doin' there. Smugglin' lumps of hash all over Europe in his knickers. Dessie would do anything for a few quid.

Maybe there's some gang after Nigel and he has to run away. Maybe that's why our Dessie went too. I wonder what they're up to. This family is turnin' into something off *Eastenders*!

***

We all went up to Farley's last night for a few drinks and the laugh we had. Marvin, Yenta's brother, got locked and we couldn't get him out of the pub at the end of the night. He's gas. I walked in tonight and the first thing he says to me is, 'how's your donkey?' I'm tryin' to work out what he was talkin' about when he smiles at me and says, 'How's your canary?' I was goin' to try and explain to him that I don't have a donkey or a canary or any other sort of animal for that matter but he can't understand a word I say to him. I was talkin' to him there tonight, tell a lie, Yenta was sittin' in the middle of us translatin' and he was sayin' that he went for a job in McDonalds. Can ya imagine Marvin in McDonalds? Every time someone walks up to him he asks them which is the coolest way to walk. He's gas though but he gets locked very easy, although would ya blame him when Jasmin's got him drinkin' Brandy, Jack Daniels and Lucozade? I told Yenta not to let him near anything Jasmin drinks but he did anyway.

Concepta told the whole pub about losin' all the weight although if you lost 19 pounds in three weeks wouldn't you be tellin' everyone? She's the talk of the area at the moment, mainly coz Celine O'Reilly that goes to the Weight Watchers with Concepta and me ma and Jasmin's ma told Misses O'Driscoll, ya know the nosey bitch, that she thought Concepta was takin' the slimmin' tablets and Misses O'Driscoll told everyone that Concepta's losin' loads of weight coz she has a drug problem. I mean, for Jayzis sake, have the auld-ones nothing better to be doin' at mass? Like prayin'? They gave poor Sister Mary Immaculate Conception an awful time that time because she was goin' out with some auld-fella or so Petulia next door told me ma. Misses O'Driscoll told Celine O'Reilly and Celine O'Reilly told Petulia so how true it is, I don't know. I just think Celine O'Reilly is jealous though coz she's still a fat cow!

***

Dave was wreckin' me head last night. I don't know what it is but there's something a bit different. He's just actin' a bit weird. Like real moody or something and he better snap out of it quickly coz I'm not puttin' up with much more of it and I told him this when I was leavin'. He just let me go and all. The bastard didn't even try to chase after me. He just looked out the window as I got in the taxi to go home.

What happened was, I met him in town about nine at McDonalds on Grafton Street and not at the Central Bank. The smelly rocker kids do be around it on the summer evenin's too and they wreck me head. I was sittin' there waitin' for Dave one night and who walks up to me only Andy, ya know Jasmin's brother and he's a really nice fella and a bit of a looker if I'll be honest, hard enough to believe with him bein' related to Jasmin. But then loads of his friends started comin' over and wreckin' me head and there must have been 20 of them by the time Dave came. I thought they were goin' to tie me to a pole and burn me coz they thought I was a witch or something!

So after that, I told Dave I wasn't meetin' him at the Central Bank anymore and he asked me where and I must have been hungry at the time coz I said McDonalds. Its grand actually coz I went in last night to get a McFlurry while I was waitin' on him.

We went up to his apartment and he rang a curry and we sat here eatin' it watchin' a DVD, cuddlin' and all that and I says something about Marvin askin' how's me donkey and he just grunts and I tell him about Concepta tryin' to snog the bouncer in Farley's and he grunts. He was really moody. So the two of us start arguin' and I tell him to cop on and I wasn't puttin' up with him and his moodswings and then I left. I was in the height of it and then he didn't even try to stop me leavin', the bastard.

**

I was on the bus today with Yenta and Concepta coz we were goin' to get the bus into town and then the Luas from Stephen's Green out to the shoppin' centre in Dundrum. I have to say, I absolutely love Dundrum. Its only mafis and it's the best place to go to get cloths and I thought to meself, seein' as I'm loaded at the moment with that

€500 that Mr O'Toole sent me for tryin' to kill me, I'll go out to Dundrum and get meself a few bits. The only thing about it though is gettin' there. We have to get a bus into town, walk to Stephen's Green and then get the Luas to Dundrum and I don't like the Luas. There's just something about it that freaks me out. I think it's the voice of that woman who announces the names of the stops. That's just freaky that is. 'The next stop is James's, alight for St James' Hospital.' Look as much as I could, I couldn't find a light for St James' anywhere. It must have been broken that day or something and then there's this ding ding ding noise that it makes when its speedin' up Abbey Street towards ya and there's people divin' out of the way, terrified of the thing. I don't know why but I don't like it.

Anyway, there's meself, Concepta and Yenta on the bus. I was tellin' them all about meself and Dave and the bit of trouble we're havin' at the moment about how he's been a bit moody and how, although I don't like to admit it but the sex isn't very good lately, well in the last week or so anyway. He just doesn't seem to want to know and Yenta and Concepta between them are there tryin' to give me the bit of advice when the bus stops, not at a bus stop or anything, it just stops and we're wonderin' what's happenin' and the door of the drivers cabin swings open and the bus driver gets out and at first we were thinkin' he was goin' to fix one of the mirrors or something but he gets off the bus and just starts runnin' away and we're all sittin' on the bus like spas for a good five minutes before we realise that for whatever reason, the bus driver is gone and isn't comin' back.

***

Bob's doin' great. Me Tamagotchi this is, although she's a bit overweight coz I haven't been exercisin' her as much as I should be although she's always happy coz I keep feedin' her sweets. She reminds me a bit of Concepta in that way. I wonder if I could get Concepta to bring me Tamagotchi to Weight Watchers with her so it'll lose a few pounds. I told her that it just goes to prove how important exercise is. Concepta this is, not the Tamagotchi.

She wants to get rollerblades. Concepta this is again, not Bob. Can ya imagine Concepta Cooney on rollerblades. She'd be like a bin truck flyin' down the road. She asked me to go rollerbladin' with her in the park. The last time I went rollerbladin' I was about 12 but all the others seem to be up for it. Bopper Ryde was up in the attic lookin' for his rollerblades this mornin' and Yenta wants to buy a pair. A good pair they are too. She was lookin' at them in Dundrum yesterday when we eventually got there. Tracy seems to be up for it as well. Can ya imagine us all on rollerblades in the park? Knowin' my luck I'd break an ankle. Me flyin' through the park and I go over a crack and go arse over tits out in front of a Volvo.

I wonder if she'll die if she doesn't get enough exercise. This is me Tamagotchi, not Concepta, although in sayin' that, it could be either one. Jayzis, I'm all worried now. I left it at home when I went to work today and when I came home, the whole screen was covered in shite. How she's still alive is beyond me, the poor whatever the fuck she is.

✳✳✳

I was on a late in work today so I was havin' a bit of a lie in and I heard a ringin' noise and I thought I might have been dreamin' but I was awake and I realised that there was someone at the door and I was hopin' whoever it was would go away but they wouldn't so I dragged meself up out of bed and went down stairs, still half asleep and I open the front door and who's standin' there only me cousin Nigel. Well I nearly died. There's me expectin' to see Jehovial witnesses and it ends up bein' me cousin. 'I'm home,' says he. 'What?' says I and he says, 'I'm comin' to live here.' And I nearly die, mainly coz I knew that I'd be back in with Bopper on a mattress on the floor but I just gave Nigel a big hug. Where we're all gonna sleep when me Uncle Dessie comes back, I don't know and I wouldn't mind but Nigel had loads of stuff with him and he says more is gettin' sent over next week. Why they can't all go to me Aunty Linda's I don't know.

I asked him why he decided to come to Ireland and he said he just got bored and wanted to do something different so fair play to him for movin' his whole life to a different country. I started givin' him the low down on everything, tellin' him about all the lads. He's met most of them before and he was delighted when I told him about how well Concepta's doin' at the Weight Watchers and I showed him Bob and he played with her for ages and she lost loads of weight. He's like a Tamagotchi pro!

I asked where me Uncle Dessie is but he doesn't know much, just the same as us, that he's in Amsterdam and would be back soon. I asked him does he know if Dessie has anything goin' on with a nun called Sister Mary Immaculate Conception but he didn't really know what I was talkin' about. I suppose it'll be a bit of laugh havin' Nigel livin' with us and I suppose he'd prefer to stay on our Boppers floor. The two of them get on great.

✱✱✱

Me ma was delighted last night after comin' back from the Weight Watchers coz she was the slimmer of the week. She lost six pounds. Concepta was snappin' coz she only lost three pounds. That makes her 15 stone 8 I think although 3 pounds is 3 pounds, ya have to give it to her like. She's still doin' great. Me ma said she was talkin' about gettin' a bike. Concepta this is. A few months ago she used to have trouble walkin' to get a Nitelink after a night out and now she wants a bike. I can imagine all 15 stone 8 of Concepta on a bike in a pair of cyclin' shorts doin' a few laps of the Phoenix Park. She'd get as far as the Hole in the Wall and stop for a vodka and Diet Coke. She still wants to get rollerblades as well. The young-one is mad.

Me ma was sayin' that Celine O'Reilly has put on six pounds since she started doin' the Weight Watchers and keeps tellin' everyone that's it doesn't work despite the fact that everyone else is losin' loads of weight. All ya have to do is look at Concepta to know how good it is. Me ma said she's always findin' things to complain about. She was tellin' everyone the scales were broken last night coz she was the only one there that didn't lose any weight. Me ma and Jasmin's ma and Concepta won't go walkin' with her anymore coz every time they talk to her about something she tells Mrs O'Driscoll and Mrs O'Driscoll tells all the auldones at the bingo so everyone around knows all our business. Everyone knows that Celine O'Reilly is nothing but a mouth. Me ma said she's goin' to tell Petulia next door that Celine O'Reilly put on six pounds since they started coz she knows Petulia will tell Misses O'Driscoll and then tell everyone. It's nothing more than comeuppance for what Celine O'Reilly's been tellin' everyone about me Uncle Dessie and the former Sister Mary Immaculate Conception.

✱✱

A women came into the shop today, a good lookin' woman she was too, tall, long hair, nice figure, could have been a model and she comes up to the till and I smile at her and she asks me is Leandra around so I go in the back and get her and as soon as Leandra sees your one, she runs up to her, kisses her on both cheeks and gives her a huge hug and meself and Julie Walsh and Amy are starin' at them. Amy's doin' a few of Dymphna's shifts coz she went to Turkey there on Wednesday.

So Leandra is huggin' this young-one and we're all thinkin', could this be the girlfriend and the two of them are all like happy and all and your woman tells Leandra she looks great and Leandra tells your woman she looks great and they hug again and I'm lookin' at Julie Walsh and Amy and they're lookin' back at me, obviously thinkin' the same thing. So Leandra asks your woman to come through to the back and ya wanna see the face on Julie Walsh. It was only comical.

'D'ya think they're gonna have sex in Leandra's office?' Julie Walsh asks, makin' sure there's no customers around but that wouldn't bother her. Subtlety isn't a word Julie Walsh knows about. 'Don't be stupid,' says I, although to be honest, I was thinkin' the same thing but I wouldn't let Julie Walsh know that. 'How do lesbians have sex?' Julie Walsh asks. 'Use your imagination,' I tell her. 'No it's their fingers,' Amy says. It was a good 20 minutes before Leandra and your woman came back out. Plenty of time for a quickie.

***

I'm in the height of it with Dave. He's still wreckin' me head and I have a feelin' there's something goin' on and even Tracy was sayin' it coz I rang her today to see what she thinks, her studyin' psychology and all and she thinks he hasn't been himself at all lately.

I haven't seen him since the night I walked out of his apartment last week although the day after I was in work and a man comes in with a bunch of flowers and a box of Milk Tray from him to say sorry for what had happened so I rang him and we had a chat about it and everything seemed to be grand and we'd been gettin' on okay all week even though we haven't seen each other and have only been talkin' on the phone so I ask him if he wanted to go for a meal the weekend and so last night comes and I got meself ready and next minute I get a phone call off him sayin' he has to work late and he's goin' to have to cancel dinner and I was in the height of it as ya can imagine, especially coz I was just gettin' ready to leave and I'd spent ages straightenin' me hair, puttin' on me false tan, doin' me make up and all the rest of it. Could he not have rang me a little earlier like? Now if the fucker thinks he's goin' to get out of this one with a bunch of flowers and a box of chocolates he has another thing comin'. I wouldn't mind but the bastard knows I have hay fever and hate Milk Tray!

***

It was gas last night. We tried to set our Nigel up with Sheila and we was havin' none of it. The poor young-fella looked terrified and to be honest, Sheila's not that bad at all, even if she still struggles to put together a sentence in English but then again, so does Jasmin and he gets on grand with her.

We brought Nigel out with us for the first time last night and the laugh we had. Anyone that knew him from him bein' here before was dyin' to see him and anyone that didn't was dyin' to meet him after all that me and Bopper had told them about him.

We were in Heaven in Blanch for the night and it was a great bit of buzz. He made the biggest mistake ya can make when you're goin' out with us coz Jasmin asked him what he wanted to drink and he said whatever she was havin' which is only askin' for trouble as he found out when she came back with a pint of Budweiser mixed with cranberry juice. The poor young-fella nearly puked all over the place so Jasmin ended up drinkin' his too, not a bother to her.

He was talkin' to Sheila at the start for a little bit so Concepta and I had an idea that we could set the two of them up although Jasmin, Bopper and Paulo said I'd be wastin' me time coz Nigel wouldn't be interested, whatever that means but they were right, he wasn't into Sheila. It was so funny coz Marvin and Yenta came in late and the first thing Marvin said to Nigel was, 'Do you want to ride with Batman?' and poor Nigel was lost until we told him about Marvin's English and the fact that he doesn't have any.

It was a great night though and we had a great laugh and it was deadly with Nigel bein' out with us. Him and Bopper are only delighted havin' each other. The two of them are always together since Nigel got back. It's good for them though coz they have a lot in common.

Dave tried to ring me as well when I was out but I didn't answer the phone. I wasn't really in the humour and Tracy says I should make him think I'm more pissed off with him than I am so he'll come runnin' back. I love when she has evil plans like that. It's coz she does psychology and English in UCD.

✷✷✷

I'm devastated. Really I am. Very upset I am. Bob died today although it was me own fault. I was the one that let her go so fat. I should have exercised her more but I didn't and now she's dead, the poor thing. Ah Jayzis. I was in work and what happened was, I looked at the screen and there she was, a little egg with wings and a halo and me heart jumped coz I didn't realise she was sick or anything but she was very fat and it was my fault coz I didn't play with her enough. It's not good enough to just feed it when its hungry and clean up its shite after it. Ya have to make sure it's fit too and I didn't and she died. I rang Yenta to tell her and I was really upset and she told me to remember that it was never ever really alive and that it's just a piece of plastic and that I'm not a murderer or anything and I suppose she's right. I just feel terrible though coz she was only about a week and a half old and ya'd think that I'd be able to keep something alive a little bit longer than that but Yenta told me not to be stupid coz I look after everyone, all our friends like, and never let anyone go home on their own or if they're cryin' in the toilets over something, I'm the first one there and she said that if our friends were Tamagotchis, they'd have lived a lot longer than a week and a half, so that was nice. I tell ya, for someone that's so intelligent, she talks an awful lot of shite.

***

I got home from work today and who's sittin' in the sittin' room only Dessie so I was only delighted that he was back and that he was okay so I ran over to him and gave him a big hug and he was delighted to see me so I asked him what had happened and he told me I better sit down so I did. This is what happened.

When me Aunt Doris left Dessie, she ran off to Holland with Nigel's best friend, Daniel. So then Dessie sold the house, gave Doris half of what he got for it and moved back here and bought his own house, the one the Filipino nurses are livin' in now but then one day, Dessie got a letter off Doris about alimony, something to do with gettin' half of everything he owned, despite the fact he'd already given her half of what he'd made from the house in England but for some reason, that couldn't be proved so the bitch was tryin' to do Dessie out of a fortune so he took a lend of a few thousand off Bernie to hire a private investigator, remember that time ages ago, but he ran out of money so he asked me ma could he move in with us for a while and rent out his own house to get together a few quid. So the private investigator tracks Doris down in Holland and in the meantime, Daniel gets on a flight to London to go home to see his parents and who's the air hostess on the flight only Bernie Boland who recognised him from pictures she'd seen that Nigel had shown her. She had a chat with him and to make sure he was stayin' with his ma and da and when she landed, she rang Nigel straight away. Nigel turns up on Daniel's doorstep that night and pretends to be all pally but he has a tape recorder in his pocket and records Daniel apologisin' for the affair between him and Doris so then it was just a case of Dessie goin' to Holland to sort it all out but Daniel got word and didn't go back to Holland so while Dessie was in Amsterdam, Daniel was tryin' to find Nigel and eventually Nigel got word that Daniel was goin' to hire someone to kill him so that's why he had to pack up and leave so quickly and why he couldn't tell Bernie where he was goin' and now me Aunt Doris and Daniel are both in shite over the money they said they never got and me Uncle Dessie doesn't have to give her a penny and now he's gonna get loads of what he gave her back, the greedy, money grabbin' bitch. He's glad it's all over though and to be honest, so am I, although where we're all gonna sleep tonight, I don't know.

✱✱

Tracy told me the funniest story ever today. She said her and Lance were out somewhere last night, at the pictures I think it was, and they went back to his apartment and they were sittin' down watchin' the telly and Lance went into his room to get something, she never said what, and he opened the door and screamed and Tracy ran over, thinkin' that Lance had just found a dead body or something from the way he screamed but she said she nearly died herself coz the whole room was silver. Everything like! The two of them stood there for a couple of seconds in shock until Lance picked something up and realised it was wrapped in tinfoil and it was only then that Tracy realised that somebody had wrapped everything in Lance's room in tinfoil for some strange reason. Like Everything! She said he opened the drawers and everything in them was wrapped and she could do nothing but laugh although she said he didn't find it very funny so they spent a good hour unwrappin' everything and there was loads of tinfoil. Tracy said she'd never seen so much tinfoil in her life so Lance was in the height of it and when his flat mate came in, he nearly killed him but all Tracy and the flatmate could do was break their shites laughin'. I kept me tinfoil off me Kit Kat that I had today to give to him. I was ragin' I wasn't there to see it!

※※※

Concepta was the slimmer of the week again this week and me ma was only ragin', accusin' Concepta of takin' slimmin' tablets and all the rest of it. Me ma's goin' mad, convinced Concepta is cheatin', that there's no way she can lose so much weight just by dietin' but I just smiled and nodded. I didn't want to get involved. The last thing I want to do is get drawn into an argument between the two of them. She nearly swung for Nigel earlier, me ma did, although he was tryin' to wind her up so he would have deserved a dig. He told her he saw her eatin' a coffee slice the day before and she was havin' none of it. She says she doesn't even like coffee slices and me da turns around and says she loves them and she goes mad and calls Nigel a shit stirin' little bollix and she goes out for a walk. I have to agree with her, Nigel is a shit stirin' little bollix. Whenever any of us are havin' an argument, he says something to cause a bit of shit and then just sits there waitin' for a reaction. I have to be honest though, its gas if I'm not involved in it.

I tell ya, there's not this much competition in the Premier League. Fair play to Concepta. She'd be top of the table coz she lost eight pounds this week which is the most anyone's lost in a week since her and me ma and Jasmin's ma joined. She's down to 15 stone now and she's only thrilled with herself and ya can notice it. She doesn't want to go out buyin' loads of new cloths yet until she's down to her target weight so her old stuff is hangin' off her. Me ma's on a mission this week though. She's like Rocky.

※※※

Leandra isn't a lesbian. We know for a fact because she told us. She actually thought it was gas that we thought she might be.

What happened was, that Jason gobshite was in work today. Remember I told ya about him, the sap that gets on with Julie Walsh, mainly coz nobody else likes either of them so they have no choice but to hang around with each other. Well he was in today and Amy was still doin' the day shifts coz Dymphna's still in Turkey with her sister and Boris and Sheila were there as well and Julie Walsh, the horrible bitch, was on tills. I was tellin' her all about Concepta losin' all the weight but she didn't really get the hint. Ya have to give it to Concepta, she's really tryin'. Julie Walsh doesn't give a fuck but still complains about it all the time. I don't have a problem with people bein' overweight but what I do have a problem with is overweight people complainin' about it but not botherin' to do anything like get up off their arses and goin' for a walk instead of sittin' in and watchin' *Hollyoaks*.

Anyway, we're sittin' there in work and Leandra is standin' there readin' this weeks hello and out of nowhere, that Jason sap says 'Leandra, what's the story, are ya a lesbian or what?' and she looks up and says, 'Why d'ya think that?' and I shoot him a look that says if he mentions my name or the fact that it was my mate Paulo that said it first I'll kill him and he looks over and says, 'Oh I just heard someone say it.' And she laughs at him and says, 'Me, a dyke? Would ya fuck off Jason. I love a bit of cock just as much as you do.' And we all just broke our shites laughin'. Except Jason.

✳✳✳

Concepta's 21st is next week and I forgot all about it til she handed me an invitation there last night when we were all up in Farley's. I nearly died though coz I didn't realise it was that soon. I thought it was another couple of weeks but we're nearly into September.

That's leaves me with two big problems though although I've a week to sort them out. The first is what to wear but I have a few quid put away so all I'll have to do is go up the Blanchardstown Shoppin' Centre and get a few bits or I might even get me Uncle Dessie to drop me out to Dundrum to get something out there. I saw a lovely pair of espadrilles in Ecco that I want to get but I have to find a little dress to go with them, something a bit classy and sexy, maybe black coz the shoes are black and gold. I'll have a look around and see what I can see. I'll have a ring around the girls to see what they're wearin' coz we don't want to all shop up in the same thing like what happened with the bikinis in Spain. I didn't even know Bernie was comin' home for it but she is.

Me second problem is what to buy Concepta and she's hard enough to buy for. I can't buy her cloths in case they get too big for her by the week after next so I don't know what to do really. I'll say it to the others and see what they're gettin' her. I'd love to get her an ice cream machine for the laugh but that's just cruel. I can see Concepta now tryin' to make diet ice cream.

✳✳✳

Me and Dave broke up. Actually he was very lucky I didn't break him up after what happened. Very lucky. I was so tempted but Nigel told me it wasn't worth the energy and he punched him for me instead and I was very nearly goin' to just walk away but I turned quickly and before the bastard knew what I was doin', I gave him such a knee in the balls that it'll take him three weeks to find them and he deserves it and that tart was lucky she was inside the apartment coz I was goin' to leave her for dead and me after stickin' up for her in the Canaries and all.

What happened was, I rang him and asked him to come out but he said he wasn't up for it and all the rest of it and that he was just goin' to sit in, so I say to meself, I'll surprise him. So our Nigel was about to go over to get something from the Filipino nurses in me Uncle Dessie's house in me Uncle Dessie's car and I tell him I need a lift into town and he says no problem coz he's dyin' to meet Dave despite the fact he's not really insured on me Uncle Dessie's car and shouldn't really be drivin' it so we're headin' into town, makin' sure to stay well under the speed limit and all the rest of it so there'd be no chance of the guards stoppin' us and we get to Dave's apartment buildin' in Christchurch and I tell Nigel I'll go up on me own but he says he just wants to meet Dave so I don't really have a problem with it. So we go up the stairs and I knock at Dave's door and there's no answer even though I can hear something inside so I knock again and after knockin' two more times, Dave finally answers the door, half naked and he nearly dies when he sees me but not as much as I nearly died when I saw Miranda McCarthy Boyle, Tracy's posh bitch of a mate from UCD, the one from the holiday, walk out of his bedroom half naked as well. 'So she's why ya couldn't come out,' I said to him and that's when Nigel punched him and I followed through with a knee into the balls and just as I'm about to walk away I say, 'And by the way Dave, you're dumped and you and the snobby cow are more than welcome to each other and by the way, your ma's a spa and I've seen ants with bigger mickeys,' but he was in too much pain to answer me and Miranda was in too much shock to do anything. I think she thought I was goin' to batter her and she's very lucky I didn't.

✳✳✳

Wanted: a man to satisfy 18-year-old young-one on Dublin's north side. Must be a bit of a ride and have all his own teeth. Stalkers or people into bondage, threesomes with flatmates, or fellas with hairy backs need not apply. Hobbies must include goin' out and gettin' locked, winter sports when we have the channel and when it's not 39 degrees outside, although we're not complainin'. Must also like spendin' loads of money on the young-one. Candidates must have mothers who are not snobby stuck up bitches from Kildare. They must also have a high tolerance to Weight Watchers, air hostesses, people who may or may not be on slimmin' tablets, smart arse students from UCD, gobshites who'd drink fairy liquid with vodka and who can't pronounce the letter S, annoyin' little brothers, Bosnian bisexuals, the bisexuals confused boyfriend from Blanchardstown, two Turks, a Chinese, and English cousin and an uncle with a thing for the young-ones. Candidates need not apply if they plan to run off with snobby south side bitches or if their name happens to be Dave Browne. However I am up for most things, especially a good ride!

September

Me ma's only gas. She does wear these rollers in her hair after she washes it in the mornin' and she went to work today with one of them still in the back of her hair and she said nobody said it to her until they were about to go for their mornin' cup of tea. I wouldn't mind but the rollers are bright pink. How she didn't notice it there I don't know but it's not the first time it happened. She went to a funeral once with not one but two of them still in the back of her hair. Two of them! All the auld-ones behind her thought it was some kind of fashion statement although knowin' me ma, it probably was and after we all started slaggin' her over it, she said it was an accident. I do be scarlet with her sometimes with the things she does but don't all mas embarrass their daughters? I used to hate it when we were goin' anywhere and she'd take out a tissue, lick it and then start wipin' me face with it. I mean, that's disgustin'. I used to be mortified. I'd prefer to walk around with a dirty face than to have it wiped by a spitty tissue. All mas do that. I'm tellin' ya, I won't be doin' it when I have kids. I'm not gonna be one of these mas that makes her kids scarlet all the time. I'll be a real cool ma listenin' to all the latest tunes and wearin' all the latest cloths and all the rest of it and I won't wear rollers in me hair so there'll be no fear of me wearin' them into work or to a funeral, although in sayin' that as well, it'll be ages before I have kids, me bein' single and all.

***

Bernie Boland came home from England today and she doesn't look a bit well. I said it to her straight away I did. She's really pale and she's after losin' loads of weight. Obviously not as much as Concepta or anything but still enough to make her look a bit sick coz Bernie was always skinny enough to begin with. She wouldn't be a stick insect or anything but kinda healthy lookin'. It just looks like she hasn't been lookin' after herself in England at all and I'm gettin' a bit worried about her. It can't be healthy havin' all the early starts and havin' nights out with that sap Dervla, the young-one she lives with, but Bernie says that Dervla's gonna be movin' to Shannon and that she's devastated coz Dervla's the closest person she has over there and she tells her everything and all the rest of it. I just grunted coz the last thing I want to do is have an argument with Bernie over Dervla, especially after what happened in the Canaries and with her lookin' so sick and all. I was actually delighted to see her and I'd been lookin' forward to her comin' over so we could hang around and have a laugh. She knocked over straight away when she came home and me, herself and Nigel sat down and we filled her in on all the news and she seems to be ragin' coz she's missin' everything bein' in England. I actually feel really sorry for her that Dervla is leavin' coz I know Bernie gets home sick. See she doesn't have the type of friends that Sheila or Yenta or Marvin have. Maybe I should give her me Tamagotchi.

✳✳✳

There was war at the Weight Watchers last night or so Jasmin's ma was tellin' me. I was in work there today and she was tellin' me all about it and I was wonderin' as well coz me ma never said a word and Concepta Cooney was on the phone to me earlier on and she never said anything about it either and usually that's all the two of them ever talk about the day after it but to be honest, it didn't even cross me mind until I saw Jasmin's ma and she asked me how me ma was after last night and I didn't have a clue what she was talkin' about.

What happened, or so she says, is that they were all doin' the weigh-in and Concepta and me ma were near the end, just before herself, Jasmin's ma was sayin', and Celine O'Reilly got on and had lost two pounds over the week, although that still makes her four pounds heavier than what she started on and then me ma gets on and she'd lost six pounds and then Concepta gets on and she's after losin' six pounds as well and the two of them are tied for slimmer of the week at the end and me ma turns around, scarlet for me, the woman's an embarrassment, and accuses Concepta of bein' on the slimmin' tablets and Concepta nearly died and accused me ma of bein' anorexic and then me ma starts tellin' Concepta what she'd eaten over the past few days and she says that she saw Concepta eatin' a Toffee Crisp on Saturday and Concepta says she can't remember the last time she had a Toffee Crisp and me ma says she mustn't have a very long memory coz she definitely had one on Saturday. Can ya imagine all this goin' on down the community hall? Jasmin's ma said it was crazy. They decided that they weren't gonna let me ma or Concepta be slimmer of the week over the argument so some auld-fella from near the shops got it coz he lost five and a half pounds. Jasmin's ma was ragin' coz she'd lost five pounds and was convinced it was goin' to be her. She bought a Terry's Chocolate Orange and three packets of Wine Gums when she was in gettin' her milk and the paper as well but she says they were for Jasmin and the triplets. My hole they were!

✳✳✳

Remember I was tellin' ya about Dymphna goin' to Turkey? Well that was two weeks ago and she was meant to be back two days ago and there's not a sign of her and she was meant to be in work yesterday and today and she never showed and it's not like Dymphna coz if she is sick, she'll give ya plenty of notice that she won't be in and I wouldn't mind but we're very short staffed at the moment coz its busy enough and it's not like we can give Amy a ring coz she's in school, although fair play to her, she came in after school yesterday for a few hours. She's a grand young-one Amy but as I told her yesterday, don't let the job get in the way of the studyin' coz she's in 5th year now and she has to knuckle down and do well in the leavin' cert and before ya say who's Joanna

Ryde to be givin' advice about the leavin', let me tell ya that I'm the best person to be givin' advice coz I never did it and I'm ragin' I never got a chance to go to college like Tracy or anything like that.

Anyway, enough about me, back to Dymphna. Yeah, we haven't heard a word from her at all so whether she even came home or not, I don't know. It wouldn't be like her though. If she didn't come home, it must be over something serious. Jasmin's little brother Andy, the big smelly rocker one, he couldn't come home from Mallorca one year they went coz his appendix burst and they wouldn't let him fly. That probably happened to Dymphna or maybe she just didn't realise she was meant to be back in work. That happens. Usually to Jasmin, but it happens.

✻✻✻

Ah the laugh we had last night. It was Concepta's 21st and I have to say, it was a great night. I do forget that she's that much older than us sometimes. Everyone was there and when I say everyone, I mean everyone. She was meant to be havin' it in Farley's but for some reason, she changed her mind and decided to have it in Chief O'Neill's hotel in Smithfield and I have to say, she made the right choice coz the place is only mafis. It's a new enough hotel and all and ya wanna see the function room in it. Beautiful it is.

The DJ was great as well and he played a good mixture, all the new stuff and then a bit of the old stuff, Abba, the Bee Gees, that sort of thing and then things like the Saturday Night dance and the Time Warp and the Macarena. We were only in our element up doin' all the moves. The auld-ones loved it as well. Me ma even went to the party but Jasmin was tellin' me her and Concepta have made up a bit since their row the other night.

Bernie Boland was lookin' a whole lot better as well although that wouldn't have been hard with the state she was in when she knocked over to my house the other day. We were tryin' to get her set up with Marvin for the buzz but I don't think it was happenin', although at one stage they got very close when the DJ was playin' a few of the tunes from *Grease*. I wouldn't be surprised if something happens there before she goes back to England or before he gets deported, whichever comes first.

Tracy said she was goin' to bring Miranda McCarthy Boyle for the laugh but after I caught her with my Dave, well my ex Dave, the bastard, I told her she wouldn't be safe in the same room as me. Tracy says it hasn't been mentioned since. I told her it better stay that way. Lance wasn't with her for some reason but she didn't say why and I didn't ask. The two of them are always all over each other or fightin'. No happy medium.

Jasmin and Bopper were up dancin' for the whole night with Nigel although they stopped for a few minutes to try to get Sheila drunk as if she wasn't bad enough with what Paulo, Kevin and Yenta had given her. I swear to god, the poor young-one gets hammered very easy but she's gas. She's totally out of her shell at this stage but I blame Paulo. He has a lot of time for Sheila and usually we wouldn't be payin' her that much attention coz she does be to quiet when we're out.

There was a table in the corner with Petulia from next door to me, Mrs O'Driscoll, Celine O'Reilly, Julie Walsh, why Concepta invited her I don't know, that's if she did invite her, the horrible cow probably just showed up and that Jason spa was there as well, ya know the gobshite from work and the five of them sat there laughin' and gigglin' and all the rest of it and I felt like goin' over and kickin' the heads off every single one of them.

I was sittin' there with Yenta, the two of us havin' a look around to see if we could see any nice lookin' fellas and this bloke walks in and catches me eye and I tell Yenta to look at him and I'm thinkin' to meself that he looks kinda familiar. He can't have been any older than 16 but he was gorgeous, black slacks, a black shirt and tie and his hair slicked back and he goes over to Jasmin's two sisters Mandy and Sandy and it was only then that I realise that its Andy, the third triplet, Jasmin's little brother, the smelly rocker kid that I do see at the Central Bank. There he was out of all his smelly rocker cloths lookin' respectable and only gorgeous. Sixteen or not 16, Jasmin's brother or not, he was still a little ride and he looks up and sees me starin' at him and I go bright red, well Yenta says I did, and I look away and she breaks her shite laughin' coz she knows how scarlet I must be after callin' Jasmin's little brother a ride. She told me to go and dance with him. Can ya imagine? I'd be put in jail with all the dirty old men. I mean, he's only 16. I think. I must find out for definite.

✳✳✳

With all the madness at the party the other night, we actually forgot to give Concepta all her presents. We got her loads. What we did was, all the close friends like meself, Bernie, Tracy, Jasmin, Bopper, Paulo, Yenta and Dessie got her a present each, something small enough and then put €50 in as well and then we got €30 each off Sheila, Kevin, Marvin and Nigel so we had loads, over €500 so we got her a smoothie maker coz she's wanted one for ages and then we booked her into a hotel in Killarney for the October weekend and she thinks it's only me goin' with her but there'll be loads of us goin'. What's goin' to happen is, the others will all be on the train and then I'll get on with Concepta and she'll get a big surprise. At least I hope she does. Ya know how our plans usually turn out. At least if we had of had Bernie here when we were sortin' it out we could have had the whole thing worked out but fair play to Yenta, she's great at that sort of thing. She got us group rates and all on the rooms. It should be a good laugh.

She was delighted with the present I got her from meself. It was this five disk workout thing that I got her in HMV and she said its only deadly and she's only dyin' to give it a go. I told her she's not meant to do all five in the same day and there's instructions but ya know Concepta. I feel a slimmer of the week comin' on.

✳✳✳

Father Mulhern said mass yesterday for Sister Mary Immaculate Conception because she's decided to leave the church.

She's goin' to still do a lot of the other stuff she did before but she won't be a nun anymore. She'll be helpin' teach the kids gymnastics and basketball and that sort of thing, she's very athletic is Sister Mary Immaculate Conception, but she'll be movin' out of the nuns residence and so yesterday, the mass was just to say thank you for all her hard work in the community and all the rest of it. Well this is what Petulia next door was tellin' me ma so it must be true although me Uncle Dessie was at mass yesterday and never said a word about it. I never knew me Uncle Dessie to be the religious type but he's been to mass a good bit since he moved in with us.

She got a huge clap and all, Sister Mary, and even one of them standin' rotations at the end, so Petulia told me ma and she heard it off Mrs O'Driscoll and we all know what she's like so how true it is, I don't know.

Petulia thinks she must have a man if she's leavin' the church and there'd be no other reason for her to stop bein' a nun but me ma told her theres loads of reasons. Petulia said Father Mulhern said that people should be ashamed of themselves about the way they've been talkin' about Sister Mary in the last few weeks and that her private life is nobody's business and that the only person who can judge her is god on the day of judgement. That's what I was thinkin' meself so fair play to Father Mulhern and if Sister Mary is gettin' it on with some fella, then fair play to her too.

※※※

Dymphna's not comin' back. I swear to god. Leandra rang her house today and her husband answered in an awful state and said that he'd been talkin' to Dymphna and that she had decided that she was goin' to stay in Turkey and then he told Leandra the whole story. What happened was, Dymphna went to Turkey, Kusadasi I think it was but I could be wrong, but she went with her sister and the two of them were havin' a great time doin' all the usual shite, goin' out and gettin' locked, sun bathin' by the pool, lyin' on the beach, goin' on day trips and all that shite and one day they're sittin' in a restaurant and the owner starts talkin' to Dymphna and the two of them are gettin' on really well, a good lookin' fella I believe, Ross his name is although it doesn't sound very Turkish. This fella was born and reared in whatever the fuck the capital of Turkey is, I'll ask Yenta, it could be Istanbul but I'd have remembered someone sayin' that and it definitely wasn't Istanbul. I think it was something like Antler but it doesn't matter the fuck. Anyway, this fella Ross told Dymphna he'd love to bring her out and show her all the islands which anyone with any bit of cop on will tell ya is Turkish for he wants to show her his willy but Dymphna went with him and he brought a picnic and all the rest of it and Dymphna ends up fallin' madly in love with this Ross fella and decides she's had enough of her husband and her kids and the shop and everything else and that she's goin' to stay in Turkey with Ross and help him in the restaurant.

We've all started callin' her Dymphna Valentine coz it's the exact same thing that happened in that film *Shirley Valentine*. Her husband's even goin' over there to persuade her to come home. It's a pity that didn't happen to Julie Walsh coz I'd much prefer Dymphna to her. Leandra's goin' mad though coz she has to find someone to replace her. I told her not to worry coz I have just the right person in mind. Needless to say, that made her even more worried.

❋❋❋

Ankara is the capital of Turkey just in case anyone gives a fuck. I certainly don't, especially after the lecture I got off Yenta about it. Ross probably does coz that's where he's from but I don't know him and let the truth be told, either does Dymphna really. Dymphna probably cares too coz she'll probably have to go there to sort out her work permit and stuff like that Yenta tells me. An hour of listenin' to the history of Turkey and all I asked Yenta was the name of the capital. I should have just looked it up in an atlas and I would have if I had of given a fuck.

❋❋❋

There was war at the Weight Watchers again last night but thank god me ma and Concepta weren't involved. Well at least they said they weren't. I asked them both and they were both stayin' out of trouble after nearly bein' kicked out last week over that argument they had and I rang Jasmin to ask her ma was it true and she said it was and I believe Jasmin's ma. She wouldn't be one to lie.

What happened was, this is what Concepta tells me, is that someone, she said she doesn't know who, said to your woman that organises the Weight Watchers that they should go metric and someone else was agreein' and Celine O'Reilly started goin' ballistic sayin' that everyone knows how much they are in stones and pounds and that nobody knows anything about kilograms or anything and how its only another way that the European Union are tryin' to force something on us and your other woman said it was fuck all to do with the European Union and that the metric system is more accurate and what would Celine O'Reilly know about it coz she never loses any weight to be measured anyway in pounds, kilograms or anything else and she was in the height of it and walked out. Concepta said it was only gas and that they're gonna have a vote on it next week. Concepta thinks they should go metric coz everything else is and it's a lot easier to work out in your head. Me ma still hasn't really made up her mind about it yet. Jasmin's ma doesn't really give a fuck. She's delighted coz she was slimmer of the week so she mustn't have been buyin' that Terry's chocolate orange and three packets of wine gums for herself. Either that or she's on the slimmin' tablets as well.

***

The 11 September freaks me out.

***

I was in the shop today doin' all the usual shite that I do when I'm in work of a Saturday, fuck all in other words and I'm there havin' a chat with Sheila about whether to put the BPM beside the Coke or the Red Bull and next minute, I hear someone say hello to me and I look up and there's Andy, Jasmin's little brother, smilin' at me. Well I went bright red. I was scarlet but don't ask me why coz he definitely hadn't heard what I said about him to Yenta at Concepta's 21st and she wouldn't be one to say anything anyway. She doesn't even know him.

I smiled back at him anyway and I think I might have managed to say hello too but I was still tryin' to regain me exposure or whatever it is Tracy says. I have to say, he wasn't lookin' as nice today, not by a long way. He was wearin' all that rocker gear and it really does nothing for him. A lot of them people are suited to the cloths and all but not Andy. I was picturin' him in that suit again and I was gettin' all embarrassed. 'Are ya alright Joanna?' he says to me with a bit of a cheeky grin on his face. 'A-one,' I says, rememberin' not to be watchin' *The Snapper* anymore. 'Ya look a bit flushed' says he, 'Are ya alright?' 'Grand,' says I, 'It's just a bit hot in here with the fridges and that. Ya know yourself.'

So we were talkin' for a few minutes. He was askin' how I got on at the 21st and did Concepta enjoy it and then we were talkin' about his ma, my ma and Concepta at the Weight Watchers and all the rest of it and when he was goin', he winked at me and said he'd see me around. I just have to keep remindin' meself he's 16 and he's Jasmin's brother. Oh but that suit.

✷✷✷

Believe it or not, Dessie's actually movin' out tomorrow. I don't mean to sound bad or anything coz I love me Uncle Dessie to bits and all but he's been livin' with us since the end of May. Fair enough, he was in Amsterdam for a few weeks but all his stuff was still here. It's after gettin' very cramped as well since Nigel moved in coz ya have to remember that we only have a three bedroom house and there's been six of us livin' in it. It's grand enough for me ma and da coz they have an en-suite but the rest of us have to use the one bathroom. It does be like something from the *Brady Bunch* in the house some mornin's.

I'm dyin' to get me own bed back as well. When Dessie got back from Amsterdam, Nigel was already in on Boppers mattress on the floor so me and Dessie had to share my double bed but after two nights of that, I'd had enough and decided to get a mattress of me own and sleep on the floor in me own room. We found it in the attic belongin' to one of them fold out beds but I would have slept on nails rather than sleep in with Dessie again. He farts as well. The bang out of the room does be unacceptable at times and the noise of them is nowhere near as bad as his snorin' though and I thought Concepta Cooney was bad for fartin' and snorin'. Dessie is ten times worse.

Nigel is stayin' here coz he said he'd prefer to live with us coz Dessie's takin' his old room in his old house back and lettin' the four Filipino nurses stay in the other two rooms and Nigel said he'd prefer to stay on Boppers floor than to live with people he doesn't know or with me Aunty Linda. Him and Bopper get on grand and Nigel's a good laugh to live with anyway so I don't mind him stayin', once he doesn't expect to take my room. I still have to put up with him and Bopper takin' over the bathroom, more cosmetics than Boots between them. I'd say they're keepin' L'Oreal in business. I wonder if Dessie would be up for swappin' Nigel and Bopper for two Filipino nurses?

**

I came home from work today and it was like the house was empty and I don't just mean that coz me Uncle Dessie was gone but when I walked into me room, it was like there was nothing in it. The mattress from the floor was gone, probably up the attic, or knowin' me Uncle Dessie, to his house so he can try fit in a few more Filipino nurses. All Dessie's stuff is gone so it's back to bein' just my room and although I have a few things meself, they don't take up half as much room as what Dessie's stuff did. Me ma even did a bit of sortin' out as well so it feels like I have loads of space. I have to be honest though, I'll be a bit nervous sleepin' in the room on me own coz I was asleep in Bopper's room on me own the night that Mister O'Toole tried to kill me. I know he's in Brazil and that he'll probably get arrested if he ever tries to get back into Ireland but ya can never be too careful. Ever since, I've just kind of been a bit nervous sleepin' on me own in the room. Before Nigel came to live with us, I'd often go and sleep on the mattress on Bopper's floor even when me Uncle Dessie was in Holland. Bopper kinda knew what the story was so he didn't mind. Even for the week or so after Nigel came, I'd wake up in me own bed with Bopper beside me. I know he doesn't say it very often but I know our Bopper does be worried about me and why wouldn't he? I'm his big sister.

Ya wanna see their room now. Bopper and Nigel spent the whole day organisin' it and its like Tracy was around helpin' them do it. They even have labels on things. Labels like? Seriously. They were even goin' to put one on the light switch sayin' 'Light' which I told them was a stupid idea coz the only time they'll need to press it is when its dark and the label will be fuck all use to them then. Ya know sometimes I think our Bopper does be around Jasmin too much.

✱✱

I had a chat with me manager Leandra yesterday in work and she said she doesn't think Dymphna is comin' back so we're gonna have to find a replacement. I reminded her that I already had someone in mind so she said to bring whoever it was I was thinkin' of in and we'll see how they got on for a few days so this mornin' I got to work early, went through a few of the orders with Leandra, did a few checks we have to do every now and then, fire alarms and that sort of thing, and opened the shop. I have to say, I hate havin' to open the shop. Seven o'clock in the mornin' is a shite time of the day. The heads on the customers comin' in and we don't be much better. The Red Bull and the BPM does fly out the door at that time of the mornin' with people on their way to work tryin' to wake themselves up. Sure I do it meself sometimes.

Anyway, there we were today and Leandra says to me, 'So Joanna, what times the new fella comin' at?' And at that moment, like it was rehearsed or somethin', in he walks, a big smile on his face and I smile back and I say, 'Leandra this is Marvin, your new employee.' And typical Marvin, he smiles back and says, 'Which is the coolest way to work?' Well her face dropped although Marvin has that effect on people but she manages to say hello and he smiles again and says, 'Don't walk on the grass, smoke it,' and at this stage, Leandra must be convinced he was another Marie but I told her that he was Turkish, wasn't into the hash and that his English wasn't great but Yenta was tryin' to teach him as quickly as she could and that he really needed the job coz he was runnin' out of money quickly and Yenta was on the verge of sendin' him back to Istanbul so fair play to Leandra, she said he could have the job so Sheila will be on the deli counter instead of Dymphna now all the time. We're gonna have to train Boris, the Ukrainian fella, how to use the tills. We'll get Marvin to work on puttin' the stock out so he won't need to speak to the customers all that much. The best part of not speakin' English is that he doesn't have a clue what Julie Walsh is sayin'. It's a blessin' in disguise.

***

Still not a word from Dymphna believe it or not. I thought she would have at least rang me to fill in on all the gossip or at least sent a postcard to the shop. We all do that when we go away. We do send a postcard to the shop and then we do hang it up in our little staff room. One of the walls is nearly full of them now. We do even get one every now and again from Greg, the old manager. We got one there off him the week before last from Namibia, wherever the fuck that is. I'll ask Tracy. I'm definitely not askin' Yenta coz she'll give me the history of the country and I've never even heard of it, let alone know where it is.

I believe Dymphna's husband's gone to look for her although how true that is, I don't know. Someone told that bitch Celine O'Reilly, Celine O'Reilly told Mrs O'Driscoll, Mrs O'Driscoll told Petulia whose real name is really Mary from next door and Petulia/Mary told me ma and me ma told me but I'd say Dymphna's husband did go coz that's the sort of man he is, not that I know him really well or anything but he does be in the shop the odd time or he does ring lookin' for Dymphna or whatever but he's goin' all the way to Turkey to look for her. Now if you were the one that had to sleep beside the smell of Dymphna every night would ya go lookin' for her? Jayzis, the Turks will be sendin' her back to us faster than ya can say Right Guard.

***

I have a pain in me tits with Weight Watchers. I swear to god, if I've to hear another thing about it I'll scream. If it wasn't bad enough listenin' to me ma and Concepta and Jasmin's ma but who comes into the shop today only that Celine O'Reilly one and its all Weight Watchers this and Concepta that and all the rest of it and she was goin' to buy a Kinder Bueno but then asked me how many Weight Watchers points were in it and I just told her straight up that I didn't know although it was more like I didn't give a fuck. A Kinder Bueno is hardly gonna pile on the pounds is it?

She started askin' me about Dymphna and I wouldn't mind but she doesn't know Dymphna from Adam, whoever the fuck Adam is. I don't know an Adam. I wouldn't tell her anything though because that cow would only go round spreadin' rumours around the area like she always does. She still hasn't lost any weight.

Concepta lost another five pounds this week so that brings her down to 13 stone which is amazin' for her coz as I've said many a time before, not one diet worked for Concepta before this although to be honest, she didn't really care before this. I think herself, me ma and Jasmin's ma seem to think it's some sort of competition to see which of them can lose the most weight. The three of them are unbelievable. Me ma ate a Malteser the other day and then started worryin' about the fat in it. A malteser like. Sure it's the lighter way to enjoy chocolate.

They had a vote on goin' metric as well and in the end they decided that from next week, everyone will be given their weight in stones and pounds as well as kilos so that should keep everyone happy except probably Celine O'Reilly coz no matter how they weigh her, she still hasn't lost any weight.

✳✳✳

There's a rumour flyin' around, although how true this is, I don't know because of all people, it was Julie Walsh that told me and ya can't believe the lord's prayer out of her mouth. She probably heard it off Petulia from next door or Celine O'Reilly or that Mrs O'Driscoll one or some other sap who goes around tryin' to spread nasty rumours about people. What she said, Julie Walsh this is, is that Sister Mary Immaculate Conception, the nun that left the church, is now livin' with me Uncle Dessie and the four Filipino nurses and at first I thought nothing of it, that it was just someone tryin' to spread a bit of scandal but the more I thought about it, the more it looked like me Uncle Dessie and Sister Mary Immaculate Conception had got a bit of a thing goin' on. It's the type of thing our Dessie would do. Here's this woman, devotin' her life to god, a nun but good lookin' and young none the less and me Uncle Dessie comes along and charms her into his, well his bed, lets call a spade a spade here and then she ends up leavin' the church to go and live with him and these four Filipino nurses he has livin' there because he needed the money so he could chase his ex-wife half way across Europe coz she was tryin' to do him out of a few thousand quid.

In fairness though she must really like him if she's leavin' the church for him. Either that or she wants his money now he has some. He's gonna go round thinkin' he's better than God now.

✳✳✳

Ah we'd a laugh out last night. Mad it was and we weren't even goin' to go out only Concepta got paid more than she was expectin' so she wanted to go and have a few drinks so she rang Tracy, Tracy rang me, I rang Paulo, Paulo rang his fella Kevin, although to be honest, it looks like the two are on the verge of breakin' up. Concepta must have got in touch with Yenta, and me cousin Nigel was in the house with nothing planned so I made him get ready and come with us.

We were just goin' to go up to Farley's for a few but someone was talkin' to Jasmin and Bopper and they were goin' into town and said they'd try to meet us so we got on the bus and headed in, havin' a bit of a buzz at the back of the bus, throwin' pieces of paper at Nigel, that sort of thing so we're all in a great mood and we walk through Temple Bar to Fitzsimons and we're all walkin' in and the bouncer stops Concepta and asks her did he not bar her before, which, as far as I can remember, he did although Concepta to this day says that other young-one walked into her fist. Anyway, Concepta smiles and says in this mad accent, 'Pub, drinks, fun, yes.' A bit like Marvin only a lot funnier and I'm wonderin' what she's up to and the bouncer asks her where she's from and she says Bulgaria. Fuckin' Bulgaria! So he asks to see her passport which she hasn't got but she takes out her garda age card and he looks at it and says, 'You're from Bulgaria and your names Concepta Cooney?' And she nods and your man says, 'Pull the other one.' And Concepta smiles and in her Bulgarian accent says, 'Pull trousers down first.' She's a dirty bitch sometimes. I wouldn't mind but he let her in and all.

***

That Yenta one has me exhausted. I don't think I've ever danced as much in me life. Me legs won't work anymore. Me arse feels like its made of steel and I was wearin' a poxy bra so me nipples are all chafed. I put a bit of the Nivea moisturiser on them so they're a little bit better but still, when I get me hands on that Yenta one I'll kill her. That's if I have the energy. I wouldn't even mind but I wasn't even goin' to go out but she rang me and said that Paulo and Kevin were after havin' a row and he wanted to do something. To be honest, I'm not surprised the way the two of them were actin' the night before. Paulo says that Kevin doesn't know what he wants and he says its' not even a case of him bein' confused about his sexuality or anything, he's just a moody fucker and it's one thing Paulo can't stand. I think that's why him and our Bopper aren't really friends anymore. Boppers mad humours get in on me.

Anyway, the three of us went around to Yentas for a drink, which turned into about seven. We were like Jasmin mixin' the stuff and then Yenta decides she wants to go dancin' so Paulo was agreein' with her so I didn't have much of a choice. We ended up in Heaven in

Blanchardstown which, I've said before, I like a lot, mainly coz it does be full of rides. Yenta had the two of us up dancin' for the night and every time I went to sit down, she pulled me back up to dance with her and I was only short of collapsin' at the end of it. Paulo told us he was goin' the toilet and disappeared for a good hour, although he was probably hidin' somewhere in case Yenta spotted him and tried to get him to dance with her. I don't know where she gets the energy from. Ya'd swear she was Concepta tryin' to lose a few pounds she was dancin' that much. I must have lost a bit meself. It definitely feels like it.

    I met this fella when we were leavin', Joe his name was, a bit of a looker and a bit of a charmer as well and I ended up snoggin' him and all and he took me number. He wanted to gimme a lift home but I was stayin' in Yentas so he said he'd ring me. He has a BMW and all. Dave didn't even have a BMX.

❋❋❋

Concepta got mugged. I know it's terrible. Or at least I thought it was til I got all the details about it and from what I hear, she left your man in a bit of a state.

    What happened was, Concepta was walkin' home from work and she was walkin' through the park like she always does. It's only a little park with like street lights and all the rest of it but she said it was only gettin' dark at the time and she was walkin' through like she always does, mindin' her own business, listenin' to Mariah Carey on her CD player, my Mariah Carey CD it is and all, and this fella grabs her handbag but ya know Concepta, there isn't a hope in hell that she's lettin' go of it and he nearly gets whiplash coz he has to stop runnin' and he goes to punch Concepta and anyone will tell ya, that's a bad move coz she ducks the punch and ends up givin' him one and then another one and she ends up batterin' your man and leavin' him there in the middle of the park but she says its only what he deserves for what he was goin' to do to her and I have to say, I agree with her. That fucker would have run off with her handbag without a second thought about Concepta so she had every right to knock the shite out of him.

***

Sheila has a fella. Ya know Sheila that I work with. The Chinese young-one. She hasn't said anything to me or anything but I know by her. Ya can tell by the way she's been actin' and I have to say, if she does have a fella, I'll be delighted for her coz she's a lovely young-one and it about time she got her hole.

She walked into work today and ya wanna see the smile on her face. Now normally, Sheila does do nothing but smile. She's like that. She's a smiley person but I know loads of people like that but today she was smilier than ever and I asked her what she was so happy about and she told me to mind me own business, the cheeky cow. It's not like Sheila at all because no matter what she does, she tells me. I've often tried to listen to her talk for a good half an hour about what she had for dinner the night before, how she made it, what she had to drink with it, how long it took her to eat it, what she was watchin' on telly as she ate it, how she washed up and all the rest of it but today she told me nothing. I even tried to get Julie Walsh to get it out of her but that was pointless coz like meself, Sheila knows well not to open her mouth in front of Julie Walsh in case it ends up gettin' spread around Dublin.

There were just a few things that she was doin' today. Sheila this is, and straight away I thought to meself this one has a fella. Either that or she bought a vibrator.

***

Yenta's after ringin' me and she told me that she thinks Marvin has a girlfriend and she wanted to know did I know anything about it seein' as he's workin' with me and all but to be honest, it's the first I've heard about it. Fair play to him and all if he does like.

Yenta asked me if I was bothered and I hadn't a clue what she was talkin' about. 'Why would I be bothered?' says I. She was quiet for a couple of seconds and then she says, 'Well don't take this the wrong way or anything Joanna but I always had a bit of a feelin' that you were into

Marvin.' Well I nearly died. 'Me into your brother?' Says I, 'ya must be jokin' Yenta.' Where she got that idea from I don't know coz I certainly have never done anything to make her or anyone else think that I like Marvin, well at least I hope I didn't, although ya know me when I'm locked. I could say anything and not realise it. True enough, I've always been friendly with him but that's it, just friendly. I don't know how anyone else could take it the wrong way. I've always just had loads of time for Marvin coz nobody else talks to him much, what with him not bein' great at English and all the rest of it but the thing is, I'm well used to that with Sheila and Boris from work and Jasmin so I was just bein' friendly like. Me and Marvin. Jayzis no!

✳︎✳︎✳︎

Concepta's still doin' great on the Weight Watchers, fair play to her. She started off eight weeks ago I think it was and at that stage she was 17 stone and now she's down to 13 stone 6 and that's nearly 4 stone, which ya have to admit is impressive and a little bit freaky at the same time. We were lookin' at the holiday pictures there the night before last and it really is amazin' how different she looks. Ya only really notice it when ya look at pictures coz when ya see her every day, ya don't really realise how much she's losin'. Ya have to give it to her though, she does look amazin' and fair play to her coz its hard work and I know because we do be goin' into McDonalds or whatever and I remember a time and not even too long ago when we'd go into McDonalds and Concepta would get two burgers and a large chips or even two small ships, a milkshake and a McFlurry and now all she'll have is a salad or a bag of fruit and ya know she's bein' serious coz Concepta Cooney never ate as much as a grape before. Even when we're out she does have just the water most nights and if she is havin' a drink, it'll be just a Bacardi and diet Coke and even at that, she won't have that many.

She's even real confident now, not that Concepta Cooney wasn't confident before but I mean with fellas. She'd never chat anyone up before but now she always doin' it. Well Irish fellas anyway. I couldn't believe it one night we were out and she brought a fella up to us and he wasn't foreign. That wouldn't be like Concepta at all so ya have to give it to her. Losin' the weight is doin' wonders for her.

She told meself and Tracy there today that she's feelin' a little bit faint lately and I told her she will do if she doesn't eat anything so I gave her a thing of these multi-vitamins we sell in the shop. They're great. I take one every day and I told her that she should take them and it'll give her a bit of energy coz she's missin' out on loads of her vitamins and minerals. I'm readin' too many women's magazines.

***

I knocked around to me Uncle Dessie today to drop in a few things that he had left in our house when he moved out and who answered the door? Not a Filipino nurse, not me Uncle Dessie but Sister Mary Immaculate Conception. Well I nearly died coz I wasn't expectin' it at all. I mean, the last person ya expect to answer the door of your uncle's house is the former nun who everyone's been sayin' he's havin' some kind of affair with but here she was, proof that after all that, the rumours actually were true and that me Uncle Dessie was the reason Sister Mary left the church. I just stood there lookin' at her when she opened the door, not able to think of something to say and she's lookin' at me, wonderin' what in the name of god I'm doin' and eventually she says to me 'Are you Dessie's niece?' And I kinda nod and she tells me to come in. How this one was ever a nun is beyond me but if that Anna Nolan one from the Afternoon Show was trainin' to be a nun then anyone could. Sister Mary is young, much too young for me Uncle Dessie and good lookin' and she seems to be really nice. I was kinda mortified coz I mean, what do ya say to your uncle's new girlfriend but she made me coffee and all. I called her Sister Mary at one stage and she laughed and said that ship had sailed, whatever fuckin' ship she was talkin' about. I certainly never said a word about a ship. Maybe she did and I didn't hear her. She said I've just to call her Mary now so I did. It's a lot nicer than what Mrs O'Driscoll and all the other auld-ones have been callin' her.

***

We had a good night last night although it ended in disaster but ya know what we're like anyway. It wouldn't be one of our nights out if someone didn't have a row.

Meself and Concepta were just goin' to go up to Farley's for a few drinks but then Tracy decides she's comin' and that she has to meet Lance in town and then Paulo and Kevin decide they're comin' too and they asked all the others but they all seemed to be busy. Jasmin and Bopper were goin' to a party in Swords with the three Nialls and Nigel. Sheila and Marvin both had dates, or that's what Yenta said anyway. I hate the way they all keep sayin' date. I feel like I'm an American television programme anytime anyone says it. Yenta herself was stayin' in coz she was knackered. I tried to persuade her to come with us but she was havin' none of it.

We ended up goin' into town anyway and we met Lance in the Q-bar and we were havin' a bit of a laugh and Lance asks me do I want him to set me up with one of his friends but after that night that him and Tracy left me sittin' there with that gobshite of a French fella, I said no thanks and went off to dance with Concepta. We came back when a shite song came on and Paulo and Kevin were sittin' there havin' some kinda argument, which I'll be honest, I didn't think it was too strange what with the way the two of them have been actin' lately. So meself and Concepta go the bar, her to get a glass of water and me to get a vodka and Coke and when we come back, Paulo and Kevin are shoutin' at each other and Tracy and Lance are sittin' there lookin' at them, not knowin' what's goin' on and eventually Kevin tells Paulo to forget about it and just walks out and Paulo sits down and Lance asks Paulo should he run after Kevin and Paulo just laughs and drags me and Concepta to the dance floor. I suppose that's the last we'll be seein' of Kevin so.

***

Ya won't believe this. Seriously ya won't. I don't know how I didn't realise it before to be honest but I think it just never crossed me mind. Ya know the way Sheila has a fella and Marvin has a girlfriend? Well believe it or not, they're goin' out with each other! I swear its true. Not a word of a lie.

What happened was, last night Yenta rings me and asks me to go over to her place and I had nothing else planned so meself and Nigel were just sittin' in watchin' the usual Saturday night shite on the telly and he was delighted as well so the two of us walked to Yentas and when we got there, Paulo was already sittin' there playin' the Playstation with Jasmin, Tracy and Concepta were in the kitchen with Yenta, tryin' to keep Jasmin away from the alcohol in case she started mixin' things together. That's why they got Paulo to play the Playstation with her, to keep them all from gettin' poisoned.

I asked Yenta where Marvin was and she said she was at the cinema with his new girlfriend and I said that it was lovely so we're there havin' a laugh, havin' a few shots on the Playstation. Paulo is great at Tekken although Concepta's not too bad either and Yenta knows all the special moves. Next minute a knock comes to the door and Yenta answers it and who is it only Marvin and Sheila and ya wanna see the looks on our faces. We couldn't believe it. Yenta just started laughin' and Concepta at last beat Paulo at Tekken when he wasn't lookin', the sly bitch.

**

I'm in work today and I'm standin' there talkin' to Leandra and Marie who, believe it or not, wasn't stoned for the first time in god knows how long and I was fillin' them in on all the details about Sheila and Marvin, makin' sure that Julie Walsh could see we were havin' a good gossip and that she wasn't involved in it. She does go mad when anyone else is talkin' and she doesn't know what to do so we do it all the time just to piss her off. She does be nearly fallin' off her stool to try and hear what we do be sayin'.

Anyway, we're there havin' a chat and who walks into the shop only Yenta so we get her to start tellin' us all about Marvin and Sheila but at this stage I know just as much of the details as she does.

The phone rings and then Leandra runs off to get it and Marie has to go make a roll for someone so once Yenta has me on me own, she tells me she has a favour to ask me and at first I was a bit worried, thinkin' what it could be and she tells me that there's an audition for this television programme on in town on Saturday and she asks me to do it with her and I tell her I've never acted before in me life and she tells me it's like one of these pop star kinda things where ya have to sing and I'll be honest, after hearin' that, I didn't have to be asked twice. I'm a great singer I am. Sure I'm always doin' great in the karaoke and didn't I tell ya about me, Bernie and the others in the school concert when we were kids. We were only great. I should easily get through to the next round coz there aren't that many singers out there as good as me. I often won bottles of peach schnapps in the karaoke on the holidays. This could be just the chance I've been waitin' for. I could be the next Mariah.

✻✻✻

I still haven't a clue about what song I'm goin' to sing on Saturday. I have a few choices ya see and at the end of the day, I think I have to pick the one that'll give me the best chance of goin' through to the next round. Yenta tells me that she already has her song picked but she won't tell me what it is, probably coz she's afraid I'm goin' to steal it on her but I have plenty of ideas meself. I could do one of the old favourites from when I do karaoke, something like Robbie Williams *Angels* coz the crowds do love that and I do sing it kinda like your woman Jessica Simpson. Concepta tried to do a Jessica Simpson song on holidays and she sounded more like Homer Simpson.

I could always do a Mariah number coz I've been told more than once that I have a voice very similar to Mariah's. I did *Hero* one night in the Canaries and everyone loved it. Mariah's hard enough to sing so if I do it right, the judges will be well impressed. That could be one way of gettin' through.

There's a few Whitney numbers I do like doin' as well like *My Love Is Your Love* or *I Will Always Love You*, ya know the one from *The*

Bodyguard. I only love that song but Yenta thinks there'll be loads of people doin' songs like that on Saturday and I should pick something different. Maybe a bit of Brandy. The singer, not the drink.

✳✳✳

I came home this evenin' and I can hear the noise of music all over the house and me ma's in the kitchen makin' a cup of tea and I go into her and ask her what the noise is all about and she says Bopper and Nigel are rehearsin'. 'Rehearsin' for what?' I ask, terrified of what the answer was goin' to be. 'Ah they're doin' some audition for the telly on Saturday,' she says. I nearly died coz it meant they were goin' to the thing as well so I went up the stairs as quiet as I could so they wouldn't know I was there and I throw Boppers bedroom door open and there's the two of them singin' to a song by Nsync or the Backstreet Boys or one of these boy bands who were famous years ago and the two of them nearly died of embarrassment when they saw me. 'What are yiz doin'?' says I, tryin' to keep in the laughter. I mean, the state of them. 'We're practicin' for *You're A Star*,' Bopper tells me, which I suddenly realise is the television programme the audition is for. 'Go way,' I says. 'Me and Yenta are goin' for it as well.'

'You can't sing,' our Nigel says, half laughin'. The cheeky bastard.

'Well you can't fuckin' dance,' I says, 'And anyways, you weren't in the Canaries to hear me singin' on the karaoke. I was only great. Even all the fellas from Cabra and the young-ones from Ballyfermot said it. What are yiz callin' yourselves anyway?'

'2 Ladz,' Bopper tells me, 'with a Z at the end.' Well I couldn't keep in the laughter. 2 Ladz. Westlife must be shittin' themselves.

October

I can't believe it. Really I can't. Of all the people, who rings me today to tell me she's comin' to the audition on Saturday only Concepta. Not a word of a lie now. I thought at first that she was just ringin' me to tell me how she got on in the Weight Watchers like she always does although she did manage to tell me about that as well. She just missed out on slimmer of the week to Jasmin's ma but she didn't really mind coz she's down to 13 stone herself now so that means that she's not too far from her target weight but she said it just like the way Dublin's not far from Nairobi. She's said that before. I just agree with her, not really knowin' what she was tryin' to say. I didn't know if that was a good thing or a bad thing but I just said nothing to be safe.

    I couldn't believe it when she told me she was comin' to the audition too coz I've heard Concepta sing and she's dreadful, can't carry a note and I wouldn't mind but she thinks she's Aretha Franklin. She says she's doin' it for all the big women out there and I told her she's not exactly big anymore and anyways, Michelle McManus already won the English *Pop Idol* thing and she was a big girl so she's too late. She says she's still gonna do it though. She wants to sing *I Say A Little Prayer For You*. She needs more than a prayer, she needs a fuckin' miracle.

✳✳✳

I'm feelin' a bit nervous about the audition tomorrow but that's only natural and besides, I think nerves are a good thing. They help ya perform. They keep ya on your toes so ya don't get too complacent or whatever the word is. I'm not studyin' English and psychology in UCD. Tracy's only gone back two weeks and it's all she's talking about.

Speakin' of Tracy, she said she's comin' to the audition tomorrow for the laugh and when she said that I thought she was comin' to laugh at us, ya know Tracy, but then Yenta tells me that Tracy's goin' to have a go at auditionin' herself. I couldn't believe it. She wouldn't be a bad singer in fairness but she'd be no Shirley Bassey if ya know what I mean. Fair enough, when she does the karaoke she does be great, but she wouldn't be what ya'd call a singer, just someone who gets up for the buzz but I think she knows herself she hasn't much chance of gettin' through to the next round so Yenta says she's just doin' it for fun.

Whatever about Tracy, I nearly died when our Bopper told me Jasmin was doin' it too. The poor girl can't even speak, let alone sing. The last time she got up in karaoke, she just kept singin' 'lalala' and when she was finished, we asked her why she didn't sing the song and she said she didn't know the words. I don't think it dawned on her that they were written on the screen in front of her, the dizzy cow. She's unreal sometimes. I can just imagine her now tomorrow. She probably thinks it's an audition for *Big Brother* or something. She actually went to the auditions for *Big Brother* and got all the way to the RDS before someone told her they were in Croke Park but she just came home coz she said she couldn't play Gaelic.

Paulo said he may as well come along seein' as everyone else will be there. He says he might sing *Like A Virgin* for the laugh and I told him he's far from bein' a virgin but he should go for it anyways. It's one way of gettin' on the telly. Ya wanna see him in the Canaries doin' Robbie Williams. I nearly wet meself laughin' when he got up on the bar and started doin' *Rock DJ* and it was even funnier when he started to strip.

I rang Bernie in England to tell her all about it and she was ragin' coz it's the type of thing she'd love to do. When she was here, she used to drag me to auditions for everything. She's a good singer, I'll give her that much and she has that look about her as well. Like she should be in Girls Aloud or something. Fair play to her, she got to the third round of

Big Brother once about two year ago and she was very nearly picked to be on that *Treasure Island* show as well. She came very close and all only she'd lied about her age and they found out.

I told her about Nigel and Boppers new group, 2 Ladz, and she thought it was gas. It was even funnier when I told her they asked me to be in it. They were gonna call it '2 Ladz and a Grrl', spelt like that. Who are they? Jasmin? I told them I'd have a much better chance on me own and I think they got a bit offended but fuck them. Poor Bernie. She misses out on all this type of stuff bein' away. Me and her could have had our own group. '2 Young-onez'. Deadly.

※※※

The buzz we had at the audition today. I swear to god, it's one of the best days we've had this long time. I really enjoyed it and it was the whole day and all and then we ended up goin' for a drink in town so it was late enough when we gettin' home.

I woke up this mornin' to the sound of 2 Ladz rehearsin'. I could have battered Bopper and Nigel coz I'd been hopin' to get a bit of a lie on what with a long day ahead of me and all but the noise of the two of them singin'. I couldn't even think about gettin' back to sleep so I had to get up and try not to listen to the two of them. I don't know what's scarier, the singin' or the dancin'. I think they're both as bad as each other and by that I mean Bopper and Nigel.

The three of us left the house early enough and headed to Yenta's where we met the others except Paulo coz he had to work for the mornin' so we all head to the bus and go into town.

The audition was in one of them fancy new hotels in the docklands and by the time we got there, there was already a bit of a queue but we didn't really mind coz we were all there havin' the bit of buzz. Paulo showed up about a half an hour after us and then five minutes later who appears only Andy, Jasmin's little brother, the smelly rocker. The one who looked like a ride when he was wearin' a suit at Concepta's 21st. I nearly died though coz I'm still a bit scarlet talkin' to him and Yenta wasn't helpin' me by nudgin' me. I could have murdered the bitch. I was talkin' to him for a minute or two but I just kind of got all embarrassed, don't ask me why. As I said before, he's only a kid.

Anyway, we eventually got to the front of the queue and Tracy went in to audition first coz she said she was only there for the laugh anyway. I went in second coz I was just dyin' to get it over with and I was glad to be honest. I decided in the end to do *Never Had A Dream Come True* by S Club 7 and personally, meself now, I thought I did it very well but the judges who were pickin' the people didn't seem too impressed. Linda Martin said she didn't think I had a great voice and Brendan O'Connor said I was too confident, the cheek. I don't know who the other fella was. They said I didn't get through to the next round and I thought they were messin' I asked them did they want me to do another song and they said no so I told them I was refusin' to leave the room til they let me do another song so Linda Martin calls the security guards to carry me out but I was still tryin' to do a bit of Mariah as they pushed me out the door. There I am being carried and I grab hold of the door frame and decide to go down a different route and start singin' *In Your Eyes* from the Eurovision and its only when the other two security guards come to help remove me and I'm outside the building that I realize that it was Niamh Kavanagh and not Linda Martin that sang *In Your Eyes*.

Believe it or not, some of them actually made it to the second round. Jasmin's brother, Andy, and 2 Ladz. I'm not jokin' ya, Bopper and Nigel's rehearsin' actually paid off coz they made it to the next stage of the auditions. They'll be impossible to live with between braggin' about it and rehearsin'. I knew I should have sang *Angels*.

✻✻✻

We had Dessie and Mary who used to be Sister Mary around for dinner today and at first it was a little bit awkward but it was nice enough. We're goin' to have to get a bigger dinin' table coz with me ma, me da, me, Bopper, Nigel, Dessie and Mary, we were kinda a bit squashed in but we managed. Me ma made a lovely roast and she got this new gravy that was only mafis. I haven't had a gravy that nice this long time.

Me da's gas. We're sittin' there havin' the dinner and he starts askin' Mary all about religion and all this shite and about what she had to do to become a nun and all the rest of it and she wasn't even scarlet or anything. She had no problem talkin' about it at all. I'd say the poor woman is sick to death of people talkin' about it but it's not nearly as bad as what people have been sayin' about her behind her back and she doesn't deserve it at all coz she's a lovely woman, a real nice person and I like her a lot. She has a lot of time for meself and Bopper as well as Nigel. I nearly died when she asked to see the song that got 2 Ladz into the second round of *You're A Star*. We were in the sittin' room after the dinner and Bopper and Nigel got up and did it and I was only scarlet for them. How they got through I'll never know but they did. The state of the two of them dancin' around our sittin' room and the curtains wide open and all so that anybody passin' by outside could see them. The two of them are goin' around thinkin' they're all that and let me be the first to inform ya that they're not.

Mary was only lovin' it. Ya wanna see her there clappin' when they were finished and all like a gobshite. She's the worse fool for encouragin' them. She doesn't have to live with them although in sayin' that, she does have to live with me Uncle Dessie and four Filipino nurses.

✳✳✳

I was in work today havin' a look through a gardenin' magazine with Sheila, showin' her the water feature that I'd love to have if I had me own garden. Jayzis, I'm lucky to have me bedroom at the moment, let alone me own garden. It was lovely though. It was like this fountain that flowed into a waterfall and then into a little stream with little steppin' stones and all over it. Mafis it was. None of these gardens in these magazines ever have sheds. Did ya ever notice that? Where do these people keep their lawnmowers I'd love to know.

Anyway, I'm there talkin' about it with Sheila and I get a text message and I look at it and its from Jasmin and it says 'What U dressin' up as 4 Halloween?' and I look at it for a couple of seconds to make sure I'm readin' it right. So I think to meself that I better ring her coz havin' a conversation over text messages with Jasmin can be confusin' at the best of times. I ring her and she answers the phone and says, 'Hello who's this?' despite the fact that me name is after flashin' up on her screen before she answered. 'Its Joanna,' I answered, 'Ya do know Halloween isn't for 4 weeks,' says I. 'Yeah I know' she says. 'Then what are ya askin' me what I'm dressin' up as?' I says. 'I just wanted to know,' she answers. Never one for givin' proper reasons is Jasmin. 'But it's ages away,' I tell her. 'Yeah I know,' she says. Now at this stage I wasn't in the humour. 'So what are ya dressin' up as?' I asked, just to humour her like. 'I don't know. It's ages away,' she says. I swear to god, that young-one gets weirder every day.

✻✻✻

I was talkin' to Yenta today and she was sayin' that she bumped into Dave in work yesterday. Ya know Dave me ex, the bastard who was doin' the dirty on me with that posh cow who used to be friends with Tracy, Miranda. I don't know whether I mentioned it before or not but Yenta and Dave work in the same company although Yenta tells me that she never sees him and she's lucky that she's not as angry about what he did on me otherwise she would have kicked his head in. She's like that Yenta. Not so much violent but she looks after her friends. She's the type of young-one ya'd know not to mess with. She'd be like Concepta in that way.

Anyway, Yenta was sayin' that when she bumped into Dave, he was tellin' her that the company were transferin' him to Poland and I'll be honest, I was only delighted coz when I was goin' out with him he used to slag people off for gettin' sent to wherever it was the company was openin' a new office although if ya ask me, Poland's not far enough away. They should really open a branch in Brazil.

Yenta said she asked him about Miranda and he said it didn't work out and I'm ragin' coz the pair of bastards deserved each other. Yenta said he even had the cheek to ask her about me and ya know Yenta, she said I was great and that breakin' up with him was the best thing that could have happened to me. She said she would have punched him as well only the boss was passin' by.

✶✶✶

Leandra made me go home from work today to get a DVD I'd promised to lend her but had forgot and I would have told her to fuck off only I'd rushed out without me phone this mornin' and wanted to get it anyway so I'm walkin' back into the shop and who's walkin' out only your man Paddy from ages back. Ya know the one that I was with on his couch last year, the one who was friends with your man Phillip who I was into. Anyway, I was thinkin' of just ignorin' him and walkin' into the shop but he stopped me and he was like, 'Ah Joanna Ryde, what's the story? I haven't seen ya this long time. What ya been up to? You're lookin' well.' And I was goin' to tell him that it was a pity I couldn't say the same about him but I thought I'd better try and be nice. I'd only be bein' honest though. He'd let himself go a little bit since the last time I was talkin' to him. He put on a little bit of weight and was nowhere near as good lookin' as he had been before. What I'd ever seen in him I don't know but I must have been really desperate or something back then.

I told him I was grand anyway and asked him what he was doin' at the shop and he just said he was over in the area coz he was seein' a girl from around here although I asked him who and he wouldn't tell me. I asked him if I knew her and he said I might and then he just smiled at me and said goodbye. Now that I come to think of it, he's actually a bit of a minger and to think I had sex with him on his couch.

✶✶✶

I went into town to meet Yenta yesterday with Jasmin, who for some reason has decided that I'm her new best friend again now that Boppers busy with Nigel practicin' for the second round of the auditions. To be honest now, I have a bit of a soft spot of Jasmin although Yenta says it's more like I have a soft spot for her brother but as I told her, I'm not like that. That young-fella is only 16 or something. She's a fucker about that Yenta. I'm ragin' I brought it up at Concepta's 21st coz she just keeps goin' on about it. I'll kill her over it one day.

Anyway, I get the bus into town with Jasmin. I'd offered to knock over to her house first but she said that she'd knock over to me coz if I was to go to her house, I'd have to pass by me own again on the way back to the bus stop. I told her I didn't mind but she said not to be silly. Not that I wanted to go to Jasmin's house for any particular reason or anything like.

We got the bus into town and met Yenta across from Trinity college and the three of us went over to Henry Street to do a bit of shoppin'. I actually picked up a few nice bits. A-Wear have some lovely stuff in and I got a mafis pair of boots in Dunnes reduced to €15. I mean, where would ya get it, ya can't go wrong.

We went to that food court place in the Jervis Street Centre and meself and Yenta are in the queue for KFC, Jasmin decided to go to Harry Ramsden's and be awkward, and we're standin' there and next minute, these two little skanger young-ones come up to me and say 'You're her aren't ya' and I'm thinkin' to meself that they must think I'm Britney Spears or someone off Fair City or something til the other young-one says 'You're the one that was in the paper coz your man tried to kill ya. Why didn't ya just give him a kick in the mickey?' I'll never be able to live that down.

***

I was in work today and me mobile rings and I look at the screen and see that it's Concepta and I answer it and she says, 'Oh my god, its you, the girl from the paper,' and starts breakin' her shite laughin'. I wouldn't mind but she'd done it three times yesterday as well. I'm goin' to batter the bitch when I see her.

***

Julie Walsh has been lookin' a bit happy with herself in work the last few days so today with it bein' Saturday and all, Amy was in so the two of us were able to have a bit of a chat about it. Julie Walsh herself wasn't workin' but her little buddy Jason was so meself and Amy were tryin' to get him to dish the dirt on his friend but he wouldn't say a word. We tried everything we could short of bribin' the bastard but he still wouldn't say anything. Them two are like that, always stickin' up for each other and all the rest of it. Nobody else in the shop likes them, not even Marvin and he's only new and he usually likes everyone. That's the type of person he is. He's like his sister in that way. Yenta usually likes everyone as well, although I think she's only met Jason once and she doesn't like him either. As I said before, he's just one of these people ya'd love to punch. He thinks he's right about everything and if he thinks he has a bit of gossip that you're dyin' to find out about, he deliberately won't tell ya just to piss ya off, but if you were to tell him something, he'd have it spread all over the place in five minutes.

 We couldn't get a thing out of him about Julie Walsh and meself and Amy were talkin' about what might be up with her when who walks in only Julie Walsh one herself and who's she with only your man Paddy, the one I'd been with before that I'd seen leavin' the shop only a few days before. When I asked him if I knew the young-one he's goin' out with he said I might and it turns out that its Julie Walsh. What he sees in her I don't know coz she's in bits although in sayin' that, Paddy's a bit of a minger himself these days.

 Ya wanna see them in the shop holdin' hands, smilin' at each other, laughin' with that gobshite Jason and all the rest of it and in the meantime, I start to fill Amy in on all the details about Paddy and she nearly wets herself laughin' when I tell her the story about meself and Jasmin hittin' Paddy's best mate Philip with the Skittles in the UGC one night so she grabs a packet of M&Ms coz we're out of Skittles, opens the packet, takes one out and throws it across the shop and it hits Paddy in the back of the head and meself and Amy are sittin' behind the Coke fridge breakin' our shites laughin' as Julie Walsh, Paddy and Jason are lookin' around, convinced something's after fallin' from the ceilin'.

✳✳✳

We had another one of our mad nights out last night. I wasn't even goin' to go anywhere only that me Uncle Dessie and Mary were comin' over for the night to have a few drinks with me ma and da and the last thing I wanted to do was sit in with them.

The one thing I'll say about me Uncle Dessie since he got back from Holland and since he met Sister Mary, sorry I mean Mary, is that he's started to act his age. No more comin' to the pub with us, no more thinkin' he's black, nothing like that at all. He's actin' like any other man of his age and it's about time, not that I didn't enjoy Dessie bein' one of us or anything but I had to look after him more than once and it's a bit embarrassin' when we're out somewhere and our uncle is sittin' with us. The fellas wouldn't come near us.

Anyway, as I was sayin', I wasn't in the mood for listenin' to me da askin' Mary more questions about the church so I decided to get a bit of a crew together and head into town. At first I could only get Yenta but then Concepta and Tracy decided to come and then Jasmin so I was well up for a bit of a girls night out and where better to go than Club M? It does be full of tourists and we do usually end up gettin' loads of snogs when we go there.

Concepta Cooney was in flyin' form and found an English fella, a Dutch fella and a Brazilian in the first hour. Jasmin was on the Jack Daniels and cranberry juice, the mad bitch, and she disappeared for ages only for Yenta to find her in the cloak room havin' a chat with the young-one doin' the coats. How she knew her or if she knew her I don't know but she was there.

I got talkin' to this bloke from Maynooth, a good enough lookin' fella and he ended up buyin' me a few drinks and all and I ended up snoggin' him for ages and then he turns around and tells me he's just after breakin' up with his girlfriend and all this shite and I wasn't in the mood for that sort of shit after what happened with Dave so I just went back to the girls. I turned around at one stage and who's sittin' behind me only Marvin and Sheila. How they got there I don't know but there they were, both of them smilin' at me. Concepta went home with the Dutch fella. Just to his apartment in Smithfield like, not to Dutchland or wherever Dutch people come from.

***

Bernie's not in the best of moods at all, although it's not unusual or anything. She's been the same every time she's rang me lately and it gets worse and worse and she won't tell me that there's anything wrong even though I know quite well that there is. I know Bernie. I know her better than anyone else and when there's something wrong I can tell and a lot of the time with Bernie she won't say a thing and I'd have to force it out of her. I usually find out some way but with her in England and all, it's hard.

To be honest, I think she's gettin' homesick. Ya have to remember that this is the first time Bernie's ever lived away from home and she's all the way in England. If she wants to talk to us all she can do is text us or give us a ring. It's not like she's here and she can knock around to me or come for a drink or whatever. Fair enough, she has your woman Dervla but Bernie says she's movin' to Shannon next week and she's not really close to anyone else. I do feel sorry for her. I think she knows she's missin' out on all the buzz here. She was ragin' she wasn't here for the audition for You're A Star. She would have loved that but she's missin' the buzz we do have with Yenta and Marvin and Nigel and all the rest of it. I told her about Julie Walsh and your man Paddy and she couldn't get over it coz the night we went out for my birthday months ago he was all over Bernie like a bad rash. Jayzis. D'ya remember that rash we all had? Mad.

I'd say bein' home for Concepta's 21st that time must have got to her and she had a great night. She didn't really wanna go back. I could tell by her. She just wasn't herself at all. She can't wait for the trip to Killarney. She asked could we share a room and all which is grand coz it means I won't have to share with Concepta. Not that I don't love Concepta to bits or anything but she does fart a lot when she's asleep.

✳✳✳

Dymphna's gone missin'. Well so Julie Walsh tells me although how she knows I don't know. Of course she's missin' I told Julie Walsh when she told me. She went to Turkey and nobody's seen her, she's obviously bleedin' missin' but Julie Walsh says that when her husband went over to find her and try to get her to come home, he saw her for the first day and then next day her and your man had just vanished and he tried to find out where they had gone. Nobody knew so he eventually had to come home after lookin' everywhere. He even went to that place that's the capital, Anchor or whatever it is but he still couldn't find her. Even the Irish embassy or consulate or whatever they have in Turkey can't find her coz they think your man might have kidnapped her. In fairness though, who'd kidnap Dymphna? Unless it was a mistake or something. They probably thought it was Mary McAleese or something, not that Dymphna looks anything like her but I don't think the Turks would know that. Dymphna probably told them she was the president for the laugh.

Knowin' Dymphna it was her choice to go with your man. She probably kidnapped him. That'd be more like her the dirty slapper. She's like that. I could picture Dymphna in all that leather dominatrix gear. H&M or something they call it, where they spank each other and all the rest of it. I'd say she's like that, makin' the Turkish fella call her mistress. 'Who's your daddy,' she'd be sayin' to him.

✳✳✳

Me cousin Jacinta, or Pussy-willow as she's called now, was arrested. Me Uncle Dessie and Mary were around in the house today and he was tellin' us he just got a phone call from her boyfriend Fudge in Birmingham. The thing is though, this isn't Pussy-willow's first time bein' arrested. Hold on. No sorry. I can't call her Pussy-willow. That's just stupid! What type of name is Pussy-willow? I couldn't give a fuck, I'm callin' her Jacinta.

Yeah it's not the first time Jacinta was arrested. Far from it. That young-one's been arrested more times than Michael Jackson. See she's one of these tree huggin' hippies that ya do hear about in the news and she does be doin' mad stuff. The first time she was at a demonstration rally in Seville and she broke the window in Starbucks and was arrested. What she was breakin' the window in Starbucks for I don't know. I mean, all they do is make coffee and nice coffee at that. I don't know what they did on Jacinta. Maybe she just doesn't like coffee or something. I don't see what breakin' a window in a coffee shop has to do with savin' the planet.

The second time she was arrested for standin' in front of this train bringin' nuclear stuff from France to Germany although what that sap was doin' standin' in front of a train, I don't know. It's a wonder the stupid bitch didn't get knocked down. Actually it's a pity she didn't get knocked down. I know she's me cousin and all but the young-one's a spa.

This time she was arrested for breakin' up a JCB near the hole she's been livin' in the path of a motorway in Birmingham, although again, don't ask me why. Why she lives in a hole, why does she not want the motorway built, why did she break up a JCB, why did she get caught. With Jacinta ya don't ask coz ya do be afraid of the answers. Dessie wants her to come to live here if she doesn't go to jail and I told me ma when he left, I said there is no way Jacinta is comin' to live with us. If she's anything like her brother though, she'll just show up one day. We still haven't got rid of Nigel.

✱✱✱

Disco died. Yeah I'm actually very upset about it coz although he was a little fucker of a dog at first, I got to like him in the end coz I mean, once he stopped barkin' all night he was grand and I was very fond of him and I don't often like dogs.

Poor Petulia next door is devastated although I don't know why. I always thought she was a bitch to him, leavin' him out at night and all but ya know me ma, she made a little bed for him in our shed so she used to always sneak in and get him and bring him in and when Petulia would come lookin' for him me ma would tell her that he came in on his own although in the end, he did start comin' in on his own. Me ma would just leave the shed door open. We were all very fond of him in our house. Ya'd often see Bopper or Nigel or ma da out the back playin' with him. Me ma used to pick up little toys for him if she was in Lidl. She'd be out the back talkin' to him and everything, havin' full blown conversations with Petulia's dog about the Weight Watchers.

I cried for a good hour when I heard about it. I was very upset but I'd grown very close to him I had. He was found just down the end of our road. The poor thing covered in blood. Somebody must have knocked him down and me da went down with a black bag and a pair of rubber gloves and picked him up and brought him up to Petulia's. We were all in an awful state and we buried him out Petulia's back between a rose bush and a rhododendron and we had a little ceremony and we were all cryin'. The poor thing must have suffered as well. Ah Jayzis I'll miss him.

✲✲✲

The laugh we had with Marvin today. It was only gas. We trained him on the tills and fair enough, he was actually very good at it, although it's hardly like flyin' a space shuttle but we decided for the bit of buzz to tell him that whenever a customer came up to him, he had to say, 'How's your muff?' and he said it a few times for us to get it right and meself and Leandra and even that Julie Walsh one were standin' there tryin' to keep a straight face so the first customer comes up to him and he smiles at her, takes her mint aero and bottle of Coke and says, 'How's your muff?' And we're still tryin' as hard as we can not to break our shites laughin' although it was nearly impossible. Leandra had to go into the back for a minute to calm down. Your woman, the customer, she just smiled back at him. I don't think she heard what he said. The next one that went up to him, he said it to her and she says, 'No sorry love, I don't have one.' Now what she thought he was askin' her for I don't know. He said it to every customer for the whole day and not one realised what he was sayin' and meself and Julie Walsh and Leandra just pissed ourselves laughin' every time.

***

I can't believe it. Like I'm scarlet. I don't think I've ever been as embarrassed in me life. I got up out of bed this mornin', not too early mind you, but I got out of bed and went down to the kitchen and surprisingly, it wasn't too much of a struggle after what Yenta made me drink last night. She had the smoothie maker flyin'. Everything was goin' into it. Jasmin was havin' a field day. She thought over to the thing she'd never get and if I had of had me way she wouldn't have. I've been on the wrong end of a Jasmin cocktail and it's not a good place to be, believe me. How I wasn't dieing this mornin' is beyond me although it might have something to do with the amount of food Yenta made me eat as well. I'm not goin' around to her apartment again. I always end up fat with a hangover.

Anyway, that has nothing to do with why I was scarlet. I walked into the kitchen this mornin' and there's me ma sittin' at the kitchen table, sprawled across the thing, a glass of water in one hand and an empty packet of Anadin in the other one.

'What in the name of Jayzis happened to you?' I says. Well she launches into it. One of the girls from her job was leavin' so they all go to a pub up behind Dame Street for a few drinks. She can't remember the name of it although it's not suprisin' with the state she must have been in. Anyway, some of the young-ones wanted to go clubbin' so me ma tells me that they brought her to the 33 and I'm thinkin' to meself where this 33 place is when it dawns on me. 'Are ya sure it wasn't TwentyOne?' I says. 'Oh that was it,' she says and falls across the table again. Well I was mortified. Can ya imagine me ma in TwentyOne with all that hiphop music? Jayzis. I'd say she was up on the dance floor and all givin' it loads. I can never go there again. Imagine someone found out we were related. I'd never get a fella!

✱✱✱

I'm tellin' ya it was a mad night out last night and I wasn't even goin' to go coz I had rang Bernie for a chat and she was really upset so that kinda put me off. I have to say, I'm livin' to see her now durin' the week. She says she'll more than likely be home Thursday night so I'm all exited about seein' her.

I told Yenta that I was in no humour to go out but she was havin' none of it. She had already told the rest of them I was goin' so I kinda had to. Sayin' that now, it was only me, Yenta, Concepta, Jasmin and Paulo but we ended up gettin' talkin' to a few people. We were in Heaven up in Blanch and we ended up sittin' at the top of the stairs with a few of Concepta's friends from work. The Jelly Babies we call them coz they work in the jelly factory like. They don't look like jelly babies or anything although one of them is a little bit like a cola bottle.

One of the fellas, we call him dancin' Tom, was sittin' there talkin' to Paulo and whatever happened, I was out the back smokin' at the time, but Tom challenged Paulo to a dance off. Well I'm not jokin' ya, it was like that film *Bring It On* in the middle of Heaven. Paulo and Tom were givin' it all the attitude and then the two of them head downstairs to the dance floor and we're all behind them and we kinda make a bit of room for ourselves on the dance floor. Concepta pushed a few people out of the way and we're all there in a circle givin' it loads to that 'You Can Do It Put Your Back In To It' song and Paulo flicks his hand like something off *Ricki Lake* and tells dancin' Tom to 'bring it.' Well it was like a squirrel tryin' to do the chicken dance. I thought he was havin' some kind of fit. I was only short of runnin' off to look for a doctor but then Paulo starts doin' his moves and he's not that bad. So the two of them are havin' turns in the middle of the circle and we're all cheerin' and then Yenta pushes them both out of the way like something out of *Save The Last Dance*, does a few moves, looks Tom up and down and turns and walks away and that was it really. Nobody's as good as Yenta at dancin'.

Your man Tom even tried it on with me later on in the night and as nice enough and all that he is, his girlfriend was sittin' beside me at the time so I didn't think it'd be a good idea to get involved and anyways, I'd be mortified if I was goin' out with someone that dances that bad.

✳✳✳

Me Uncle Dessie was around today tellin' me and me ma all about Jacinta. None of us are callin' her Pussy-willow coz we think it's stupid although Bopper keeps doin' it to piss me Uncle Dessie off.

Me Uncle Dessie was sayin' that her case went to court today and she was fined and has this barrin' order thing sayin' she has to stay away from wherever it was her hole in the ground was. The thing is, that's kinda where Jacinta's been livin' the last while in a tent or something so she hasn't really got anywhere to go which sounds to me like Jacinta is gonna end up livin' with us or Dessie, Mary and the four Filipino nurses and either way, there's very little room for her. I know she's me cousin and all but at the end of the day, I'm not too fond of her and there's not a hope in hell that after livin' in a hole for god knows how long that she's goin' to come into my house, take my bed, start usin' my Herbal Essences Shampoo and conditioner, borrow my cloths and start preachin' to me about the effects that hair straighteners have on the environment. Whatever about me, she'll fuckin' die when she see's all the cosmetics that Nigel and Bopper have. Talk about pollution. I blame 2 Ladz!

✳✳✳

I'm in work today havin' to listen to Julie Walsh go on about what her and your man Paddy got up to over the weekend and ya know what Julie Walsh is like, givin' more information than I needed to know. I was nearly gettin' sick listenin' to her tellin' me about sexual positions. There's just some things ya don't need to know when you're tryin' to eat a sausage roll. And I thought that story about her ear ring in the spicy wedges was bad.

Anyway, there I was in work and who walks in only Jasmin's little brother Andy and one of his mates. Andy's the one that Yenta thinks I fancy but I don't even though he is gettin' better lookin' every time I see him. That doesn't mean I fancy him or anythin though. The only reason I go scarlet when I see him is coz Yenta is always slaggin' me over him and anyways he's only 16 and I'm two years older than him and that means I'm too old for him although in sayin' that, I know plenty of couples that have an age gap of two years and some of them even more. It's nothing strange but as I said, I don't even fancy him so it doesn't matter.

He walked in anyway and there was meself and Julie Walsh havin' a chat and ya know me, it won't be often that you'll see me and Julie Walsh havin' a chat. I do just try and ignore her if I can but Marvin and Sheila were busy behind the deli counter, makin' rolls and that, nothing else. Jayzis, the hygiene people would kill us.

Anyway, Andy and his mate walks in and Andy picks up a can of Red Bull and his mate looks over at me and says hello and who is it only Keith O'Reilly, who's ma is none other than Celine O'Reilly, the auld-one that does go to the Weight Watchers. I'll be honest now, Keith is a bit of a sap as well, nothing compared to his ma or anything but the type of annoyin' little kid ya'd love to give a sly slap to when no one else is lookin'. What Andy is doin' hangin' around with a gobshite like him for I don't know. He's not even one of these mosher rockers like Andy and he's scruffy as well. I'd love to grab a hold of him and wash him. He just looks dirty or something.

The two of them were talkin' to me and I could tell by the look on Andy's face that I wasn't the only one who Keith was annoyin'. He is gas though Andy. He has a great sense of humour. The two of us are very alike in a lot of ways. We have a few things in common. I'd say we'd get on very well if we were goin' out together although I don't fancy him or anything.

***

I swear to god, I could kill Marvin. I'm convinced that bastard can speak a lot more English than he's lettin' on. He's just pretendin' he doesn't for the laugh so he can laugh at us makin' gobshites of ourselves tryin' to communicate with him.

I was in work today and I was tellin' Leandra how it had just dawned on me that Dymphna had run off to Turkey and the person takin' her job turns out to be Turkish. It was like Marvin was meant to work with us or something. It's like god's work or something. Jayzis, I've been around Mary too much. I'm goin' all holy.

So I'm in the office talkin' to Leandra and who walks in only Marvin himself and he says, 'Yes Joanna, a lady would like to speak with you. You no give her change.' And already I know the fucker he's talkin' about, a dope of a woman she was so I says to him, 'Yeah I'll be out in a minute.' And I'm about to go back to talkin' to Leandra when he says 'This woman, she angry. What I tell her?' So I says to him, 'Tell her I called her a sap.' So he gives me a confused look and off he goes. So I finish talkin' to Leandra and go out and your woman's standin' there not lookin' very happy and she says, 'Not only do ya leave me short changed but ya tell the foreign fella to call me a sap.' She was disgusted. I could have killed Marvin. The bastard knew I was only jokin'.

***

Jasmin's gas. It was her birthday last night and with us goin' to Killarney this weekend and all she said she didn't want to have a night out til we got down there, which is understandable. I could understand totally where she was comin' from but ya know Concepta, she tells Jasmin she has to go for a drink the night of her birthday but she wasn't too mad about the idea coz it was Wednesday and most of us had to be up for work so after a bit of a chat about it, text messages goin' back and forward between everyone, we decide to head down to Farley's for a quiet drink but with Concepta Cooney involved, ya could hardly expect it to be quiet.

Meself and Jasmin went up about eight o'clock with Yenta, Paulo, Sheila and Marvin. We were like a meetin' of the United Nations sittin' there and Bopper and Nigel show up with two of the three Nialls, ya know Bopper's friends, and we're all sittin' there havin' a drink and who walks in only Concepta and me ma and Jasmin's ma and half the Weight Watchers. She's down to 12 stone 4 now Concepta so she hasn't that much to go to her target weight. She was delighted last night.

Anyway, we're sittin' there havin' the few drinks havin' taken over half the pub at this stage and Jasmin gets a phone call and I ask her who it is and she says it's her brother Andy, the one that I don't fancy, and Yenta asks Jasmin can she talk to him and takes the phone and tells Andy to come to the pub and winks over at me. Well I could have killed her. I went the toilet a few minutes later and come back and there he is sittin' there with your man Keith, that scruffy little young-fella, and I just said hello and Yenta starts nudgin' me when I sit down, the bitch. I was scarlet talkin' to Andy though coz she was there. I'll murder her I will.

I think your man Keith fancies me. He scares the shite out of me. He was there starin' me out of it and sayin' filthy things and I was kinda disgusted coz the state of him. How they let him in, I don't know coz he looks about 12 and about five times he heard people slaggin' his ma although it's well known that no one from the Weight Watchers likes Celine O'Reilly, the horrible cow. By the way, Killarney is fucked if last night is anything to go by!

※※※

Bernie got home yesterday evenin' so I got Nigel to bring us up to Dunnes in Blanchardstown coz he had a lend of me Uncle

Dessie's car and they had a special on the Ben and Jerry's Ice Cream and we're just plannin' on gettin' a few bits to eat and go back to the house and watch a DVD just so we could do something together, just the two of us although Nigel had no other plans so we said he could hang out with us as well, although what else could we say after him drivin' us up for ice cream and all. We could hardly tell him to fuck off could we? Although ya know Bernie, I wouldn't have put it past her.

Anyway, we park the car and head into the supermarket and we're goin' around pickin' up the few bits, Pringles and that sort of thing and we come to where they sell the vinegar and whatever and there was a young-one and a young-fella a bit older than meself, 22 or 23 maybe, standin' there in the middle of Dunnes snoggin' the faces off one another, no word of a lie. Now I was disgusted although Nigel thought it was gas. He wanted to throw a packet of cupcakes at them for a laugh but I told him not to. I work in a shop and battered cup cakes are a bastard to sell. I went up and told the manager though. I told him they should make an announcement or something like, 'Customer announcement, there is to be no French kissin' on the condiments aisle.' They'd be scarlet then and would think twice about doin' it next time. Could they not wait til they got home or something? I've heard of people doin' it in public but Dunnes is a different story.

***

Well I have to say, I very much doubt the hotel in Killarney had any idea what they were lettin' themselves in for. I can imagine the look on their faces when we all showed up yesterday. It hadn't even dawned on me how many of us there was goin' until we got to the train station. We made sure we had plenty of time before we had to get on the train so we could all go to Supermacs for a bite to eat after what happened goin' to Galway.

We got on the train anyway and we must have taken up a whole carriage ourselves. There was meself, Bernie, Concepta, Tracy, her fella Lance, Jasmin and Bopper, Paulo, Yenta and Nigel. Loads of us! So we're on the train anyway and Nigel puts a Dunnes bag up on the table and what's in it only three bottles of that €8 peach schnapps. Well ya wanna see us lowerin' it back straight although Jasmin had some of that Vanilla Coke and she mixed it with it. Trust her.

The hotel we're stayin' in is only mafis. The Plaza it's called and its real posh. Yenta had been given this voucher from work so it was dirt cheap and we had already paid for Concepta and Jasmin's weekends for their birthdays between us.

Needless to say, we were locked and all by half eight and we ended up in a pub called the Grand which ended up havin' a nightclub and all at the end of the night. We were all locked by the end of it. Concepta Cooney was in heaven coz the place is full of tourists and she made loads of friends. I have to say I was that locked I can hardly remember anything about it. Why I woke up in our Boppers cloths I'll never know.

***

They say Rome wasn't built in a day, not that I've ever been there but I'm startin' to think Killarney was. We went to get a few drinks last night and we found this off licence and went in and it was in someone's front room. Ya had to ring a bell to get your woman's attention and there she was sittin' there watchin' *Ros Na Rún* or whatever it is people watch on telly in Kerry and we ask her for the drink, me and Concepta it was, and she asks us for ID. Now Concepta just laughed in her face, her bein' 21 and me 18. I mean, we don't get asked for ID anywhere. So I says to her 'Love we come from Dublin. We don't need our passports to get here.' And eventually she just let it go although can ya blame her with the amount of alcohol we bought.

We ended up back in the Grand last night. Don't ask me how but we kinda just drifted towards it and we had a good night there the night before, not that I remember or anything. I was told. The hangover I had yesterday mornin'. I woke up and there's Bernie in her bed, lines of mascara runnin' down her face. The two of us were in bits and next minute a knock comes to the door and Bernie manages to haul herself out of the bed to get it and there's Jasmin standin' there fresh as a tube of Aquafresh, tellin' us she's tryin' to get everyone to go sightseein'. 'This is Killarney, not Paris' I tell her but Jasmin's havin' none of it and she's goin' around knockin' at all our hotel doors to get us all up to go see some house so we all had to go to keep her happy and we were all dyin' and how Jasmin wasn't I don't know but in fairness, the country air did help clear me head a bit and the house was nice.

We went into a restaurant for lunch and the face on the waiter when we asked him for a table for 10. He kinda counted us again just to make sure. I wouldn't mind but ya wanna see the bill and then the row that started over it. I wasn't gettin' involved coz I know well what they're all like and Nigel as usual sittin' there stirin' the shit to see a fight. It was a nice enough meal I'll be honest.

We came back to the hotel and got changed and then headed out again and we were told by these Americans earlier in the day that the Granary was a great spot so we headed there and ended up havin' a bit of laugh sittin' there with all these yanks and all the rest of it. I don't know who said it but someone suggested that we head to the Grand again so we all trouped off; us, these Americans and three Canadians Concepta had been talkin' to. It was like an invasion when we arrived at the Grand. We had a great night in there though and thank god I didn't get as locked as the night before, although I can't remember how locked I was the night before as I already said. I ended up gettin' chatted up by loads of culchies and all but I ended up snoggin' one of the Canadian fellas. Kyle his name was and he was from Toronto and he told me that he works in television. I asked him had he got his own TV show and he told me he was a camera man. He wanted me to go back to his hotel room with him and all only it was his last night and it would have meant Bernie would have been on her own and I wouldn't do that to her. He gave me his e-mail address and told me to e-mail him. I told him I can't even spell e-mail but I took it anyway. He was a ride. Pity he's Canadian. Not that I don't like Canadians or anything, I just meant that he lives there and doesn't live here and Tracy says 'it's a tragedy of life that someone I click with so well lives so far away.' And she'd know coz she studies English and psychology in UCD and her Lance is from Cork.

Today I was grand gettin' up but I decided to leave Bernie coz the poor young-one was only exhausted. I found Yenta and Paulo and the three of us decided to go down to the leisure centre. Well it was only deadly. We were in the Jacuzzi for nearly an hour and then we got into the sauna and we're sittin' there and this big fat American auld-fella with man diddies comes in and we're tryin' not to laugh and Yenta says to me, 'Joanna did you bring your wonder bra with you?' And the three of us start breakin' our shites laughin' and your man gets paranoid and leaves and the three of us are still laughin'.

We get back to the hotel and there'd been a search party out for the three of us coz none of us had told anyone where we were goin' and none of us had our phones with us so they were all goin' mad, askin' where we were and all the rest of it. Bernie and Concepta had even been around the town, although we found out later off Concepta that they'd gone as far as McDonalds and come back. Bernie was in a mood with me for a good 10 minutes until I said I was goin' to the offo and she said she'd come with me only then our Bopper and Nigel wanted to go to the leisure centre so she went with them and meself and Concepta took the orders and went the offo and as I said, it was well worth it and all with it bein' someone's front room and all. It would have been grand if she hadn't of been so disgusted that we disturbed her durin' Ros Na Rún, the narky cow.

※

Bernie makes me laugh, she really does. There I was the other night sayin' to meself I won't go back to the hotel with Kyle the Canadian coz I didn't want to leave her on her own, bein' the great mate that I am and all. So there we are last night, surprise surprise back in the Grand and she comes up to me holdin' this fellas hand, a ride I'll be honest, kinda a bit like your man Christiano Ronaldo and Bernie tells me he's from Portugal and all and Jasmin's there like a spa speakin'

Spanish to him before I tell her they speak Brazilian in Portugal. So she disappears for hours and comes back at the end of the night with Christiano or whatever his name is and the two of them are all lovey dovey and she tells me she's goin' to go back to his hotel room with him so I couldn't really say anything so I just let it go, thinkin' to meself that there was a good half hour left and I might find meself a fella and I'm comin' off the dance floor and Yenta stops me and tells me Concepta's after hookin' up with some Portuguese fella and wants to bring him back to the room and I tell her about Bernie and ask her does she want to stay in my room and she's only delighted. So the end of the night comes and everyone has vanished at this state, like everyone. I'm half tempted to go look for Jasmin, half expectin' her to have ended up findin' one of them donkeys and flyin' around the centre of town on it. I know Jasmin and that's what she's like. I ring her and Nigel answers the phone and tells me that she's with him and Bopper at the chipper. Then I'm worried about where Paulo is and I ring him as well and he's already back in the hotel with Tracy and Lance so it suddenly dawns on me that we still have a bit of drink left in the room so meself and Yenta get loads of food and head back to the hotel and find Tracy, Lance and Paulo sittin' in the lobby havin' a chat and the five of us go up to my room and have a bit to eat and start on the drink that's left over and we hear someone in the corridor and I sneak out and look and who is it only Concepta and the Portuguese fella goin' into Concepta's room two doors up and I go back in and tell the others and Tracy looks out to make sure they're gone in and then runs up to the door, knocks on it and legs it back to my room and the five of us are breakin' our shite laughin' and we hear the door openin' and closin' again and we're still laughin' and then she goes out to do it again only this time when we hear the door openin' we hear people talkin' and then its gettin' louder and I open the door a little to look out and theres Jasmin, Bopper and Nigel havin' an argument with Concepta. What happened was, they'd come up the stairs just after Tracy had closed the door and Concepta found them standin' there and went mad at them for knockin' at her door and she calls them immature and next thing, meself and the others start pissin' ourselves laughin' and were about to close the door so they don't hear us when Tracy falls forward and lands out in the hallway and that only makes us laugh louder and the others are there lookin' at us and its only then that we realise just how locked we are. Concepta wasn't even slightly amused.

***

Well we were all pretty knackered gettin' the train this mornin' although d'ya think that'd stop me, Bernie and Yenta goin' to the outlet centre to do a bit of shoppin'? I'm actually delighted at how well Bernie and Yenta are gettin' on coz they don't really know each other that well coz we only started hangin' around with Yenta after Bernie went to live in England and even though they've met each other before they've had very little chance to get to know each other. They're very alike in a lot of ways, Bernie and Yenta, so I think that's why I got on so well with Yenta. It was kinda like she filled in a lot when Bernie was gone, not that she'd ever replace Bernie as me best friend. Jayzis, Bernie would go mad and Concepta and probably Tracy would be pissed off as well thinkin' they'd be next in line. To be honest, I can't see Bernie stayin' in England much longer but I wouldn't let her hear me sayin' that.

We got onto the train, the three of us were nearly late but I blame Yenta for spendin' ages gettin' a pair of runners in the Nike shop and the carriage was a little bit more packed so some auld-one ended up sittin' in with us as far as Limerick Junction, takin' her life into her hands the poor cow, and I'm not jokin' ya, ya wanna get the smell of her. I wouldn't even know how to describe it. Kinda like a cross between a sewer and grass that's after been cut. It was rotten and we were tryin' to annoy her to get her to move but she wouldn't so we were delighted when we got to Limerick Junction and she got off. I know it's bad and all but if there's a bang off the woman, there's a bang off her. It's just a pity that the mingin' cow had to sit beside us.

***

I couldn't believe it when I got home. I nearly died. There I was walkin' into the house with Nigel and our Bopper and me da's there smilin' like a sap and I ask him what's wrong with him and he just smiles and ignores me so I think nothing of it and go straight into the kitchen to see if me ma's there and next minute I hear this barkin' and I stop for a second and think maybe it's me imagination coz the only barkin' I'd hear at the back of the house is Disco and god love him, he's up in doggy heaven but then I hear it again and it sounds just like Disco so I go to the back door and open it and there's a little jack russell there barkin' at me, a gorgeous little thing, dark brown with light brown speckles here and there and I bend down to pet him and me da comes up behind and asks me what I'm goin' to call him and I'm kinda confused for a minute before Bopper comes up behind me and shouts 'You bought us a dog!' and he runs out and picks it up. 'Can we call him Disco?' he says, still holdin' him and I look up at him and tell him he can't call the dog Disco after Petulia's dog dyin' so Nigel says 'Disco 2' and we think about it for a second and me and Bopper both say yes, thrilled with ourselves that we have a new dog. I can just imagine what me ma was like.

※※※

I'd almost forgotten about Concepta's diet and by the sound of things, I think she did too. Me ma said when they went to the Weight Watchers last night, Concepta got on the scales and your woman told her she'd put on two pounds and me ma said ya wanna see the face on Concepta, gettin' your woman to check the scales and everything but she said there was nothing wrong with the scales. Concepta was disgusted. Me ma said Celine O'Reilly had this big grin on her face and then she ends up bein' slimmer of the week and she only beat Jasmin's ma by a quarter of a pound or whatever that is in Kilograms.

See the thing about it is, Concepta wasn't really stickin' to her diet that much in Killarney and she didn't go for a walk, although Jasmin made us walk far enough to see that bleedin' house but she hadn't got the exercise bike and she was eatin' and drinkin' a good bit and the other thing is and she can deny it all she likes, in fact she has done but we all know she's on the slimmin' tablets and she probably didn't bring them with her in case Yenta found them. Me ma was tellin' me there's these great slimmin' tablets ya get in Sweden that break down the fat in your body and that's what Concepta would be on coz she knows Swedish people.

I was tellin' Bernie all this on the way to the airport but she wasn't really listenin'. The poor young-one was in an awful state in the car, now an awful state. Nigel brought her to the airport in me Uncle Dessie's car so we could say goodbye but she didn't want to go and she just cried and cried and cried and I felt dreadful lettin' her go back. She was mad into that Portuguese fella she met the weekend and he told her he's movin' here soon and all. Ah the poor young-one. I have a feelin' she'll be back soon.

✳✳✳

Bopper and our Nigel are in an awful state and I have to be honest. I'm tryin' as hard as I can not to be relieved. See they went to the second round of *You're A Star* and they said they were doin' deadly and all right up to the end and then they got eliminated and after all that rehearsin' and all. I'll even be honest and admit that they were startin' to get a little bit better. Just a little bit. They even ended up rehearsin' a few times when we were down in Killarney and Yenta even helped them with their dancin'. She's great at that sort of thing and everyone knows how deadly she is at the dancin' but it wasn't enough in the end. It wasn't like they hadn't got the confidence or anything. Jayzis no. They had loads of that. Too much if ya ask me, plannin' world tours and practicin' for bein' on the *Late Late Show* and *Top Of The Pops*. They had a logo and everything. 2 Ladz is written everywhere in our house. I went to blow me nose the other day and it was written on the tissue.

Our Bopper hasn't left his room since although maybe that's a good thing. Nigel's not as bad although he's still a bit depressed over it. He was sayin' that Andy got through to the next round. Andy as in Jasmin's little brother, the good-lookin' one. All I'm sayin' is that he's good lookin' though. Like I don't fancy him or anything. I'm delighted though coz he's a deadly singer and our Bopper and Nigel wouldn't have a patch. Like he's good lookin' and funny and he has a deadly personality and he's a great singer for the show like. As I said, I don't fancy him or anything.

✳✳✳

Halloween has to be the weirdest day of the year and I didn't know this but Tracy tells me that Halloween comes from this festival they had back in ancient Ireland and the Americans turned it into what it is now. Trust us to come up with a night for loopers and then the Americans to make it worse.

    I was in work til six and then I had to walk home on me own and it was like a war zone with them rockets goin' off everywhere. This little young-fella tried to throw a banger at me only it missed and he was the lucky one coz if a banger had have come anywhere near me it would have been shoved up the little fucker's hole followed very closely by my right foot.

    I was only in the door when the kids started knockin' and me and da were like gobshites, in their element askin' who all the kids were and given them packets of Smarties and Mini Maltesers. I don't know how many Spidermans knocked on the door.

    We'd all been very quiet about our costumes coz we were all goin' to the Halloween night up in Farley's and I was thinkin' to meself mine was only deadly after gettin' out me ma's old sewin' machine for it and all. I could hear our Bopper and Nigel in their room gettin' dressed and tried to go in but the door was locked so I just got meself ready. I piled on the fake tan coz I needed to be really dark dressin' up as Pocahontas. Ya wanna see me in all the gear, the exact same as she looks in the film. So our Bopper comes into me room in some kind of green outfit, green tights and all he has on, and I'm wonderin' why he's dressed up as a frog and before I say anything, he tells me that he's Peter Pan and then Nigel comes in dressed as a pirate, supposed to be Captain Hook and him and Bopper start havin' this sword fight with their plastic swords in me bedroom, the pair of gobshites.

Can ya imagine the three of us walkin' down to Farley's? I mean, scarlet, although in sayin' that, everyone else was as bad. There was witches and wizards and all the rest of it and we got into Farley's and theres Tracy and Lance sittin' there with Jasmin, Paulo and Yenta and I'm tryin' to work out what everybody is meant to be. Tracy tells me that her and Lance are Aladdin and Princess Jasmine, our own Jasmin is Snow White, Paulo is Hercules and Yenta is Cinderella and its only when Concepta walks in dressed as the Little Mermaid that I realise that every single one of us is dressed up as a character from a Disney Cartoon. I swear to god! And I was wonderin' why everyone was givin' us strange looks. It was like the Disneyland in the middle of Farley's.

I turned to Yenta and asked her what her brother Marvin was dressin' up as and she just laughed and said him and Sheila were on their way and next minute the two of them walk in the door, Sheila lookin' lovely as Mulan, believe it or not, and Marvin as fuckin' Batman! I swear to Jayzis. Can ya imagine how out of place he looked in the middle of all us gobshites? I was only mortified and I was ragin' coz I thought me costume was only great although the funniest thing had to have been Concepta Cooney fallin' over her tail fin on the way to the toilet. That was hilarious.

We were tryin' to work out how in the name of god we all ended up as Disney characters when it suddenly dawned on me. Pocahontas was Bernie's idea, the bitch. She did it for a laugh when we were in Kerry and she'd been talkin' to Sheila in the Spar and she doesn't know Marvin so that's the only reason he turned up as Batman and not Pinocchio. Thank god we all saw the funny side of it, for her sake anyway. Needless to say she got seven or eight text messages at the same time sayin' 'HA HA HA,' although I have to admit, it was funny. Other than endin' up lookin' like a sap though it was a great night. God knows where me bow and arrows ended up.

November

Jayzis, November already. Can ya believe it? I thought I was seein' things today when I walked into Dunnes and saw the Christmas decorations gettin' put up. I swear to god, not a word of a lie. I mean, it's far too early as far as I'm concerned. The bonfires haven't even gone out after Halloween yet. Sayin' that now, I did get a lovely top in Dunnes reduced to a fiver. I mean, where would ya get it? Ya can't go wrong and I wasn't even in the mood for goin' shoppin' after Halloween only Yenta was dyin' to get a pair of shoes she'd seen and Nigel had Dessie's car so we got him to drop us up only he was worse than meself and Yenta put together. We were in the Blanchardstown Shoppin' Centre and he had us dragged around every shop tryin' on everything. I nearly killed him after one place he brought us into and tried on six things and bought none of them, although I don't blame him coz they all looked shite on him. I wouldn't mind but all the bastard came home with in the end was a shirt. Yenta on the other hand bought half the shoppin' centre and she does buy mafis stuff and all. She got a dress in that BT2 and it cost more than I get paid in a week. I was delighted with me top I got reduced to a fiver. Mafis it is.

✳✳✳

I was havin' a bit of a lie in this mornin' coz I wasn't in work til 12 and I get up to go the toilet about half nine and I just get back into bed when the door bell rings and I was goin' mad coz whoever it is has their hand stuck to the button and it's still ringin' as I go downstairs and open the door and I nearly died. Who's standin' there only me cousin Jacinta. Not a word of a lie. I didn't know what to say. She screams and throws her arms around me and I still don't say anything. I have to be honest, she's lookin' a bit rough but then again, wouldn't you if you've been livin' in a hole in the ground for ages. It's only when she goes to walk past me into the house with her enormous back pack that I notice that she has this fella with her, a big hippie kinda like Bob Geldof only dirtier and he hugs me as well and introduces himself as Fudge, the famous boyfriend I've heard so much about. Well I'm still in shock after they walk into the house and it takes me a couple of seconds to realise what has just happened and I eventually close the door and follow them into the kitchen.

'So what's it like having your favourite cousin home?' Jacinta, or Pussywillow as she calls herself these days, says to me in her English accent. 'Ah great,' I says to her 'Nigel's a great laugh.' The face on her.

I'm not goin' to lie now, meself and Jacinta have never really seen eye to eye. I don't really know why like, with us bein' the two girls and all. Look at Bopper and Nigel. They get on like a house on fire. The two of them are always together these days. Nigel is grand to live with but there's no way Pussywillow and Bob Geldof are stayin'. What could I do though now that they were in the house only make a cup of tea and whip out a few Danish's coz at the end of the day, it's not really my house to be throwin' people out of, despite the fact I've been livin' here this past 20 years.

I take out the milk and ask Fudge if he wants any and he tells me that he's a vegan. 'Go way,' I says to him 'I have a friend who went there on her holidays.' And I just leave the milk down so he can take some if he wants it.

'So,' I say to Jacinta at last, 'Are ya stayin' here then?' I was dyin' to find out coz if the answer was yes I was ready to run up the stairs and lock the door of me bedroom. 'Just for a day or two,' she tells me with a little smile, 'It'll give me and you a chance to catch up Joanna.' And I'm sittin' there thinkin' to meself whether this mad bitch is for real. Obviously she is coz the silly cow is grinnin' across the table at me and all I can think about is givin' Fudge a wash.

***

They're in a tent out the back. I swear to god. I dropped into Jasmin last night on the way home from work to see how she was and for a chat like. Her brother wasn't even there and I don't fancy him anyway.

Anyway, when I got back to me own house, I had already forgot about Jacinta and Fudge and its only when I let Disco 2 out the back to go the toilet do I see the tent and it dawns on me what's goin' on. For the laugh I go up and knock on it and Jacinta pokes her head out and says hello and I tell her I have to let Disco 2 out for a few minutes to go the toilet and she says grand and then starts tryin' to have a chat with me, me standin' there and her with her head pokin' out of a tent in the middle of me back garden and I ask her is she not a bit cold and she starts tellin' me all about her hole in the ground in the path of a motorway in Birmingham and how she'd got used to the cold weather and all the rest of it and I'm standin' there not really givin' a fuck, hopin' to god that Disco 2 would hurry up and have a piss before I have to listen to any more stories and then Fudge pops his head out too and starts tellin' this other story about when they were in Norway for some kind of march and how he was involved in a riot and I'm startin' to realise that this Fudge bloke is a nutter. I've never been happier to see the dog piss.

***

Well ya'd never guess who we got a postcard from today? I nearly died. I'm in work this mornin' with Leandra, Sheila and Boris and we're havin' a chat about Pamela Anderson Lee and her breast implants, although tryin' to get Boris to stop workin' to ask him a question is impossible which is the opposite of Julie Walsh who we can't get to start workin'.

Anyway the postman comes in as he often does of a mornin', says hello to us and hands Leandra the mail and it's a bill, two invoices and then a postcard with a picture of what looks like a desert and Lebanon written across the front of it and I'm wonderin' who in the name of holy Jayzis do we know in Lebanon and I can see by the look on Leandra's face as she's readin' it that she's in shock. 'What is it?' I ask her and she starts readin' it. 'To everyone in Spar. How are yiz? Sorry I never got to say goodbye but for the first time in my life I'm in love. I'm living in Lebanon and love it here but miss you all and miss making the rolls. I'll ring soon. All my love, Dymphna.'

Now I'll be honest, I could feel the tears comin' into me eyes coz it was kinda sad. I like Dymphna and ya do miss her around the place, d'ya know that kinda way but if she says she's happy then that's all that matters. I wonder why she's not in Turkey anymore. Where the fuck is Lebanon? I'll ask Tracy or Yenta.

I hope I'm there when she rings. I'm dyin' to tell her all the news. I know what Dymphna's like. If Julie Walsh answers she'll just hang up, although in fairness, d'ya think Julie Walsh would get up off the stool to answer the phone, the lazy cow.

✳✳✳

That Concepta Cooney one is a dirty bitch. I went over to Yenta's last night for a chat and a few glasses of wine, a good few now, but anyway, we're there and next minute me phone rings and who is it only Concepta just out of the Weight Watchers and she asks me where I am and I tell her I'm in Yenta's and she says she's droppin' over coz she wants to show the two of us something and straight away I'm terrified coz I know what Concepta's like.

Anyway, about 15 minutes later, she arrives. Don't ask me where Marvin was coz I didn't even ask Yenta. He was probably off somewhere with Sheila. The two of them are always together.

So Concepta comes in anyway, all smiles and all the rest of it and straight off she tells us that she's down to 12 stone 2 which is great news after her puttin' on the 2 pounds last week but she's only 2 pounds less than what she was two weeks ago and some other auld-one was slimmer of the week this week.

I ask her what it is she wants to show us and I couldn't believe what the dirty bitch did. She opened the string of her tracksuit bottoms, pulled them down and then pulled down her knickers and meself and Yenta turn away in shock but Concepta tells us to look and we turn slowly and it was like a caterpillar crawlin' up her thingy.

'What is it?' Yenta asks at last, tryin' to figure out what it was. 'It's a Brazillian.' Concepta tells us, still standin' there with her knickers around her ankles. 'A Brazilian?' Yenta asks. 'I've met a few Brazilians and not one of them looks like that.'

※※

I'm only mortified I am. I was in work today and who comes in only Jasmin's brother Andy and his scruffy little mate Keith and I was talkin' to the two of them for a minute. Andy was askin' me all about how Nigel and Bopper were after gettin' knocked out of *You're A Star* and askin' how Halloween was. He said he'd been talkin' to Bernie Boland and she'd very nearly got him to go up to Farley's dressed up as Tarzan as if we didn't look bad enough. He thought the Disney thing was only gas. And when I think of Lance and that gobshite Dave that I used to go out with bringin' Andy to that gig in the Temple Bar Music Centre. It's only a few months ago but he was a kid then and now it's like he's a man, not that I'm into him or anything.

Anyway, we're chattin' away and next minute, scruffy little Keith, who I'll be honest, as scruffy as he is, hasn't a patch on Fudge, asks me is it true about the family of Sudanese refugees livin' out me back garden in a tent and I just laugh, wonderin' what in the name of Jayzis a Sudanese is. I told him me ma put the tent up for the dog but that Petulia bitch next door is probably tellin' everyone. I'm scarlet. I knew there'd be rumours flyin' around about that. What can ya do when that Petulia one is livin' next door to ya and we all know she's a friend of that Mrs O'Driscoll one who has the biggest mouth in the country and then Mrs O'Driscoll is friends with that Celine O'Reilly one and we know what she's like and don't forget that Keith is Celine O'Reilly's son and he's as bad at spreadin' rumours as his ma. He even goes on like her. What a nice, respectable, good-lookin' young-fella like Andy is doin' with that dope Keith I don't know.

I'm tellin' ya one thing though, Jacinta, sorry Pussy-willow, and her tent and herbal tea and scruffy boyfriend have to go. I don't care where but I am not listenin' to another lecture about how shampoo is causin' all sorts of harm to the environment. I wouldn't mind but I use Herbal Essences.

**

I rang Tracy and asked her what a Sudenese was and she told me it was kinda like a Brazilian and said she'd only kill me if I even attempted to shave me fanny.

**

I swear to god, that Jacinta one is unreal. She doesn't even live in the house, well sleep in it anyway and she has us recyclin' everything. Like in fairness, we did recycle anyway, me ma was always a great one for it but Jacinta has taken it to a whole new level. Her and Fudge were out the back today showin' me da how to make a compost heap so we can recycle all our left over food and Disco 2's shite and all the rest of it. The back smells bad enough as it is with Fudge sleepin' in it. We don't need it to get any worse.

I'm tellin' ya theres something I don't like about that chap. I can't place it or anything but I just have this kinda feelin' any time he's around, other than wantin' to throw up. Don't ask me what it is though. Call it women's constuition or whatever but I'm keepin' an eye on him, a very close eye. One step out of line and I'll have the fucker by the bollix. He's a lazy bastard as well. He does nothin' around the house when he's in it and I wouldn't mind but we're feedin' the bollix and he's not even payin' any rent. In fairness to Jacinta, at least she cleans, even if she only uses natural products but she'll wash the pots and pans and everything, like the ones that won't go in the dishwasher after dinner while he just sits there tryin' to enforce his views on us like he's Jesus. I can't have milk on me cornflakes without him talkin' about cows bein' held captive to make the milk for me and he has a manner with Jacinta I don't like, whatever about me not gettin' on with her, she is me cousin and I don't like the idea of her fella treatin' her like shite. He ate her there the day before yesterday coz I gave her a wine gum and they're made from part of a cow, which is news to me. Like what harm is a wine gum? The bleedin' cow is dead whether she eats it or not. He wouldn't say anything in front of us but I happened to hear him after I left and I felt like goin' back in and shovin' the rest of the pack down his throat. This is comin' from the bloke who said that I must have killed a whole herd of cows coz of the amount of leather stuff I have as if I went out and killed them meself. If I'm doin' any killin', he's the first in line.

✳︎

I'm scarlet. No really I am. We were sittin' there watchin' the telly last night, meself, me ma and Jacinta. Fudge was out, god knows where, probably up in the Phoenix Park huggin' the trees or savin' the squirrels, but for some reason, Jacinta only watches telly when he's not there. I don't think he lets her to be honest but who am I to get involved in someone else's relationship?

So there we are watchin' the telly and what comes on only *You're A Star* and I didn't even know it had started yet and we're watchin' it and who comes on only Tracy, I swear to god and its only then that I found out what song she had sang coz she said she'd do something mad so they'd put her on telly and there she is on the telly in front of the whole of Ireland singin' the theme song off the *Teletubbies* in a kinda gospel style and the judges on the telly are as speechless as I am and tryin' as hard as they can not to laugh and then Brendan O'Connor just bursts out and Linda Martin can't contain herself. I still don't know who the other fella is.

Anyway, Tracy leaves and who walks in next only me. I was mortified coz I'd forgotten all about it goin' to be on the telly but there

I am and I give the judges a huge smile and wink at Brendan O'Connor which I can't actually remember doin' at the time and then I launch into the song and I'm not only sayin' this but I did a great job of it. How they said no to me is beyond me coz I was better than most of them that were on the programme. I have to be honest though, it was only gas when I refused to move when they wouldn't let me sing another song and the security guards had to come and carry me out of the room. Well at least I did something a bit different on the telly. Bopper and Nigel were absolutely shite doin' the audition but they were lickin' the judges holes so that's why they got through. Linda Martin thought there was nothing like them. It was Jacinta's first time seein' them too and she agreed with me that they were shite.

Andy was only great on it, ya know Jasmin's little brother. I have to say, I was very impressed with him. He's still on the programme so he has a very good chance of gettin' into the final. I hope he does coz he's a lovely young-fella, although not that I fancy him or anything. Our Jacinta couldn't get over the fact that it was Andy. She remembers the triplets from when she used to come over and she'd be a good six or seven years older than them.

Jayzis. Me on the telly. I'll be signin' autographs and all, wait and see.

***

I had the day off work today and I was mopin' around the house doin' the usual shite like listenin' to a few songs in me room and watchin' a bit of Trisha on the telly and I go into the kitchen to get a drink and look out the window and who's starin' in at me only Jacinta. It was kinda like something out of one of them horror films the way she just appeared. I had flashbacks of Mister O'Toole in me bedroom tryin' to kill me until Jacinta holds up the dog to have a look at me, smiles, puts him down and comes into the kitchen.

Now ever since she arrived, Jacinta's been lickin' me arse, really tryin' to be all pally with me and with the way that gobshite Fudge has been treatin' her, I feel kinda sorry for her. I hadn't even realised she was at home. Me ma and me Uncle Dessie made Fudge go out today to look for a job and it's about bleedin' time. We asked him what he was goin' to do for work and he said probably go on the dole and me ma went ballistic. She asked Jacinta would she not move into the house and leave him outside in the tent. I don't blame her. The smell off him is unacceptable.

Anyway, so Jacinta comes into the kitchen and asks me can she ask me a favour and I say yeah of course and she asks me will I bring her to the Blanchardstown Shoppin' Centre coz she's never been to it and it's been years since she was in a shoppin' centre and I remember the way Fudge was givin' out to her about globalisation and chain shops and all and think to meself what an arsehole he really is. Fair enough, he's entitled to his views and I wouldn't have a problem with that but what I do have a problem with is the way he's makin' Jacinta go along with his views. I can't understand why she puts up with him. I know I wouldn't.

I have to be honest, I was in no mood for goin' to get the bus to Blanchardstown so I give Nigel a ring and ask him if he's up to much and as luck would have it, he has a few hours free so I get him to come get meself and Jacinta and drop us to the shoppin' centre.

Well it was an experience to say the least. I mean, to go shoppin' with a young-one who's never been in Miss Selfridges in her life. Sayin' that now, she didn't buy anything but I'm thinkin' that's coz Fudge wouldn't be too impressed with her wearin' a pair of hipsters and a pale blue halter neck from Zara, despite the fact they looked mafis on her.

We got on great as well, meself and Jacinta, havin' a laugh and all that hippie shite started to disappear. She's a totally different person when Fudge isn't around. It's like he's holdin' her back or something. I'm even goin' to be honest and admit that I'm startin' to like Jacinta. Now there's something I thought I'd never say!

✳✳✳

We had a bit of a laugh today in work coz it was Sheila's birthday and we thought it'd be funny to pretend that we didn't know anything about it at all and then to surprise her. We said nothing about this to Marvin coz he wouldn't have been able to understand us and I was kinda tempted to ring Yenta to get her to explain it to him in Turkish but then we just said fuck it, we'll ignore him if he says anything about it. So there we all were, meself, Leandra, Julie Walsh, Marie and Boris, goin' about our own business and Sheila and Marvin are all lovey dovey like usual. It'd make ya sick. But anyway, the days goin' on and not a mention of it and we all know that Sheila's present is locked in Leandra's desk in the office, a lovely necklace and matchin' bracelet. They're only mafis. I picked them out and all and was very nearly tempted to keep them for meself.

So we'd kinda forgotten about it with stuff goin' on like magazine deliveries that got messed up. That Celine O'Reilly one got a copy of *Amateur Housewives* instead of her regular copy of *Women's Way* and she came in and had a conniption, although I'd say that scruffy little son of hers Keith, ya know Andy's mate, I'd say he made use of the amateur housewives, the dirty little pervert. The young-fella makes me vomit.

Anyway, I go into the stockroom and there's Sheila sittin' on a crate of Red Bull cryin' her eyes out and I was kinda a bit shocked and go over and put me arm around her and ask her what's wrong and she tells me it's her birthday and nobody even said happy birthday to her and I kinda felt bad for playin' the joke on her so I get the others together and got Marvin to go on the till so Julie Walsh could come in too, although she wasn't too happy we made her get up off her stool, and we all gave Sheila her present and she starts cryin' again and starts sayin' how nice we are to her and she starts huggin' us all, even Boris and he starts cryin' as well, despite the fact that he's about seven feet tall and just a big stocky Ukrainian in general like. She's 26 Sheila and I didn't even know. Twenty-six! She looks about 15.

※※※

I'm in the shop today, potterin' around givin' the place a bit of a tidy, straightenin' the Pot Noodles, puttin' the crisps into neat lines and that sort of thing when these two young-ones come up to me, only about nine I'd say, definitely still in primary school coz I could tell by their uniforms and they come up to me and they were like 'Here missus' and I don't pay them any attention coz I'd never have anyone, even a nine year old, call me missus. Misses and me only 18. The cheek of them like.

So anyway, they stand in front of me and one of them says 'Aren't you that girl that was singin' on the telly last week?' and I smile and say yes, thinkin' that they want me autograph and the one that had asked me turns to her friend and says, 'See Chantelle, I told ya it was her' and then she turns back to me and goes, 'Yeah, you were shite.' Cheeky little bitch.

✳✳✳

Oh good Jayzis. I don't think I'll ever get over the shock of last night. I swear to god, my heart can't handle any more shite this year. I really just amn't able for it. I can see meself endin' up in an early grave although that would have more to do with the stress than the nut jobs tryin' to kill me. Thank god that Mister O'Toole is in Brazil and can't get near me although in sayin' that, he could be back and following me everywhere I go and I don't know.

There was a bit of a do on last night in Farley's for Amy's ma's 40th, ya know Amy, the young-one that does the weekends with me in the Spar, the one I do always be slaggin' Julie Walsh with. Well anyway it was her ma's 40th up in Farley's there last night and half of Finglas was there. I went up with our Bopper, Jasmin, Sheila, Marvin and Concepta. Tracy wouldn't come coz she was off doin' something with Lance and Nigel. Yenta and Paulo were goin' to see some concert in town and they wouldn't come up either and I'd say they're delighted after what happened.

There we were, the six of us at our table, havin' our drink, havin' the bit of laugh, chattin' to Amy, slaggin' Julie Walsh who was sittin' across from us with her new fella Paddy, who, may I remind ya, I was with last year and who's now a total minger if ever I saw one and we were throwin' peanuts at that gobshite Jason who's sittin' with them, thinkin' your man Paddy is only the greatest thing since your woman Evita, even though he's far from it, believe me.

So we're havin' a laugh when this auld-one that goes to the Weight Watchers passes by and throws Concepta this filthy look. Dolly this auld-one's name is and I kinda know her from bein' in and out of the shop, a right grumpy cow she is, never has a smile on her, ya know one of these types of people. The type who if ya kicked the ball over the back wall when ya were a kid she wouldn't give it back, although we used to make our Bopper go in himself to get it.

So anyway, nobody else notices the look she's after throwin' Concepta except me and I kinda ask Concepta quietly what it's all about and she says that there'd been a bit of a row earlier on in the week at the Weight Watchers coz Celine O'Reilly and this Dolly auld-one accused Concepta of cheatin' coz of the slimmin' tablets and that Concepta doesn't deserve to be slimmer of the week and they all know she's well on course to win slimmer of the year too. Of course, Concepta denied it down to the ground. She's disgusted any time anyone says anything to her about the slimmin' tablets despite the fact that everyone knows she's on them. Jasmin's ma even knows who's gettin' them for her she says, someone smugglin' them in from Hungary she said. Jasmin's ma knows coz she's been tryin' to get a few herself.

Anyway, I wasn't too impressed with this Dolly auld-one givin' our Concepta dirty looks, walkin' around Farley's thinkin' she's all that and a packet of Mentos. So as the night goes on, she's still givin' Concepta dirty looks and Concepta, fair play to her, ignores her, knowin' theres no point in startin' something in the middle of Farley's, although let the truth be told, that's never stopped her before. I don't know how many times they're tried to bar her at this stage, not that she'd listen to them anyway.

So Concepta was up gettin' a drink at one stage, actually it was two drinks, one for me and one for her, and she's on her way back down and your woman Dolly is passin' by and on purpose, it definitely was coz I was watchin', she bumps into Concepta and knocks both of the drinks out of her hand and Concepta looks up at her and says to her, as cool as ya like, not like Concepta at all, she says 'That was a vodka and a Bacardi and Diet Coke Dolly. We're sittin' over there,' and your one Dolly says 'Ya must be jokin'' and Concepta says 'No Dolly, I'm deadly fuckin' serious.' At this stage everyone in the pub is lookin', the barmen, the owner, Amy's ma, everyone. The DJ has even lowered the music so that everyone can hear what's goin' on. It was like an episode of Eastenders in the middle of Farley's.

So your one Dolly says, 'Concepta Cooney, are you threatenin' me?' and Concepta just smiles and goes to move away and Dolly grabs her arm and swings her back around and Concepta pulls her arm away and says, 'Don't you touch me,' and your woman Dolly pushes Concepta backwards, a grown auld-one this is, and says, 'Or else what?' So Concepta gave her a right hook into the nose. All hell broke loose then and the two of them are goin' at it in the middle of the pub and it's like one of them fights ya see in a school when all the kids are around and I can see your one Celine O'Reilly right up the front givin' Concepta a few sly kicks and the bouncers are runnin' in to split them up but the crowd think it's the Jerry Springer show shoutin' things like 'Hit her with a stool' and all the rest of it and eventually they get pulled apart and the crowd start to go back to their seats when next minute all ya can hear is someone shoutin' 'I need help here' and coz the music hasn't come back on yet, everyone looks and there's some woman kneelin' in front of that Mrs O'Driscoll one who talks about everyone and I can't see too well from where I'm sittin' but it looks like there's something wrong with Mrs O'Driscoll and the woman shouts for help again and some man goes up to her and your one goes 'Are you a doctor?' And your man says 'No I'm a vet' and I can see your woman is thinkin' twice before lettin' him anywhere near Mrs O'Driscoll but she either thinks that she has no choice or Mrs O'Driscoll is a bit of a dog coz she lets him have a look at her and straight away he calls for someone to call an ambulance and the whole pub spends the next fifteen minutes waitin' for it to come to find out what's wrong with her, although meself and a few others took the opportunity to go outside, have a smoke and have a chat about who won the fight, although nearly everyone said Concepta, especially after the right hook she started with. Neither Dolly or Concepta went home, out of principle Concepta said so I made our Bopper and Jasmin keep and eye on her to make sure she didn't get into any more trouble.

Eventually the ambulance comes and the ambulance man and woman go into the pub and we all follow and they have a look at Mrs O'Driscoll and the word starts to go round that she's after havin' a heart attack. All the excitement over the fight, that's what it was. They carried her away on a stretcher and all.

The poor DJ hadn't a clue what to play. *Congratulations* was definitely out the window, and clearly so was *Rock The Boat*.

***

A bit of bad news. Mrs O'Driscoll died this mornin' in hospital. I swear to god. They said she didn't really stand a chance after such a bad heart attack and she wasn't even that old. Like she was old enough but she was only a couple of years older than me ma, like about ten years or something.

I couldn't really believe it when I heard coz I got a phone call off Tracy askin' me what happened coz she heard there'd been a fight at the party and someone killed Mrs O'Driscoll, ya know the way these rumours spread. Luckily enough Mrs O'Driscoll wasn't helpin' to spread them like she usually does or there'd be rumours about riot police havin' to be called in to break things up.

I told Tracy the whole thing about Concepta and Dolly and about Mrs O'Driscoll havin' a heart attack and Tracy said she definitely heard she was dead and I was thinkin' to meself maybe she is and I hadn't heard so I says to meself I'll go to Jasmin's to see what's goin' on coz she'll know, or at least her ma would so I knock at the door and the first thing Jasmin says to me when she answers, not a hello or anything, is 'Did ya hear? She's dead.' And I'm kinda a bit shocked, more at the way she said it then anything else coz it wasn't like she was pretendin' to be shocked or anything. She seemed to be happy if anything, although in fairness, I'm not goin' to pretend that I'm devastated that she's dead. I mean, come on, the auld-one spent her time goin' around talkin' about people, gossipin' and spreadin' rumours. She said horrible things about me that time Mister O'Toole tried to kill me and then she said horrible things about Dessie's girlfriend or whatever she is, Mary, the one that used to be a nun.

Me ma said Petulia next door is in bits over Mrs O'Driscoll coz the two of them were kinda friends. Between the two of them and Celine O'Reilly, they kept the whole area goin' with gossip. I've seen them many a mornin', not so much now but in the summer, standin' outside the church havin' a chat for hours and ya do know as soon as ya pass they do be sayin' stuff about ya. Ah poor Mrs O'Driscoll won't be spreadin' any rumours from now on. I bet ya that bitch will haunt Farley's now, if only to see who's goin' home with who.

✱✱

I gave Bernie a ring today to fill her in on all the news goin' down over here and she didn't seem in any form to talk at all, even when I told her about Mrs O'Driscoll. I asked her what was wrong with her but do ya think she'd tell me? She never does anymore. I really don't like the idea of her bein' over there in England on her own. It's been nearly eight months now and she still hasn't settled in at all. She's still homesick and I know she is. She can deny it down to the ground but I'm her best friend in the world and I can see straight through it. She might think I can't but believe me, I can.

I have to be honest and say that I don't think she'll last very much longer over there and I'm not bein' bad by sayin' that, it's just that I know Bernie and she'll try to prove herself to everyone and when she thinks she has, then she'll try make up an excuse like she's applyin' for a job here in Dublin and come home. The thing is, Bernie doesn't realise that she doesn't have to prove herself to anyone. I have to be honest, our group of mates is great like that coz it never matters how long ya can last away on your own or how much weight ya've lost or how well ya did in your exams or how many languages ya speak or how far ya get in *You're A Star*. Them things don't matter and Bernie needs to realise that. All we want is that she's happy and I know for a fact she's not. She doesn't have to say it but I know. She didn't even laugh when I told her about Concepta bein' in a fight with your one Dolly although she did ask me had me ma set up a camp for the homeless out our back. I don't know where she heard that from.

***

Me ma is very close to throwin' Fudge out coz he's been here two weeks and there's still no sign of him gettin' a job. She says whatever about Jacinta, she's family but that other waste of space has his shite if the rest of us are goin' to support him. I agree with me ma. I like the young-fella less and less every time I see him and I've overheard him bein' a bastard to our Jacinta a few times and only for when I said to her she said it was grand and not to get involved, I would have battered him. I mean, where does he get off comin' into our house, eatin' our food, whatever it is that's organic. Me ma's tryin' to buy stuff with loads of food colourin' and all in it so he won't eat. She's starvin' the bastard out. He gave her a lecture the other day about feedin' the dog Pedigree Chum. He wants us to make the dog vegetarian. Now who ever heard of a vegetarian Jack Russell? Its gettin' to the stage now where he'll be fucked out on his ear, him and his tent and his herbal tea and all the rest of it.

He had a fit at Jacinta the night before last when he came home from a walk in the park to find her watchin' You're A Star with me and me ma, sayin' that television is the demon that spreads capitalism, whatever that means. The young-fella has issues and he's draggin' our Jacinta into his war on life and whatever about her, I for one have had more than enough.

Me ma warned him today, she said if he doesn't get a job by the end of the week she's fuckin' him out and doesn't care where he goes and Jacinta isn't goin' with him even if it means lockin' her in the shed and believe me, me ma would do it and all.

✳✳✳

Tracy asked me to go into town today with her to get some book she needed but she said it's been ages since just the two of us did anything together so I had to. To be honest though, we all know it's a lot more Tracy's fault than it is mine. Any time I ask her to do something she's doin' this or that with Lance and I mean, fair enough, he is her boyfriend but I don't know how many times I'd ring her to come into town and she says she can't and then when she rings me I'm expected to jump. Only for it matters to me that I stay close to all me mates, I would have told her I couldn't go although I knew it'd be an excuse not to go to Mrs O'Driscoll's removal in case anyone asked me to go to it, which they did and I said no. I was only gettin' off the bus in O'Connell Street when Jasmin rang to ask me to go, then Concepta when we were in HMV and then Jacinta rings and says that if I need someone to go with, she'd come even though religion isn't really her thing. I have to be honest, I hate funerals. I just don't like them at all. They were all askin' me to go in the mornin' to the mass but me hole am I goin'. I'll just meet them all after when they're goin' to the pub.

Meself and Tracy are walkin' down Henry Street anyways, chattin' away about things when who do I notice walkin' towards us only that posh cow Miranda McCarthy Boyle, the one that robbed Dave, me ex, on me. I swear to god. She got the fright of her life though coz by the time she noticed us, she was right in front of us and Tracy says hello to her and she says hello back, walkin' quicker to get away and I say, 'Heya Miranda love. How's Dave? Oh I forgot he dumped ya and moved to Poland.' And she doesn't answer and walks off. Very fast but she walked and Tracy calls me a bitch although come on, in fairness, it could have been a lot worse. I wanted to punch the bitch.

✳✳✳

Fair play to Leandra, she let me off really early to go and meet the others after the funeral. I have to be honest, she's only great with stuff like that. All I have to do is ask.

Jasmin, Paulo and Concepta went to the funeral and from what Paulo tells me, Concepta and that Dolly one were standin' on opposite sides of the grave givin' each other dirty looks. Can ya imagine it?

They said it was a crap funeral anyways. Everyone went back to Farley's afterwards and they had laid on a spread and all and we ended up sittin' with me ma and Jasmin's ma and me Uncle Dessie and your one Mary who used to be a nun and we were havin' a great bit of laugh slaggin' off your one Celine O'Reilly. Ya wanna see the state of her, dressed in all black with a black hat and sunglasses, even in the pub like. She was like Jackie Onasis sittin' in the middle of Farley's. At one stage she just starts wailin' all of a sudden and everyone was starin' at her. I wouldn't even mind but it's not that big of a secret that Celine O'Reilly and Mrs O'Driscoll couldn't stand each other really, even though they were always together. Funny that. I heard they used to fight all the time. It's mad isn't it.

Jasmin's ma's phone rang at one stage and all I heard her sayin' was, 'Where are ya? Come up to the pub.' She just hangs up and Jasmin asks her who it was and she says, 'Andy,' and for some reason, I don't know why, I kinda go scarlet and go to the toilets to check me hair and make-up and when I get back, Andy's sittin' in me seat and without sayin', he smiles and stands up askin' me how I am and I kinda just nod back at him as I sit down. He still looks a bit like a rocker but he's wearin' this navy tee-shirt with these like baby blue patches on it and his hair is all spiky and he looks really muscley or something. I look away and pray to god that nobody else has noticed how scarlet I've gone, although I look over at Paulo and he's starin' me out of it, then he raises his eyebrows at me and looks away. Jasmin's ma tells me to move around a little bit to let Andy in and he sits down beside me and I go scarlet again and the more the time passes, the more me and Andy start to forget that the others are there and we're deep in our own conversation when me phone beeps and I take it out and it's a message from Paulo sayin' 'I'm on 2 u' and I look across the table at him and give him the filthiest look and he kind of nods his head towards Andy and I think to meself that as soon as I get Paulo Corancovich on his own, I'm goin' to batter him.

Meself and Andy just sit there talkin' up til we were leavin' and it was just, I don't know what the word is. Great? Brilliant? Special? Ah I don't know. He's just really easy to get on with and I know I said so many times before that I didn't fancy him but I'll be honest now and say I do just a little bit. Just a little bit mind you.

***

I'm tellin' ya, it's worse that Jasmin young-one is gettin'. The things she comes out with sometimes. At this stage I'm convinced the young-one is slow, convinced of it.

She rings me today in the joys of spring even though it's the middle of November and the weathers gettin' so cold that me nipples freeze if I don't wear a heavy enough jumper. So she says to me that she'll meet me after work and we can go around to Tracy's for a chat, which I'll be honest, was a nice enough idea, fair play to her, coz I haven't been in Tracy's in ages and she's just started this project and she's stuck in the books, although we all know how much work she puts in. Ya have to when you're doin' English and Psychology in UCD. She's doin' something about the workin's of the human mind. It's a pity Jasmin's mind wouldn't work every now and again.

We get to Tracy's and were talkin' to her ma and she's only delighted we're there, dyin' to show us the back garden she's only after gettin' done although why in the middle of November I don't know and she brings us out the back and turns on the lights so we can look. Mafis I'll be honest. So all of a sudden Jasmin says, 'Ah Jayzis, someone broke the arms off your statue,' and Tracy's ma tells her it's the Venus De Milo and Jasmin says, 'Would ya not try to stick the arms back on with something?' and we didn't even bother tryin' to explain it to her. Jasmin can't even spell art.

✱✱✱

There has to be something about me that I attract so many weirdos, like there has to be. It's like I walk into a pub and they just start to swarm around me like they knew I was comin'. There was Mister O'Toole and the whole thing with him tryin' to kill me and then there was your man with the nipple clamps in the Westbury and the fella that wanted a threesome and even me ex Dave wouldn't even be what ya'd call normal. Far from it.

Then there was Lawrence last night and I swear to god, when I get that Tracy Murtagh one I'll kill her. We went out to this thing with her out in a good friend of her's, this big huge mansion out in Killiney. Ya wanna see it, like a palace it was. I was only delighted that Jasmin wasn't with us coz she'd have ended up breakin' something, probably her back comin' down the sweepin' staircase. As it was, there was meself, Paulo, Yenta and Nigel and why Tracy asked us, I don't know. I mean, we don't even know the young-one who's house it was. I was warned on the way over in the car, Nigel was drivin', that if that posh cow Miranda was at the party that I wasn't to go lookin' for her to start a fight but she wasn't there. I know coz I searched.

I'm standin' there anyway tryin' to be nice to all Tracy's posh mates, one of them, a right snobby cow, turns around to me and says, 'Tell me Joanna, what do you work at?' and I say, 'I'm in retail,' and she's like, 'How spiffing. A boutique?' And I'm like, 'No, a Spar.' Ya wanna see her face drop.

Tracy called me over and introduced me to a bloke called Lawrence, maybe a little older than meself, a bit plump and ugly as fuck and straight off he sticks out his hand for me to shake it and says 'I'm a jeweller you know,' and that was it. I had to stand there listenin' to him go on about jewellery, and fond as I am of a bit of bling, I don't need to know how it's made, how it's tested to see if its real, where it comes from and all this shite and he followed me for the whole night. All the fella was short of doin' was humpin' me leg and I just kept ignorin' him and walkin' away and talkin' to other people hopin' he'd get the hint but he didn't and then he even went and asked me for me number. I gave him Jasmin's for the laugh and he was delighted, the gobshite. If I ever meet anyone that borin' again I'll throw meself in front of a bus.

✳✳✳

I was hopin' to get a bit of a lie in this mornin' with it bein' Sunday and all but I was woken up by Fudge and Jacinta havin' an argument. I mean, could they not do it out in the tent? Although in sayin' that, the weathers freezin' at the moment and as much as me ma doesn't like Fudge, she doesn't want him to die of hypothermia out our back garden, although she still won't let him sleep in the house. Jacinta told me the other day she was seriously thinkin' of leavin' him out there and movin' onto our couch which I think she should. After all, she is related to us.

This latest row, or what I could hear of it, was because Fudge could smell shampoo in Jacinta's hair and straight away she tells him that its Herbal Essences and its natural but he's not impressed and storms out of the house and Jacinta comes up the stairs and comes into my room and I ask her what's wrong but she ignores me, takes me hair brush and turns to me and says, 'Joanna do me hair for me.' I'm kinda shocked coz Jacinta's hair is this tangled mess and she hasn't brushed it once since she arrived at our house and that was a few weeks ago and although I want nothing better than to go back to sleep, I know Jacinta is upset so I get her to sit down in front of me, get a bit of spray in conditioner and get rid of all the tangles and I'm brushin' away and I have an idea. I get her to come into the bathroom and I get a scissors and take a bit off the length of the hair coz it was so long she was sittin' on it. She was only delighted and still smilin' when me Uncle Dessie and Mary who used to be a nun knocked around for dinner and we all sat down and had a big family dinner and we're gettin' the drinks and out of nowhere, Jacinta says she wants Coke, which to me was a surprise seein' as she told me on the day she arrived that Coke was the drink of the devil.

It was late when Fudge came home but she refused to talk to him even when he asked her what happened her hair. She made him sleep out in the tent on his own and she came and slept on the floor in my room in her sleepin' bag. Me ma's only delighted.

***

Jasmin's gas. She came into the shop today and god love her, she looked a bit confused although let's face it, Jasmin always looks confused and I ask her what's wrong with her and she tells me that some fella rang her and asked her to go for a drink with her and I'm wonderin' what could be so bad about that so I say 'That's a good thing Jasmin,' and she's like, 'I suppose so but the thing is, I haven't a clue who he is.' And I'm thinkin' she must have got drunk one night, ya know how she gets and got chattin' to some fella and just can't remember it so she's tellin' me what he said to her on the phone and she's makin' guesses at who it could be and that confused look comes back on her face and she says to me, 'And the funniest thing was, he kept talkin' to me about jewellery,' and it's only then that I remember givin' that Lawrence fella her number the other night and I'm so tempted to tell her but decide its funnier not to, especially with that look on her face.

***

Bernie rang me today in an awful state and by the sound of her all she wants to do is get on a plane and come home although she didn't go as far as sayin' that. She didn't have to though. I know Bernie Boland this many a year and as I said before, she tries to put a brave face on things so meself and the others won't worry about her.

She said she was on a flight to Malmo which I think is in Switzerland and she said all through the flight she wasn't feelin' well but she didn't say anything coz she had to look after the passengers on the plane and make people buy drinks and maps and all the rest of it and she said on the way back she was in a bit of a state so she had to go into the toilet for a few minutes to get sick and your one that's in charge of the air hostesses on the plane was goin' mad at Bernie, tellin' her she shouldn't be sick in work and that it made the company look bad as if poor Bernie had a choice. The only thing is, Bernie said it's the third flight she's been sick on in the last week and it can't be from flyin' coz she was sick on her two days off as well. I asked her could she have food poisonin' but she doesn't think it'd last a week. I can't think of any other reason she'd be sick in the mornin's though. It's weird like. I told her to go the doctor but Bernie's not one for doctor's at all. I'm very worried about her over there but there's nothing I can do. I told her to just come home for a few days but she hates missin' work. Loads of water I told her and a bit of rest but whether she listens to me or not is another story.

✳✳✳

Julie Walsh is engaged. I swear to god. She came in today and showed us the ring. I wouldn't even mind but she wasn't even in work. She just came in to let us all know, as if any of us really give a shite. I mean, it's not as if any of us actually like her and we don't pretend to either. Well I certainly don't.

The face on Leandra when she heard though. It was kinda less like shock and more like disgust. The thoughts of anyone marryin' Julie Walsh is sickenin', even your man Paddy. Actually the thoughts of him as well. He's rotten lookin' and he gets worse every time I see him. He definitely wasn't that bad when I was seein' him. Definitely. My taste isn't that bad although I'm sure some of the girls would disagree about that. Tracy would anyways although she can't talk. Her Lance is hardly Johnny Depp.

We had to explain to Sheila what was goin' on three times although she understood well enough the first time. I think it was just that she couldn't understand why Julie Walsh is engaged after goin' out with someone for only two months. I asked her would herself and Marvin not think about gettin' engaged and she just said 'Me hoop,' and walked away. They were her exact words. I'm tellin' ya, that young-ones been workin' with us too long.

She does have a point though. I mean, two months is a very short amount of time to be goin' out with someone before gettin' engaged. When I was goin' out with Dave I would have battered him if he even attempted to ask me to marry him. I'm far too young to think about settlin' down and havin' kids and all that. I mean, I amn't even 19 and Julie Walsh isn't much older than me. Like in the old days people got married younger but a lot of the time that was coz a fella got a young-one pregnant and had to marry her. Oh good Jayzis, I'm just after havin' a thought. What if Julie Walsh is pregnant? What if that's the reason why Paddy asked her to marry him? There has to be some kind of reason behind it. I'll have to follow her now in work to see if she has mornin' sickness. Her gettin' her hole up off that stool to go the toilet is a sure sign that she's up the pole.

※

I'm just sittin' down to watch telly last night when I get a text message off Paulo sayin' 'Goin to Farley's to meet Concepta. C U there in 15!' and I'm thinkin' to meself that I'll text him back and tell him I'll stay where I am coz the weather's a bit shite when I hear the back door openin' and Jacinta and Fudge come in shoutin' at each other again. It's all I've heard this week and at this stage, I've had enough. I wish they'd ever fuck off with their tent and live out someone else's back. I'm sure Tracy's ma would love to have them in her deckin' with her rhododendrons. Can ya imagine?

So I say to meself, fuck this, and go upstairs to get changed into something else, although not too fancy. I mean, it was only Farley's I was goin' to. I slapped on a bit of make-up just in case anyone a bit decent made an appearance and left the gaff without sayin' goodbye to the happy couple, afraid I'd be dragged into an argument. Fudge is disgusted at me for doin' Jacinta's hair but I think he's just afraid of me doin' his when he's asleep. There's not a chance of me touchin' his hair.

I got to the pub anyway and Concepta and Paulo are already sittin' there with the drinks in front of them and I go the bar, get meself a vodka and Coke and sit down with them and straight away, Concepta starts tellin' me about the Weight Watchers and how half the auld-ones are on your woman Dolly's side and half of them are on Concepta's side and all Dolly's crowd are sayin' that it's Concepta's fault Misses O'Driscoll is dead although we all know that's a load of bollix. Concepta was nowhere near Mrs O'Driscoll. She was too busy fightin' Dolly. Concepta says there's goin' to be a civil war next week at the weigh-in though. I'd love to go and watch. It'd be like *When Fat People Go Bad* or something.

We're chattin' away and all of a sudden Paulo says, 'So Joanna, what's the story with Andy?' and I go scarlet and throw him filthy look but Concepta goes, 'Who's Andy?' and Paulo says, 'Jasmin's brother Andy,' and Concepta says, 'What about him?' and I'm still scarlet and I give Paulo such a kick under the table but he doesn't feel it. Concepta looks at me and goes, 'What about Andy? Tell us Joanna,' and I'm tryin' to think up something when Paulo just smiles at me and says. 'Well to be honest, I think he's a bit of a ride as well, Joanna,' and Concepta's mouth drops open as if her chin's after gettin' really heavy all of a sudden and she goes, 'Joanna Ryde, ya don't fancy Jasmin's little brother do ya?' and I don't even have a chance to answer coz Paulo says, 'Yeah she does. Did you not see her all over him the day of the funeral?' And Concepta thinks about it and says, 'I knew it. Yenta was sayin' something about it as well and I never thought. But he's Jasmin's brother like.' I'm mortified at this stage and I say, 'I don't fancy him. I just get on well with him,' and Paulo says, 'Me hole,' and I'm thinkin' that's exactly where I'd love to kick the little bollix.

✳✳✳

Julie Walsh is unbearable in work at the moment. I swear to god, ya don't know how close I came to punchin' the young-one today. She's engaged a few days and she's already plannin' the weddin'. Where she'll have the reception, what type of food there'll be, what type of car she'll have to bring her to the church and of course everyone's all over her like a bad case of syphilis. She was showin' all the customers the ring and all and its hardly anything special. I'm sure I seen one very similar in the Elizabeth Duke collection in Argos and all the auld-ones are like, 'Who's the lucky fella?' Lucky? Bein' lumped with Julie Walsh for the rest of your life. That's not lucky. He'd be luckier if he walked out in front of a bus.

Leandra, Marie and Sheila were all over her helpin' to pick out weddin' dresses and Julie Walsh turns around to them and says 'I might have to lose a few pounds before then,' and I'm thinkin' to meself a few? The size of her. Even if she does lose a few pounds she'll still have to get married wearin' a circus tent, the fat bitch.

Its an awful pity Dymphna's not here. She would have found it all gas. She's like that Dymphna. She loves a good laugh at someone else's expense. I must get in touch with her to tell her about Julie Walsh. I can just imagine the look on Dymphna's face. She won't believe it when I tell her Julie Walsh is engaged. She wasn't even goin' out with anyone when Dymphna ran off to Turkey or wherever she is now and when I tell her its Paddy she'll die after all the stories I told her about him and his couch.

※※※

I was in no fit mood to go out last night what with bein' so tired after work and with the weather bein' so shite. I swear to god, it feels like it's been rainin' for weeks. Me ma's only delighted coz it means Fudge has to sleep out in the tent in the pissin's of rain. She even has the dog sleepin' in the kitchen and she bought Jacinta a blow up bed and she's on my floor now.

I was just sittin' down watchin' *Coronation Street* when the phone rings and who is it only Yenta tellin' me herself and Concepta are goin' out and I was about to tell her I wasn't movin' when she told me she'd come down and drag me and knowin' Yenta, she probably would so I got meself ready and walked to Yenta's apartment. I had only got a new jacket in Dunnes and I was delighted coz it kept me nice and dry. Mafis it is and only €60 and all. I mean, where would ya get it? Ya can't pass it.

Concepta and Paulo were already there with Yenta and were already gettin' a few drinks into them. I had got a card for Bernie in work so I brought it for them to write something on, just a little something to show her how much we miss her and that so she knows we're thinkin' of her. Paulo's unreal. I think he thought it was a novel he was writin' on the card. I had to tell him to stop or else there'd be no room for Jasmin, Tracy and the others. I'll send it to her when I find them to sign it and put a sanitary towel in as a bit of a joke. She'll find that funny. She put a sanitary towel into Jasmin's birthday card and Jasmin, the dizzy bitch, turned around and asked her had it been used.

We were goin' to go into town but Marvin and Sheila were in Heaven in Blanchardstown so we ended up goin' there and I was delighted coz I do usually have a great night up there. They're gas Marvin and Sheila. I don't know how they do it. They work with each other all day and then spend all their spare time together. It's grand though coz they both have to speak English all the time so they're gettin' that little bit easier to understand, although in work, all Sheila does is slag Julie Walsh with meself of course and Marvin won't say a bad word about anyone. He's decent like that.

We had a great bit of laugh in Heaven, havin' a few drinks and dancin' and that sort of thing. Concepta met a bloke from some place called Azerbaijan, wherever that is. She was all over him for the night although in fairness to her, he was a ride apart from the wooly jumper. The thing had patterns on it. It was the type of thing ya'd have seen on Pat Kenny years ago. I hadn't a clue what the bloke was tryin' to say to me but Concepta had no problem of course. She's unreal.

I was standin' at the bar at one stage with Paulo and I looked up and I nearly died coz who's walkin' towards me only Nigel and Jacinta. I swear to god, our Jacinta in a nightclub and she looked only mafis. Bopper had done her hair and gave her a few of my things to wear. He even did her make-up and I've never seen her look so well. I couldn't believe she was there though coz when she first came she kept sayin' how nightclubs were evil. She even got a vodka and Coke, the first drink she had in years. I asked her why she decided to come and she just said

'Bastard' and went to the dance floor with Nigel. She can't dance for shite mind you but we'll get Yenta to give her a few lessons. I'm presumin' it was Fudge she was callin' a bastard. They do nothin' but argue these days and she's doin' everything she can to annoy him, although fair play to her. He is a bastard. I even saw a few fellas tryin' to chat her up and she was havin' a great time and all. I think she was locked on three drinks although ya would be if ya haven't drank in years. Nigel was lookin' after her though and makin' sure she didn't do anything stupid. She just kept laughin' though and the noise of her gettin' into the house. Me ma said it sounded like a herd of elephants comin' in. She's mad though. She better be comin' out with us more often. She should ditch that loser and find a new fella.

※

Andy got knocked out of You're A Star and at first I was devastated coz out of all of us, he was the best by far, even better than me and that's sayin' something but only a few minutes after the programme is over, Tracy rings me and says, 'Did ya see Andy got knocked out?' I told her I did and she's goin' on about how it's a disgrace and then she says, 'Joanna there's something I have to tell ya,' and I'm a bit worried and I tell her to go on and she says, 'D'ya know your one Cheryl off *You're A Star*?' and I tell her I do. Cheryl is one of the other contestants, about 17, great voice, kinda looks like Jessica Simpson and she has a huge pair of tits and I'm wonderin' why Tracy's askin' me about her and she goes, 'Look someone had to tell ya Joanna, Andy is goin' out with that one Cheryl,' and I say, 'I don't know what that has to do with me,' and she tells me Concepta told her that I'm into him and I'm thinkin' to meself that I'm goin' to batter Concepta for tellin' her, I'm gonna batter Paulo for tellin' Concepta and I'm gonna batter Yenta for startin' it all in the first place and I'm gonna batter that Cheryl fucker just because she's goin' out with Andy.

Tracy starts tryin' to council me over the phone and at first I pretend it's not true but there's no foolin' Tracy Murtagh. I mean, she does study English and psychology in UCD and I eventually give in and start tellin' her about how I thought he was mafia the night of Concepta's 21st and how it kind of went on from there and she could tell I was kinda upset by my voice and she asked me why I hadn't just said it to him but I told her I'd have been scarlet. I mean that and the fact that he's 16 and Jasmin's brother but Tracy thinks Jasmin would be delighted. I wasn't goin' to risk her not bein'. I really believe ya should put your friends before fellas. I'm not bein' bad or anything but I think it's time Tracy started to think like that herself. I see less and less of her the longer she's with Lance.

I'll be honest though. I am a bit devastated over Andy goin' out with that Cheryl one coz I'll admit that I thought he was into me as well coz we got on so well and all the rest of it but I must have been wrong. I probably would have made a show of meself though. Why would Andy go out with someone like me with young-ones like that Cheryl around him all the time? I was goin' to send him a text message, I got his number off our Bopper, but I'd never sent him one yet and I was thinkin' of sayin' something like '4get Cheryl, go out with me!' but in the end I just sent 'It's Joanna. Hard luck. X.' He didn't write back.

***

There was war in the house last night. I was expectin' Jerry Springer to jump out and all it got so bad and it happened so quickly and all.

See what happened is, our Bopper went and opened his big mouth about Jacinta bein' out with us on Friday night in front of Fudge and Fudge starts havin' a go at her in the kitchen in front of meself and Bopper and the dog. Thank god me ma wasn't there coz she'd batter him. I mean, she hates him as it is without hearin' him talkin' to her niece like that.

Anyway, meself and Bopper kinda grab our sambwhiches and go to go inside to watch telly and we're about to sit down and Fudge and Jacinta are still shoutin' at each other and next thing I hear is a kind of a thump and then her screamin' and I drop me plate with the sambwhich on it and run back into the kitchen with Bopper behind me and Jacinta's on the ground, blood comin' out of her nose and Fudge is standin' there lookin' at me and I realise that the bastards after punchin' her so I grab the nearest thing I could find, one of Disco 2's toys and throw it at him and start screamin' at him to get out and he's about to try to say something to Jacinta but she tells him to get out too and he doesn't get a chance to say anything coz the candle I've just thrown at him hits him in the head and he's thinkin' about standin' up to me, I could see it in him, but I grab a knife out of the drawer and start movin' quickly towards him. He moved quick enough then, out the front door with me chasin' him, shoutin' at him the whole time and he turns back as I'm chasin' him and says, 'What about my stuff?' and I say, 'What fuckin' stuff?' and he says, 'My clothes and my tent.' And I just shout, 'I'm goin' to fuckin' burn them and if you ever come back near this house again, I'll burn you too ya scruffy little bollix,' and I go back inside and shut the door behind me. I go into the kitchen and there's Jacinta still on the floor, the blood comin' out of her nose and our Bopper with his arms around her and she's cryin' and lookin' at her, I just break down meself and get on me knees and hug her and she's sobbin' onto me shoulder and the blood is destroyin' me top but I don't care because that bastard is gone out of her life and she can be the person she really is instead of who he was makin' her be. Pussy-willow is gone but no one cares coz she was never half the person Jacinta Digge was, and that's bein' honest.

December

I have to say, I've a pain in me tits with Christmas already and it's only the start of December. Not that I don't like Christmas or anything, Jayzis no, but when Christmas starts in the middle of October, that's what pisses me off.

I'm in the shop today, on the till coz Julie Walsh was on a day off although I didn't mind coz I was a bit knackered havin' been up with Jacinta half the night. I was there anyway, servin' away and listenin' to the Jackson 5 singin' about some snowman when some woman, a biggish woman, bigger than Julie Walsh, she comes in and asks me for 18 selection boxes. Now what in the name of Jayzis would she want with eighteen selection boxes? She can't know that many kids, although by the size of her, they could have easily been for herself. Eighteen selection boxes!

The world goes mad at Christmas though doesn't it. One minute you're walkin' down Henry Street thinkin' to yourself what to dress up as for Halloween for the bit of a laugh and next thing ya know you're lookin' at the Dunnes Christmas shop and listenin' to *Do They Know It's Christmas Time?* Of course they know. How could they not know? If ya stand still long enough in a shop someone will come up and put tinsel on ya.

Tracy rings me today and asked me what I thought about doin' a Kris Kringle with our group of friends and at first I didn't know what she was talkin' about but she said we were all gonna put our names into a hat and everyone pulls one out and then ya just buy that person something big instead of buyin' everyone something small. I have to be honest, I think it's a great idea, although everyone will have to agree to it. I'm even gettin' them to do it in work. That'd be a bit of buzz although I swear, Julie Walsh better not get me!

***

I was sittin' down tonight to watch a repeat of that Lost programme, which is how I feel when I watch it, when a knock comes to the door and seein' as everyone else is upstairs, I get up and answer it, although I'll be honest, I had a good mind to get Bopper to come down and get it.

I walk into the hall anyway and open the door and who is it standin' there only Jasmin, the big happy head on her and she's standin' there with a big smile on her face, not even sayin' hello and after a few seconds, I eventually just tell her to come in and go back to the sittin' room to watch the telly. She follows me in and sits down, still smilin' like a gobshite and I ask her is she alright and she just nods at me. At this stage I'm wonderin' should I call Bopper coz I'm thinkin' she must have wanted him but all of a sudden she says 'I need clothes,' and I'm wonderin' if maybe she's after mistaken my gaff for Dunnes or something when all of a sudden she starts tellin' me she's goin' to the pictures with some fella and she wants to wear something nice and that she has nothing and she wants to borrow something off me. Of course I don't mind and I ask her who it is she's goin' to the pictures with and she just smiles and says 'I don't know,' and I look at her for a second and I says, 'Ya don't know?' She just nods and I says, 'What d'ya mean ya don't know? How d'ya know this bloke?' She just smiles again and says 'He rang me,' and I'm like, 'He rang ya?' and she says, 'Yeah on the phone,' and nods. So I'm thinkin' Jasmin has finally lost the plot, although some people would argue and say she lost the plot a long time ago and I say, 'What does this fella look like?' and she says, 'I dunno. I've never met him.' I can't believe what I'm hearin' and I say to her, 'Why are ya goin' the pictures with a bloke ya never met?' and she's like, 'He rang me and said I met him at a party in some house out in Kiliney and we just got textin' and all. I can't even remember bein' in a house in Kiliney. Ever.' The look on Jasmin's face was comical. She looked so confused and then she says, 'For some reason Joanna, he thought I was you,' and I smile and say, 'Jasmin, is his name Lawrence?' and she asks how I know and I just tell her that she mentioned him the other day. I'm hopin' to Jayzis the gobshite realised Jasmin isn't me. 'I think Tracy gave him me number,' Jasmin says, that confused look still on her face. 'Yeah she must have,' I says, feelin' like Cilla Black!

✷✷✷

I'm lyin' in bed about six o'clock this mornin' and I'm convinced I hear a noise but I think nothing of it and go down stairs to get meself a drink and I get the orange juice out of the fridge, pour it into a glass and I walk to the kitchen window and look out as I'm drinkin' it when all of a sudden, a face appears at the window and I get such a fright that I nearly dropped the glass and for a second I think to meself that its Mister O'Toole after comin' back from Brazil to kill me and I'm shitin' bricks, I'll be honest with ya, but then I realise it's that bastard Fudge and he sticks out his tongue, sticks his finger up at me and runs away to climb over Petulia's wall with something under his arm and I'm still standin' there in the kitchen after gettin' the shite scared out of me. Only for the door bein' locked I would have been out after the bastard. The cheek of him comin' anywhere near our gaff after what he did, the bollix!

    I'm wonderin' to meself what it was Fudge had under his arm, thinkin' that I'm gonna hunt the bastard down if he robbed anything on us, when I realise the tent was gone. Me ma had left it out there, afraid to bring it into the house in case it was infested or something, although she didn't tell Jacinta as much. She wouldn't give a care now though. I've never seen a person change as much in me life. She was even eatin' a packet of Tayto yesterday and before she said Tayto was the food of the devil. She's growin' her nails and all now and she had an interview for Next up in Blanchardstown and all today. Jacinta hasn't had a job in her life. They'll ask her for a reference and she'll have to give them the number of the tree she was chained to in Birmingham.

Me ma's delighted the tent is gone. She was goin' to throw it out anyways but I think she was afraid to touch it in case she caught anything. She's disgusted coz all the grass underneath it is dead. That's what Fudge is gonna be if I ever get me hands on him.

***

We did the Kris Kringle in work today and guess who I got? Marie. Now can ya believe it? Out of everyone I'd have to go and get mad Marie. I would have even preferred to get Julie Walsh. I mean, at least with Julie Walsh it's just a matter of gettin' her a cheap pair of ear rings or a chain from Elizabeth Duke at Argos and she would have been delighted, although in sayin' that, her taste is up her hole.

What do I get for Marie though? Ya wouldn't know with that woman. I would get her a pot plant only she still has Tinky Winky, Dipsy, Lala and Cliff and they're gettin' kinda big. She has them in the toilet in work and I feel like Tarzan every time I have a piss. I'm sure I'll find something for her. Maybe I'll just buy her a bit of hash. She'd like that.

Tracy did the other Kris Kringle with Lance last night coz she said it'd be too hard to get us all together and Lance was a witness that she didn't do anything dodgy. She said only to spend about fifty quid on each one so that's grand. She said I got Nigel at first but seein' as I'd be gettin' him something anyway, she did it again and I got Paulo. That's grand. He's easy enough to buy for. I'll either get him a bottle of the Jean Paul Gautier for men that he wears of a game for that little Playstation thing he does play on the bus. I have the strangest feelin' that Jasmin got me. I could be wrong but I did get a text message off her today askin' if there was anything I needed for Christmas.

***

I'm in work today havin' a good chat with Amy about the state of Julie Walsh's new hair do when I get a text message and I look at it and It says 'Hi Joanna. Wanna go 4 a drink sumtime?' and I'm wonderin' who it is coz I don't recognise the number so I send back, 'Who's this?' and before I even put the phone back in me pocket I get a reply sayin', 'Keith' and I'm wonderin' who in the name of Jayzis Keith is and thinkin' did I give me number to anyone one night when I was out but I can't think of anyone so I send back, 'Keith who?' And I get a message back straight away sayin' 'Keith O'Reilly, Andy Spi's friend,' and I'm fuckin' disgusted and I tell Amy that Celine O'Reilly's scruffy little son is after askin' me out and I'm half tempted to send him her number for the buzz but decide it's better to just ignore him and I'm about to call him a flea ridden pox when who walks in the door only his best friend Andy with that tart Cheryl from that *You're A Star* and I have to be honest, I nearly died. Don't ask me why, but I did. He says hello to me and I kinda just grunt back at him and walk towards the stockroom before he has a chance to say anything else and I could see by the look on his face that he was wonderin' what he had done while his little Barbie doll of a girlfriend tried to decide whether a Toffee Crisp was less fattenin' than a Lion Bar.

✳✳✳

Jacinta got her job and I'm only delighted coz she really wanted it. She's goin' to be workin' in the ladies section of Next up in Blanchardstown and she's only thrilled coz she didn't think she'd get a job so close to Christmas. She's only temporary at the moment but she's hopin' that they keep her on after Christmas. She's real nervous about startin' and all coz she's never had a job before in her life. I was wonderin' did she put eco warrior down on her CV but I doubt she did. I wouldn't even mind but she knows nothing about cloths although now she's not a hippie, she's wearin' loads of my clothes and Nigel even took her out to Dundrum and bought her loads although I wouldn't let her go on her own. I'd be afraid she'd come back lookin' like a Christmas tree so I sent our Bopper to help her. I would have gone meself only I was workin' and mores the pity coz I need cloths for the Christmas and

I do always find a few lovely bits out in Dundrum. I come home broke mind you but the stuff does be mafis.

I have to say, it's great to see Jacinta so happy. She was miserable with that Fudge bollix but she still kinda missed him a bit when he ran off. After all, they did go out together for ages so ya can kinda understand. I nearly cried today coz we were havin' a chat in me bedroom while I was straightenin' her hair and she says to me 'D'ya know Joanna, I've always admired you. You're such a lovely person.' And I swear to god, there was a tear in me eye. That's such a lovely thing to say to someone and I felt terrible coz I couldn't stand Jacinta last month. Although I have to agree with her. I am a lovely person.

※※※

I'm sittin' at home last night havin' a curry and a bottle of wine with Jacinta to celebrate her gettin' her job even though when she came home from England she said curry was made from the fires of hell and wine was the devils piss. But anyway, there we are watchin' a DVD when all of a sudden, me phone rings and who is it only Paulo whose around in Yenta's and he asks me do I wanna go into town and I'm in no more of a humour but Jacinta is askin' me who it is and what he's askin' and I'm tellin' her and she gets all excited and says she wants to go out so I had no choice but to go really.

So upstairs the two of us go and get ready as quickly as we can and only an hour later we meet Yenta and Paulo and get the bus into town and Yenta says we should go to Fitzsimons coz that's where Jasmin was with your man Lawrence and they were dyin' to meet him but I said nothing about him bein' the most borin' person in the world coz I'd only met him the once and I maybe didn't give him a proper chance.

But no, I was right. He is the most borin' person I've ever met. He says hello to me when I saw him and says 'I think ya might have given me Jasmin's number by mistake that night I met you,' and I says 'I'm always doin' that, ah sure it all worked out for the best didn't it' and I run off to find Yenta before he has a chance to inspect me jewellery.

Jasmin's only mad about him and he seems to be mad about her so I'm only thrilled for them. They actually look great together. True enough, he's as interestin' as a tin of Dulux but she seems to like him and that's what matters.

✱✱✱

If I hear another culchie I'll die. Good Jesus, they're everywhere. I had the day off so Concepta and Yenta took the day off too and we went into town for the bit of shoppin'. This is Yenta's first Christmas believe it or not. She's a Muslim and they don't really have Christmas so she can hardly sleep with all the excitement, god love her.

Yeah so the three of us hopped on a bus and went into town. We were goin' to go to Blanchardstown so we could drop in to see Jacinta in her new job but Yenta had to pick something up from her job in town so we went there instead.

Well I'm not jokin' ya, the place was overrun with people up from the country. It was like an invasion. See I forgot about it bein' culchie day. I didn't realise it was today. See what it is, everyone gets the 8 December off coz its some kind of religious holiday, something like the immaculate collection or something and all the kids get the day off school so all the auld-ones come up to Dublin to do their shoppin' coz they don't have H&M and Zara down the country.

I did manage to get a few bits in between the madness. Like I got this mafis pair of furry boots in a kinda beige colour in River Island and a skirt and top to match in Vero Moda. They're lovely now. Can't wait to wear them Christmas mornin'. I'll be only gorgeous. I got me two Kris Kringle presents as well so I'm all organised. I got Marie a book in Eason's called *Caring For Houseplants*. She'll like that I hope. Paulo was easy to buy for. Jean Paul Gautier have this new aftershave out so I just got him that. He'll be delighted. Well he better be for the price of it.

✱✱✱

I'm sittin' down watchin' Coronation Street waitin' for Paulo to ring me so we can go down to Farley's for a drink to meet the Concepta one after the Weight Watchers. I'm in the gaff on my own on me own coz Jacinta's in work, Bopper is out with Nigel, me da's at some football thing and me ma's at the Weight Watchers with Concepta and Jasmin's ma. So I tell Jasmin to come down to the house and I'm sittin' there havin' a cup of Nescafe Cappuccino, the one from the packet, waitin' for Jasmin to knock and Paulo to ring when next thing a knock comes to the door and I put me coffee down on the table, makin' sure it's on a coaster coz me ma would kill me if she found a mark on it and I get up and go into the hall and open the front door and standin' there cryin', lookin' like I've never seen her before, like she's upset badly, like she has no one else in the world, like she's alone. Standin' there on me doorstep cryin' was Bernie.

***

I'll be honest now, seein' Bernie arrive at me door like that had the maddest effect on me. Like I fainted. I just collapsed. I swear to god. Bernie says it's lucky she caught me or else I'd have smacked me head off the wooden floor in the hall. She said it took me a good five minutes to wake up and I only did coz she poured a pint of water over me. I woke up soakin'. I thought I was on the beach until I realised me ma would batter me if she came home and found water all over her good wooden floor.

Bernie had stopped cryin' when I woke up so I got off the floor and gave her a big hug and told her I was delighted to see her and she tells me she's delighted to see me and I ask her what she's doin' back in Dublin and she says she had loads to tell me and put the kettle on.

So I make Bernie one of them Cappuccino things and the two of us go into the sittin' room and she's not really sayin' anything so I say to her, 'Why did ya come home Bernie?' And she looks at me with this big sad look on her face and says, 'Joanna, I'm not goin' back. I hate it.' And I tell her she doesn't have to and she says, 'I was so lonely and missed me family and I missed all of youse and the bit of laugh we used to have. I had no friends over there, not real friends like you and Concepta and Tracy and the others. Not me mates like.' And at this stage I'm in tears and she says 'And then they said it was best if I don't fly,' and I'm like 'The bastards. Why wouldn't they let ya fly?' And she looks away for a second, wipes the tears out of her eyes then comes over to the sofa I'm on and sits down beside me and takes me hand in hers and says, 'D'ya remember we were in Killarney for the October weekend?' And I tell her I do and she says, 'D'ya remember I was with the Portuguese fella?' And I tell her I do and she says, 'D'ya remember I was tellin' ya how I was gettin' sick all the time, especially in the mornin'?' And I tell her I do and she looks into me eyes and says, 'Joanna, I'm pregnant.' And that's when I fainted again.

✻✻

Well needless to say, Bernie comin' home is still the main topic of conversation between all of us. I asked her after I woke up from faintin' was she goin' to tell the others about bein' pregnant and she just said she may as well coz they'll find out soon enough.

    We were sittin' there and Bernie was tryin' to get me to drink loads of water after me faintin' twice when next thing a knock comes to the door and Bernie says she'll get it and she opens the door and next minute all I can hear is Jasmin screamin' the place down, like screamin'. It was like a scene from Jurassic Park and she comes in and Bernie tells her about bein' pregnant and Jasmin screams the place down again so we say nothing to Paulo when he rings and the three of us go down to Farley's to meet him and Concepta and we walk in and the two of them are sittin' there and we sit down and Paulo goes to get the drinks and when he comes back, Bernie tells the two of them her news and they're both silent for a minute and then Concepta says 'I had a feelin'' And Bernie says 'That was just wind Concepta' and we all laugh and it kinda feels special with Bernie bein' back, like the gang of us all together.

    Anyway, ya know yourself, text messages were sent out and Tracy and Lance arrive and Jacinta comes in after work and Bopper and Nigel appear and Marvin and Sheila and Yenta shows up with a bunch of flowers for Bernie even though she hardly knows her and there we all are havin' a great laugh and it's like old times and Bernie turns to me and says 'D'ya know what Joanna? Its great havin' mates like all of youse.' And as I look around at them all, I have to agree with her.

✱✱✱

I'm in work today on the tills, me head only melted with auld-ones buyin' selection boxes and 15 years old young-fellas tryin' to buy cans of Dutch Gold. I was only on the tills coz Julie Walsh is out sick and whether she really is or not is another story. She told Leandra on the phone that she has piles but I don't believe her coz I think ya can only get it once in a year and she's already had it when she got back from Tunisia. I sat there one day while I was havin' a chicken salsa wrap listenin' to her goin' on about her piles, although not that it stopped her from spendin' her whole day sittin' on her hole on that stool, the horrible cow.

Marvin and Sheila were all lovey dovey too coz they had a fight over something that night we were in Farley's, although what it was over, we don't know coz nobody understands a word of what they do be sayin'. They were blowin' kisses across the shop at each other and all today. At one stage, some man thought Marvin was blowin' kisses at him and went and complained about him to Leandra and all Leandra could do was laugh, right into your man's face and all and he was none too impressed either.

I'm standin' there at the till anyways and I look up and who's walkin' into the shop only Andy and I'll be honest now, when I saw him me heart kinda jumped but at the same time I go kinda scarlet so I'm lookin' at him as he picks up a bottle of Pepsi Max and comes to the counter and its only then that he realises it's me and he says, 'Heya Joanna,' with a big smile and I say, 'Heya,' a bit more bitchier than I should have and scan in the Pepsi Max and he says, 'Any news Joanna?' I just say, 'Not much Andy. You?' And he says, 'I'm just goin' over to see Cheryl,' and I tell him how much his drink is and says, 'That's nice,' in a way that sounded like I thought him goin' to see his girlfriend was anything but nice and I could tell he was a little bit taken aback by the way I was bein' so short with him although I couldn't help it. It was all jealousy. Like I'll be the first one to admit it but it's totally me own fault for not tellin' him about how I felt about him, not that he'd look twice at me with girls like that Cheryl hangin' out of him.

In the end anyway, he just picked up his bottle of Pepsi Max, said goodbye and left and as he walked out the door, all I could think of was how much I'm crazy about him and what a lovely arse he has.

✳✳✳

I swear to god, I can't take any more shocks. First Bernie arrives at me door and tells me she's havin' a baby and now I find out about our Bopper's little secret, although I always had a good idea to be honest.

What happened was, I was sittin' in Bernie's, the two of us watchin' the *Muriel's Weddin'* like old times and next minute I get a phone call off Paulo and he's tellin' me he's meetin' Yenta and Concepta in town coz his Christmas party is shite and he's askin' me and Bernie to go and to be honest, I'm in no more of a humour but Bernie's there askin' me who it is and I tell her its Paulo askin' me to go out and she thinks about it for a minute and she gets me to ask where they're goin' and I ask Paulo and he says The George and when I tell Bernie she gets all excited and says we have to go so I couldn't exactly say no at that stage, although I'll be honest now, I've always wanted to go there coz I've never been and I heard it's a great night out. So I run back to me own house to get me cloths and get back to Bernie's and the two of us get ready and get a taxi into town and meet Yenta, Concepta and Paulo at the Central Bank and the five of us head up to The George.

Well I'll be honest, it was nothing like what I expected it to be, ya know, bein' a gay bar and that. I was expectin' fellas dressed in leather with the arse cut out of the trousers kissin' each other and all but it was nothing like that at all. Most of the fellas are rides and they can't all have been gay. I'm sure there was a few bisexuals like Paulo around too.

I went out to the smokin' area at one stage and there's Concepta Cooney in the middle of loads of people havin' a great laugh. That young-one would make friends anywhere. Another time I look over the balcony and there's Yenta on the dance floor givin' it loads to some song with loads of these fellas, fair play to her.

Anyway, I'm there on the dance floor at one stagin' havin' a dance with Bernie and all of a sudden I see this young-fella who I could have sworn was our Bopper so I leave Bernie there with some young-fella who thought he was Kylie Minogue and go and look to see if it really is our Bopper and then the young-fella is all up against this other young-fella and I'm right behind him and he turns around and true enough it is our Bopper and me mouth just dropped and he nearly died, like really died. The poor young-fella got the shock of his life. I've never seen our Bopper as quiet in all me life. I just smile eventually and say, 'Heya Bopper,' and he's like, 'Joanna what are ya doin' here?' And I'm like, 'I'm the one that should be askin' you that,' and he's like, 'Are you a lesbian?' And I'm like, 'Will ya fuck off. I'm too mad into the fellas to be a lesbian,' so he says, 'Joanna I have something to tell ya. I'm gay.' And I say, 'Well I kinda have that figured out at this stage Bopper.' Then he asks me am I bothered and I tell him that of course I'm not coz he's me brother and I love him no matter what and he asks me did I have an idea and I tell him I did although to be honest, it never really crossed me mind before, although it would explain why he has a big poster of David Beckham hanging up in his room. Our Bopper knows fuck all about football.

✳✳✳

It's unbelievable. I'm the last person out of everyone to find out about our Bopper. I rang Tracy this mornin' and she says he told her all the way back when we were bookin' the Canaries and that was in January or February. She said she was one of the first ones to know coz he went to her lookin' for a bit of advice, her studyin' English and Psychology in UCD and all.

Bernie found out around the same time and so did Concepta and I was talkin' to Concepta about it and I asked her how she found out and she saw him and Paulo one night and I asked her what did she mean and what did she see and she just laughed. So of course I had to find Paulo to ask him and he laughed as well and then just said 'Why d'ya think me and Bopper weren't talking for ages?' And I'm like 'I don't know Paulo, yiz had a fallin' out over something did yiz not?' And he laughs and shakes his head and says 'We broke up Joanna,' and the penny finally dropped. I can't believe I never noticed it. The two of them were always together and our Bopper would come home from Paulo's covered in hickeys.

I can't believe Jasmin kept it quiet as well. I would have thought she'd have let it slip at some stage. That one can't hold her piss. I said to Jacinta and of course she knew and so did Nigel. Actually, now that I come to think of it, I think our Nigel is gay too. I didn't go as far as sayin' it to anyone but it'd make sense. I must ask Tracy. She'd know.

I nearly died when I found out that Sheila, Yenta and Marvin knew, whatever about Yenta, he hardly knows Sheila and Marvin. I even tried to set our Bopper up with Sheila at one stage and there was me wonderin' how he couldn't be into a good lookin' girl like her.

I rang me Uncle Dessie too and he said that Bopper sat down with him and me ma and da one night after Dessie started livin' with us and told them. That was in May or something. Even Petulia next door knows so half the area probably knows, knowin' her and her big mouth and I only found out now, the little bastard. I'm never tellin' him anything again. Never. He can take his Kylie's *Greatest Hits* and fuck off.

✳✳✳

The hassle just to put up a Christmas tree, I swear to god. There was pandemonium in the house last night over it and there was more than one fight nearly breakin' out and we're very lucky there wasn't.

See what was to happen was Nigel was to get the decorations out of the attic and leave in the sittin' room for me ma to put up. Simple enough ya'd think. So I come in after work and start givin' me ma a hand and next minute me da comes in and that's where the madness started. He starts complainin' about everything as he always does and starts tryin' to do things his way coz he thinks his way is better than everyone else's although he just ends up doin' everything arseways.

Bernie knocked over for me then and I tried to get her to just come to me room to have a chat but she gets talkin' to me ma and da and starts givin' a few suggestions and me da's only delighted coz she's agreein' with him and he thinks he's gettin' his way and next minute, Bopper and Jacinta arrive home and that's when it turned into a disaster. Bopper starts goin' on as if its Buckingham Palace he's decoratin' and then Jacinta starts and she thinks she's your one Carole Smilie from that *Changin' Rooms* programme and her and Bopper start arguein' with me da and Bopper tells him he lacks vision and me da tells him he'll be lackin' half his face if he doesn't shut the fuck up and then Bernie starts agreein' with me da again and Boppers only disgusted with her and then me da, half jokin', tells Jacinta she should know enough about trees havin' been tied to one for long enough and she's not impressed at all and Bopper tells him it's a low blow and Bernie tells our Bopper he should be well used to low blows and me ma tells her she has a filthy mind and Bernie agrees with her so eventually I just go out and knock up to Concepta for an hour for a chat and I come back and they're all still there arguein', not even noticin' that I've been gone over an hour so I just went up to bed and I woke up this mornin' and went downstairs and the Christmas tree was standin' in the sittin' room with nothing on it, I swear to Jayzis. Not a bauble or a bit of tinsel. Naked. I just got a cup of coffee and ended up doin' it meself before I went into work. At the end of the day it's a fuckin' Christmas tree, not the Mona Lisa.

✶✶✶

I'm in work yesterday sortin' out the newspapers when next minute me phone beeps and I look at the text message and it's from Jasmin and it says 'Shorqim afves wrl?' and I'm lookin' at it tryin' to make out what the dizzy bitch is tryin' to say to me and eventually I ring her back and when she answers I ask her what the fuck 'Shorqim' means and poor Jasmin is lost already. She says 'I don't know what you're talkin' about, Joanna. Have you been drinkin'?'

'Of course I haven't been drinkin' Jasmin,' I says 'Its quarter to one in the day and I'm in work. Ya sent me a mad text message.' She goes all quiet for a couple of seconds and then says 'Ah no Joanna, it said shoppin' after work?' And it's only then that I realise Jasmin's textin' without her contact lenses in again. She's always doin' it. I think I do be readin' German sometimes with her.

Anyway, she asks me will I go to the Blanchardstown Centre with her after work and I tell her I will coz even though it's a Tuesday, all the shops are open til nine and ten with it bein' Christmas next week. I needed to get a few more bits for the Christmas anyway and I still have a few quid in the bank for some mad reason.

So I knock down after work and Jasmin's ma answers and tells me Jasmin's still dryin' her hair and she makes me go into the sittin' room to have a look at the Christmas tree, which I'll be honest, looks great despite the fact Jasmin decorated it.

One of the triplets, I think it was Mandy although it could easily have been Sandy, popped her head in the door to say hello and left again before I even had a chance to answer and have a chance to find out which one of them it was.

I'm sittin' there for a minute or two while Jasmin's ma is makin' me a cappuccino in the kitchen and next thing the door opens and I'm thinkin' it must be Jasmin's ma with the coffee or Jasmin or even Mandy or Sandy but I look up and who's standin' in front of me in a pair of shorts and nothing else only Andy. I have to say, I nearly died. There he was, his beautiful six-pack and pecks and a cheeky little grin on his face and whatever about me bein' into Andy before, seein' him half naked made me want to be with him so much more.

He says, 'Heya Joanna' and comes into the room and sits down on the arm chair, his legs slightly apart so I can kinda see up them a little bit and I kinda mumble what's meant to be a hello but he catches me havin' a sly look up the leg of his shorts but does nothing except grin at me again and starts to ask me am I set for the Christmas and all the rest of it and I'm tryin' to chat away to him but he's bein' really seductive as Tracy would say, pullin' the leg of his shorts up a little to scratch his leg and just givin' me this kinda smile and I'm grinnin' back at him like a sap and the two of us are just flirtin' like mad and we're havin' a great laugh until all of a sudden, the door opens and Jasmin's ma walks in with the coffee and asks him if he's not meant to be gettin' ready to go meet his girlfriend and the little moment we're after been havin' is ruined and he gets up and says he'll see me around and leaves while his ma's askin' me what I think of the Christmas tree but me mind is a blur thinkin' about Andy and wonderin' what it'd be like to kiss him or even just to hold his hand and I know I'm crazy about him and I'm just ragin' I never told him before he started goin' out with that other sap.

***

Me ma came home last night from the Weight Watchers only delighted with herself bein' slimmer of the week although she said a few of them weren't there this week what with it bein' the week before Christmas and all. She was sayin' Celine O'Reilly is in Tenerife for a few days to see some relatives of hers but everyone knows she's after the cheap Christmas presents and cheap booze. Me ma was surprised as well not to see Concepta there coz as far as I know, it's the first night she's missed since she started. It's not like her to miss it and me ma agrees with me. It'd have to be something serious for Concepta to miss Weight Watchers. So I thought I better give her a ring to see if everything's okay but when I do, there's no answer on her phone and I think nothing of it until I'm in work today and try to ring her and there's still no answer and when I ring her job they tell me she's called in sick and I started thinkin' it might be something really serious like that bird flu that's goin' around so on the way home from work I knock around to her house and she answers the door and is a little bit surprised to see me, which I found a bit weird coz I do often knock around to Concepta, mainly to see which of me CDs she's robbin'.

She asks me in and I notice straight away that she's wearin' a housecoat that probably would have fit her a few months ago but now since she's lost the weight it's like a tent on her. We go into the sittin' room and I ask her why she wasn't at the Weight Watchers and what's wrong with her and she lifts up her arm and she has this rash, the very same one as what meself and all the others had a few months back and I laugh coz of her sayin' she was keepin' away from us not to catch it and she ended up catchin' it in the end. God only knows how she got it and for all the slaggin' she gave us. She told me not to tell anyone and I told her I wouldn't. Paulo, Yenta, Bernie, Tracy and me ma thought it was gas but.

✳✳✳

I'm lookin' through the Christmas cards this mornin', the ones that were just delivered like and I come across one that looks a bit different and I look at the stamp and it says BRASIL on it and I'm wonderin' who I know in Brazil and wonder why it's my name on the envelope and not the Ryde Family and the usual shite so I open it and there's a card inside and I open the card and this Brazilian money falls out and I read the card and it says 'My dearest Joanna. Wishing you the nicest possible Christmas this year and my apologies for what I did. I hope you have it in your heart at this time of year to forgive me for what happened. I am now living a very happy life in Brazil and have no plans to ever return to Ireland, mainly for fear of being arrested. Once again, a very merry Christmas and prosperous new year.' And it's only then I realise its from Mister O'Toole, despite the fact that he hasn't signed it or anything. Like I mean, what a cheek to try and kill me and then send me a Christmas card to try and say sorry. I just fucked the card straight into the bin. I kept the money but the card went into the bin.

✳✳✳

I swear to god, I really can't take anymore surprises. I mean, here I am 19 in a month and I'm close to a heart attack and then there's all the stress of the Christmas and all. First there was Fudge scarin' the shite out of me the night he was robbin' the tent, then Bernie turns up on me door and tells me she's pregnant and then I find out our Bopper is gay and then there was last night. At this stage I'm goin' to have to see one of them paediatricians about me heart.

See it was the Christmas party for the Spar last night and we all went to that Hard Rock Café in town, meself, Marie, Leandra, Julie Walsh, Sheila, Marvin, Boris, that Jason sap and Amy and I have to say, it was a great bit of laugh. We walked in and straight away I made sure that I got a seat between Amy and Leandra coz my hole did I wanna sit beside Julie Walsh while she was eatin' but then her and that Jason gobshite ended up sittin' in front of me. Amy was in no more of a humour for them. There was one stage where I thought she was actually goin' to get up and batter Jason over something. What it was I don't know coz I was too busy talkin' to Leandra about the state of Julie Walsh's outfit. Ya wanna see her. She was in this kinda sari effect dress and fair enough, it was nice but just not on her. I mean, she's at least 20 stone if not more.

I couldn't believe it when we were orderin' coz she got the barbeque ribs and chicken wings and chips, the fat fuck. Lookin' at her eatin' them was even worse. She looked like something out of Jurassic Park.

I have to say, we were havin' a great night and a bit of laugh sittin' there havin' our meal and a nice chat and we were plannin' to go somewhere for a drink after, probably Fitzsimons and at one stage I was talkin' to Amy about whether or not Jason is gay, which she thinks he is and next thing I hear a voice sayin' hello, a familiar voice, one I hadn't heard in months and I look up to see a tanned woman who looked like a completely different person to when I last saw her. There was no mistakin' who it was though. Dymphna was back.

***

Well with all the excitement over Dymphna comin' back from her Shirley Valentine adventure I really needed to do something to calm down. To be honest, I still can't believe she just arrived in the restaurant. I've never seen her lookin' so well. The tan really suits her and she's real clean or something. She'd been a bit of a scruffy cow before as everyone knows well but the six months in Turkey and then some place called Syria and then Lebanon did her well. She says your man asked her to marry him and it was only then that she realised how much she loves her husband and kids and came home. She says she's a better person coz of the experience and she seems it. Fair play to her for givin' it a go I say.

Anyway, I'm on the phone to Tracy tellin' her all about it and she tells me that Lance is bringin' her ice skatin' in Smithfield and I told her whether she liked it or not, I was comin' too coz it's been ages since I was ice skatin' and I used to be only rapid at it. Me and Tracy and Bernie used to go all the time.

So I get on to Yenta, Concepta, Jasmin and Paulo and they say they'll come and our Nigel is sittin' in with nothing to do even though it's the Saturday before Christmas so he says he might as well too even though he's never been ice skatin' before in his life and I tell him not to worry coz Yenta is from Turkey and it'll be her first time too coz they don't have ice rinks in Turkey.

So we all get the bus together, the whole seven of us. I was ragin' Bernie couldn't come but she said she wouldn't be up to it and she hasn't been feelin' that good the last few days anyway. I asked her to come watch but she said she just needed rest so I didn't want to force her or anything.

We show up at the ice rink, the big group of us and Lance is standin' there and nearly dies when he sees the whole group coz I'd say he thought it was gonna be nice to go skatin' with just Tracy but fuck him.

We go and get our skates and sit there in the changin' area and Yentas the first one ready and skates onto the ice and starts doin' these twirls and all the rest of it and Nigel gives me a look to say no ice rinks in Turkey me hole and I just shrug me shoulders and look back at Yenta who's on the ice standin' there lookin' at something and its only when I skate up to her to ask what's wrong that I see what she's been lookin' at and its only when Tracy skates up to me that she sees it too and all of us are just starin' at it. There's a big banner hangin' over the edge of the rink that says, 'Tracy I love you. Please marry me – Lance XXX,' and she turns to him and jumps into his arms knockin' him flyin' on his arse. I have to say, it was lovely. I hate bein' single.

✱✱✱

I got home from work early enough tonight and Jacinta is there only after gettin' in herself and she tells me she still has to get a few bits for the Christmas and tells me I'm goin' into town with her to go shoppin' and seein' as it's not even six yet I say I may as well and we're just leavin' when Nigel pulls up in the car and says he'll drop us in which is handy enough for us. So he drops us there on Parnell Street and the two of us go into the Ilac and are shoppin' away, tryin' loads of things on and all the rest of it. I got a few nice bits in Zara and then we went across to Next and I got a few more bits on Jacinta's discount.

The two of us are walkin' down Henry Street about to go into Arnotts when Jacinta nudges me and says 'Isn't that Jasmin's little brother? God he looks gorgeous. I remember him when he was a scrawny lookin' smelly rocker. He looks better in real life than he does on the telly.' And true enough Andy is walkin' towards us with that Cheryl one although Jacinta is one to be callin' anyone a smelly rocker. Only a month ago she was a smelly eco-warrior.

He says hello as he walks up to us and he tells Jacinta she looks great and she tells him the same and he introduces her to Cheryl who's actin' a little bit snotty and he starts talkin' to me about the Christmas and that and tells me I'm gonna love the present Jasmin got me and that it always reminds him of me and he kinda smiles as he says it, kinda flirtin' even in front of his girlfriend. I know it's a bottle of the Ultra Violet by Paco Rabane coz if there's one thing Jasmin Spi can't do its subtlety. She was only short of givin' me the money to get it meself that night we went shoppin' last week. He asks me what kinda cloths I got for Christmas and I show him what I got in Next and he says they're lovely and that I always look well of a Christmas. I tell him he should drop down to the house on Christmas mornin' with his ma and da and Jasmin and he says he probably will but it depends on what Cheryl is doin' and I look at her and she has a face on her, the moany cow, and Jacinta tells me to come on and I say goodbye to them and Andy says he'll try come down to the gaff on Christmas mornin' or that I might even see him at mass on Christmas Eve night and as I'm walkin' away, Jacinta nudges me and says 'What are you like?' And I ask her what she's talkin' about and she tells me not to play stupid, that she knows I'm mad into him and I end up tellin' her everything and she hugs me there in the middle of Henry Street and tells me the best thing to do is just tell him and I'm half tempted to run after him but in the end we just go into Arnotts.

✻✻✻

I gave Bernie a ring on me way home from work and she sounded a bit down so I thought to meself I better do something to try and cheer her up so I give the others a ring and everyone's either workin' or doin' something except Concepta and Jasmin so I meet them at the Chinese and we go in and get loads of food and go into the Spar and get two bottles of the Blossom Hill white wine and then the three of us walk to Bernie's and knock on the door and she's only delighted to see us and we go in and sit down and enjoy our Chinese and our glasses of wine and Bernie puts on the video of all of us in the school concert when we were kids and were havin' a great laugh at that. Jayzis the state of us. Every time I see it I think it's even funnier. How I didn't know our Bopper is gay is mad. Like lookin' at that video it was obvious even then.

When it's over, we're just sittin' there havin' a chat with our glasses of wine and Bernie starts gettin' upset coz she says her baby won't know its father and Concepta tries to make her laugh by sayin' that at least Bernie doesn't know the father either and she kinda laughs and I tell her the babies gonna be gorgeous coz that Portuguese fella was a ride and we're tellin' her she'll have to call it a Portuguese name and Jasmin says Fatima if it's a girl and we all laugh but I can tell by Bernie that she's really upset about the baby not havin' a da so I say 'D'ya know what Bernie. Who needs a da when the baby has all of us. I'll teach her to sing, Concepta will teach her how to meet loads of strangers, Tracy will teach her English and psychology, Paulo will teach her Bosnian, Bopper will teach her how to dance to Kylie, Sheila will teach her Chinese, Marvin will teach her the coolest way to walk, Jacinta will get her discounts in Next, Nigel will get a baby seat, Jasmin will babysit, Yenta will teach her to fight, dance, ice skate and speak six languages and every single one of us will love her to bits' and at this stage Bernie is in tears and I look at Jasmin and she is too but Bernie knows I'm right. We may not make up for the fact that the baby's da is in Portugal somewhere but we'll be just as good if not better.

*＊＊

I swear to god, what a mad day in work. It's the day before Christmas Eve so the place is packed with people buyin' selection boxes and drink and everything else. We have Dymphna in doin' a few hours and its kinda mad havin' her back in. Marvin took her job when she ran off to Turkey so we have her on a temporary contract for the moment but she'll be back to her full time after Christmas if she wants to.

Marie is a bit upset coz she came in today and Cliff was dead but he hasn't been lookin' the best the last few weeks. She still has Tinky Winky, Dipsy and Lala so it's not too bad. Dypmhna went out on her lunch and came back with some kind of plant so Marie was only delighted. I think it's a hash plant but I didn't say anything in case I'm wrong. I don't want to be accusin' Dymphna of anything and her only back. She's after callin' the plant Po, although I could see that happenin'. I hope it's not a hash plant coz if the health and safety people come round and we have drugs growin' in the toilet we'll be shut down. I was goin' to get Marie another plant for her kris kringle in work but the toilet is already like *The Jungle Book* so I got her a book about plants and *Bob Marley's Greatest Hits* on CD coz she's always sayin' she wants to get it. I was right about Julie Walsh gettin' me and I was dreadin' opening' the envelope but I nearly died coz there was a fifty euro gift voucher for Mac in Brown Thomas. I couldn't believe it. Julie Walsh gettin' me a present for €50 and something I can use too. The Christmas must be goin' to her head. We all chipped in and got Dymphna something coz she hasn't been here. I know she hasn't been smelly since she got back from wherever she was but I thought it'd be a good idea to get her a bottle of perfume. We got her the Chanel Number 5 coz its only mafis. I picked it out.

The phone rang at one stage and I answered it and some fella in a mad accent asked was he through to Spar and I tell him he is, wonderin' who it is and it turns out that its Greg ringin' us all the way from South Africa to wish everyone a Happy Christmas. It was lovely hearin' from him though. He was askin' how the shop was gettin' on now that he's not the manager and I told him we were copin'. Needless to say, the phone got passed around to everyone, even Leandra and Marvin and they'd never ever met him. I ended up talkin' to him for about twenty minutes, tellin' him about everything that's happened since he left. He was shocked about Sheila goin' out with Marvin and Julie Walsh bein' engaged and Dymphna runnin' off with some strange man. Ah isn't it lovely to hear from people far away at Christmas.

***

Christmas Eve. My favourite day of the year. I love it. As a kid and all I even preferred Christmas Eve to Christmas Day. I can remember meself and Bopper goin' into town with me ma and da and then gettin' a McDonalds on the way home and havin' our baths and gettin' into our pyjamas and then snugglin' up in front of the fire to watch the *Muppets Christmas Carol*. As we got older we'd sit in one of our houses and then when we got older still we'd go to the pub of a Christmas Eve although last year we all just went to nine o'clock mass and then to Bernie's and all of us sat there and watched the Muppets Christmas Carol together.

This was the best Christmas Eve ever though. I was in work til about five and we were all havin' the bit of laugh and all the rest of it.

Marvin came in dressed as Santy but with him bein' Turkish and not wearin' the big white beard he looked a bit stupid.

I got home and everyone was already sittin' there and we made me da go the chipper and meself and him and me ma and Jacinta and Nigel and Bopper sat there watchin' the telly havin' a few glasses of wine until about twenty to nine and then me, Jacinta, Nigel and Bopper started walkin' down to the church to meet the others and they're all standin' at the garage as I get there and straight away me heart gives a little jump coz I notice Jasmin's little brother Andy is standin' there with Jasmin, Bernie, Tracy, Lance and Paulo and we all head into the church and try and get a good seat. I end up sittin' beside Andy and he's tryin' to make me laugh and Jacinta is sittin' behind me pokin' her finger into me to make me shut up coz there's a few auld-ones givin' us looks but I don't care coz its Andy.

I'm wonderin' where Concepta is when all of a sudden I hear a commotion down the back of the church where there's a big crowd who couldn't get seats and Concepta is shovin' her way through them and starts lookin' around for us and eventually she spots us and half the church is lookin' at her as she comes to where we're sittin' and makes about twelve people move so she can sit in between Paulo and Bernie. I was a little bit surprised to see her wearin' a belly top under her ankle length leather jacket but she won the slimmer of the year by a good bit last night at the Weight Watchers although she didn't get down to her ten stone by Christmas she wanted, although ten stone ten is still amazin', fair play to her, even if she clearly cheated by takin' illegal drugs.

It was half ten again the mass was over and we'd all promised to go to Yenta's coz she doesn't go to mass what with not bein' a Christian so the whole lot of us arrive at her door and Sheila and Marvin are already there and she has the Christmas songs on and a bit of food and loads of drinks and we're all havin' a good bit of laugh and we're dancin' and me and Andy are gettin' on great and flirtin' like mad and I'm gettin' dirty looks off Jacinta and Paulo over it and I go to have a smoke on the balcony and I'm the only one out there and next minute the door opens and who is it only Andy and we're talkin' and I'm lookin' at him thinkin' to meself how amazin' he is and how for the first time in me life I actually feel like I'm in love and I'm lookin' into his eyes and he's lookin' into mine and I decide I'm just gonna go ahead and tell him how I feel and I say, 'Andy there's something I really need to tell ya,' and he gives me this smile that makes me feel like I'm doin' the right thing and I'm about to continue when his phone rings and the moment just vanishes. He takes out his phone, tells me it's his girlfriend Cheryl and answers it and I just leave him there on the balcony and slip away from the party without anyone noticin' and I'm devastated walkin' home, like someone has put their hand down me throat and pulled out me heart and I'm so close to just cryin' me eyes out and I go into me house and close the door and I'm about to go upstairs to cry me eyes out when the door bell rings and I answer it and who's standin' there in front of me only Andy and I don't get a chance to say anything coz he just takes hold of me and kisses me and the happiest feelin' in the world came over me and it felt like it lasted forever. God bless us, everyone.

✲✲

I have to say, it was a lovely Christmas. Sayin' that, I do always have a lovely Christmas but for some reason, this Christmas just seemed lovelier than ever. Maybe it has something to do with Andy. I couldn't believe he'd just shown up on me doorstep like that but he had. I was askin' him what he was goin' to do about your one Cheryl and he said it'd probably be best to wait til the day after Stephen's Day to break up with her coz it's not very nice to break up with someone on Christmas Day, which I have to agree with him about. I'm just delighted that he likes me too though. It's the best Christmas present I ever got, even better than me GHD I got off me ma last year. I didn't even get to sleep late coz Bopper came into the room and started shoutin' at me and Jacinta to wake up and I'd understand if we were kids and we were goin' down to see what Santy was after leavin' us but at this age it's ridiculous and at half eight in the mornin' too I wouldn't mind. If he had of stayed still long enough I would have found something to throw at him. Needless to say, the whole house had to get up at that stage and Nigel was already in the kitchen makin' all of us a fry, although Bopper wouldn't let anyone eat til we'd opened all our Christmas presents. I got a few nice things off them all so I was delighted with meself. Me ma and da got me ten drivin' lessons despite the fact I don't have a car or even a provisional licence. Bopper got me a €50 gift voucher for the Blanchardstown Centre, Jacinta got me a €50 voucher for Next and Nigel got me a bottle of Coolwater for women. Mafis it is.

We hadn't even the fry eaten when we all were runnin' upstairs to try get the shower first coz we only have the one in me ma's en-suite coz Bopper slipped in the bath in the big bathroom and pulled the shower off the wall, the sap.

We were hardly dressed when people started knockin' on the door. It's a thing we do every Christmas mornin' that everyone comes to our house. Years we've been doin' it. Me Uncle Dessie and Mary were there as well as the four Filipino nurses that live with them, then there was a few other uncles and aunts and cousins I hardly ever see and don't like much, although not me Aunty Linda coz Dessie and me ma still don't talk to her. Then there was Concepta, her two brothers and her ma and da, Tracy and Lance, Jasmin, Andy, Mandy, Sandy and their ma and da, Bernie and her ma and da, Petulia from next door and the news about me and Andy was already spread around. Jasmin even came over to me and said she was delighted and I was worried about her bein' pissed off with me.

It must have been about two by the time everyone had gone although Dessie and Mary were stayin' for dinner coz Jacinta and Nigel live with us and Dessie's their da, although in sayin' that, he's always in our house anyway. I'm helpin' me ma with the dinner when a knock comes to the door and I go to answer it and who is it only Yenta, Marvin and Sheila and me ma's standin' behind me goin' 'Surprise! I invited your friends over for dinner so they wouldn't be on their own.' And I'm only delighted and Yenta can't thank her enough although I know for a fact that me ma is dyin' to feed them. If it's one thing mas love doin' its feedin' people, despite the fact they don't like ya thinkin' they eat coz they're on the Weight Watchers.

The dinner was only mafis and there was plenty to go round all eleven of us and we had mafis desserts and all and then just flaked out with a few drinks and then we started playin' charades and Trivial Pursuit and all the rest of it and havin' a great laugh and Andy even rang to talk to me for a few minutes and I'm lookin' around at everyone thinkin' how deadly Christmas is.

∗∗∗

Isn't it mad how one minute you feel like life can't get any better and the next, your whole world comes crashin' down on top of you. That one day ya can feel so happy and the next ya feel like life isn't worth livin'.

 I was enjoyin' me Stephens' Day sittin' at home with Andy in front of the telly watchin' *Willy Wonka and the Chocolate Factory*, havin' a drink when me phone starts ringin' and I look at it and I see Bernie's name and presume she's ringin' to tell me she's on the way over or something and I pick it up and say 'Heya love' but it's not Bernie, it's her ma and she's cryin' and before she even starts talkin' I have a feelin' about why she's ringin'. 'The baby. Bernie's been rushed to hospital' she says and me heart sinks. 'She's in the Rotunda Joanna. She said she wants ya to go up to her.' and I just let the phone drop onto the chair beside Andy and he's lookin' at me to see what's goin' on but I just run out of the sittin' room and up the stairs and I can feel the tears rollin' down me face as I go into Bopper and Nigel's room and Nigel's lyin' there on the bed readin' a book and I kinda shout at him 'I need a lift,' and he looks at me to see what's up and I shout 'Bernie's in hospital Nigel, I need a fuckin' lift,' and he jumps up and puts his runners on as I turn to Andy and tell him he needs to get in touch with Tracy, Jasmin and Concepta and let them know and me and Nigel run to the car and we drive a lot faster than we should have to the Rotunda and as I get out of the car, I see Bernie's da havin' a smoke, his eyes red from cryin' and he tells me what way to go and I rush in the direction he's after showin' me and I go into the room and there's Bernie, a drip in one hand and her ma holdin' the other and I couldn't get over the look on her face when she looked at me. In all the time I've known Bernie, I don't think I've ever seen her lookin' as sad and Bernie's ma gets up and tells me that me and Bernie should be alone and her and Nigel leave the room and Bernie is still lookin' up at me with that sad look on her face and as soon as her ma is gone, I take her hand and she's the first to speak. 'It's gone Joanna' she says to me, startin' to cry 'The baby is gone' and hearin' her say it makes me feel like the whole worlds after fallin' out from under me and I'm standin' there holdin' her hand tryin' not to cry coz I want to try and be strong for her. 'I was only havin' a bath' she says to me and at this stage I can feel the tears rollin' down me cheek. She says 'I was just lyin' there and I'd been gettin' pains for a few hours. That's why I was havin' the bath, to make it stop and next thing blood starts comin' out of me and I panicked. I just screamed and me ma came runnin' in. Me babies dead Joanna.' And at this stage I couldn't hold it in any longer. I just broke down and the two of us are there cryin' and she pulls me towards her and the two of us hug and I'm thinkin' that the sadness I'm feelin' must be nothing compared to Bernie's and I'm prayin' to god that I'm gonna wake up and its all after bein' a dream but I open me eyes and I'm still there in the hospital holdin' Bernie and all either of us can do is cry.

✻✻✻

Jayzis poor Bernie. I can't stop thinkin' about her and how horrible it must all be for her. I mean, imagine losin' your baby like that. It's awful. It's the type of thing that'd effect ya for the rest of your life.

    I stayed with her for ages after I went in to see her. I was gettin' phone calls off everyone askin' me what was goin' on and every time I had to tell someone I broke down and cried again. Thank god Nigel was there coz he was lookin' after me as much as he could and stayin' with me outside while I had a smoke. Bernie told me to tell the others not to come to the hospital coz she wasn't really ready to face them all yet. Ya can understand though. The last thing ya want when you're upset is loads of people hangin' around ya, even if they are your friends. Ya can understand too that they're just worried about her and upset about the whole thing but at the end of the day, the best thing they can do is just give her a few days to get better.

At about two o'clock this mornin' they gave Bernie something to make her sleep so her ma made me go home. Nigel had gone a while earlier coz I didn't want him just waitin' around for me for hours. I couldn't get me mind off it when I went home. It was too late to go out for a walk to clear me mind and it was freezin' anyway so I poured meself a Baileys and tried to watch telly to relax but I couldn't. I went up and tried to sleep but I just couldn't. When I eventually did get to sleep, I had a horrible nightmare that I can't even remember and woke up sweatin'. Jacinta was beside the bed askin' was I okay and I just started cryin' and she hugged me and told me Bernie was goin' to be alright and although I know she's right, that Bernie is as strong a person as I know, it's still hard not to be upset over what's happened. I'm just devastated every time I think of what poor Bernie is goin' through and how she must feel. For a few short weeks she had a life growin' inside her. She was goin' to be a mother. Now she's left with nothing but painful memories and a horrible experience, god love her.

✳︎✳︎✳︎

I have to say now, she's lookin' a whole lot better today than she did yesterday and she even ended up lettin' the others go and visit her. It's actually cheered her up a good bit seein' them all, especially when Concepta came in covered in bandages coz of the rash she has. She got a great laugh out of that Bernie did and it was great to see her smilin'. She even brought her a big bag of jellies from the jelly factory so Bernie was delighted with herself. Yenta sent five books that she got in Eason's in with Concepta coz she said she didn't really know Bernie that well and wouldn't want to be imposin'. Bernie would have loved to see her though. She's very fond of Yenta.

I got a text off Jasmin at one stage sayin' she was outside and half an hour later there's still no sign of her so I give her a ring and ask her where she is and she tells me she doesn't know so meself and Concepta and Paulo have to go around the Rotunda lookin' for her and I end up findin' her wanderin' around the premature unit lookin' at people she doesn't know. The look on her face was priceless when I found her.

Tracy's in Cork with Lance til New Years Eve and Bernie told her to stay where she was but I have to say, seein' all the others made the world of difference. She was a whole lot better after it and she was millin' into the jellies Concepta had left her. She was smilin' anyway so I suppose it's a good sign.

***

I went to work today even though I was in no more of a humour but I was in the hospital with Bernie last night and she made me promise to just go back to work and stop worryin' about her and I could hardly say no. I tried to make meself stop worryin' about it but I couldn't. It just stuck in me mind the whole time. It's just horrible. For it to happen is bad enough but for it to happen like that is even worse. How poor Bernie can cope after that I don't know but as me Uncle Dessie says, she's resilient. She'll get through it and she'll come out a stronger person. That's the way Bernie is and always has been and she'll just accept that it wasn't meant to be and move on.

I have to admit, workin' was great to get me mind off things. I spent the mornin' sortin' out the magazine orders so that kept me busy. I had a good inspection of Marie's new pot plant as well to see if it was a hash plant but I can't tell really. I'll only find out when I see her rollin' up the leaves and smokin' them.

I have to say, Julie Walsh was one person I was dreadin' talkin' to coz if she had of found out about Bernie she'd just keep goin' on about it and I was thinkin' she'd more than likely know, thinkin' Marvin or Sheila would have said somethin' but if she did know, she kept it very quiet. She wasn't her usual self at all this mornin' Julie Walsh and she even got off the stool for ages and at one stage she'd been missin' for a good ten minutes and I'm thinkin' she's havin' a doss in the stockroom so I ask Dymphna to look after the tills while I go to see where Julie Walsh is and the toilet door is locked and I can hear cryin' so I knock on it and she tells me she'll be out in minute and I ask her is she okay and I can still hear her cryin' so I tell her to let me in and there she is sittin' on the toilet cryin' her eyes out and I ask her what's wrong with her and she says, 'He was cheatin' on me Joanna. The bastard was ridin' some other young-one. The engagements off,' and she breaks down cryin' and I tell her that I told her at the start he was nothing but a bollix and she starts pourin' her guts out to me there in the toilet tellin' me everything about everything and I'm listenin' and for the first time in me life I actually feel sorry for Julie Walsh. Me heart really did go out to her as she was tellin' me about what had happened and all of a sudden she says 'No one likes me' and I tell her not to be so stupid and she says 'It's true. Nobody can stand me. Everyone hates me. Even you Joanna and you like everyone. Everyone except me.' 'That's not true' I say although she can tell I'm lyin' and I feel terrible, especially seein' her in this state. 'It is true' she goes on 'I know ya don't like me and the funny thing is that I think you're deadly Joanna. I've always thought ya were lovely even though ya slag me and are mean to me all the time, even though ya bitch about me behind me back and ignore me when I'm talkin' to ya. I still think you're deadly and I've tried so hard for ya to like me but ya don't. You're great mates with Amy and Sheila and Marvin and Leandra and Dymphna and even Marie and no matter how hard I try, ya don't want anything to do with me. All I wanted was for ya to like me Joanna.' and she breaks down again and I realise that over the past few months, years even, that without realisin' it I've been terrible to Julie Walsh and it makes me feel shit, like I'm a horrible bitch but she still tells me that despite everything that she still likes me and that makes me realise how wrong I've been about her and I promise meself that I'll do everything I can to make it up to Julie Walsh.

✳✳✳

Dymphna said she'd work for me today so I was delighted to just be able to sit at home and relax after what's bein' goin' on lately.

Bernie's got out of hospital and I was goin' to go up to her this mornin' but she told me to have a few hours to meself coz she didn't think I looked the best meself lately and I'll be honest, I'm exhausted with everything happenin' and not gettin' much sleep.

I was only sittin' down to watch *Trisha* when a knock comes to the door and who is it only Andy and I haven't even seen him since St Stephens Day but he just gives me a big hug and tells me not to worry about anything and that he'll look after me and all I can think of is how lucky I am to have him at last. That Cheryl young-one he was goin' out with was bitch. When he broke up with her she just laughed and said she was seein' someone else anyway.

As I said, I just wanted to relax but Andy wouldn't let me. He told me he was goin' to bring me somewhere and I was thinkin' to meself its goin' to be a fancy restaurant or something but we get the bus into town and then we walk to Tara Street and get the Dart to Bray and when we get off he brings me down to the beach and says 'We're here.' And I'm like, 'Andy it's December and you're bringin' me the beach, ya mad sap.' But he just took me hand and we walked for about two hours while he listened to me talkin' about everything and it felt great to get things off me chest. He's just such a great listener and I feel I can talk to him about everything. We even found this lovely little restaurant and had a nice meal and then for the laugh we went into one of them arcades and played the slot machines. He even won a big teddy and handed it to me and says 'I think Bernie will like this' and it was nice to know he was thinkin' of her too.

It was about nine when I got home and Andy was only gone when the door bell rings and I answer it and there Bernie standin' there smilin' and for a second it's like we're kids again, like Bernie's knockin' into me to come out and play skippin' or to go to school or to go down to the Spar to get someone to get us drink so we can go drinkin' in the fields and I give her a big hug and tell her how great it is to have a best friend like her and she tells me she's freezin' her nipples off and to let her inside and I realise that at last Bernie's back to her old self, the way she was before she went to England and she comes in and the two of us go up to me room and put on the Sugababes and we're chattin' away and she says 'D'ya know Joanna, I think it was for the best,' and I don't say anything. I just listen and she says, 'I was too young to have a baby anyway and just because I made one stupid mistake, it wouldn't be fair to bring a baby up without a da. Sayin' that, if I hadn't of lost it I would have been a great ma but it happened and there's nothing I can do about it. I just have to move on with me life and learn from it.' And I look at her as she manages a soft smile and I think to meself that she's goin' to be okay. We're all goin' to be okay.

✳✳✳

God I actually can't believe it's New Year's already. That year flew in. It's mad when ya think about it and all the stuff that happened but now I'll be honest, I think that I've come through it a much stronger person. It had its ups and downs but I suppose that's just life isn't it. I've learned a few things about meself and about other people and I feel a better person for it. Jayzis though, when I think back on everything that's happened.

There was that mad rash that Concepta's only gettin' over now and goin' to Galway for Tracy's birthday and havin' to run away from a hairy bloke and goin' for promotion in work and then goin' out with Dave and Mister O'Toole tryin' to kill me, goin' the Canaries and to England and the weekend in Killarney and Misses O'Driscoll dyin' and then Andy arrivin' on me doorstep. Jayzis how I didn't have heart failure. What a year.

Bernie had a rough one as well but she'll be grand. I know she will. It's mad when I think she wasn't here for most of it. It's like she never even left. I'm just glad she's home and to be honest, so is she. Life is so much easier when ya have a best mate like her.

Concepta Cooney is like a totally different person to what she was. She lost nearly seven stone in six months although the slimmin' pills helped her along but lets lie, it can't be healthy. The thing I learned about Concepta though, especially with Bernie bein' away is how good of a friend she really is and that even though her belly's a lot smaller now, her heart's a lot bigger.

It's mad to think that Tracy's engaged. Out of all of us I wouldn't have pictured her bein' the first engaged but it's great to see her so happy. She's doin' great in college and soon enough she'll have a degree in English and psychology and be married and have a house in Castleknock or somewhere like that but I know she'll always be on the end of the phone to listen to me problems or even just to tell me the capital city of New Zealand or whatever.

Jasmin, god love her, is still Jasmin but she just doesn't give a fuck and that's what I love about her. She's found a nice fella in Lawrence and the two of them are mad about each other already. She even thought herself Spanish this year and surprised me and everyone else I'd say. Yentas helpin' her learn Arabic now for next year, although god love her, the poor young-one still struggles with English. I have no doubt she'll do it though.

It's mad to think about Paulo bein' such a good mate. This time last year I would have thought of him as a friend of Bopper's although at that stage I knew little about how close they actually were. Durin' the year though we just got closer and he always seems to be there when I need someone to cheer me up.

I have to say, meetin' Yenta was probably one of the best things to happen all year. God love her, there was the poor young-one sittin' on the bus and next minute, Concepta gets talkin' to her and she just becomes part of our little gang. A lovelier young-one ya couldn't meet and she has everything goin' for her; looks, brains and she's just deadly at everything she does. Above everything though, she's a deadly mate.

Sheila and Marvin, god love them, are as cute goin' out together. Sheila, even though she still can hardly speak a word of English, is great to have in work and Marvin is probably the maddest bastard I know. Together. They're deadly.

Then there's our Bopper. My Jayzis. I'm still gettin' over him bein' gay but he's happy and so I'm happy. I have one brother and I'm glad its him. He can be as annoyin' as fuck sometimes but I love him to bits and wouldn't change him for anything. Although, I wouldn't mind our Wanda back from Australia.

Havin' Nigel here with us is deadly. Ever since he arrived he's just been great and he's such a lovely bloke, always goin' out of his way to do something for ya and he's been more than me cousin, he's been me friend too.

Jacinta is the same. I used to think she was a spa but she changed so much since she came home and got rid of that Fudge gobshite and now she's a totally different person and I'm after gettin' very close to her. She's happy in Ireland though and it's good to see.

Me Uncle Dessie couldn't be happier either. He has his two kids livin' here and he's after fallin' madly in love with Mary and he's even actin' his age now which is good to see. The whole ghetto auld-fella look just wasn't workin' for him. He even managed to sort out that cow of an ex-wife at last.

It was a mad year in work too. Greg left and now we have Leandra and as far as bosses go, she's only deadly. Its great havin' Dymphna back and she's changed loads as well. She's back with her husband though and she's happy and I'm delighted for her. Marie is still a mad cow and young Amy is growin' up fast and Boris the Ukrainian is still mixin' up the Coke and Pepsi but I'll be honest, I love me job to bits. The one thing I thought I'd never see though is me and Julie Walsh becomin' mates but its goin' to happen. She's not that bad really and I'm actually lookin' forward to gettin' to know her better.

Then there's Andy who started off the year as me mates little brother but who grew up and became me fella and the first person I've ever been madly in love with. I know it's early days but it took long enough and we got together in the end.

So that's it really, the end of the year. We're all headin' over to Bernie's tonight for a big party and I can't wait coz there's no better way to spend New Years than with all your friends. I even invited Julie Walsh and she's only delighted. Concepta said she'll persuade her to join the Weight Watchers. We're even lettin' Jasmin make a punch although I still haven't decided whether I'll be brave and try it. I just hope she has no Milk of Magnesia at home. We might even whip out the karaoke machine although if Concepta Cooney sings *My Heart Will Go On*, I'm leavin'.

Jayzis New Years Eve. When I think of it. The thing is though, one years endin' but another ones only beginnin'.

About the Author

Joanna Ryde is an all singing, all dancing comedy sensation from Finglas, in Dublin's north side, described by some as Ryvita, Dublin's answer to Eva Peron. Her rise to superstardom began in 2007 when she won the prestigious Alternative Miss Ireland and began performing in venues throughout Ireland. Appearances on TV and radio followed, most notably in 2010 when she was chosen as a finalist on RTE's *The All Ireland Talent Show* prompting Daithi O'Se to suggest she had the nicest legs he'd ever seen. She someday hopes to represent Ireland or Liechtenstein in the *Eurovision Song Contest*.

Joanna currently lives in Waterford where she has a residency in the legendary Dignity Bar and can be found online at www.JoannaRyde.com or on the beach in Tramore on nice days.

Kolyn Byrne plays the fictional character 'Joanna Ryde' and won the Alternative Miss Ireland title in 2007. He has gained a large amount of exposure since then on the gay scene around the country. He currently has four weekly shows in Ireland as well as a column in *THE Magazine* and a weekly slot on *The Cosmo* on RTE Pulse. He is also studying web design and marketing in his free time. Kolyn currently lives in Waterford.